Contents

Maigret Has Doubts

Translated from the French
by Lyn Moir

1. Madame Pardon's Rice Mould

The maid had just placed the rice mould on the circular table and Maigret had to make an effort to appear both surprised and gratified, while Madame Pardon, blushing, gave him a sharp look.

This was the forty-fourth rice mould that they had had in the four years that the Maigrets had dined regularly once a month at the Pardons', while they in turn came on the intervening fortnights to the Boulevard Richard-Lenoir, where it was up to Madame Maigret to provide a good meal.

Five or six months after the visits had started, Madame Pardon had served a rice mould. Maigret had had three helpings, saying that it reminded him of his childhood and that for forty years he hadn't eaten one as good, which was true.

After that, every dinner at the Pardons' new flat in the Boulevard Voltaire finished with the same creamy pudding which underlined the character of these get-togethers – sweet, soothing and a little dull.

Since neither Maigret nor his wife had any family in Paris, they had practically no experience of those evenings spent on a fixed day with sisters or sisters-in-law, and the dinners with the Pardons reminded them of childhood visits to aunts and uncles.

This evening the Pardons' daughter Alice, whom they had known as a schoolgirl and who had been married a year ago, was at the dinner with her husband. She was seven months pregnant and had the 'mask of pregnancy', particularly the red blotches on her nose and under her eyes, and her young husband watched her diet carefully.

Maigret was going to say once again how delicious his hostess's rice mould was when the phone rang for the third time since the soup. They were used to it. It had become a kind of game at the beginning of the meal to guess if the doctor would get to the pudding without being called by one of his patients.

The telephone stood on a wall-shelf with a mirror above it. Pardon, napkin in hand, grabbed the receiver.

'Hello. Doctor Pardon here . . .'

The others were silent, watching him, when suddenly they heard a voice so shrill that it made the phone vibrate. No one except the doctor could make out the words. They were only sounds piled one after the other like a record played too fast.

Maigret, however, frowned as he saw his friend's face become grave, a worried look spreading over it.

'Yes. . . . I'm listening, Madame Kruger. . . . Yes.'

The woman at the other end of the line needed no encouraging. The sounds fell over each other like a litany, incomprehensible but pathetic to those who didn't have their ear to the receiver.

A wordless drama was being acted out in the slight variations of expression on Pardon's face. The local doctor, who had been watching the by-play with the rice mould a few minutes before, now seemed to be far away from the quiet middle-class dining-room.

'I understand, Madame Kruger. . . . Yes, I know. . . . If it would help you, I'll come and . . .'

Madame Pardon threw a look at the Maigrets which said 'See! Another dinner to be finished without him.'

She was wrong. The voice shrilled on. The doctor grew more uneasy.

'Yes. . . . Of course. . . . Try to put them to bed . . .'

They could see that he felt discouraged and helpless.

'I know. . . . I know. . . . I can do no more than you can . . .'

No one was eating. No one in the room spoke.

'You understand that if this goes on it's you who . . .'

He sighed and wiped his forehead with his hand. At forty-five, he was almost bald.

He finished by sighing wearily, as if he were giving in to unbearable pressure:

'Then give him a pink pill. . . . No. . . . One only. . . . If that hasn't had any effect in half an hour . . .'

10

Everyone sensed a certain relief in the voice coming over the phone.

'I won't leave the house. . . . Good night, Madame Kruger.'

He hung up and sat down again. The others avoided asking him what it was all about. It took several minutes to get the conversation going again. Pardon took no part in it. The evening kept to its traditional rhythm. They got up from the table and had their coffee in the living-room, its table covered with magazines because that room was used as the waiting-room during surgery hours.

Both windows were open. It was May. The evening was warm and the air of Paris had quite a springlike feel, in spite of the buses and the cars. Local families were out strolling on the Boulevard Voltaire and there were two men in shirt-sleeves on the terrace of the café across the street.

Cups filled, the women took up their knitting in their usual corner. Pardon and Maigret sat by one of the windows, while Alice's husband didn't really know which group to join and ended up by sitting beside his wife.

It had already been decided that Madame Maigret would be the child's godmother, and she was knitting a little jacket for it.

Pardon lit a cigar. Maigret filled his pipe. They didn't particularly feel like talking, and quite a while went by in silence broken only by the hum of the women's voices.

The doctor finally spoke in a low voice, almost to himself:

'It's another of those evenings when I wish I'd chosen another profession.'

Maigret didn't press him, didn't urge him to speak. He liked Pardon. He felt he was a real man, in the full sense of the word.

The other glanced at his watch.

'This could go on for three or four hours, but she might ring at any minute.'

He went on without giving any details, so that Maigret had to pick up the sense for himself:

'A tailor in a small way, a Polish Jew, living in the Rue Popincourt above a herbalist's. . . . Five children, the eldest only nine, and the wife pregnant with the sixth . . .'

11

He shot an involuntary look at his daughter's increasing girth.

'No drug so far discovered can save his life, and he has been on the point of death for five weeks. . . . I've done all I can to get him to go into hospital. . . . As soon as I mention it he gets into a real state, calls his family to him, weeps, groans, begs them not to let him be carried off . . .'

Pardon was finding no pleasure in his one cigar of the day.

'They live in two rooms. . . . The kids cry. . . . The wife's at the end of her tether. . . . She's the one I ought to be taking care of, but as long as this goes on there's nothing I can do. . . . I went there before dinner. . . . I gave the man an injection and his wife a sedative. . . . They have no effect on them any more. . . . While we were at dinner he began to groan again, then to shriek with pain, and his wife, with no strength left . . .'

Maigret pulled on his pipe and murmured:

'I think I've got the picture.'

'Legally, medically, I haven't the right to prescribe another dose. . . . This isn't the first telephone call like that. . . . Up until now I've managed to convince her . . .'

He looked pleadingly at the inspector.

'Put yourself in my place . . .'

He glanced at his watch again. How much longer would the sick man fight on?

The evening was soft, with a trace of heaviness in the air. The wives were still chatting in low voices in a corner of the room, their kitting needles marking the rhythm of the conversation.

Maigret said hesitantly, 'It's not quite the same sort of case, of course. . . . Sometimes I too have wished I had chosen another profession . . .'

It wasn't a real conversation, with the dialogue following a logical pattern. There were gaps, silences, slow puffs of smoke rising from the inspector's pipe.

'For some time now we policemen haven't had the same powers we used to have, nor, in consequence, the same responsibilities . . .'

He was thinking aloud and felt very close to Pardon, a feeling which was shared by the other man.

12

'In the course of my career I've seen our duties grow less and less while the magistrates have taken more and more. . . . I don't know if it's a good thing or not. . . . In any case, we've never had to pass judgement. . . . It's the job of the courts and the juries to decide whether or not a man is guilty and to what extent he is responsible.'

He kept on talking because he felt that his friend was tense, his mind elsewhere, in the two rooms in the Rue Popincourt where the Polish tailor was dying.

'Even with the law as it is at present, though we are only the instruments of the Public Prosecutor's Office and of the examining magistrate, there is still a moment when we have to take a decision on which a lot depends. . . . Because after all the magistrates, and the juries eventually, form their opinions according to our investigations, according to the facts we have amassed . . .

'Just to treat a man as a suspect, to take him to the Quai des Orfèvres, to question his family, his friends, his concierge and his neighbours about him can change the entire course of his life.'

It was Pardon's turn to murmur, 'I understand.'

'Was a certain person capable of committing a certain crime? . . . Whatever happens, it is almost always we who have to be the first to ask ourselves that question. Material evidence is often non-existent or hardly convincing.'

The telephone rang. Pardon seemed afraid to answer it and it was his daughter who picked up the receiver.

'Yes, monsieur. . . . No, monsieur. . . . No. . . . You have the wrong number . . .'

Smiling, she explained to the others, 'The Bal des Vertus again.'

A dance-hall in the Rue du Chemin-Vert whose telephone number was similar to that of the Pardons.

Maigret went on in a subdued voice.

'This man in front of you, who seems so normal, could he have killed someone? . . . Do you see what I mean, Pardon? All right, so it's not a matter of deciding whether he is guilty or not. That's not the business of Central Police Headquarters. But we still have to ask ourselves *if it is possible*. . . . And that's a kind of judging! I hate that. ... If that had occurred to me when I joined the force, I'm not sure if ...'

A longer silence. He emptied his pipe and took another from his pocket, filling it slowly, seeming to caress the bowl.

'I remember one case, not so long ago. ... Did you follow the Josset case?'

'The name rings a bell.'

'It had a lot of publicity in the papers, but the truth, if truth there was, has never been told.'

It was rare for him to talk of a case in which he had taken part. Sometimes in the Quai des Orfèvres, among themselves, they would mention a well-known case or a difficult investigation, but it was always in few words.

'I can see Josset at the end of his first interrogation, for that was when I had to ask myself the question. I could let you read the report and see what you think. ... But you wouldn't have had the man in front of you for two hours. ... You wouldn't have heard his voice, watched his face and expressions ...'

*

The place was Maigret's office in the Quai des Orfèvres; the day, he remembered, was a Tuesday, the time about three in the afternoon. And it was spring then too, the end of April or the beginning of May.

When the inspector arrived at the Quai that morning he had heard nothing about the case, and he was only contacted at ten o'clock, first by the inspector at the Auteuil police station, then by Coméliau, the examining magistrate.

There was some confusion about everything that day. The Auteuil police claimed that they had informed Police Headquarters in the early hours of the morning, but for one reason or another the message didn't appear to have got through.

It was nearly eleven when Maigret climbed out of his car in the Rue Lopert, two or three hundred metres from the parish church of Auteuil, and he found himself last by a long way. The reporters and photographers were there, surrounded by about a hundred spectators held back by policemen. The men from the Public Prosecutor's Office were already on the spot and those from the Criminal Identity Division arrived five minutes later.

At 12.10 the inspector ushered Adrien Josset into his office. He was a handsome man of about forty, only just beginning to put on weight, and, in spite of being unshaven and wearing rather crumpled clothes, he was still elegant.

'Please come in. . . . Sit down . . .'

He opened the door of the detectives' office and called young Lapointe.

'Bring a pad of paper and a pencil.'

The office was bathed in sunlight and the sounds of Paris filtered in through the open window. Lapointe, who had understood that he was to take down the interrogation in shorthand, seated himself at one corner of the table. Maigret filled his pipe and watched a row of barges going up the Seine while a man in a small boat kept out of their way.

'I'm sorry, Monsieur Josset, but I have to make note of your answers. You aren't too tired, are you?'

The man indicated that he was not with a slightly bitter smile. He had not slept the previous night and the Auteuil police had already questioned him at length.

Maigret did not wish to read their report, preferring to make his own judgement.

'Let's begin with the usual questions of identity – surname, Christian names, age, profession . . .'

'Adrien Josset, aged forty, born in Sète in the Hérault region . . .'

One would have had to know that to pick out the slight accent of the Midi.

'What does your father do?'

'He was a primary school teacher. He died ten years ago.'

'Is your mother still alive?'

'Yes. She still lives in the same little house in Sète.'

'Did you take your degree in Paris?'

'In Montpellier.'

'I believe you are a pharmacist.'

'I did pharmacy, then a year of medicine. I didn't go on with that degree.'

'Why?'

15

He hesitated, and Maigret saw that it was from a kind of honesty. One could sense that he was trying very hard to answer correctly, truthfully, up to now at any rate.

'There were probably several reasons. The most obvious is that I had a girl-friend who went to Paris with her family.'

'Did you marry her?'

'No. In fact we broke it off a few months later. I think too that I felt I wasn't cut out to be a doctor. . . . My parents weren't well off. . . . They had to go without to pay for my studies. . . . And then when I had qualified I would have had difficulty in getting into a practice . . .'

Because of his tiredness it was hard for him to follow his own train of thought, and he sometimes looked at Maigret as if to reassure himself that the inspector understood him.

'Is that important?'

'Everything may be important.'

'I see. I wonder if I ever had a real vocation. . . . I had heard of jobs being offered in laboratories – most big drug firms have research laboratories. When I got to Paris, diploma in hand, I tried to get one of those jobs.'

'Without success?'

'All I found was a locum's post in a chemist's shop, then another . . .'

He was hot. So was Maigret, who was walking up and down the room, stopping from time to time in front of the window.

'Did they ask you these things at Auteuil?'

'No. Different things. I can see that you're trying to find out what kind of person I am. As you see, I'm trying to answer you truthfully. I suppose that basically I'm no better and no worse than anybody else.'

He mopped his brow.

'Are you thirsty?'

'A bit.'

Maigret opened the door of the detectives' room.

'Janvier! Bring us up something to drink.'

He turned to Josset.

'Beer?'

'That's fine.'

'Aren't you hungry?'

Without waiting for an answer he went on, to Janvier:

'Beer and some sandwiches, please.'

Josset gave a sad smile.

'I've read about that,' he murmured.

'Read about what?'

'Beer, sandwiches. The inspector and the detectives taking it in turns to ask questions. . . . It's quite well known, isn't it? . . . I never thought that one day . . .'

He had delicate hands which betrayed his nervousness from time to time.

'One knows what it means when one comes in here, but . . .'

'Calm yourself, Monsieur Josset. I can tell you now that I have no preconceived ideas about you.'

'The detective at Auteuil did.'

'Was he rough with you?'

'Fairly rough. He used some words which. . . . Never mind! Maybe in his place I would . . .'

'Let's go back to your first days in Paris. . . . How long was it before you met the woman you eventually married?'

'About a year. I was twenty-five and working in an English chemist's in the Rue du Faubourg Saint-Honoré when I met her.'

'Was she a customer?'

'Yes.'

'What was her maiden name?'

'Fontane. Christine Fontane. But she was still using the name of her former husband, who had died a few months before. Lowell, of the English brewery family. . . . You must have seen that name on bottles . . .'

'So she had been a widow for several months. How old was she?'

'Twenty-nine.'

'No children?'

'No.'

'Rich?'

'Very. She was one of the best customers of the fashionable shops in the Faubourg Saint-Honoré.'

'And you became her lover?'

'She led a very free life.'

'Even when her husband was alive?'

'I have reason to think so.'

'What kind of family did she come from?'

'Middle-class. Not rich, but comfortably off. She had spent her childhood in the XVIth *arrondissement* and her father was a director on the boards of several companies.'

'You fell in love with her.'

'Very quickly, yes.'

'Had you already broken off with your friend from Montpellier?'

'Several months before.'

'Did the question of marriage between Christine Lowell and you come up straight away?'

He hesitated only a second

'No.'

There was a knock at the door. It was the waiter from the Brasserie Dauphine, carrying beer and sandwiches. That made a break. Josset didn't eat, but he drank half his beer while Maigret marched to and fro munching a sandwich.

'Can you tell me how it came about?'

'I'll try. It's not easy. It was fifteen years ago. I was young, I see that now. Looking back, I think life was different then, things weren't as important as they are now.

'I was earning very little. I lived in a furnished room near the Place des Ternes, and I ate in cheap restaurants when I could afford more than croissants. I spent more on clothes than I did on food.'

He had kept his taste for clothes, and the suit he was wearing came from one of the best tailors in Paris. His monogrammed shirt had been made to measure, as had his shoes.

'Christine lived in a different world, one which I didn't know and which dazzled me. . . . I was still a provincial boy, a primary-teacher's son, and in Montpellier my student friends were hardly any better off than I was.'

'Did she introduce you to her friends?'

'A long time afterwards. There was one thing about our relationship which I didn't notice until later.'

'What was that?'

'One often speaks of businessmen, industrialists or financiers

18

having an affair with a salesgirl or a model. It was a bit like that for her, the other way round. She made dates with a poor, inexperienced pharmacist's assistant. She had to know where I lived – it was a cheap hotel, with delft tiles on the walls of the staircase. You could hear everything through the walls. She loved it. On Sundays she drove me to an inn in the country . . .'

His voice had grown duller, tinged both with nostalgia and with a little resentment.

'At first I too thought it was just one of those affairs which wouldn't last.'

'Were you in love with her?'

'I grew to love her.'

'Were you jealous?'

'That's how it all started. She used to tell me about her boy-friends and even about her lovers. She found it amusing to give me details. At first I said nothing. Then, in a fit of jealousy, I called her every name under the sun and ended up by hitting her. I was sure she was laughing at me behind my back and that when she left my little iron bed she went away to tell other men about my awkwardness and ingenuousness. . . . We had several quarrels like that. . . . I went without seeing her for a month . . .'

'Was it she who came back?'

'She or me, one of us. One of us always asked to be forgiven. We were really in love, Inspector.'

'Who first spoke of marriage?'

'I don't know. Frankly, I couldn't say. We got to the point where we hurt each other on purpose. . . . Sometimes she knocked at my door, half-drunk, at 3 a.m. If I was sulking and didn't answer at once the neighbours complained of the noise. I can't count the times they threatened to throw me out – at the pharmacy too, for I was late and half asleep on several mornings.'

'Did she drink a lot?'

'We both did. . . . I don't know why. . . . It was a habit. The affair excited us too much. Finally we realized that I couldn't live without her and she couldn't live without me . . .'

'Where did she live at that time?'

'In the house you saw in the Rue Lopert. . . . It was about two or three o'clock one morning, in a night club, that we looked into each other's eyes and suddenly sobered and asked ourselves seriously what we were going to do.'

'Don't you know who asked the question?'

'Frankly, no. For the first time someone had mentioned the word "marriage", at first as a joke, or almost. It's hard to say when it was so long ago.'

'She was five years older than you?'

'And several millions richer. Once married to her I couldn't go on working behind the counter of a chemist's shop. She knew a man Virieu who had been left a small drug firm by his parents. Virieu wasn't a pharmacist. He was thirty-five and had spent his life flitting between Fouquet's, Maxim's and the casino in Deauville. Christine put some money into the Virieu company and I became the head of it.'

'So in fact you were achieving your ambition?'

'It looks like that, I know. If one looks back on the sequence of events it does look as if I must have prepared each step carefully. In spite of that, I can tell you it's not a bit true.

'I married Christine because I was passionately in love with her and if I had had to leave her I would definitely have committed suicide. She in turn begged me to live legally with her.

'There was a long period when she had no more affairs and it was her turn to be jealous. She began to hate the customers at the pharmacy and came to spy on me.

'A chance came up which would give me a job commensurate with her style of living. The money put into the business stayed in her name and the marriage was legally one of separate maintenance.

'Some people took me for a gigolo and I haven't always been well received in the new society I had to live in from then on.'

'Were you happy together?'

'I think so. I worked hard. The laboratories used to be little known, but now they're considered one of the four biggest in Paris. We went out a lot too, so there weren't any gaps, so to speak, in either my days or my nights.'

'Don't you want anything to eat?'

'I'm not hungry. Perhaps I might have another glass of beer?'

'Were you drunk last night?'

'That's what they asked me about most this morning. I must have been at one point, but my memory isn't any the less clear for it.'

'I didn't want to read the statement you made at Auteuil, which I have here . . .'

Maigret flicked over the pages carelessly.

'Would you like to change any of it?'

'I told the truth, perhaps in rather strong language because of the detective's attitude. As soon as he started to question me I realized that he thought I was a murderer. Later, when the men from the Public Prosecutor's Office came to the Rue Lopert, I felt that the magistrate had the same idea . . .'

He was silent for a few moments.

'I can see their point. I was wrong to get angry.'

Maigret murmured, without too much stress,

'You didn't kill your wife?'

And Josset shook his head. He no longer made his protests angrily. He seemed tired, despondent . . .

'I know it's hard to explain . . .'

'Would you like to lie down for a little?'

The man hesitated. He shifted his weight slightly in the chair.

'I'd better go on. But would you let me get up and walk around?'

He too wanted to go to the window, to look at the world of those who were carrying on with their normal life in the sunlight.

The previous evening he had still belonged to that world. Maigret watched him dreamily. Lapointe waited, his pencil poised.

*

Now, in the peaceful room in the Boulevard Voltaire – a little too peaceful, almost oppressive in its calm – where the women still knitted and chatted, Doctor Pardon listened to Maigret's every word.

Nevertheless Maigret felt that he was just a link between the other man and the telephone on the shelf, between the doctor and the Polish tailor who was fighting his last battle among his five children and his hysterical wife.

A bus passed, stopped, started again after setting down two shadowy figures, and a drunk kept bumping against the walls without even faltering in his song.

2. The Geraniums in the Rue Caulaincourt

'Good heavens!' Alice cried suddenly and stood up. 'I forgot the liqueurs!'

She had changed completely. Before she was married she hardly ever came to these dinners which must have been boring for her. In the first months of her marriage she was rarely seen, only once or twice when she was basking in her new role as a married woman, as her mother's equal, in fact.

Since she had been expecting a child she often came to the Boulevard Voltaire, where she willingly acted as hostess, and she suddenly began to give more importance to the tiniest details of housewifery than even her mother did.

Her husband, a recently qualified veterinary surgeon, leaped from his chair, made his wife sit down again and went into the dining-room to get armagnac for the men and, for the women, a Dutch liqueur found hardly anywhere but at the Pardons'.

Like most doctors' waiting-rooms, this room was badly lit, and the furniture was drab and shabby. Maigret and Pardon, facing the open window, had a good view of the glaring lights of the boulevard where the leaves on the trees were beginning to rustle. Was there to be a change in the weather?

'Armagnac, Inspector?'

Maigret smiled vaguely at the young man, for although he realized where he was his thoughts were still in his sunny office on that Tuesday when Josset was being interrogated.

He felt duller than he had at dinner, with the same thing weighing on his mind as on the doctor's. Pardon and he, although they had met late in life, when the working life of both was well advanced, had always been able to understand each other's half-spoken sentences. There had been a bond between them on first meeting, and they respected each other greatly.

Wasn't this because they had the same kind of honesty, not only towards others, but self-knowledge? They didn't cheat, they didn't gild the pill, they looked things squarely in the face.

And if Maigret had suddenly begun to talk that evening, it was less to distract his friend than because the phone call had reawakened in him feelings much like Pardon's.

It wasn't that he had a guilt complex. Besides, Maigret detested that word. Nor was it a question of remorse.

Each man was obliged sometimes, through his job, the job he had chosen, to make a choice, a choice determining the fate of another. In Pardon's case it was whether a man should live or die.

There was nothing romantic in their attitude. Nor was there any dejection or rebellion, only a rather melancholy seriousness.

Young Bruart didn't quite dare to sit near them. He would have liked to know what they were talking about so quietly. But he knew that he didn't yet belong to that group, so he sat down again beside his wife.

'There were three of us in my office,' Maigret was saying. 'Young Lapointe, who was taking the whole thing down in shorthand, looking at me from time to time; Adrien Josset, who sometimes stood and sometimes sat on the chair; and me. I spent most of the time standing with my back to the window.

'I could see that the man was tired. He hadn't slept. He had had a lot to drink, first in the evening and then again in the middle of the night. I could see waves of lassitude sweeping over him. Sometimes he had real dizzy spells, and his rather worried eyes would become fixed, expressionless, as if he were sinking into a torpor and forcing himself to snap out of it again.

'It seems cruel to have gone on in spite of that with this first interrogation, which was going to last more than three hours.

'Yet it was for his sake as much as for duty's that I kept on.

On the one hand I had no right to let slip a chance of getting a confession, if he had anything to confess. On the other, he was in such a state of nerves that he wouldn't have been able to relax without an injection or a sedative.

'He felt the need of talking, of talking right then, and if I had sent him to the cells he would have gone on talking to himself.

'There were reporters and photographers waiting in the corridors. I could hear sudden snatches of loud conversation and laughter coming from there.

'By that time the afternoon papers had just come out and I was sure that they featured the Auteuil murder, and that photographs of Josset taken that morning in the Rue Lopert were blazoned over the front pages.

'It wasn't long before I had a call from Coméliau, the magistrate, who is always anxious to get a quick solution to his cases.

' "Is Josset there with you?"

' "Yes."

' "Has he confessed?"

'The man looked at me, guessing that it was about him.

' "I'm very busy," I said, giving no details.

' "Does he deny it?"

' "I don't know."

' "See that he understands that it's in his own interests . . ."

' "I'll try."

'Coméliau isn't a bad man. He has been called my dear enemy, because we've sometimes clashed with each other.

'It's not really his fault. It stems from the idea he has of his role and therefore of his duty. In his eyes, since he is paid to defend society he must show no pity to anything which threatens to disturb the established order. I don't think he has ever known what it is to have doubts. He calmly divides the sheep from the goats and is incapable of imagining that anyone could be a mixture of the two.

'If I had told him that I hadn't yet formed an opinion he wouldn't have believed me, or else he would have accused me of neglecting my duties.

'And yet after an hour, after two hours of questioning, I was

24

unable to answer the silent question which Josset kept asking with pleading looks:

' "You believe me, don't you?"

'The evening before, I hadn't met the man. I had never heard of him. If his name seemed familiar to me it was because I had had medicines with the names "Josset et Virieu" on the box.

'Oddly enough, I had never set foot in the Rue Lopert, which I had been rather surprised to discover that morning.

'In the little area around the parish church of Auteuil crimes are rare. And the Rue Lopert, which doesn't lead anywhere, is more a private lane than a real street. It only has about twenty houses of the kind you find in any avenue in a provincial town.

'It's only a stone's throw from the Rue Chardon-Lagache and yet one feels far away from the noises of Paris. The neighbouring streets, instead of being called after great men of the Republic, have authors' names: Rue Boileau, Rue Théophile-Gautier, Rue Leconte-de-Lisle . . .

'I wanted to go back to the house, which was different from all the others in the street. It was almost all glass and unexpected angles, built about 1925, in the Decorative Arts period.

'Everything was strange to me – the décor, the colours, the furniture, the layout of the rooms, and I would have been hard put to it to say what kind of life was lived there.

'The man in front of me, fighting exhaustion and a hangover, kept on asking with anxious but resigned look:

' "You believe me, don't you?"

'The inspector at Auteuil hadn't believed him and seemed to have treated him with no consideration at all.

'At one moment I had to open the door to silence the reporters in the corridor, who were making too much noise.'

*

For the second or third time Josset refused the sandwich he was offered. It seemed as if, knowing that his strength might fail him at any minute, he wanted to go on as far as he could, whatever the cost.

And perhaps it wasn't only because he had a divisional inspector facing him, a man who would have a say in his future.

He needed to convince someone, anyone, someone other than himself.

'Were you and your wife happy together?'

What would Maigret or Pardon have answered to the same question?

Josset hesitated too.

'I think that at certain times we were very happy. . . . Especially when we were alone. . . . Especially at night. . . . We were real lovers. . . . Do you understand? . . . If we could have been alone more often . . .'

He wanted so much to express himself exactly.

'I don't know if you know that class of people – I didn't either before I was a part of it. Christine had been brought up in it. . . . She needed it. . . . She had many friends. . . . She piled up social duties. . . . Whenever she had a free minute she was on the phone. . . . There were lunches, cocktail parties, dinners, dress-rehearsals, late suppers in night clubs. . . . There were hundreds of people we were on Christian name terms with and who were always to be found at these functions.

'She loved me once, I'm sure of that. . . . And certainly, in one sense, she still loved me . . .'

'And you?' Maigret asked.

'I loved her too. No one will believe it. Even our friends, who know all about us, will say it wasn't so. Yet what held us together was perhaps stronger than what is usually called love.

'We weren't lovers any more, except on rare occasions.'

'How long had that been so?'

'For a few years – four or five – I don't know exactly. I couldn't even say how it came about.'

'Did you quarrel?'

'Yes and no. It depends in what sense. We knew each other too well. We had no illusions left, and we couldn't cheat each other either. We had no mercy left.'

'No mercy on what?'

'On all the little faults, the tiny treacheries everyone commits. The first few times one doesn't know about them, or if one finds out one is tempted to see them in such a light that they become delightful . . .'

'One changes their qualities?'

'Let's say that the other one grows more human, more vulnerable, because of them, so that one wants to protect her, to surround her with love. . . . You see, at the bottom of everything is the fact that I wasn't prepared for that kind of life . . .

'Do you know our offices in the Avenue Marceau? We have laboratories at Saint-Mandé too, and in Switzerland and Belgium. That was, it still is, a big part of my life, the most important part. You asked me a moment ago if I was happy. There, running a business which was growing more important every day, I had a feeling of fulfilment – then, suddenly, the phone would ring. Christine would ask me to meet her some place . . .'

'Did you have a feeling of inferiority towards her, because of her money?'

'I don't think so. People thought that and no doubt still think that I married her for her money.'

'Didn't you? Didn't money come into it at all?'

'No, I swear it didn't.'

'Did the business remain in your wife's name?'

'Unfortunately, no. She kept a large part, but I was given an almost equal share six years ago.'

'At your request?'

'At Christine's. You must understand that it wasn't a question, as far as she was concerned, of recognizing the results of my hard work, but of avoiding taxes without giving shares to a third party. But I can't prove that and it will count against me – as will the fact that Christine made a will in my favour. I haven't read it; I haven't seen it; I don't know where it is. She told me about it one evening when she was very depressed and thought she had cancer.'

'Was her health good?'

He hesitated, still giving the impression of a man scrupulous about details, a man who must give words their exact meaning.

'She didn't have cancer, or a bad heart, or any of those diseases you read about every week in the papers and for which people collect money in the streets. As I see it she was none the less very ill. This last while she only had a few hours a day of complete lucidity and she sometimes spent two or three days shut in her room.'

'Didn't you sleep in the same room?'

'We did for years. Then, because I got up early and that wakened her, I moved into the room next door.'

'Did she drink a lot?'

'If you ask her friends, as you must, they will tell you that she didn't drink any more than many of them. They only saw her at her best, don't you see? They didn't know that an outing of two or three hours was preceded by several hours in bed and that the next day she had to start drinking or taking drugs as soon as she woke.'

'Don't *you* drink?'

Josset shrugged his shoulders as if to say that Maigret had only to look at him to see the answer.

'Less than she did, though. And not in such a morbid way. If I had, the laboratories would have folded up long ago. But when I drink I act like a drunk, so those same friends will tell you that I drank more than she did. Especially since I get violent when I drink. If you haven't been in the same position, how could you understand?'

'I'm trying,' sighed Maigret.

And then, point-blank:

'Do you have a mistress?'

'I thought we'd get to that before long! They asked me that this morning and when I answered the detective pounced on it triumphantly, as if he'd just put his finger right on the vital fact.'

'How long have you had one?'

'A year.'

'In that case it started long after things grew worse between you and your wife. That began five or six years ago, didn't you say?'

'Yes, it was a long time after and had nothing to do with it. Before that I had a few affairs like anyone else, mostly short ones.'

'But you've been in love for a year now?'

'It's embarrassing to use the same word I used for Christine, because it's quite different. But how else can I put it?'

28

'Who is she?'

'My secretary. When I said that to the detective I could tell that he had expected that answer and he was delighted with his own foreknowledge. Because it's so common it has become a joke, hasn't it? And yet . . .'

There was no more beer in the glasses. Most of the passers-by who had been walking on the bridge and on the banks of the Seine had been swallowed up again by offices and shops where work had begun again after lunch.

'Her name is Annette Duché, she is twenty, and her father is head clerk in the sous-préfecture at Fontenay-le-Comte. He is in Paris just now, and I am surprised that he hasn't come here to see you since the papers came out.'

'To accuse you?'

'Possibly. I don't know. Because something happens, because someone dies in dubious circumstances, everything becomes very confused from one minute to the next. Do you understand what I'm trying to say? Nothing natural, obvious or fortuitous is left. Every action, every word takes on a damning sense. I assure you I am aware of what I am saying. I need time to organize my thoughts, but right now I want you to know that I am hiding nothing from you and that I will try as hard as I can to help you to find the truth.

'Annette had been working in the Avenue Marceau for six months before I ever set eyes on her, for Monsieur Jules, the personnel officer, had put her in the shipping department, which is on another floor in the building, one I rarely go to. One afternoon my secretary was sick and I had an important report to dictate, so they sent her. We worked until 11 p.m. in the empty building, and since I felt guilty about depriving her of her dinner I took her to a local restaurant for a bite.

'That's all, really. I'm just forty and she's twenty. She reminds me of some of the girls I knew in Sète and in Montpellier. I hesitated for a long time. First I had her transferred to an office near mine, where I could keep an eye on her. I found out all about her. I was told that she was a nice girl, that when she first came to Paris she lived with an aunt in the Rue Lamarck, and that after quarrelling with her she had rented a small flat in the Rue Caulaincourt.

'All right, so it's silly! I even walked down the Rue Caulaincourt and I saw the pots of geraniums on her fourth-floor window-sill.

'Nothing happened for almost three months. Then, since we were setting up a branch in Brussels, I sent my secretary there and put Annette in her place . . .'

'Did your wife know about it?'

'I never hid anything from her. She didn't either, from me.'

'Did she have lovers?'

'If I answer that, people will say that I'm blackening her memory in order to save myself. People become sacred when they die.'

'How did she react?'

'Christine? At first she didn't react at all, just looked at me with a trace of pity in her eyes.

' "Poor Adrien! Have you sunk that far? . . ."

'She kept asking me about "the little girl", as she called her.

' "Not pregnant yet? What will you do when that happens? Will you ask for a divorce?" '

Maigret, frowning, looked at the other man with more interest.

'Is Annette pregnant?' he asked.

'No! That at least will be easy to prove.'

'Does she still live in the Rue Caulaincourt?'

'She hasn't changed her way of life at all. I didn't furnish her flat for her; I didn't buy her a car, or jewels, or a fur coat. There are still geraniums on the window-sill. There's still a walnut wardrobe with a mirror in her bedroom, and you still have to eat in the kitchen.'

His lip trembled, as if he were issuing a challenge.

'Didn't you want to change that?'

'No.'

'Did you often spend the night in the Rue Caulaincourt?'

'Once or twice a week.'

'Can you tell me as exactly as possible what you did yesterday and last night?'

'At what point shall I begin?'

'In the morning.'

Maigret turned to Lapointe as if to tell him to take down the times very carefully.

'I got up at 7.30, as usual, and went out on to the terrace for my exercises.'

'That was in the Rue Lopert, then?'

'Yes.'

'What did you do the evening before?'

'Christine and I went to the première of *Témoins* at the Théâtre de la Madeleine and then we ate at a night-club in the Place Pigalle.'

'Did you quarrel at all?'

'No. I had a hard day ahead of me. We were thinking of changing the packaging of some of our products, and this matter of how things are presented to the public has tremendous influence on sales.'

'At what time did you go to bed?'

'About 2 a.m.'

'Did your wife go to bed at the same time?'

'No. I left her in Montmartre with some friends we met.'

'Their name?'

'Joublin. Gaston Joublin is a lawyer. They live in the Rue Washington.'

'Do you know what time it was when your wife got home?'

'No. I'm a sound sleeper.'

'Had you been drinking?'

'A few glasses of champagne. My head was quite clear – I was thinking only of the next day's work.'

'Did you go into your wife's room in the morning?'

'I opened the door a crack and saw she was sleeping.'

'Didn't you waken her?'

'No.'

'Why did you open the door?'

'To see if she had come home.'

'Did she ever not come home?'

'Sometimes.'

'Was she alone?'

'As far as I know she has never brought any man back to the house.'

'How many servants have you?'

'Very few for a house the size of ours. Of course we rarely ate at home. The cook, Madame Siran, who is really a house-keeper, doesn't live in, but lives with her son in Javel, across the Pont Mirabeau. Her son must be about thirty. He's a bachelor, his health is poor, and he works on the Métro.

'Sleeping in, there's only the housemaid – Carlotta, a Spanish girl.'

'Who gets your breakfast?'

'Carlotta. Madame Siran only arrives as I am leaving.'

'Was everything the same as usual this morning?'

'Yes. . . . I'm thinking. . . . I can't think of anything special. I had a bath, dressed, went downstairs for a bite of breakfast, and as I was getting into my car, which is parked in front of the door all night, I saw Madame Siran coming round the corner carrying her shopping basket, for she does the shopping on the way.'

'Do you have only the one car?'

'Two. I use an English two-seater, because I'm mad about sports cars. Christine has an American car.'

'Was your wife's car parked at the side of the road?'

'Yes. The Rue Lopert is quiet, there's little traffic and it's easy to park there.'

'Did you go straight to the Avenue Marceau?'

Josset blushed and shrugged his shoulders slightly.

'No! And naturally that will count against me too. I went to the Rue Caulincourt to pick Annette up.'

'Do you go there every morning?'

'Almost. My car's a convertible. It's delightful to cross Paris early in the morning in spring . . .'

'Do you and your secretary arrive at the office together?'

'For a long time I put her down at the nearest Métro station. Some employees saw us. Since everyone knew about us I pre-ferred to be open about it and I think I derived some pleasure from hiding nothing, from facing up to public opinion. You see, I hate that kind of smirk, those whispers, the knowing looks. Since there is nothing wrong in our relationship I don't see why . . .'

He looked for approval, but the inspector remained impass-ive. It was his job.

The weather was the same as it had been the previous day, a delightful spring morning, and the little sports car coming down from Montmartre had threaded its way through the traffic, running along beside the gold-tipped railings of the Parc Monceau, crossing the Place des Ternes, rounding the Arc de Triomphe at a time when the crowds, still fresh at the day's start, were hurrying to their work.

'I spent the morning in discussions with my department managers, the sales manager in particular.'

'In front of Annette?'

'Her desk is in my office.'

It probably had tall windows looking out on to the elegant avenue with its luxury cars parked along either side.

'Did you take her to lunch?'

'No. I took an important English client who had just come over to the Berkeley.'

'Did you have any word from your wife?'

'I phoned her at 2.30, when I got back to the office.'

'Was she up?'

'She had just wakened. She told me she was going to do some shopping and then have dinner with a friend, a woman.'

'Did she say her name?'

'I don't think so. I would have remembered. Since it often happened, I didn't pay much attention, and we went on with the talks we had broken off at midday.'

'Did anything out of the ordinary happen during the afternoon?'

'It's not something out of the ordinary, but it has a certain importance: at about four o'clock I sent one of our errand-boys to a shop in the Madeleine to buy some hors d'oeuvres, a lobster, some Russian salad and some fruit. I told him to buy two punnets of cherries if there were any. He put it all in my car. At six o'clock my colleagues left, as did most of the employees. At 6.15 Monsieur Jules, the oldest employee, came to see if I needed him any longer and he left too.'

'And your partner, Monsieur Virieu?'

'He left the office at five. In spite of his years of experience, he's still an amateur and his role is largely public relations. He's the one who usually invites our foreign colleagues and our big provincial clients to lunch or dinner.'

'So he should have lunched with the Englishman?'

'Yes. He goes to conferences too.'

'So you and your secretary were alone in the building?'

'Yes, except of course for the concierge. That often happens. We went down and when we were in the car I decided to take advantage of the good weather to go and have a drink somewhere out of town. Driving relaxes me. We got to the Chevreuse valley quite quickly and had a drink in an inn.'

'Didn't you and Annette ever eat in a restaurant?'

'Hardly ever. At first I avoided doing so because I was keeping our relationship more or less secret. Then I grew fond of our little dinners in the Rue Caulaincourt.'

'With the geraniums at the window.'

Josset looked hurt.

'Does that seem funny to you?' he asked, a little aggressively.

'No.'

'Can't you understand?'

'I think so.'

'Even the lobster should give you some clue – in my family, when I was a child, we only had lobster on special occasions. The same in Annette's family. When we had what we called our little dinners we tried to have dishes we had wanted when we were young. In fact I did give her one present with that idea in mind – a refrigerator. It stands out a bit in the flat, which isn't very modern. It lets us have chilled white wine and sometimes a bottle of champagne. . . . You're not laughing at me?'

Maigret made a reassuring gesture. It was Lapointe who was smiling, as if it brought back recent memories.

'It was a little after eight when we got to the Rue Caulaincourt. I must add something else. The concierge, who was motherly towards Annette at first, before I came on the scene, took a dislike to her then. She used to growl obscenities at her when she passed and turned her back on me. We went by the room where her family were seated at table, and I'd swear that the woman gave us a malicious smile when she saw us . . .

'It had enough effect on me to make me want to go back and ask her what was making her look so happy.

'I didn't do it, but we found out why half an hour later. Once upstairs I took my jacket off and set the table while Annette changed. I make no secret of it – that gives me pleasure, makes me feel younger. She talked to me from the next room while I looked through the half-open door at her from time to time. Her skin is fresh and clear, her body refreshing.

'I suppose this will all come out in public. . . . Unless I find someone who'll believe me.'

His eyes closed with tiredness and Maigret went to the wall-cupboard to get him a glass of water. He didn't yet want to give him a small glass of the brandy which he always had in reserve. It was too soon. Maigret was afraid to put him into a state of nervous excitement.

'Just as we were sitting down to eat in front of the open windows Annette thought she heard something and a moment later I too heard footsteps on the stairs. There was nothing strange about that, because the building has five floors and there were three flats on the floor above us.

'I wondered why she suddenly seemed embarrassed to be wearing only a blue satin peignoir. The steps halted on our landing. No one knocked at the door but a voice said:

' "I know you're in there! Open up!"

'It was her father. He had never come to Paris as long as I had known Annette. I'd never seen him. She had described him to me as a melancholy man, stern and withdrawn. He had been a widower for several years and lived alone, completely intro-verted, with nothing to take him out of himself.

' "Just a moment, Papa!"

'She hadn't time to dress. I didn't think of putting my jacket on. She opened the door. It was me he looked at straight away, his eyes hard under bushy grey eyebrows.

' "Is this the man who keeps you?" he asked his daughter.

' "This is Monsieur Josset . . ."

'His look turned to the table and fell on the red splash of the lobster, on the bottle of Rhine wine.

' "Just as they said," he muttered as he sat down.

'He hadn't taken off his hat. He looked me over from head to foot with an unpleasant expression on his face.

' "I suppose you keep your pyjamas and slippers in the wardrobe?"

'He was right and I blushed. If he had gone into the bathroom he would have found a razor and a shaving brush, my toothbrush and my favourite toothpaste.

'Annette, who hadn't dared look at him at first, began to watch him and saw that he was breathing oddly, as if the climb up the stairs had had an effect on him. He was holding his body in an odd way, too.

' "Papa, have you been drinking?" she cried.

'He never drank. He must have come to the Rue Caulaincourt earlier in the day and met the concierge. Maybe she was the one who had written to tell him about the affair.

'While he waited he must have gone into the little bar across the street, from where he must have seen us go in.

'He had drunk to give himself courage. He had a greyish complexion, and his clothes hung on him as if he had once been a big man and had shrunk.

' "So, it's true . . ."

'He peered at each of us in turn, trying to find words. Probably he was as ill at ease as we were.

'Finally he turned to me and, in a voice both threatening and ashamed, asked:

' "What are you going to do about it?" '

3. The Concierge who Wanted her Picture in the Paper

Maigret had condensed this part of the interrogation into twenty or thirty interchanges which he considered to be the most important. His narrative was not continuous. His talks with the doctor were usually sprinkled with silences during which he pulled on his pipe as if he were giving the meaning of the sentences time to take form. He knew that for his friend the words had the same meaning, evoked the same feelings as they did for him.

'A situation so common that it's only a subject for hoary old jokes. There must be tens of thousands of men in the same situation in Paris alone. Things work out all right for most of them. Drama, if there is any, is restricted to a scene between husband and wife, to the separation, sometimes to the divorce, and life goes on . . .'

The man facing Maigret in the office which smelled of spring and tobacco was fighting a desperate battle for survival, and from time to time he looked at the inspector to see if there was any hope left.

The scene in the flat in the Rue Caulaincourt, with its three characters, had been both dramatic and sordid. It is this particular mixture of sincerity and farce which is so difficult to make clear, difficult even to imagine after the event, and Maigret understood Josset's discouragement as he searched for his words, never satisfied with the ones he found.

'I am sure, Inspector, that Annette's father is a good man. And yet. . . . He doesn't drink, I've told you that already. . . . He seems to be eating his heart out. . . . I don't know. . . . It's only a guess. . . . Perhaps it's due to remorse at not having made her happier? . . .

'Well, yesterday, while waiting for us to get to the Rue Caulaincourt, he had a few drinks. . . . He was in a bar, the only place he could watch the house from. . . . He asked for a drink mechanically, or perhaps to give himself courage, and he went on without realizing it.

'When he stood in front of me he hadn't lost control of himself, but one couldn't have argued with him in his state.

'What answer could I give to his question?

'He repeated it, still giving me a hard look:

' "What are you going to do?"

'And I, who few minutes before had nothing to blame myself for, I who was so proud of our love that I couldn't keep from showing it to everyone, I suddenly felt guilty.

'We had hardly begun to eat. I can see the red of the lobster and the red of the geraniums, and Annette clutching her blue peignoir tight about her and not crying.

'Truly moved, I blurted, "I assure you, Monsieur Duché . . ."

'He went on:

' "You realized, I hope, that she was a virgin?"

'I didn't find the words funny when spoken by her father. Besides, it wasn't true. Annette wasn't quite a virgin when I met her and she hadn't tried to pretend she was.

'The funny thing is that it was indirectly because of her father that she wasn't. That solitary misanthrope admired one man only, a man of his own age who was his superior at work, whom he regarded humbly as his friend, and for whom he felt a sort of hero-worship.

'Annette had her first job as a typist in this man's office, and Duché was as proud of that as some fathers are when their sons give their lives for their country.

'It's stupid, isn't it? It was with this man that Annette had her first sexual experience, which was incomplete anyway because her partner was unable to reach a climax. So because she was obsessed by the memory of the occasion, and also to prevent its happening again, she came to Paris.

'I hadn't the courage to say that to her father. I kept my mouth shut, trying to find words.

'He kept on, his voice thick:

' "Have you told your wife?"

'I said "yes" without thinking, without any heed for the consequences.

' "Does she consent to a divorce?"

'I must admit I said "yes" again.'

Maigret gave him a hard look and asked in his turn:

'You didn't really want a divorce, did you?'

'I don't know. . . . You want the truth, don't you? . . . Perhaps I thought of it, but not seriously. . . . I was happy. . . . Let's say I had enough little pleasures to think myself a happy man and I didn't have the courage to . . .'

He was still forcing himself to be exact, but since he was trying to achieve an impossible degree of exactness, he grew discouraged.

'So in fact you had no reason to wish to change the status quo?'

'It's more complicated than that. . . . With Christine too I had known a time. . . . Let's say a time when things were different. . . . One of those times when life seems brighter. . . . Do you understand? . . . Then reality broke through, bit by bit. . . . I saw her change into another woman. . . . I wasn't annoyed with her. . . . I knew it had to happen. . . . I hadn't seen the truth at the beginning, that's what it was.

'The woman that Christine became before my very eyes is exciting too, perhaps more so than the other was. . . . It's just that she doesn't inspire flights of rapture. . . . It's a different world . . .'

He wiped his hand across his brow in a gesture which was becoming more and more frequent.

'I wish you could believe me! . . . I'm trying to make you understand everything. . . . Annette isn't the same as Christine was. . . . I'm different too. . . . And I'm older now . . . I was happy with what she gave me and I didn't want any more. . . . You must find my attitude selfish, maybe even cynical . . .'

'You didn't want to make Annette your wife and have the whole thing begin all over again. . . . But you didn't say that to her father.'

'I don't remember exactly what I said. . . . I was ashamed, looking at him. . . . I felt guilty. . . . Besides, I wanted to avoid a scene. . . . I swore I loved Annette, which is true. . . . I promised to marry her as soon as possible . . .'

'Did you use those exact words?'

'Perhaps. . . . At any rate I spoke heatedly enough for Duché to be moved. . . . I said it was a question of how long the formalities would take. . . . To have done with the whole episode of the Rue Caulaincourt, I'll tell you quickly one detail which is sillier than the rest. . . . By the end I felt myself so much his son-in-law that I uncorked the champagne which we always kept in the refrigerator, and we drank each other's health.

'It was dark when I left. I got into the car and for a while I drove about the streets without knowing where I was going.

'I didn't know any longer whether I had done right or wrong. . . . I felt I had betrayed Christine. . . . I've never been able to kill anything. . . . And yet once, when we were staying with friends in the country, I was asked to chop off a chicken's head

39

and I didn't dare funk it. . . . Everyone was watching me. It took me two attempts and I felt I was conducting an execution . . .

'That was a bit like what I'd just done. . . . Because a half-drunk old man had acted the heavy father in front of me I had rejected fifteen years of life with Christine. . . . I had promised, I had sworn to sacrifice her . . .

'I began to drink too, in the first bar I came to. . . . It wasn't far from the Place de la République, where I was surprised to find myself when I left the bar. . . . Then I got to the Champs-Elysées. . . . Another bar. . . . I had three or four drinks there, one after the other, trying to think what I should say to my wife . . .

'I made up sentences which I mumbled to myself to see how they sounded . . .'

He looked at Maigret, suddenly pleading.

'I'm sorry. It's probably not the thing to do. . . . You wouldn't have anything to drink, would you? . . . I've held on up to now. . . . But it's physical, you know. . . . When you've had too much the night before . . .'

And Maigret went over to the wall-cupboard, took out the bottle of brandy and poured a glass for Josset.

'Thank you. . . . I'm still ashamed of myself. . . . I have been since yesterday evening, since that grotesque scene, but not for the reasons people will think . . .

'I didn't kill Christine. . . . The idea never entered my head for a minute. . . . I found many solutions to my problem, unlikely solutions, it's true, for *I* was drunk now. . . . Even if I'd wanted to kill her, I wouldn't have had the guts . . .'

*

The Pardons' telephone still hadn't rung. So the little tailor hadn't yet died and his wife was still waiting, while the children slept.

'At that moment,' said Maigret, 'I thought the time had come . . .'

He didn't say the time for what.

'I tried to decide, I weighed the pros and cons. . . . My phone rang. . . . It was Janvier, asking me to come into the detectives' office. . . . I excused myself and went out . . .

'Janvier had a new edition of an afternoon paper to show me. The ink on it was still wet. A bold headline read:

Double Life of Adrien Josset
Violent Scene in the Rue Caulaincourt

' "Do the other papers have this too?"

' "No, only this one."

' "Phone the editorial office and find out where they got it from." '

While he waited Maigret read the article:

We are able to give some details of the private life of Adrien Josset, whose wife was murdered last night in their house in Auteuil – see the preceding article.

While friends of the couple believed them to be very close, the pharmacist had in reality been leading a double life for about a year.

He had become the lover of his secretary, Annette D—, aged 20, and had set her up in a flat in the Rue Caulaincourt, where he went every morning to pick her up in his sports car and where he took her back almost every evening.

Two or three times a week Adrien Josset dined there with his mistress and he often spent the night there.

Now last night a dramatic incident took place in the Rue Caulaincourt. The young lady's father, a very respectable civil servant from Fontenay-le-Comte, paying an unexpected visit to his daughter, found the couple, whose intimacy was beyond doubt, together.

The two men confronted each other in an angry exchange. We have unfortunately not been able to interview Monsieur D—, who must have left the capital this morning, but the events in the Rue Caulaincourt must have some connection with the drama which later took place in the house in Auteuil.

Janvier put down the telephone.

'I didn't manage to speak to the reporter, because he's not there just now.'

'He must be here, waiting in the corridor with the others.'

'That's possible. The girl who answered didn't want to tell me anything. She did say something about an anonymous telephone call to the editor's office at about noon, immediately after the murder was announced on the wireless. I got the impression that it was the concierge who rang.'

Half an hour before, Josset had still had a chance of putting his case to an impartial audience. He hadn't been charged. He might be a suspect, but there was no material evidence against him.

Coméliau was in his chambers, waiting for the results of Maigret's questioning, and although he wanted to have a guilty man to put before the public he would not make a decision against the inspector's advice.

A concierge who wanted her picture in the paper had changed the entire situation.

In the public eye Josset would now be 'The Man with the Double Life', and even the thousands of men in like situation would see that there lay the motive for his wife's death.

All this was so true that Maigret heard the telephone in his office ringing already. When he went in Lapointe, who had answered it, was saying:

'He's right here, Monsieur Coméliau. . . . Just a moment . . .'

Coméliau, of course!

'Have you read it, Maigret?'

'I knew all about that already,' Maigret answered rather drily.

Josset couldn't but know that it was about him and was trying to overhear.

'Did you give the information to the paper? Did the concierge tell you?'

'No. *He* did.'

'Of his own free will?'

'Yes.'

'Did he really meet the girl's father yesterday evening?'

'He did.'

'In that case, don't you think . . .?'

'I don't know, Monsieur Coméliau. The interrogation is still going on.'

'Will you be long?'

'Probably not.'

'Let me know as soon as possible and don't give the press any statement until you've seen me.'

'You have my word on that.'

Should he tell Josset? Would it be right? The phone call had upset him.

'I suppose the magistrate . . .'

'He won't do anything before he has seen me. Sit down. Try to keep calm. I still have a few questions to ask you.'

'Something has happened, hasn't it?'

'Yes.'

'Something that makes things worse for me?'

'In a way. . . . I'll tell you about it in a minute. . . . Where were you? . . . In a bar near the Étoile. . . . That will all be checked – not because we doubt your word, but as routine. Do you know the name of the bar?'

'The Select. Jean, the bartender, has known me for years.'

'What time was it?'

'I didn't look at my watch, nor at the clock in the bar, but I'd say half past nine.'

'Did you speak to anyone?'

'To the bartender.'

'Did you tell him your troubles?'

'No. He knew I was upset because of the way I was drinking, because I wasn't myself. He said something like:

' "Things not going well, Monsieur Josset?"

'And I said something like:

' "Not very . . ."

'Yes, that's it. I added, for self-respect, afraid to be taken for drunk,

' "I've eaten something that doesn't agree with me . . ." '

'Were you clear-headed then?'

'I knew where I was, what I was doing, where I'd left my car. . . . A little later I stopped at a red light. . . . Is that what you mean by being clear-headed? . . . Still, things *were* a bit confused. . . . Indeed, the fact that I was sorry for myself, that I was getting maudlin about myself, which isn't normal for me . . .'

But he was a weak man, his story showed that clearly, and it was no less obvious in his expressions and his attitudes.

'I kept saying to myself, "Why me?"

'I felt I'd been the victim of a plot. I even went so far as to suspect Annette of telling her father and getting him to come to Paris to make a scene which would put me in a tight corner . . .

'At other times I blamed Christine. Everyone will say that I

43

owe my success to her and that it's through her that I've attained any position of importance. . . . Maybe it's true. . . . Who knows what my career would have been like without her? . . .

'But, on the other hand, it was she who plunged me into a world which wasn't my world, where I have never felt at ease. . . . Only in the office did I . . .'

He shook his head.

'When I'm less tired I'll try to say it more clearly. . . . Christine taught me a lot. . . . There is good *and* bad in her. . . . She isn't happy and never has been. . . . I was going to say she never will be. . . . You see I can't manage to convince myself that she is dead. . . . Doesn't that prove I didn't do it?'

Unfortunately, as other cases had shown Maigret, it didn't.

'Did you go home when you left the Select?'

'Yes.'

'What were you planning to do?'

'To talk to Christine, to tell her everything, to discuss with her what I should do.'

'Were you thinking about a divorce at that time?'

'It seemed the simplest solution to me, but . . .'

'But what?'

'I realized it would be difficult to get my wife to agree to it. . . . To understand that, you'd have had to know her, and even her closest friends only knew superficial things about her. . . . It's true that our relationship wasn't what it had been. . . . I've already told you we didn't sleep together any more. . . . We quarrelled and sometimes we hated each other. . . . But I was still the only person who really understood her, and she knew it. . . . She could be herself only with me. . . . I never judged her. . . . Wouldn't she have missed me? . . . She was so afraid of being left alone. . . . That was why she hated growing old, because age and loneliness were the same in her eyes.

' "As long as I have money I'll be able to buy friends, won't I?"

'She used to laugh when she said that, but it was no joke to her.

'Was I going to tell her just like that that I was going to leave her?'

'But you'd made up your mind?'

44

'Yes. . . . Not quite. . . . Not like that. . . . I would have told her what had happened in the Rue Caulaincourt and asked her advice . . .'

'Did you often ask her advice?'

'Yes.'

'Even about business matters?'

'Important ones, yes, always.'

'Do you believe that honesty was your only motive for needing to tell her all about your relationship with Annette?'

He thought about it, truly surprised by the question.

'I see what you mean. . . . For a start, she was older than I. . . . When I met her I hardly knew Paris and had only seen what a poor student can see here. . . . She taught me everything about a certain type of life, a certain social class . . .'

'What happened when you got back to the Rue Lopert?'

'I wondered if Christine was back. It wasn't likely and I expected to have to wait a while. That thought cheeered me up a bit, for I needed to bolster up my courage.'

'With another drink?'

'I suppose so. Once you've begun, you keep thinking one more glass will set you right. I saw the Cadillac parked at the door.'

'Were there any lights on in the house?'

'I only noticed Carlotta's, upstairs. I let myself in with my key.'

'Did you bolt the door after you?'

'I expected you'd ask that, because they asked me this morning. I suppose I did it mechanically, as it's a habit, but I don't remember.'

'Were you still unaware of the time?'

'No. I looked at the clock in the hall. It was five past ten.'

'Weren't you surprised that your wife was home so early?'

'No. She has never kept to a strict timetable and it's hard to know exactly what she'll decide to do next.'

He continued to speak of her in the present tense, as if she were still alive.

'Have you been to the house?' he asked.

Maigret had hardly seen it, because the men from the Public Prosecutor's Office were there, and Doctor Paul and the local

45

inspector, and seven or eight experts from Criminal Records.

'I must go back there,' he murmured.

'You'll find a bar on the ground floor . . .'

The ground floor was in fact one huge room of an odd shape, with unexpected corners and bits of wall, and Maigret did indeed remember a bar almost as big as any in the Champs-Elysées.

'I poured myself a whisky. . . . My wife only drinks that. . . . I flopped into an armchair; I needed time to draw my breath . . .'

'Did you put the lights on?'

'I put the hall light on when I came in, but I turned it off at once. There are no shutters on the windows. A street lamp about ten metres away lights the room well enough. . . . Besides, it was full moon. . . . I remember looking at the moon for a while and even calling it to witness . . .

'I got up to pour another drink. . . . Our glasses are very big. . . . I sat down again in the chair, whisky in hand, and began to think again . . .

'And that, Inspector, is how I fell asleep.

'The inspector this morning didn't believe me and told me to change my story. When I refused he got angry.

'But it's true. . . . If it happened while I was asleep I didn't hear a thing. . . . I didn't dream, either. . . . I don't remember anything, only a big blank – I can't find a better word for it . . .

'A pain in my side, a cramp, woke me up bit by bit . . .

'It took me some time to organize my thoughts before I stood up . . .'

'Did you feel drunk?'

'I don't know. . . . Now it all seems a nightmare. . . . I put the light on, drank a glass of water, after considering having another whisky. . . . Finally I started to go upstairs . . .'

'With the idea of waking your wife and discussing the situation with her?'

He didn't answer, but looked at the inspector with surprise, reproachfully, even. He seemed to be saying, 'Do *you* ask me that?'

And Maigret, a little embarrassed, muttered, 'Go on.'

'I went into my room, put on the light and looked at myself in the mirror. I had a headache. My beard and the bags under my eyes looked repulsive.

'I opened Christine's door out of habit. . . . That's when I saw her as you did this morning . . .'

The body half out of bed, head hanging on a fur rug spotted with blood, as were the sheets and the satin coverlet . . .

Doctor Paul, in a hasty examination — he was performing the autopsy while Maigret was questioning Josset — had counted twenty-one wounds inflicted by what the report, in its official language, called a sharp instrument.

So sharp in fact, and wielded with such force that the head had almost been severed from the body.

There was silence in Maigret's office. It seemed impossible that on the other side of the windows life went on as before, that the sun was as bright, the air as soft. Two tramps were asleep under the Pont Saint-Michel, newspapers over their faces, indifferent to the noise. And two lovers sitting on the stone parapet dangled their feet above the water reflecting them.

'Try not to forget anything.'

Josset indicated that he would do his best.

'Did you put the light in your wife's room on?'

'I hadn't the courage.'

'Did you go up close to her?'

'I could see enough from where I was.'

'Didn't you make sure that she was dead?'

'It was obvious.'

'What was your first reaction?'

'To telephone. I went to the phone and even lifted the receiver . . .'

'To call whom?'

'I didn't know. . . . It didn't occur to me at first to call the police. . . . I thought first of our doctor, Doctor Badel, who is a friend . . .'

'Why didn't you call him?'

In a whisper he repeated, 'I don't know.'

He put his head in his hands and thought. He fitted the part perfectly.

'It was the words, I suppose, that stopped me from phoning. . . . What should I say? . . .

' "Someone has just killed Christine. . . . Come . . ."

'Then I'd be asked questions. . . . The police would take over the house. . . . I couldn't face them. . . . I felt that if they pressed me, I'd collapse . . .'

'You weren't alone in the house. The maid was upstairs.'

'I know. . . . Everything I did seems illogical, and yet you must believe that there was a certain logic in it since I acted that way and I'm not mad . . .

'It's also true that I had to rush to the bathroom to vomit. . . . That wasted some time. . . . As I leaned over the basin I thought a bit. . . . I told myself that no one would believe me, that I'd be arrested and thrown into prison . . .

'And I felt exhausted. . . . If I could only have a few hours, a few days. . . . I didn't want to escape, but to have time to think. . . . Maybe that's panic. . . . Hasn't anyone ever told you that? . . .'

Josset knew that many others had passed through that same office before him, people just as exhausted, just as haggard, and piece by piece had put together their string of lies or the truths which they couldn't express.

'. . . I washed my face in cold water. . . . I looked at myself in the mirror again. . . . Then I rubbed my hands over my cheeks and began to shave.'

'Why, *exactly*, did you shave?'

'I was thinking quickly, maybe not logically, and I was trying not to mix up the ideas which were rushing into my mind.

'I had decided to go away. Not by car, for I'd risk being caught too soon, and besides, I didn't have the strength for a long drive. The easiest thing would be to catch a plane, any plane, at Orly. My business requires me to travel a lot, sometimes at a moment's notice, and my passport always has some current visas.

'I calculated the time I'd need to get to Orly. . . . I had hardly any money on me, perhaps twenty or thirty thousand francs, and there wouldn't be more than that in my wife's room, since we were in the habit of paying for everything by cheque. . . . That was a complication . . .

'These worries stopped me thinking about what had happened to Christine. . . . The mind fixes on small things. . . . It was because of a little thing that I shaved. . . . The customs officers at Orly know me. . . . Since they know that I'm very careful about my person, perhaps too much so, they would be very surprised to see me go off on a trip unshaven . . .

'I had to go to the office in the Avenue Marceau. . . . Although the safe didn't hold a lot, I was sure I'd find several hundred thousand francs . . .

'I needed a suitcase, if only for appearance's sake, and I stuffed one full of underwear and toilet things. . . . I thought of my watches. . . . I have four, two of them valuable. . . . That would bring me money if I needed any . . .

'The watches made me think of my wife's jewels. . . . I didn't know what was going to happen. . . . The plane might take me to the other end of Europe or to South America. . . . I still didn't know if I would take Annette . . .'

'Had you thought of taking her?'

'I think so, yes. . . . Partly so as not to be alone. . . . As my duty, too.'

'Not for love?'

'I don't think so. I'm being frank. Our love was . . .'

He began again.

'Our love *is* something clearly defined: her presence in my office, the route we take every morning from the Rue Caulaincourt to the Avenue Marceau, our little dinners in her flat. . . . I didn't *see* Annette with me in Brussels, in London or in Buenos Aires, for example . . .'

'But you still thought of taking her?'

'. . . Perhaps because of my promise to her father. . . . Then I was afraid that he might have spent the night in her flat. . . . What would I say to him if I found myself face to face with him in the middle of the night?'

'Did you take your wife's jewels?'

'Some of them. The ones she kept in her dressing-table. That is, the ones she had worn recently . . .'

'Did you do anything else?'

He hesitated, hung his head.

'No. I can't think of anything else. . . . I put out the light. . . .

I went downstairs without making a noise. . . . I hesitated again about having a drink, as I felt sick to my stomach, but I had one . . .'

'Did you take your car?'

'I decided it wasn't wise. . . . Carlotta might have heard the engine and come down, who knows? . . . There's a taxi-rank by the church in Auteuil and I walked there . . .'

He picked up his empty glass and held it out to Maigret with a timid look.

'May I?'

4. How Adrien Josset Spent the Rest of the Night

Once, talking of the notorious grillings of the French police, gentle but surprisingly effective, and the no less legendary American third degree, Maigret had said that the suspects most likely to get away with it are the simpletons. This got to the ears of a journalist, and the joke had become a stock item which the press brought out from time to time in different guises.

What he had really meant to say, what he still believed, was that a simple-minded person is naturally mistrustful, always on the defensive, answers with the minimum of words without worrying about seeming truthful, and when he is later cross-examined he doesn't get upset but sticks firmly to his story.

The intelligent man, on the other hand, needs to explain himself, to dispel any doubts his questioner may have. Trying to be convincing, he anticipates questions, gives too many details and, determined to build up a watertight case, ends up by catching himself out.

So, when his logic is shown up, it is rare for him not to get upset and, ashamed of himself, to confess.

Adrien Josset was one of those who anticipated questions, anxious to explain facts and actions which seemed disconnected.

Not only did he admit that they didn't fit together, but he

underlined it, sometimes seeming to be seeking the key to the mystery in speaking aloud.

Guilty or innocent, he knew enough about the mechanics of an investigation to realize that, once it had started, everything he had said and done that night would be fed through the machine sooner or later.

He said everything with so much passion that two or three times Maigret could hardly prevent a confession of the kind which came too early for his taste.

Because Maigret usually chose the time for a confession to be made. He preferred to have a wider and more personal understanding of the case first. This morning he had hardly looked at the house in the Rue Lopert and he knew nothing about the people who lived there and almost nothing about the crime.

He hadn't questioned anyone else, neither the Spanish housemaid nor Madame Siran, the cook whose son worked on the Métro and who went home to Javel every evening.

He had no idea what the neighbours were like, hadn't seen Annette Duché or the father who had been summoned rather mysteriously from Fontenay-le-Comte. And he had yet to see the head office of Josset and Virieu, Pharmaceutical Products, in the Avenue Marceau, and Josset's friends, and many other more or less important people.

Doctor Paul would have finished his autopsy and must have been surprised not to have the usual phone call from the inspector, who rarely had the patience to wait for the written report. Up there too, in Criminal Records, they were working on the fingerprints found that morning.

Torrence, Lucas and perhaps ten or twelve detectives were carrying out the routine jobs, and in various offices in the Quai des Orfèvres Carlotta and other minor witnesses were being questioned.

Maigret could have broken off the interrogation to find out what was going on, and even Lapointe, still hunched over his pad of notes, was surprised to see him listening patiently, without steering the interview in any particular direction, without trying to catch Josset out.

The questions he asked were rarely technical and some of

them seemed to have only a distant connection with the night's happenings.

'Tell me, Monsieur Josset, I suppose that at your offices in the Avenue Marceau or the laboratories of Saint-Mandé you sometimes have to give people the sack?'

'One has to do that in all businesses.'

'Do you yourself do it?'

'No, I leave that to Monsieur Jules.'

'Have you ever had business problems?'

'That's unavoidable too. For example, three years ago people said one of our products wasn't absolutely pure and had been the cause of several deaths.'

'Who dealt with that?'

'Monsieur Jules.'

'I thought he was the personnel manager, not a business manager. It seems, then . . .'

Mairgret interrupted himself, then added after a bit of thought:

'You can't bear to say unpleasant things to people, can you? I note that when you saw Monsieur Duché in the Rue Caulaincourt you promised him anything, to get a divorce, to marry his daughter, anything rather than speak frankly.

'When you found your wife dead you kept away from her and didn't even put on the light. Your first thought was to run away.'

Josset hung his head.

'It's true. I panicked, there's no other word for it.'

'You got a taxi near the church in Auteuil?'

'Yes. A grey 403. The driver was from the Midi, by his accent.'

'You asked to go to the Avenue Marceau?'

'Yes.'

'What time was it?'

'I don't know.'

'You must have passed several lighted clocks. You meant to take a plane. You often travel by plane. Therefore you know the timetables of several airlines. It was very important for you to know the time . . .'

'I know all that, but I can't explain it. Things don't happen the way one expects when one thinks about them in cold blood.'

'Did you have the taxi wait when you got to the Avenue Marceau?'

'I didn't want to attract attention. I paid the man and walked across the pavement. For a moment, as I went through my pockets, I thought I had forgotten my key.'

'Did that worry you?'

'No. I meant to leave Paris, but I was fatalistic about it. Besides, I found the key in a pocket I don't normally put it in. I went in.'

'Wasn't there a risk of wakening the concierge?'

'If I had done so, I would have said that I needed some papers for a last-minute business trip. It didn't worry me.'

'Did he hear you?'

'No. I went up to my office. I opened the safe, took the four hundred and fifty thousand francs in it and wondered where to hide them in case I was searched at the customs. I didn't worry too much about it, as I never have been searched. I sat in my chair, not moving, for about ten minutes, looking around me.'

'Was that when you decided not to go?'

'I felt too tired. I had no strength left.'

'Strength for what?'

'For going to Orly, for buying a ticket, waiting, showing my passport, being afraid . . .'

'Afraid of being arrested?'

'Of being questioned. I kept thinking of Carlotta. She might have come downstairs. Even when I landed at a foreign airport, there was still the risk of being questioned. At best, I would have had to start a new life, alone . . .'

'Did you put the money back in the safe?'

'Yes.'

'What did you do then?'

'The suitcase was hampering me. I wanted a drink. It became an obsession. I was sure that even though it hadn't helped before a little alcohol would restore my self-control. I had to walk to the Étoile to get another taxi. I said:

' "First of all, stop at a bar." '

'The taxi had only to go about two hundred metres. I left the suitcase in it and I went into a strip-tease place without noticing which one it was. I refused to follow the maître d'hôtel to a table. I leaned on the bar and ordered a whisky. A hostess asked me to buy her a drink, and I did, to avoid a scene.

'On the dance-floor another woman was taking off black underclothes and uncovering more and more white skin.

'I had two drinks. I paid. I went out and got into my taxi again.

' "Which station do you want?" the driver asked.

' "I want to go to Auteuil. Go by the Rue Chardon-Lagache. I'll tell you when to stop . . ."

'My suitcase was making me feel guilty. I stopped the taxi about a hundred and fifty metres from my house and before I went in I reassured myself that there were no lights on in the house. I only lit what lights I had to and I put my wife's jewels back, and put away my clothes and toilet articles. I expect they'll find my fingerprints on the dressing-table and on the jewels if they haven't done so already.'

'So you went into her bedroom again?'

'I had to.'

'Didn't you look?'

'No.'

'And you still didn't think of phoning the police?'

'I kept putting it off.'

'What did you do then?'

'I went out and wandered around the streets.'

'Which way did you go?'

Josset hesitated and Maigret, watching him, frowned and pressed the point rather impatiently.

'It's an area you're familiar with. You've lived there for fifteen years. Even if you were preoccupied or upset you must have recognized some places you passed . . .'

'I do remember the Pont Mirabeau, where I found myself. I couldn't think how I'd got there.'

'Did you cross it?'

'Not all the way. I leaned on the parapet somewhere near the middle of the bridge and watched the Seine go by.'

'What were you thinking about?'

54

'That I really was going to be arrested and that for weeks, if not months, I would be struggling with tiring and painful problems.'

'Did you go home again?'

'Yes. I would have liked another drink before going to the police, but there wasn't anywhere open. I had to take a taxi again.'

'Has Annette Duché a telephone?'

'I had one put in for her.'

'Did you never think of ringing her to tell her what had happened?'

He thought.

'Perhaps. I don't remember. Anyway, I didn't.'

'Did you wonder at all who could have killed your wife?'

'I was more concerned with the fact that I would be the one who would be accused.'

'According to the report I have here you presented yourself at 3.30 at the Auteuil police station at the corner of the Boulevard Exelmans and the Rue Chardon-Lagache. You gave your card to the policeman on duty and asked to see the inspector in person. He told you that wasn't possible at that hour of the night and took you to Detective Jeannet's office.'

'He didn't tell me his name.'

'First the detective questioned you briefly, and when you had given him your key he sent a car to the Rue Lopert. I have here the more detailed statements you made later. I haven't read them. Are they correct?'

'I think so. It was very hot in that office. I suddenly felt exhausted and wanted to sleep. The detective's manner of asking questions, sometimes brutal, sometimes ironical, annoyed me.'

'You seem to have been able to sleep for two hours.'

'I don't know how long it was.'

'Have you anything to add?'

'I don't think so. . . . Perhaps some things will come back later. . . . I'm exhausted. . . . It seems as if everything is against me, that I'll never be able to prove the truth. . . . I didn't kill Christine. . . . I have always tried never to hurt anyone. . . . Do you believe me?'

'I haven't any opinion. ... Will you type out your notes, Lapointe?'

And, to Josset:

'You've had enough for just now. When they bring you the typed statement, read it and sign it.'

He went into the neighbouring office and sent Janvier to keep Josset company.

The performance had taken three hours.

*

While he was silently watching the lights in the Boulevard Voltaire Maigret heard his wife cough slightly. He turned towards her and saw her make a little sign to him.

She was reminding him of the time. It was later than they usually stayed. Alice was saying good night to her mother, because she and her husband had to go home to Maisons-Alfort. Pardon kissed his daughter on the forehead.

'Good night!'

Just as the young people reached the door the phone rang loudly, more loudly, it seemed, than usual. Madame Pardon looked at her husband and he went slowly to answer it.

'Doctor Pardon here.'

It was Madame Kruger. Her voice was less shrill, less vibrant than it had been a short while before. Now those standing at a distance could barely hear a murmur from the receiver.

'No, no,' Pardon was saying gently. 'You can't blame yourself at all.... It's not your fault, I assure you.... Are the children up? ... Haven't you got a neighbour you can take them to? .. Listen, I'll be with you in half an hour at the latest ...'

He listened a little longer, murmuring something from time to time.

'Yes. ... Yes, of course. ... You've done all you could. ... I'll take care of that. ... Yes. ... Yes. ... I'll see you in a few minutes ...'

He hung up and sighed. Maigret was standing up. Madame Maigret had wrapped up her knitting and put on her spring coat.

'Is he dead?'

'He died a few minutes ago. I must go over there. She's going to need taking care of.'

They went downstairs together The doctor's car was parked at the kerb.

'Don't you want a lift?'

'No, thank you. We'd prefer to walk a little.'

That was part of the tradition. Madame Maigret took her husband's arm automatically, and they walked home slowly in the calm evening air along the empty pavements.

'Were you telling him about the Josset case?'

'Yes.'

'Were you able to get to the end?'

'No. I'll tell him the rest some other time.'

'You did all you could . . .'

'Like Pardon this evening. . . . Like the tailor's wife . . .'

She gripped his arm more tightly.

'It's not your fault.'

'I know.'

There were some cases like that which he didn't like to remember, and, paradoxically, they were the ones he had taken most to heart.

For Pardon, the Jewish tailor in the Rue Popincourt had previously been almost unknown, one sick person among many. Now, because of a high-pitched voice on the telephone, because of a decision taken at the end of a family dinner, because of some words spoken wearily, Maigret was sure that his friend would always remember him.

Josset too had had an important place in Maigret's thoughts for a time.

While Lapointe was typing his shorthand notes, while telephones shrilled in all the offices, while the journalists and the photographers grew more impatient, Maigret wandered here and there in the premises of the Police Headquarters, grave, preoccupied, his shoulders hunched.

As he had expected, he found the Spanish maid being questioned by Torrence in a distant office. She was a woman of about thirty, quite pretty, with a cheeky look, but her lips were thin and hard.

Maigret looked her over from head to foot, then turned to Torrence.

'What does she say?'

'She says she knows nothing. She was sleeping and was wakened by the Auteuil police who were making a racket on the first floor.'

'At what time did her mistress come home?'

'She doesn't know.'

'Wasn't she in the house?'

'I had permission to go out,' the young woman interrupted. She hadn't been asked, but she was annoyed to see how little notice was being taken of her.

'She had to meet her boy-friend by the Seine.'

'At what time?'

'Half past eight.'

'When did she get back?'

'At ten.'

'Didn't she see any lights on in the house?'

'She says not.'

'I don't just say so! I didn't!'

She still had a strong accent.

'Did you go through the big room on the ground floor?' Maigret asked her.

'No. I went in the back door.'

'Were there any cars in front of the house?'

'I saw Madame's was there.'

'And Monsieur's?'

'I didn't notice.'

'Don't you usually make sure that they don't need anything when you come in?'

'No. What they did in the evenings was their own affair, not mine.'

'Didn't you hear any noises?'

'I would have said so if I had.'

'Did you go straight to sleep?'

'As soon as I had washed.'

Maigret growled to Torrence:

'Get hold of her boy-friend and check.'

Carlotta's spiteful look followed him to the door.

Back in the detectives' office, he picked up a phone.

'Get me Doctor Paul, please. He may still be at the Medico-Legal Institute. If not, call his house.'

He had to wait for a few minutes.

'Maigret here . . . Have you any news?'

He took notes out of habit. He didn't have to, since he would get the full report a little later.

The throat wound had been one of the first and was enough to cause death within a minute at the outside. The killer had therefore kept on stabbing viciously at a body already drained of most of its blood.

The alcohol level of the blood showed, according to the forensic surgeon, that Christine Josset was drunk when she was killed.

She had not eaten. No food was being digested in the stomach. Her liver was in fact in a very bad state.

As to the time of death, Doctor Paul placed it tentatively between 10 p.m. and 1 a.m.

'Can't you be more precise?'

'Not just now. One more detail which may interest you. The woman had had sexual intercourse a few hours before death, at the earliest.'

'Could it have been half an hour before?'

'It's possible.'

'Ten minutes?'

'Scientifically, I can't answer that.'

'Thank you, doctor.'

'What does he say?'

'Who?'

'The husband.'

'That he's innocent.'

'Do you believe him?'

'I don't know.'

Another phone rang. A detective signalled to Maigret that it was for him.

'Is that you, Inspector? Coméliau here. Have you finished your interrogation?'

'A few minutes ago.'

'I'd like to see you.'

'I'll be straight over.'

He was just leaving the room when Bonfils came in, excited.

'I was just going to knock on your door, Chief. . . . I've just come from the house. . . . I spent two hours with Madame Siran, questioning her and making another careful inspection of the house. I've got something new.'

'What?'

'Has Josset confessed?'

'No.'

'Hasn't he told you about the dagger?'

'What dagger?'

'Madame Siran and I were examining Josset's room when I saw she was looking for something and seemed rather surprised. It was difficult for me to get her to speak, for I think she likes the master better than the mistress, for whom she didn't have a very high regard. Finally she muttered:

' "The German dagger."

'It seems it's one of those commando knives that some people keep as a war souvenir.'

Maigret looked surprised.

'Was Josset in the Commandos in the war?'

'No, he wasn't in the war at all. He was invalided out. It was someone in his office, a Monsieur Jules, who brought it back and gave it to him.'

'What did Josset do with it?'

'Nothing. It sat on a small desk in his bedroom and he probably used it as a letter-opener. It has disappeared.'

'Has it been gone long?'

'Since this morning. Madame Siran is quite sure about that. She does her employer's room, while the Spanish girl does Madame Josset's room and clothes.'

'Did you look everywhere?'

'I searched the house from top to bottom, including the attic and the cellar.'

Maigret almost went back to his office to ask Josset about it. He didn't do so because the magistrate was waiting for him, and Coméliau was hard to please. Then again, he needed time to think.

He passed through the glass door separating Police Head-quarters from the Palais de Justice and went along several corridors before knocking at the familiar door.

'Sit down, Maigret.'

The afternoon newspapers were spread out on the desk, showing their banner headlines and their photographs.

'Have you read those?'

'Yes.'

'Does he still deny it?'

'Yes.'

'But he admits that the scene in the Rue Caulaincourt did take place yesterday evening, a few hours before his wife's death?'

'He told me about it of his own accord.'

'I suppose he says it's a coincidence?'

As usual, Coméliau, moustaches trembling, was beginning to lose his temper.

'At eight o'clock in the evening the father finds him with his young daughter, Josset's mistress. The two men face each other, and the father demands redress.'

Maigret sighed wearily:

'Josset promised him he would divorce his wife.'

'And marry the daughter?'

'Yes.'

'But to do that, Josset would have had to give up his wealth and his position.'

'That's not quite true. For some years Josset has owned one third of the drug firm.'

'Do you think his wife would have agreed to the divorce?'

'I don't think anything, sir.'

'Where is he?'

'In my office. One of my detectives is typing out the record of the interrogation. Josset will read it and sign.'

'And then? What are you going to do with him then?'

Coméliau felt Maigret's reluctance to speak, and that angered him.

'I expect you're going to ask me to let him go free, to tell me that you wish to have him watched by your detectives in the hope that he'll betray himself in some way or other.'

'No.'

That cut the magistrate short.

'Do you think he's guilty?'

'I don't know.'

'Listen, Maigret. . . . If ever a case was clear-cut, it's this one. Four or five of my friends who knew Josset and his wife well have been on the phone to me . . .'

'Are they against him?'

'They've always known what he is.'

'And what is that?'

'An ambitious and unscrupulous man who took advantage of Christine's passion. But when she began to grow old he found he needed a younger mistress and didn't hesitate to take one.'

'I'll send you the statement when it's ready.'

'And until then?'

'I'm keeping Josset in my office. You'll decide what to do with him.'

'No one would stand for my letting him free.'

'That's quite likely.'

'No one, you understand, no one, will believe he is innocent. I will read your report before I sign his committal, but you may take it that my mind is already made up.'

He didn't like the look on the inspector's face. He called him back.

'Have you anything to say in his favour?'

Maigret didn't answer. He hadn't anything to say. Except that Josset had told him that he hadn't killed his wife.

Perhaps that was too easy, too obvious.

He went back to his office, where Janvier showed him the man asleep in his chair.

'You may go. Tell Lapointe I'm back.'

Maigret sat down, fiddled about with his pipes and chose one which he was lighting when Josset opened his eyes and looked at him without saying anything.

'Do you want to go on sleeping?'

'No. I'm sorry. Have you been here long?'

'A few minutes.'

'Have you seen the magistrate?'

'I've just come from his office.'

'Am I to be arrested?'

'I think so.'

'It was inevitable, wasn't it?'

'Do you know a good lawyer?'

'Several of my friends are good lawyers. I wonder if I wouldn't rather have a complete stranger.'

'Tell me, Josset . . .'

The man shuddered, sensing that something unpleasant was coming after those simple words.

'Yes?'

'Where did you hide the knife?'

There was a slight pause.

'I did wrong. I should have told you about it.'

'You went to throw it in the Seine from the Pont Mirabeau, didn't you?'

'Has it been found?'

'Not yet. Tomorrow morning divers will go down for it and they'll find it.'

The man was silent.

'Did you kill Christine?'

'No.'

'Yet you took the trouble to go all the way to the Pont Mirabeau to throw your knife into the Seine.'

'No one will believe me, not even you.'

The 'not even you' was a compliment to Maigret.

'Tell me the truth.'

'It was when I went home and put my suitcase away. I saw the dagger in my room . . .'

'Were there any bloodstains on it?'

'No. At that time I was thinking of what I was going to say to the police. I already realized that my story would seem hard to believe. Although I hadn't looked carefully at the body, what I had seen made a knife seem the likely weapon.

'When I saw mine lying out on my desk I told myself that the police would make the connection at once.'

'But there wasn't any blood on it!'

'If I had killed her, and if there had been any, wouldn't I have been careful to clean the weapon? I hadn't thought carefully enough when I fastened my suitcase with the intention of taking a plane. The presence of the knife a few feet away from the body overwhelmed me, and I removed it. It was Carlotta who told you, wasn't it? She has never been able to stand me . . .'

'It was Madame Siran.'

'I'm a little surprised at that. But I should have expected it. From now on I suppose I can't count on anyone any more . . .'

Lapointe came into the office holding some typewritten pages which he placed in front of his superior. Maigret handed one copy to Josset and scanned the other himself.

'Get hold of a diver for tomorrow morning. At dawn by the Pont Mirabeau.'

One hour later the photographers were finally able to take pictures of Adrien Josset leaving Maigret's office with handcuffs on.

It was precisely because of the reporters and photographers that Coméliau had insisted on handcuffs.

5. *The Obstinate Silence of Doctor Liorant*

Certain details of the case were etched more sharply than others on Maigret's memory, and several years later he could remember the taste and smell of the sudden shower in the Rue Caulaincourt as clearly as any childhood recollection.

It was 6.30 in the evening and when it began to rain the sun, already turning red above the roof-tops, was not obscured: the sky continued to glow and some windows still reflected the light, while a solitary pearly-grey cloud with silver edges, slightly darker at the centre, floated like a balloon over the area.

It didn't rain everywhere in Paris, and in the evening Madame Maigret assured her husband that none had fallen in the Boulevard Richard-Lenoir.

The raindrops seemed wetter, more transparent than usual and at first they left big black rings on the dusty road as they landed one by one.

As he raised his head the inspector saw four pots of geraniums on the sill of an open window, and then he was hit in the eye by a raindrop so large that it almost hurt.

The open window made him think that Annette was already home, and he went into the building, passing the concierge's room, and looked in vain for a lift. He was about to start climbing the stairs when a door opened behind him. An unpleasant voice called:

'Where do you think you're going?'

He found himself face to face with the concierge, who wasn't at all like the idea he had formed from Josset's tale. He had imagined her as middle-aged and careless about her appearance. But she was an attractive woman of about thirty, with a good figure. Only her voice grated, vulgar and aggressive.

'To see Mademoiselle Duché,' he answered politely.

'She isn't back yet.'

Later he was to remember that it was at this precise moment that he wondered why some people seem disagreeable at once, for no particular reason.

'It must be about time for her to come in, isn't it?'

'She comes and goes as she likes.'

'Was it you who phoned the newspaper?'

She stood in her doorway and did not invite him in.

'What of it?' she asked defiantly.

'I am a policeman.'

'I know. I recognized you. You don't impress me.'

'When Monsieur Duché came to see his daughter yesterday, did he tell you his name?'

'He even stayed a quarter of an hour in my room, chatting.'

'So he came before, when his daughter wasn't in. In the afternoon, I suppose?'

'About five o'clock.'

'Was it you who wrote to Fontenay?'

'If I had I would only have been doing my duty, and it wouldn't be any concern of anybody's. But it wasn't me. It was the young lady's aunt.'

'Do you know her aunt?'

'We shop in the same shops.'

'Did you tell her what was going on?'

'She guessed all by herself.'

'Did she tell you she was going to write?'

'We talked about it.'

'When Monsieur Duché came, did you tell him about Monsieur Josset?'

'I answered his questions and advised him to come back a little later, after seven.'

'When the girl came in, didn't you warn her?'

'I'm not paid to do that.'

'Was Monsieur Duché very angry?'

'He could hardly believe it, poor man.'

'Did you go up a little later to find out what was going on?'

'I took a letter up to the fifth floor?'

'Did you stop on the fourth-floor landing?'

'I might have done, to catch my breath. What are you trying to make me say?'

'You spoke of a violent scene.'

'To whom?'

'To the reporter.'

'The papers print what they choose to. Look! There she is, *your* young lady.'

It wasn't one girl, but two, who came into the building and went towards the stairs without even looking at the concierge or at Maigret. The first was blonde and very young. She wore a navy blue suit and a light-coloured hat. The second, thinner, harder, must have been about thirty-five and walked like a man.

'I thought you came to talk to her.'

Maigret controlled his anger, for this uncalled-for spitefulness hit him like a physical blow in the stomach.

'I'll talk to her, don't you fret. It's quite likely I'll have another word with you too.'

He could have kicked himself for this rather childish threat. He waited to go upstairs until he had heard a door open and close again above.

He stopped for a moment on the third floor to get his breath back, and knocked at the door a minute later. He heard whispering, then footsteps. It was not Annette, but her friend, who opened the door a crack.

'What do you want?'

'Inspector Maigret from Police Headquarters.'

'Annette, it's the police!'

She must have been in her bedroom, perhaps changing her suit which must have got wet in the rain.

'I'm coming.'

Everything was disappointing. The geraniums were certainly in place, but they were the only things which corresponded with the inspector's mental picture. The flat was commonplace, without a single personal touch. The famous dining-room-cum-kitchen where the little dinners had been held had dull grey walls and the furniture was just like that in any other cheap room.

Annette hadn't changed, only run a comb through her hair. She too was a disappointment. She had a kind of freshness, that was true, the kind of freshness one has at twenty, but she was ordinary, with large, prominent blue eyes. She reminded Maigret of the photographs found in provincial photographer's windows, and he would have bet that at forty she would be very fat, with a hard mouth.

'I'm sorry, mademoiselle . . .'

The friend went reluctantly towards the door.

'I'll leave you.'

'Why? You're not in the way.'

And, to Maigret:

'This is Jeanine, who works with me in the Avenue Marceau. She was kind enough to come home with me. Sit down, inspector . . .'

He would have found it difficult to say what he felt was wrong. He felt annoyed with Josset for having idealized this chit of a girl who, although her eyes were a little red, hardly seemed upset at all.

'Has he been arrested?' she asked, mechanically tidying things about her.

'The magistrate signed a committal order this afternoon.'

And Jeanine advised her:

'You'd better let the inspector speak.'

It wasn't an official questioning, and Coméliau would have been furious had he known that Maigret had taken this step on his own initiative.

'What time was it when you heard about the murder?'

'Just when we were leaving the office for lunch. One of the store-keepers has a transistor radio. He told the others what had happened, and Jeanine told me.'

'Did you have lunch as usual?'

'What else could I do?'

'She wasn't hungry, Inspector. I had to take her upstairs again. She kept bursting into tears.'

'Is your father still in Paris?'

'He left at nine this morning. He wanted to be back in Fontenay today because he only took two days' leave and he starts work again tomorrow.'

'Did he stay in a hotel?'

'Yes. Near the station. I don't know which one.'

'Did he stay here long yesterday evening?'

'About an hour. He was tired.'

'Did Josset promise him he would get a divorce and marry you?'

She blushed and looked at her friend as if asking advice.

'Did Adrien tell you that?'

'Did he?'

'It was mentioned.'

'Was there a formal promise?'

'I believe so.'

'Before that, did you hope he would marry you one day?'

'I didn't think of it.'

'Didn't he ever speak of the future?'

'No, not really.'

'Were you happy?'

'He was kind to me, very attentive.'

Maigret didn't dare to ask her if she loved him, because he feared she would lie again, and Annette asked:

'Do you think he'll be convicted?'

'Do you think he killed his wife?'

She blushed and again looked to her friend for advice.

'I don't know. The wireless says he did, and the newspapers . . .'

'You know him well. Do you think he had it in him to kill his wife?'

Instead of answering directly she muttered:

'Do you suspect anyone else?'

'Was your father hard on him?'

'Papa was sad, quite overwhelmed. He never thought such a thing could happen to his daughter. He still thinks I'm a little girl.'

'Did he threaten Josset?'

'No. He wouldn't threaten anyone. He just asked him what he was planning to do and suddenly, of his own accord, Adrien started talking about divorce.'

'Wasn't there any quarrel, any shouting?'

'Certainly not. I don't know how it came about, but we ended up by all three drinking champagne. My father seemed relieved. There was even a gay light in his eyes which I've hardly ever seen before.'

'And after Adrien left?'

'We talked about the wedding. My father was sorry that it couldn't be a white wedding, in Fontenay, because people would snigger.'

'Did he have any more to drink?'

'He emptied the bottle which we hadn't finished before Adrien left.'

Her friend gave her a look warning her not to say too much.

'Did you take him back to his hotel?'

'I offered, but he didn't want me to.'

'Didn't your father seem upset to you, different from usual?'

'No.'

'He's not a drinking man, I believe. Have you ever seen him have a drink in Fontenay?'

'Never. Only a little wine with water, at mealtimes. When he had to meet someone in a café he ordered mineral water.'

'But he had been drinking yesterday before he made his unexpected visit.'

'Don't answer without thinking,' advised Jeanine with a knowing look.

'What should I say?'

'The truth,' answered Maigret.

'I think he'd had a glass or two while he was waiting.'

'Didn't you notice his speech was awkward?'

'His speech was a bit slurred, I noticed that. Still, he knew what he was saying and what he was doing.'

'Didn't you ring his hotel to make sure he'd got back safely?'

'No. Why?'

'Didn't he ring you this morning to say good-bye?'

'No. We never phone each other. We've never got into the habit. At home in Fontenay we don't have a telephone . . .'

Maigret preferred not to pursue the matter.

'Thank you, mademoiselle.'

'What does he say?' she asked, worried again.

'Josset?'

'Yes.'

'He says he didn't kill his wife.'

'Do you believe him?'

'I don't know.'

'How is he? Does he need anything? He isn't too depressed?'

Each word was badly chosen, not strong enough in proportion to what had happened.

'He's quite depressed. He spoke a lot about you.'

'Didn't he ask to see me?'

'That's not up to me now, but to the magistrate.'

'Didn't he give you any message?'

'He didn't know I was coming to see you.'

'I expect I'll be called as a witness?'

'Very likely. That depends on the magistrate too.'

'May I keep on going to the office?'

'I don't see why not.'

He felt he had better leave. As he went through the main door, Maigret glimpsed the concierge. She was eating, sitting opposite a man in shirt-sleeves. She threw him a mocking look.

It was perhaps the inspector's state of mind which made him find everything and everyone disappointing. He crossed the street and went into a little local bar where four men were playing belote, while two others, elbows on the counter, were talking to the proprietor.

He didn't know what to drink, asked for the first drink he saw the label of, and remained silent for quite a long time, scowling, in about the same place Annette's father must have stood the previous evening.

If he turned his head he could see the entire front of the building across the street, with four pots of geraniums at one of the windows. Jeanine, hiding in the shadows, had seen him cross the street and was talking to her invisible friend.

'You had a customer who spent a long time here yesterday, didn't you?'

The proprietor picked up a newspaper and tapped the article about the Josset case.

'You mean the father?'

And, turning to the others:

'It's funny, I knew straight away something was up. In the first place he wasn't the kind of man to lean at the bar for over an hour. He asked for some mineral water, and I had already picked up the bottle when he changed his mind.

' "No, give me . . ."

'He looked at the bottles and seemed unable to make up his mind.

' "A glass of spirits. . . . Any kind . . ."

'It's not common for someone to ask for spirits before dinner.

' "A brandy? . . . A calvados? . . ."

' "A calvados, please."

'It made him cough. It was easy to see he wasn't used to it. He kept on looking at the door across the street, then at the Métro exit, a little farther away. Two or three times I saw his lips move as if he were talking to himself.'

The proprietor interrupted himself, frowning.

'Aren't you Inspector Maigret?'

And since Maigret didn't deny it:

'Hey, you lot, it's the famous Inspector Maigret. So that pharmacist has confessed, has he? . . . I've had my eye on him too, for a long time. . . . Because of his car. . . You don't get many sports cars round here . . .

'It was mostly in the mornings I used to see him, when he came to get the girl. . . . He parked by the pavement right in

71

front of the door and looked up. . . . The young lady would wave at the window and she'd come out to join him a minute or two later . . .'

'How many glasses of calvados did your customer have?'

'Four. . . . Each time he asked for another he looked ashamed, as if he was afraid I would take him for an alcoholic . . .'

'Did he come back later?'

'I didn't see him again. . . . This morning I saw the girl. She waited a while on the pavement, then took herself off to the Métro.'

Maigret paid and went down towards the Place Clichy, looking for a taxi as he went. He found a free one just as he was passing the Montmartre cemetery.

'Boulevard Richard-Lenoir, please.'

Nothing else happened that evening. He dined alone with his wife, to whom he said nothing at all, while she, knowing his moods, took care not to ask him any questions.

The investigation went on as usual in other ways. The machinery of the police force had been set in motion, and the inspector would find several reports on his desk the next day.

For this case, for no particular reason and against his usual practice, he decided to make a sort of private dossier.

The times, in particular, seemed to have a great importance, and he racked his brains to reconstruct the sequence of events, hour by hour.

Since the crime had been discovered in the morning, or rather towards the end of the night, the morning papers couldn't have anything on it, and it was the wireless which first made public the drama of the Rue Lopert.

At the time of this broadcast the reporters were camped in front of Josset's house in Auteuil, where the men from the Public Prosecutor's office had descended in force.

Between noon and one o'clock the first afternoon papers spoke briefly of the event.

One daily only, contacted by the concierge of the building in the Rue Caulaincourt, brought out the story of Duché's visit to his daughter and his meeting with Annette's lover, in its third edition.

72

All this time the head clerk's train was travelling to Fontenay-le-Comte, and the fresh news couldn't reach him.

Later on they found at least one of his travelling companions, a grain merchant from near Niort. The two men were strangers to each other. When the train left Paris the compartment was full, but after Poitiers only the two of them remained.

'I thought I knew him by sight though I couldn't remember where I had met him. I nodded to him politely. He looked startled, a bit annoyed, and huddled into his corner.

'He seemed a bit off-colour. His eyelids were red, as if he hadn't slept. When the train stopped at Poitiers he went to the buffet for a bottle of Vichy water which he gulped down.'

'Was he reading?'

'No. He watched the countryside going by, in a vague sort of way. From time to time he closed his eyes and finally he went to sleep. When I got home I suddenly remembered where I'd seen him – at the sous-préfecture at Fontenay, where I sometimes have to go to sign papers . . .'

Maigret, who had made the trip especially to see the grain merchant – his name was Lousteau – tried to find out more. He seemed to be looking for something which he couldn't explain.

'Did you notice his clothes?'

'I couldn't say what colour they were – they were dark, not very well cut . . .'

'Weren't they crumpled, as if he had spent the night out of doors?'

'I didn't notice. . . . I was looking at his face. . . . Wait! . . . There was a raincoat in the luggage rack, on top of his suitcase . . .'

It took some time to find the hotel where Annette's father had stayed, the Hôtel de la Reine et de Poitiers, near the Gare d'Austerlitz.

It was a cheap hotel, dimly lit and gloomy, but clean, mainly patronized by regulars. Martin Duché had stayed there several times. His previous visit had been two years before, when he had brought his daughter to Paris.

'He had room 53. . . . He didn't take any meals in the hotel. . . . He arrived on Tuesday by the 3.53 p.m. train and went out almost immediately after filling in his form, saying he would only be staying one night.'

'What time did he come in in the evening?'

There they ran into difficulties. The night porter, who had a camp bed in the office, was a Czech who hardly spoke any French and who had twice been a patient in Sainte-Anne, the mental hospital. The name Duché didn't mean anything to him, nor did a description. When asked about room 53, he looked at the key-board, scratching his head.

'He comes . . . he goes . . . he comes back . . . he leaves . . .' he muttered angrily.

'When did you go to bed?'

'Not before midnight. I always shut the door and go to bed at midnight. That's orders.'

'Don't you know if number 53 was back?'

The poor man did what he could but he couldn't do much. He hadn't been working at the hotel two years previously, when Duché had last stayed there.

He was shown a photograph.

'Who is it?' he asked, anxious to please his questioners.

Maigret, stubborn as usual, had gone so far as to look for the two people who had had rooms on either side of number 53. One of them lived in Marseilles and could be reached by telephone.

'I don't know a thing. I came in at eleven and I didn't hear a thing.'

'Were you alone?'

'Of course.'

He was a married man. He had come to Paris without his wife. And they were sure that he at least had not spent the night alone.

As for number 51, a Belgian who was only travelling through France, it proved impossible to trace him.

At a quarter to eight in the morning, at any rate, Duché had been in his room and had rung for breakfast. The maid hadn't noticed anything odd except that he had asked for three cups of coffee.

'He seemed tired . . .'

That was vague. It was impossible to get her to say any more.

74

At half past eight, without having taken a bath, Duché had gone downstairs and paid his bill to the cashier, who knew him.

'He was the same as usual. I've never seen him look happy. He looked like a sick man. He stood still as if to listen to his heart beating. I knew someone else like that, a good customer, a man who came once a month. He had the same look, the same gestures, and one morning he fell dead on the stairs without even having time to call for help . . .'

Duché had caught his train. He was still there, sitting opposite the grain merchant, when Maigret was interrogating Josset in the Quai des Orfèvres.

At that same time a reporter on a morning paper, after rushing to the Rue Caulaincourt, rang his correspondent in Fontenay-le-Comte.

The concierge hadn't told Maigret about the visit of this journalist, to whom she had given Annette's father's name and address.

These tiny facts were all mixed up together, and it took time and patience to make a more or less logical picture from them.

When the train stopped at Fontenay-le-Comte that afternoon Martin Duché still didn't know anything about it. Nor did the people of Fontenay, for the wireless had not yet given the name of their fellow-citizen, and only by guessing could they have made a connection between the head clerk and the sous-préfecture and the drama of the Rue Lopert.

Only the newspaper correspondent knew what was going on. He had got hold of a photographer. They were both waiting on the platform, and when Duché stepped out of the train he was surprised to be welcomed by a flash-gun.

'May I, Monsieur Duché?'

He blinked, bewildered and confused.

'I suppose you haven't heard the news?'

The reporter was polite. The head clerk seemed like a man who doesn't understand what is happening to him. Suitcase in hand, raincoat over his arm, he went towards the exit, handing his ticket to the ticket collector, who greeted him by touching his hand to his cap. The photographer took another picture. The reporter drew closer to Annette's father.

They went down the Rue de la République together in the sunshine.

'Madame Josset was murdered last night.'

The newspaperman, Pecqueur by name, had a baby face, plump cheeks, and the same protuberant eyes as Annette. He had red hair, his whole appearance was casual and, in order to make himself look important, he was smoking a pipe which was much too big for him.

Maigret interviewed him too, in the back room of the Café de la Poste, by the empty billiard table.

'What was his reaction?'

'He stopped in his tracks and stared at me as if he suspected me of setting a trap for him.'

'A trap? Why?'

'No one in Fontenay knew as yet that his daughter was having an affair. He must have thought that I had found out and was trying to get him to talk.'

'What did he say?'

'After a moment he said in a hard voice:

' "I don't know any Madame Josset."

'So I told him that my paper would have it the next day and would give all the details of the case. I added what I had just learned by telephone:

' "Already one of the evening papers has the story of your meeting with your daughter and Adrien Josset in the Rue Caulaincourt." '

Maigret asked:

'Did you know him well?'

'As well as anyone in Fontenay did. I've seen him at the préfecture and when he passed by in the street.'

'Did he ever stop short while he was walking?'

'To look in the shop windows, of course.'

'Was he a sick man?'

'I don't know. He lived alone, didn't go to the café, and didn't talk much.'

'Did you get the interview you wanted?'

'He kept on walking in silence. I asked him questions, whatever came into my head:

' "Do you believe Josset killed his wife?"

' "Did he really mean to marry your daughter?"

'He scowled and didn't listen to me. Two or three times he growled:

' "I have nothing to say."

' "But you did meet Adrien Josset?"

' "I have nothing to say."

'We reached the bridge. He turned left, along the quay, where he lives in a little brick house which a daily woman comes in to clean for him. I took a picture of the house, since the paper never has enough pictures.'

'Was the cleaning-woman waiting for him?'

'No. She only worked for him in the mornings.'

'Who got his meals?'

'At lunch-time he used to eat at the Trois Pigeons. He made his own dinner in the evenings.'

'And he didn't go out?'

'Hardly ever. Once a week to the cinema.'

'Alone?'

'Always.'

'Did anyone hear anything that evening or during the night?'

'No. A cyclist going by at about one in the morning saw a light. When the cleaning woman came in that morning the light was still burning.'

Martin Duché had not undressed, nor had he eaten. Everything in the house was tidy.

As far as his actions could be reconstructed, he had taken a photograph album out of a drawer in the dining-room. On the first pages there were yellowing portraits of his parents and those of his wife; one of him as an artilleryman on national service; his wedding photograph; Annette a few months old, lying on a bearskin; then Annette at five, at ten, as a first communicant, and finally in a class group at the convent where she had been to school.

The album, open at that page, was lying on a little table by an armchair.

How long had Duché remained seated there before making his decision? He must have gone upstairs to his bedroom to take his revolver from the drawer in the bedside table. He had left the drawer open.

77

He had gone downstairs again, taken his seat in the armchair once more, and shot himself in the head.

The next morning the newspapers announced in banner headlines:

A SECOND VICTIM IN THE JOSSET CASE

In the minds of the readers it was almost as if Josset had killed Annette's father with his own hands.

The papers spoke of the head clerk's life as a widower, dignified and lonely, of his love for his only daughter and of the shock he had received on reaching the flat in the Rue Caulaincourt and learning of his daughter's affair with her employer.

For Josset it meant almost certain conviction. Even Coméliau, who ought to have seen the facts from a purely professional point of view, became very excited when he spoke to Maigret on the telephone.

'Have you read about it?'

It was Thursday morning. The inspector, who had just arrived in his office, had read the papers while standing on the platform of the bus.

'I hope that Josset has chosen a lawyer, for I intend to have him in my office this morning and hurry the case up. The public wouldn't understand if we let things drag on.'

That meant that Maigret had no more to do with it. The magistrate was taking the case into his own hands, and theoretically from that point on the inspector would only act under his instructions.

Perhaps he would never see Josset again except in court. And he would only know what the magistrate saw fit to tell him about further interrogations.

It wasn't that day that he went to Niort and Fontenay, because Coméliau would certainly have heard about it and would have reprimanded him severely.

The rules forbade him even the most innocent excursion outside Paris.

Even his first phone call to Doctor Liorant, who lived in the Rue Rabelais, Fontenay-le-Comte, and whom he had met previously in that town, was irregular.

'Maigret here. . . . Do you remember me, doctor?'

The doctor answered coldly and carefully, and Maigret was immediately suspicious.

'I would like, in my personal capacity, to ask you for some information.'

'Go on.'

'I wonder if Martin Duché was by any chance one of your patients.'

There was a silence.

'I suppose it would not be a breach of professional etiquette . . .'

'He has consulted me.'

'Did he suffer from a serious illness?'

'I am afraid I cannot answer that.'

'One moment, Doctor. . . . Forgive me if I press the matter. . . . A man's life may depend on it. . . . I have heard that Duché sometimes stood still suddenly, in the street or elsewhere, like a man suffering from angina pectoris.'

'Did a doctor tell you that? If he did, he should not have done so.'

'It was not a doctor.'

'In that case it is only an unfounded supposition.'

'Can you not tell me if he could have died at any time?'

'I have nothing to say. I am sorry, Inspector, but I have several patients waiting to see me . . .'

Maigret saw him again, with no more success, after his journey to Niort and Fontenay, when the doctor paid a secret visit to Coméliau and even to the Quai des Orfèvres, between trains.

6. *The Old Man who Couldn't Sleep*

Rarely had spring been so lovely, and the newspapers vied with each other in announcing records of temperature and of drought. Rarely, too, in the Quai des Orfèvres, had Maigret been seen so gloomy and so touchy, to such an extent that those who didn't know what it was all about inquired anxiously after his wife's health.

Coméliau had taken the bit between his teeth, enforcing the law to the very last letter, somehow managing to keep Josset hidden away, so that the inspector hadn't even the chance to speak a word to him.

Every day, or almost every day, the drug manufacturer was taken from the Santé prison to the magistrate's office where his lawyer, Maître Lenain, was waiting for him.

He was a bad choice, and if Maigret had had the chance he would have advised Josset against him. Lenain was one of the three or four leading lights of the bar, specializing in court trials attracting nation-wide interest. As soon as he took over a spectacular case he occupied as much space in the newspapers as any film star.

Reporters waited for his almost daily statements, his biting words, always to some extent fierce, and, because of two or three acquittals which had been thought impossible, he was called the counsel for lost causes.

After these interrogations Maigret would get unexpected orders from Coméliau, mostly without explanation: witnesses to hunt out, details to be checked, tasks even more irksome because they seemed to have little connection with the crime in the Rue Lopert.

The magistrate did not act in this way through animosity, and if Coméliau had always distrusted the inspector and his methods it was due to the gulf separating their points of view.

It all went back to the question of social classes. The magistrate had remained a man of an unchanging background in a changing world. His grandfather had presided over the highest Courts of Appeal, in Paris, and his father still sat on the Council of State, while one of his uncles was French Ambassador at Helsinki.

He himself had studied to enter the Inspection des Finances, and it was only after failing the examination that he had taken up the law.

He was the typical product of his society, the slave of its ways, of its rules of conduct, even of its language.

One would have thought that his daily experiences in the Palais de Justice would have given him a different idea of human nature, but that was not so, and he was invariably influenced by the point of view held by his class.

In his eyes Josset, if not a born criminal, was the guilty type. Had he not fraudulently entered a class which was not his own, first through a sinful affair, then through an ill-suited marriage? Did not his affair with Annette and his promise to marry her confirm this opinion?

On the other hand the young girl's father, Martin Duché, who had committed suicide rather than face dishonour, was a man after Coméliau's own heart. He was, according to popular belief, the model of the honest civil servant, humble and self-effacing, for whom nothing could soften the blow of his wife's death.

The fact that he had been drunk that evening in the Rue Caulaincourt was of no importance to Coméliau, while that detail had significance to the inspector.

Maigret could have sworn that Annette's father had been ill for a long time, probably with an incurable disease.

And his dignity, wasn't it all really based on pride?

He had returned to Fontenay sick at heart, ashamed, in fact, of his behaviour of the previous evening, and, instead of finding peace and silence, he immediately ran into a journalist and a photographer on the station platform.

That worried Maigret, as did Doctor Liorant's attitude. He determined to come back to those points, to try to bring the matter into the open, even though his hands were tied.

His men had covered kilometres in Paris while verifying facts, and Maigret had drawn up a time-table of Josset's actions on the night of the crime. He didn't know that this time-table would be of vital importance.

During the course of his only interrogation at the Quai des Orfèvres, Josset had stated that he had wandered around after leaving the Rue Caulaincourt at about 8.30, and that his first stop had been at a bar near the Place de la République.

This bar, La Bonne Chope, had been found in the Boulevard du Temple, and a waiter remembered him. Because of a customer who came every day on the stroke of nine and who had not yet arrived when Josset left, his visit to the Boulevard du

Temple could be fixed between a quarter to nine and nine o'clock.

That checked, then.

At the Select, in the Avenue des Champs-Elyseés, it was even easier, for Jean, the barman, had known the drug manufacturer for years.

'He came in at 9.20 and asked for a whisky.'

'Was that his usual drink?'

'No. He usually had a quarter-bottle of champagne. I had even reached for the bucket where there's always some on ice when I saw him come in.'

'Did anything about his manner strike you as odd?'

'He drank his whisky in one gulp, held the glass out to be refilled, and instead of talking he stared straight ahead. I asked him:

' "Things not going well, Monsieur Josset?"

' "Not very."

'He added something about some food which hadn't agreed with him, and I offered him some bicarbonate of soda.

'He refused and drank a third whisky before he went off, still very preoccupied.'

That checked too.

Still according to Josset, he had then gone towards the Rue Lopert, where he arrived at five past ten.

Torrence had questioned all the people living in the street. Most houses had had their shutters closed at that time. One of the neighbours had come home at a quarter past ten and hadn't noticed anything odd.

'Were there any cars parked in front of Josset's house?'

'I think so. A big one, anyway.'

'And the little one?'

'I couldn't say.'

'Did you see any lights on?'

'I think so. . . . I couldn't swear to it.'

Only the owner of the house across the street was certain of what he had seen, so certain that Torrence had repeated his questions three or four times and had written down the answers word for word.

He was one François Lalinde, seventy-six years of age, a

colonial administrator retired some years previously. As he was not in the best of health – he was subject to frequent bouts of fever – he never left the house where he lived. He was cared for by a coloured maid whom he had brought back from Africa and whom he called Julie.

He stated that, according to his custom, he had not gone to bed before four in the morning, and that he had spent the first part of the night in his armchair by the window.

He showed this armchair to Torrence. It was on the first floor, in a room which was bedroom, library, living-room and curiosity shop all at once. It was the only room in the house he really used and he rarely left it except to go to the bathroom next door.

He was an impatient, easily-angered man who could not bear to be contradicted.

'Do you know your neighbours across the street?'

'By sight, sir, only by sight!'

He seemed to be sneering unpleasantly.

'Those people have chosen to live so that everyone may see them. They haven't even the decency to have shutters on the windows.'

'Of whom are you speaking?'

'Of both of them. The woman as well as the man. The servants aren't any better.'

'Did you see Josset come home on Tuesday evening?'

'How would I not see him, since I was seated by the window?'

'Were you doing nothing but looking out into the street?'

'I was reading. Every noise made me jump. I hate noises, particularly the noise of motor cars.'

'Did you hear a car stop in front of the Josset's house?'

'And I jumped, as usual. I consider noise to be a personal insult.'

'So you heard Monsieur Josset's car, and probably the shutting of the car door?'

'I heard that too, yes indeed, young man!'

'Did you look out?'

'I looked out and saw him going into the house.'

'Were you wearing a wristwatch?'

83

'No. There is a clock on the wall, exactly opposite my chair, as you can see. It is never more than three minutes out in a month.'

'What time was it?'

'10.45.'

Torrence, who had read Josset's statement, as had all Maigret's colleagues, pressed the point.'

'Are you sure it wasn't 10.05?'

'Positive. I am a man of precision. I have been so all my life.'

'Do you never fall asleep in your chair in the evening or at night?'

This time Monsieur Lalinde was angry, and poor Torrence had a dreadful job to calm him down. The old man could not allow himself to be in the wrong, even less about his sleep than about any other subject, for he prided himself on not sleeping.

'Did you recognize Monsieur Josset?'

'Who else could it have been?'

'I am asking you if you recognized him?'

'Of course.'

'Could you make out his features?'

'The street lamp is not far away and there was a moon.'

'Were there any windows lit up at that time?'

'No, monsieur.'

'Not even in the maid's room?'

'The maid had gone to bed half an hour before.'

'How do you know?'

'Because I saw her shut her window and her light went out immediately afterwards.'

'What time was that?'

'At a quarter past ten.'

'Did Monsieur Josset put on the light on the ground floor?'

'He most certainly did.'

'Do you remember seeing the ground floor lit up after he went in?'

'Perfectly.'

'And then?'

'Then what always happened, happened. The ground floor was in darkness once more, and the lights went on on the first floor.'

'In which room?'

Josset's bedroom and his wife's both looked out on to the street, Josset's on the right, Christine's on the left.

'In both.'

'Did you see anything of what was going on in the house?'

'No. I wasn't interested.'

'Can you see through the curtains?'

'Only a shadow when someone goes between the lights and the windows.'

'So you didn't look even for a minute?'

'I went straight back to my book.'

'Until when?'

'Until I heard a door across the street open and shut.'

'When was that?'

'Twenty minutes past twelve.'

'Did you hear a car engine?'

'No. The man went towards the church on foot. He was carrying a suitcase.'

'Were there any lights still on in the house?'

'No.'

After that the last few hours tallied with the timetable Josset had given Maigret. And from then on there were plenty of witnesses. They had found the driver of the 403 from the taxi-rank by Auteuil church, Brugnali by name.

'The fare engaged me at 12.30. I noted the trip in my book. He was carrying a suitcase, and I took him to the Avenue Marceau.'

'What was he like?'

'A real softy, reeking of alcohol. I asked him which station he wanted, because of the suitcase.'

In the Avenue Marceau Josset had paid the fare and gone towards a large building which stood alone. It had a brass plate to the left of the door.

They found the second taxi too, the one Josset had taken when he left the offices.

The night club he had gone into at 1.30 was a small place called Le Parc aux Cerfs. The tout and the bartender remembered him.

'He didn't want a table. He seemed surprised to find himself in a place like this, and he seemed embarrassed watching Ninouche doing her strip act on the dance floor – Ninouche comes on at the end of the first show, so I can fix the time. He drank a whisky and bought one for Marina, one of the hostesses, but he didn't pay any attention to her.'

Meanwhile, outside, the taxi-driver was having an argument with another taxi-driver. He worked in league with the tout and was trying to stop him parking there.

'Go and get your money and I'll pick up your fare when he comes out.'

Josset's arrival put an end to the argument, and the taxi in which he had left his case took him back to the Rue Lopert. Although he knew the neighbourhood the driver took a wrong turning, and Josset had had to set him right.

'It was 1.45, maybe 1.50, when I set him down.'

'What was he like?'

'Drunker than when he went in.'

Lalinde, the former colonial administrator, confirmed the return. The lights had gone on again.

'On the ground floor?'

'Certainly. Then upstairs.'

'In both rooms?'

'And in the bathroom, which has frosted glass windows.'

'Did Josset go out again?'

'At 2.30, after he had put out all the lights.'

'Did he take his car?'

'No. And this time he went towards the Rue Chardon-Lagache, carrying a parcel.'

'What size of parcel?'

'Quite big, longer than it was wide.'

'Twelve inches long? Fifteen?'

'I would say sixteen.'

'And how wide?'

'About eight.'

'Weren't you in bed?'

'No. At 3.48 exactly I heard a police siren and saw half a dozen policemen leap out on to the pavement and go into the house.'

'So, if I've got it right, you didn't leave your chair either in the evening or at night.'

'Only at half past four, to go to bed.'

'Did you hear anything after that?'

'Motor cars coming and going.'

Here too the times coincided, for Josset had reached the Auteuil police station at half past three, and the van had been sent to the Rue Lopert a few moments afterwards, when he was just beginning to make his statement.

Maigret had passed this report on to Coméliau. A little later the magistrate asked him to come to his office where he was sitting alone.

'Have you read it?'

'Of course.'

'Has anything struck you?'

'One point. I'll tell you about it later.'

'What strikes me is that Josset has told the truth about most things, those which have no direct bearing on the crime. His timetable is correct for most of the night.

'But while he says he went in at 10.05 at the latest, Monsieur Lalinde saw him go in at 10.45.

'So he wasn't asleep in the lounge, as he says he was, at that time.

'He went upstairs at 10.45 and put on the lights *in both rooms*.

'Note that the time corresponds with what Doctor Paul considers the probable time of the murder. What do you think?'

'I would like to make a simple observation. According to Torrence, Monsieur Lalinde smoked very black cigars continuously throughout the interview, those little Italian cigars people call coffin nails.'

'I don't see the connection . . .'

'I expect he smokes at night too, in his armchair. If that is so, he almost certainly finds he needs to drink.'

'He could have everything within reach.'

'Of course. He is seventy-six, according to the report.'

The magistrate still didn't understand.

'I wonder,' Maigret continued, 'if he didn't at any time have to relieve his bladder. . . . Old men generally . . .'

'He states that he did not leave his chair, and everything points to his being a man whose word can be trusted.'

'And he is an obstinate man who must be right whatever the cost.'

'Since he only knew Josset by sight he had no reason to . . .'

Maigret would have liked to see Monsieur Lalinde's doctor. It was the second time he had wanted to call on that type of witness.

'You are forgetting professional etiquette.'

'I am not forgetting it, unfortunately.'

'And you are forgetting that it is in Josset's interests to lie . . .'

Duché's suicide in Fontenay-le-Comte had definitely turned public opinion against Josset. The press had given it good coverage. They had printed photographs of Annette weeping as she boarded the train for Fontenay:

'Poor Papa! Had I but known . . .'

They had interviewed employees at the sous-préfecture and shopkeepers of Fontenay-le-Comte, all of whom sang the head-clerk's praises.

'A worthy man, of quite exceptional rectitude. Already worn out by grief at his wife's death, he was unable to bear the disgrace . . .'

Maître Lenain answered the reporters' questions like a man preparing a crushing retort:

'Wait! The investigation is only in its early stages . . .'

'Have you any new evidence?'

'I am keeping it for my good friend Maître Coméliau.'

He named the day, the hour when all would be told, keeping their curiosity alive. When, as he himself said, he dropped the bomb, there were so many reporters and photographers in the corridors of the Palais de Justice that the police had to be called in to control them.

The 'suspense' lasted three hours, during which four men were shut in the magistrate's chambers: Adrien Josset, who had been much photographed as he arrived; Maître Lenain, who had been no less popular; Coméliau; and his clerk of the court.

As for Maigret, he was attending to various administrative matters in his office in the Quai des Orfèvres.

Two hours after the meeting he was brought the newspapers. They all had more or less the same headline:

JOSSET ACCUSES!

The sub-heads were varied:

Josset, Cornered, Turns to the Offensive.

And:

The Defence Attempts a Desperate Manoeuvre.

Coméliau, as usual, refused to make a statement and remained in his chambers.

Lenain, as was usual for him, not only gave a written statement to the reporters, but held what was in fact a press conference in the corridors of the Palais de Justice immediately after his client had left accompanied by two policemen.

The statement was brief.

Up to now Adrien Josset, who has been accused of the murder of his wife, has chivalrously kept silent on her private life and secret habits.

On the advice of Counsel he has finally decided that when his case is brought before the Grand Jury he will lift a corner of this veil of secrecy, and as a result of this the investigation will take a new turn.

It will be shown that many people could have killed Christine Josset, of whom little has been said until now, so busy have people been in condemning her husband.

Maigret would have liked to know what had prompted this decision, to have known what was going on in the meetings which had taken place between lawyer and client in the cell in the Santé prison.

It reminded him more than somewhat of the scene in the Rue Caulaincourt. Annette's father had come in and had said almost nothing. He had only said, 'What are you planning to do?'

At once Josset, who hid behind Monsieur Jules when he had to sack an employee, had promised to divorce his wife and marry the girl.

Couldn't a clever and unscrupulous man like Lenain make Josset say anything he wanted?

Naturally the reporters had bombarded the lawyer with questions.

'Do you mean to say that Madame Josset had a lover?'

The barrister smiled mysteriously.

'No, gentlemen, not a lover.'

'Lovers?'

'That's putting it too simply, and wouldn't explain anything.'

They didn't understand. He alone knew what he was getting at.

'Madame Josset, as was her privilege, remember, had protégés. Her friends will confirm this, and in some circles the protégés were spoken of as if they were racehorses belonging to some well-known owner.'

Complacently he explained:

'When she was very young she married a well-known man, Sir Austin Lowell, who formed her tastes and taught her the ways of the world – the world of power, of those who pull the strings. At first, like so many others, she was only an ornament . . .

'You must understand this: she was not Austin Lowell. She was the beautiful Lady Lowell, the woman he dressed and covered with jewels, showed off at the races, at first-nights, in night-clubs and in drawing-rooms.

'When, at less than thirty years of age, she was widowed, she wanted to go on like this, but *on her own terms*, if I may put it that way.

'She did not wish to be the subsidiary element of a couple, the accessory or ornament, but the first.

'That is why, instead of marrying a man of her own class, which would have been easy for her, she sought out Josset, who was serving in a chemist's shop.

'She in her turn needed to dominate, needed to have beside her someone who would owe her everything, who would be her property.

'Unfortunately it happened that the young pharmacist had a stronger personality than she had thought.

'He got on so well in the drug manufacturing business that he became a person in his own right.

'That is all. Therein lies the drama.

'She was growing older and felt that the time when she would no longer be attractive to men would soon be upon her . . .'

'Excuse me,' interrupted a journalist. 'Did she have lovers before this?'

'Let us say that she had never lived according to the bourgeois moral code. The day came when she no longer dominated her husband, and so she looked for others to dominate.

'It is these whom I called her protégés, using the word she herself chose, and which it appears she uttered with a complacent smile.

'There were many of them. Only some are known. There were certainly others who are not known, but whom I hope the investigation will uncover.

'For the most part they are unknown artists – painters, musicians, singers, whom she found God knows where and whom she determined to launch on their careers.

'I could name you one singer very popular today, who owes his success solely to his chance encounter with Madame Josset, who met him in the garage where he worked as a mechanic.

'Although some succeeded, others proved to be without talent and after a few weeks or a few months she dropped them.

'Need I add that these young men did not always become resigned to returning to obscurity?

'She had presented them to her friends as the future stars of the stage, of painting, or of the screen. She had given them clothes and a good home. They had lived in her shadow, in her wake . . .

'Then, from one day to the next, they were nobodies again.'

'Can you give names?'

'I leave that to the magistrate. I have given him a list of people among whom are certainly some fine young men. We do not accuse anyone. We say only that some people had reason to resent Christine Josset.'

'Anyone in particular?'

'Obviously one must look at her most recent protégés . . .'

Maigret had thought of that. From the first he had felt he should find out about the victim's private life and her circle of friends.

Until now he had come up against a wall. And again it was,

as in dealing with Coméliau, a question of class, of caste almost.

Christine Josset had moved in a world even more limited than that of the magistrate – a handful of people whose names were always in the papers, whose every word and deed were reported, about whom many strange news items were published but who were in fact hardly known at all by the general public.

Maigret had only been a detective when he had made a witty remark about this type of thing, a remark which was often repeated to newcomers to the Quai des Orfèvres. Told to watch a banker – a man who was arrested several months later – he had said to his chief:

'To understand how his mind works I must breakfast with financiers . . .'

Has not each social class its own jargon, its taboos, its weaknesses?

When he asked, 'What's your opinion of Madame Josset?' people invariably answered, 'Christine? What a fabulous woman . . .' (For in her circle she was not a Josset, she was Christine.) '. . . a woman interested in everything, passionate, in love with life . . .'

'And her husband?'

'A good chap . . .'

This was said more coldly, showing that, in spite of his commercial success, Josset had never been completely taken up by his wife's friends. He was tolerated, like the mistress or wife of a celebrity, and they said:

'After all, if she likes him . . .'

Coméliau would be furious. He would be even more so when he had read all the papers. He had made up a case which satisfied him, and the time was coming when he had to put it to the Grand Jury.

Now the investigation had to begin all over again. It wasn't possible to ignore Lenain's accusations, since he had taken care to give them as much publicity as possible.

It was no longer a matter of questioning concierges, taxi-drivers, neighbours.

It was necessary to enter a new circle, to get confidences, names, to make up a list of these now notorious protégés, and it would obviously fall to Maigret to check their alibis.

'But,' objected one reporter, 'Josset says he was asleep in the living-room, in an armchair, after he got home at 10.05. A reliable witness who lives across the street says that he only arrived home at 10.45.'

'A witness can be mistaken in good faith,' retorted the lawyer. 'Monsieur Lalinde, for that is the man you are speaking of, no doubt did see a man enter the house at 10.45, while my client was asleep.'

'Would that be the killer?'

'Probably.'

'Could he have got past Josset without seeing him?'

'The living-room was in darkness. The more I think of it the more certain I am that, at the time of the murder, there were not two but three cars parked in front of the house. I have checked the positions. I have not been in Monsieur Lalinde's house, as the maid was not very welcoming. Nevertheless, I am sure that from the old man's window one can see the Cadillac and a car parked in front of it, *but not a car parked behind*. I have asked for this theory to be checked. If I am right, I am ready to swear that there were three cars there . . .'

Madame Maigret was quite excited that evening. She had held out for a long time, but she finally became passionately interested in a case which everyone in the shops was talking about.

'Do you think Lenain was right to attack?'

'No.'

'Is Josset innocent?'

He looked at her without seeing her.

'It's a fifty-fifty chance.'

'Will he be convicted?'

'Probably, especially now.'

'Can't you do anything?'

This time he merely shrugged his shoulders.

7. *Monsieur Jules and Madame Chairman*

Maigret, powerless to intervene, watched a phenomenon which he had observed several times and which still surprised him. His old friend Lombras, head of the municipal police, responsible for public order, for all demonstrations, and for regulating crowds, used to swear that the whole city of Paris, like any private individual, could sometimes sleep on the wrong side and wake up in a bad temper, ready to jump at any opportunity to indulge it.

It happens like that in criminal cases. A cold-blooded murder, revolting in detail, may pass unnoticed, the investigation and then the trial taking place with the public, if not exactly amenable, indifferent.

Then, for some unknown reason, a quite ordinary crime raises public indignation.

There was no organized campaign. Those who purported to be in the know said there was no one pulling strings, no one mounting a campaign against Josset.

Certainly the newspapers had made much of the case and continued to do so, but newspapers only reflect opinion and give their readers what they want to read.

Why had Josset had the whole world against him from the first?

The twenty-one stab-wounds had something to do with it. When a murderer loses his head and keeps on attacking a dead body, people talk of savagery; and where a psychiatrist might see that as a sign of diminished responsibility, the general public, on the other hand, sees it as an aggravating circumstance.

Of all the people in the case Josset had immediately become the 'baddy', the villain, and perhaps there was an explanation for that: from the newspaper articles even those who had never seen him could sense that he was a weak man, a 'softy', and mediocrity is not easily pardoned.

One doesn't forgive someone who denies what seems to be a fact, and, as far as the world at large was concerned, Josset's guilt was a fact.

If he had confessed, if he had pleaded a moment of passion, of mental aberration, and had asked forgiveness contritely, most people would have been inclined to leniency.

He chose, however, to defy *logic* and *reason*, and that was like a slap in the face to the people's intelligence.

Ever since the Tuesday when he had questioned him, Maigret had known that it would be like that. Coméliau's reactions had been one indication of it. The first headlines and sub-heads in the afternoon newspapers had been another.

Since then feelings against him had only increased, and it was rare to hear someone doubt Josset's guilt or to find, if not excuses for him, extenuating circumstances at least.

Martin Duché's suicide had made matters worse, for the ex-pharmacist was now considered not guilty of one murder, but of two.

Finally his lawyer, Maître Lenain, had added fuel to the fire by his ill-timed statements and by his accusations.

In these circumstances it was difficult to question witnesses. The most honest of them, in all good faith, tended only to remember things which went against the prisoner.

In fact Josset was unlucky. Take the matter of the knife, for example. He had said in his statement that he had thrown it into the Seine from the middle of the Pont Mirabeau. Ever since Wednesday a diver had searched the muddy bottom for hours, watched by hundreds of idlers hanging over the parapet, while photographers and even television cameramen started taking pictures every time the big brass helmet appeared.

The diver came up empty-handed every time and he continued his search the next day with no better results.

For those who know the bed of the Seine, this wasn't surprising. The current is strong against the piles of the bridge and makes undertows which can carry quite a heavy object a considerable distance.

In other parts the mud is thick and rubbish of all kinds sinks deep in it.

Josset could not point out the exact place where he had been standing, which, in the state of mind he was supposed to have been in, was only to be expected.

In the mind of the public, all this was proof that he had lied. He was accused of having hidden the weapon somewhere else, for some unknown reason. It wasn't only a question of the dagger. Monsieur Lalinde, the ex-Colonial administrator, whose word no one doubted and whom it would have been dangerous to call even a slightly dotty old man, had described a parcel *of some bulk,* whose dimensions were much greater than those of a commando knife.

What could the packet Josset carried off after the murder contain?

Even a discovery which at first seemed in the prisoner's favour and which the lawyer was careless enough to boast about too soon turned against him in the end.

The Criminal Identity division had taken several fingerprints from the house in the Rue Lopert which, because of its modern architecture, was now being called 'the glass house'. These fingerprints, once classified, had been compared with those of Josset, of his wife, of the two servants, and of an employee of the gas board who had been in to read the meter on Monday afternoon, some hours before the crime.

One set of prints remained unidentified. They were found on the banisters and, more thickly, in the victim's bedroom and in her husband's.

They were the prints of a man with a broad thumb marked with a small, round, easily identifiable scar.

When questioned, Madame Siran stated that neither Madame Josset nor her husband had had any visitors in the last few days, and that, as far as she knew, no stranger had been up to the bedrooms.

Carlotta, who was still on duty in the evenings after the cook had left, confirmed this statement.

In the papers this became:

A MYSTERY VISITOR?

Naturally Maître Lenain made a great fuss about this discovery, which he made the starting-point of an important line of defence.

According to him, Doctor Paul could have made an error of judgement. There was nothing, said the lawyer, to prevent the murder having taken place a little before ten, that is, before Josset's arrival.

Even if the police surgeon were right, one must not reject the hypothesis of a stranger entering the house while Josset, who had had a lot to drink, slept soundly in a chair in the unlighted living-room.

Lenain had conducted an experiment on the spot, at the same time of night. He had taken up his position in the chair which Christine's husband had occupied, and six unsuspecting people were asked to pass through the room in the dark, one after the other, and to climb the stairs. Only two of them noticed that he was there.

To this it was objected that the moon was not in the same position as it had been on the night of the crime, and that the sky was overcast.

In any case, Lalinde's statement remained and he refused to alter a word of it.

It was Maigret who had a visit from the decorator. This man had just read the papers and, worried, had gone to the Quai des Orfèvres to tell what he knew. He had worked regularly for the Jossets. It was he who, some years previously, had put in new curtains and wallpaper. Some months ago he had changed some of the curtains, including those in Madame Josset's bedroom, which had just been refurnished.

'The servants seem to have forgotten my visit,' he said. 'They mentioned the gas-man, but not me. Three days ago I went to the Rue Lopert because Madame Josset had told me that the curtain cords had come loose. That often happens. So on Monday at about three I happened to be passing nearby and took advantage of the occasion to call in.'

'Whom did you see?'

'Madame Siran opened the door. She didn't come upstairs with me because she hates stairs, and she knows I know the house.'

'Were you alone?'

'Yes. I'd left my mate on another job in the Avenue de Versailles. My job only took a few minutes.'

'Did you see the maid?'

'She came into the room where I was working, for a minute, and I said "Hello" to her.'

Neither of the women had remembered the decorator when they had been questioned.

Maigret took the man to Criminal Identity. His fingerprints were taken and they corresponded exactly with those of the mysterious visitor.

The next day it was again Maigret who received the anonymous letter which was to increase public anger – a sheet of paper torn from a school exercise book and folded in four, then slipped into a cheap envelope which bore some grease marks, as if the message had been written on a kitchen table.

The postmark was that of the XVIIIth *arrondissement*, where Annette Duché lived.

'Inspector Maigret, who thinks he's so clever, should question a certain Hortense Malletier, in the Rue Lepic, who is a filthy abortionist. She had a visit from the Duché girl and her lover three months ago.'

The way things stood, the inspector decided to take the letter himself to Coméliau.

'Read this.'

The magistrate read the letter twice.

'Have you checked?'

'I didn't want to do anything without your instructions.'

'You'd better see this Hortense Malletier yourself. Is she on your records?'

Maigret had already looked up the Vice Squad's records.

'She has been arrested once, ten years ago, but nothing could be proved.'

The Malletier woman lived on the fifth floor of an old building near the Moulin de la Galette. She was over sixty and suffered from dropsy, so she wore bedroom slippers and couldn't move without a stick. There was a sickening smell in the flat, and ten or twelve canaries flew around in a large cage by the window.

'What do the police want with me? I'm a poor old woman who doesn't want anything from anyone any more . . .'

Grey hair, so thin that her scalp showed through, framed her pallid face.

Maigret began by showing her a photograph of Annette Duché.

'Do you recognize her?'

'Her picture's been in the papers enough!'

'Did she come here to see you about three months ago?'

'What would she do here? I haven't read the cards for a long time.'

'Did you read the cards too?'

'So? Everyone earns their living as best they can.'

'She was pregnant, and after you saw her she wasn't any more.'

'Who made up that story? It's a lie!'

Janvier, who was with his superior, searched the drawers and found nothing, as Maigret had expected.

'We must know the truth. She didn't come here alone. There was a man with her.'

'It's been years since any man set foot in my flat.'

She stuck to her story. She knew the routine. The concierge of the building, when she was questioned, said she hadn't seen Annette or Josset.

'Doesn't Madame Malletier often have young girls to visit her?'

'Long ago, when she used to read the cards, she did, young and old, and even men, whom you wouldn't expect to believe in such things. But she hasn't done that for a long time now . . .'

That could all have been foreseen. Annette's attitude, when she was summoned by Maigret to the Quai des Orfèvres, was less so. The inspector began with a blunt question:

'How long had you been pregnant when you went to Madame Malletier in the Rue Lepic?'

Didn't Annette know how to lie? Was she taken by surprise? Didn't she realize what depended on her reply?

She blushed, looked around her as if for help and glanced nervously at Lapointe, who was once again taking everything down in shorthand.

'I suppose I must answer that?'

'It would be wise to do so.'

'Two months.'

'Who gave you the address in the Rue Lepic?'

Maigret was annoyed without knowing why, possibly because he thought she gave in too quickly. The concierge had played the game. So had the old abortionist – naturally, for she had more reason.

'Adrien.'

'So you told him you were pregnant, and he talked about an abortion?'

'It wasn't quite like that. I had been worried for about six weeks, and he kept on asking what was wrong with me. He even accused me of loving him less than before. One evening I asked him if he knew of a midwife or a doctor who would . . .'

'Didn't he object?'

'He was very upset. He said, "*Are you sure?*"'

'I said yes, that it wouldn't be long before it showed, and I'd have to do something.'

'Did he know Madame Malletier?'

'No, I don't think so. He begged me to wait a few days and not to do anything before he decided.'

'Decided what?'

'I don't know.'

Josset had no children by his wife. Had he been moved by the idea of Annette giving him a son or a daughter?

Maigret, for his own satisfaction, would have liked to ask him this question amongst others, but all the interrogations were now Coméliau's prerogative, and he didn't see things the same way.

'Do you think he was tempted to make you have the child?'

'I don't know.'

'Did he say anything about it?'

'For a week he was very gentle, very attentive.'

'Wasn't he usually gentle?'

'He was kind and loving, but it wasn't the same thing.'

'Do you think he told his wife about that?'

She jumped.

'His wife!'

One would have said that she was afraid of Christine even when she was dead.

'He wouldn't have done that, surely . . .'

'Why not?'

'I don't know. A man doesn't tell his wife that another woman is expecting his child.'

'Was he afraid of her?'

'He didn't hide anything from her. When I advised him to be careful, not to be seen with me in certain restaurants, for example, he assured me that she knew all about it, and that it didn't matter to her.'

'Did you believe him?'

'Not entirely. I don't believe it's possible . . .'

'Did you ever meet Christine Josset?'

'Several times.'

'Where?'

'In the office.'

'Do you mean in her husband's office?'

'Yes. . . . I worked there too. . . . When she came to the Avenue Marceau . . .'

'Did she go there frequently?'

'Two or three times a month.'

'To see her husband, to take him somewhere?'

'No. Mostly to see Monsieur Jules. She was chairman of the Board.'

'Did she take an active interest in the business?'

'Not active.. . . . She kept up with things, though, saw the accounts, had certain methods explained to her . . .'

This was a side of Christine which no one had yet talked about.

'I suppose she was curious about you?'

'The first few times, yes. The very first time, she looked me up and down, from head to foot, shrugged her shoulders and said to her husband, "Not bad".'

'So she knew already?'

'Adrien had told her.'

'Did she never speak to you privately? Did she never get the idea that she was afraid of you?'

'Of me? Why would she be afraid of me?'

'If her husband had told her you were expecting his child . . .'

'That would have been different, of course. But I would never have let him tell her. Not only because of her, but the others . . .'

'Your fellow-workers?'

'Everybody. . . . And my father too . . .'

'What happened at the end of the week?'

'One morning in the office, before opening the mail, he whispered quickly:

' "I have an address. . . . We have an appointment there this evening . . ."

'That evening when we left the office he didn't take me straight home to the Rue Caulaincourt. He left the car in the Boulevard de Clichy, as a precaution, and we walked to the Rue Lepic . . .'

'Weren't you tempted to change your mind?'

'The woman frightened me, but I'd made up my mind.'

'What about him?'

'After a few minutes he went outside to wait for me.'

Maigret had taken his report to Coméliau, as he had to. Had there been any leakage from the magistrate's office? Coméliau was not the sort of man to spread about information of that kind. Would Lenain, who had had to be told professionally, be less discreet? Publicity about this was not in his client's interests and, in spite of his earlier faux-pas, he wouldn't have done that.

It was more likely that the person who had written the anonymous letter, annoyed that nothing about it had been printed, had gone directly to the newspapers. They had carried out their own investigation.

Madame Malletier, still denying everything, had been arrested, and the case was once more on the front pages.

Coméliau had been obliged to charge the girl too, but she was given bail.

JOSSET AND MISTRESS ACCUSED OF SECOND CRIME

If Annette was spoken about, it was in tones of pity, all responsibility being placed on her lover.

One could feel a real wave of hate growing around him every day. Even those who had been his friends could only malign him and tried to minimize their friendship.

'I knew him, like everyone else. . . . But I was really Christine's friend. . . . What an amazing woman . . .'

Amazingly vital, yes indeed. But what else?

'He wasn't the man she needed.'

When pressed, they were unable to say just what kind of man she did need. As far as could be seen, she had been created to live her own life with complete independence.

'For a while he was her great love. Everyone wondered why,

because Josset has never been sexy, he was no Don Juan. Besides, he's a weakling.'

It hadn't occurred to anyone that Christine might have crushed all life out of that weakling.

'Had she stopped loving him?

'They lived apart more and more. Especially since he became infatuated with that typist.'

'Did it upset her?'

'It's hard to know just what Christine felt. She kept her feelings to herself.'

'Even about her lovers?'

They would look reproachfully at Maigret, as if he weren't playing the game.

'She liked to help young people on, didn't she?'

'She went to lots of art shows and things . . .'

'She had her colts, so to speak, didn't she?'

'She may have helped a beginner . . .'

'Can you give me an example?'

'It's difficult. . . . She was tactful enough not to make a lot of it. . . . I remember she helped a young painter, particularly by bringing her friends and some reporters she knew to his first exhibition . . .'

'What was his name?'

'I don't remember it. . . . I think he was Italian . . .'

'Is that all?'

As each day went by he met a more and more organized resistance.

After the bomb he had so heedlessly dropped, Maître Lenain, for his part, tried to draw up a list of the protégés he had sworn existed. Maigret knew that he had the help of a detective agency run by one of his own former detectives. They had a freer hand than Police Headquarters and didn't have Coméliau always on top of them.

In spite of that, he hadn't found anything clear-cut. He had rung Maigret to tell him of one Daunard, a former hotel porter in Deauville who was now a singer in Saint-Germain-des-Prés.

Although he wasn't yet widely known, he was beginning to make a name in the night-clubs on the Right Bank, and he was to open soon in music-hall, at the Bobino.

Maigret went to see him in his hotel room in the Rue Pon-thieu. He was a well-built lad, unpolished, the same aggressive type as some young American stars.

At two in the afternoon he opened the door, wearing crumpled pyjamas. Only the blonde hair of the woman curled up in the sheets could be seen.

'Maigret, eh?'

He had been expecting this visit at any time. He lit a cigarette and began to act like a film tough.

'I could forbid you to come in unless you have a warrant. Do you?'

'No.'

Maigret was not prepared to discuss the legality of his visit.

'I warn you now I have nothing to say.'

'Did you know Christine Josset?'

'So what? There are thousands of people in Paris who did.'

'Did you know her intimately?'

'In the first place, that's none of your business. In the second, if you look hard enough you'll find several dozen young men who've slept with her. And when I say dozens . . .'

'When did you last see her?'

'About a year ago. And if you're going to say that she started me off, you've got it wrong. When I was in Deauville the owner of a club in Saint-Germain had seen me already and given me his card so that I would come to Paris to see him.'

The woman in the bed pulled the sheet back a few inches and risked a one-eyed look.

'Don't you worry, love! I've got nothing to fear from these men. I can prove that I was in Marseilles the night Madame Christine was bumped off. They'll even find my name in big print on the programme at the Miramar . . .'

'Did you know any others?'

'Other whats?'

'Other friends of Madame Josset's.'

'Do you think we were a club, maybe, or a guild? Then why didn't we wear a badge, eh?'

He was very pleased with himself. His girl-friend, still wrapped in the sheet, was doubled up with laughter.

'Is that all you want? Then, with your permission, I have better things to do. Right, love?'

There were obviously others, the same type or different, who evidently didn't want to make themselves known. The painter who had been mentioned now lived in Brittany, where he painted seascapes, and there was nothing to show that he had been in Paris at the time.

A different kind of investigation, among the taxi-drivers, hadn't brought any results either. Still, even after quite a long time, it is rare not to find the driver who has made a particular trip.

Several detectives had divided the companies, the taxi-ranks and the small owners between them.

Each one was asked if he had taken anyone to the Rue Lopert on the night of the crime. That brought no results. They had only learned that a couple who lived three doors away from the Jossets had come back from the theatre by taxi a little before midnight.

Neither the driver nor the couple could remember if there had been any lights on in the glass house at that time.

However, the fact that there had been a taxi in the street at that time did have something good about it, for the former colonial administrator, who had said that not a thing of what had been going on in the street had escaped him, hadn't mentioned that vehicle. And yet the taxi had been parked there, engine running, for three or four minutes, because the customer, who had had no change, had gone into the house to get some.

A photograph of Martin Duché had been shown to thousands of drivers, particularly those who usually stand in the Caulaincourt area.

They had all seen it in the papers already. According to Annette, her father had left her about 9.30 that evening. He didn't appear to have got back to his hotel by the Gare d'Austerlitz before midnight, and the night-watchman didn't remember having seen him come in at all.

What had the head clerk from Fontenay-le-Comte been doing all that time?

It appeared to be a complete blank. No driver remembered picking him up, although his figure and his face were easily recognizable.

Annette had admitted that he was not really in his normal state of mind – although he was a total abstainer, he had had a considerable quantity to drink.

Even though it had had a calm enough ending, the scene in the Rue Caulaincourt must nevertheless have upset him.

The fact remained that no taxi appeared to have taken him to the Rue Lopert or anywhere else.

He had not been seen in the Métro station either, which, given the number of people passing through, didn't prove a thing.

And there were still the buses, in which he could have travelled completely unnoticed.

Was he the type of man to sneak stealthily into the Josset's house? Would he not have rung the doorbell? Had he found the door open?

And how was it possible that, since he didn't know the place, he could have crossed the living-room in the dark and climbed the stairs to Christine's bedroom?

The murderer, if he wasn't the husband, wore gloves. He had either brought with him a fairly heavy weapon with which to inflict the wounds described by Doctor Paul, or he had used the commando dagger which had been in Adrien's bedroom.

Who, apart from close friends, could have known that that dagger was there? Moreover, it had to be admitted that, having committed the crime, the unknown man had cleaned the weapon and left no trace whatsoever on a cloth, since the drug manufacturer had not seen any blood on the dagger.

The public was aware of these contradictions, for the journalists exercised their ingenuity by going in detail into every imaginable hypothesis. One of them had even printed the arguments for and those against in parallel columns.

Maigret went to the Avenue Marceau for the first time, to the mansion built at the end of the last century and now converted into offices.

Apart from the switchboards and a little room where visitors left their cards and filled out forms, the ground floor, with its panelling and its over-decorated ceilings, was only used for exhibition rooms.

The products of 'Josset et Virieu' were displayed in glass cases and there were also, sumptuously framed, diagrams and doctors' testimonials. And on huge oak tables lay the various medical publications which helped to sell the firm's products.

This time it was Monsieur Jules whom Maigret had come to see. He had already learned that Jules was not his Christian name but his surname, so that he was not called that as a mark of familiarity.

The bright, almost bare room where two secretaries were working separated his office from Josset's, which was the largest in the building, and had tall windows looking out over the trees in the avenue.

Monsieur Jules was sixty-five, with bushy eyebrows and dark hairs sprouting out of his nose and his ears. He was a little like Martin Duché but less humble. Like him he typified the image usually brought to mind by the words 'honest servant'.

In fact he had been in the firm long before Josset, indeed from the time of Virieu's father, and although his official title was head of personnel, he had the right to supervise everything else.

Maigret wanted to talk to him of Christine.

'Don't put yourself to any trouble, Monsieur Jules. I'm only passing by, and I am really not too sure what I wanted to ask you. . . . By chance I learned that Madame Josset was chairman of your board of directors.'

'That is true.'

'Was this only an honorary title or did she take an active interest in the firm's business?'

He could already sense the unwillingness to speak that he was finding everywhere. Was it not precisely to avoid this that it is so important to act quickly in a criminal investigation? Madame Maigret knew this better than anyone, since she saw her husband come home so often in the early hours of the morning, if indeed he hadn't spent several nights on the job.

When people read newspapers they soon form an opinion, and, even when they believe themselves to be sincere and truthful, they tend to distort the truth.

107

'She was really interested in the business, in which, moreover, she had a considerable financial interest.'

'A third of the registered capital, I believe?'

'A third of the shares, yes, another third belonging to Monsieur Virieu and the remaining third, for the past few years, to her husband.'

'I understand that she came to see you two or three times a month.'

'It was not quite as regular as that. She came from time to time, not only to see me, but also to see the managing director and, sometimes, the chief accountant.'

'Did she know what was what?'

'She had a very good business sense. She played the stock market with her own money, and I may say that she made a handsome profit out of it.'

'In your opinion, did she distrust the way her husband ran things?'

'Not only her husband. Everyone.'

'Didn't this attitude make enemies for her?'

'Everyone has enemies.'

'Did she have enemies in this firm? Did she ever take action against anyone in particular?'

Monsieur Jules scratched his nose, a malicious gleam in his eye, not in the least embarrassed, but he hesitated a little before speaking.

'Have you studied the management and the personnel of a big business firm before, Inspector? As long as there are enough interested parties, and as long as departments are in more or less open competition, there are bound to be cliques . . .'

It was true even of the Quai des Orfèvres, as Maigret knew only too well.

'Were there cliques in this firm?'

'There probably still are.'

'May I ask to which you belong?'

Monsieur Jules frowned, grew more serious and stared at his pigskin desk-set.

'I was quite devoted to Madame Josset,' he said finally, weighing his words.

'And to her husband?'

At that Monsieur Jules got up to reassure himself that there was no one listening behind the door.

8. *Madame Maigret's Coq au Vin*

It was the Maigret's turn to have their friends the Pardons to dinner in the Boulevard Richard-Lenoir. Madame Maigret had spent all day cooking amidst a veritable symphony of noises, for the season of wide-open windows had begun, and the life of Paris swept into the flats with the warm breezes.

Alice had not come, and it was her mother's turn to listen for the telephone, since they were waiting to hear at any moment that the young woman had been rushed off to hospital for the delivery.

When dinner was over, the table cleared and coffee served, Maigret offered the doctor a cigar while the two women began to whisper in a corner. Among other things Madame Pardon could be heard to say:

'I've always wondered how you make it.'

They were talking about the coq au vin which had been the main dish at dinner. Madame Pardon continued:

'There's a faint taste of something, hardly noticeable, which makes all the difference and I can't decide what it is.'

'But it's quite simple really – I suppose you add a glass of cognac at the last moment?'

'Cognac or armagnac, whichever I have to hand.'

'Well, although it's not orthodox, I put in a little Alsatian plum brandy. That's all there is to it . . .'

All during dinner Maigret had been in a very gay mood.

'Have you much work on hand?' Pardon asked.

'Yes, a lot.'

It was true, but it was amusing work.

'I'm living in the midst of a circus!'

For some time now there had been a series of burglaries carried out in such a way that the perpetrator could only be a professional acrobat, probably a contortionist of either sex, so that Maigret and his colleagues spent the entire day among people of the circus and the music-halls, and the oddest people were to be seen at the Quai des Orfèvres.

They were dealing with a newcomer who used new methods, which is much rarer than one might think. Everything had to be learned afresh, and a peculiar excitement reigned over the Crime Squad.

'Last month you didn't have time to tell me the end of the Josset case,' murmured Doctor Pardon, once he was settled in his armchair with a drink in his hand.

He never had more than one glass, but he swallowed it in tiny sips which he held on his tongue, the better to savour the bouquet.

A different expression crossed the inspector's face when he thought of the crime in the Rue Lopert.

'I don't remember now exactly where I'd got to. From the beginning I had guessed that Coméliau wouldn't let me see Josset again, and that is exactly what happened. He held on to him so tightly that one might have thought he was jealous of him . . .

'The preliminary investigation took place between the walls of his chambers, so that we in the Quai des Orfèvres knew no more about it than what we could read in the papers.

'For nearly two months ten of my men, sometimes more, carried out depressing inquiries.

'Our investigation was carried out on several levels at once. First there was the purely technical side, the reconstruction of each person's time-table on the night of the crime, the searching, twenty times over, of the houses in the Rue Lopert, where we kept hoping to find a clue which had previously escaped our notice, including the notorious commando knife.

'I myself questioned the two servants, the tradesmen and the neighbours heaven knows how many times. And to complicate matters there was the flood of letters, both anonymous and signed, mostly signed, which couldn't be ignored.

'That is inevitable when a case takes the public fancy.

'Madmen, crackpots, people who have had it in for their neighbours for years, or just people who think they know something, they all come to the police, and we have to separate the true from the false.

'I went to Fontenay in secret, almost illegally, without any result, as I think I told you.

'You see, Pardon, once a crime has been committed, nothing is simple any more. The deeds and words of ten or twenty people, which a few hours before seemed so natural, are suddenly seen in a more or less incriminating light.

'*Everything is possible!*

'There is no theory which is in itself ridiculous. Nor is there an infallible way of being sure of a witness's good faith or his memory.

'The public makes up its mind by instinct, prompted by sentimental considerations and elementary logic.

'But *we* have to doubt everything, to look everywhere, not to leave any theory untested . . .

'So, on the one hand, the Rue Lopert; on the other, the Avenue Marceau.

'I didn't know anything about the drug business and, in order to do my job, I had to learn how this one, which, together with its laboratories, employed more than three hundred people, was run.

'How could I, in a few interviews, see how Monsieur Jules' mind worked?

'He wasn't the only one who played an important part in the Avenue Marceau. There was Virieu, the founder's son; then there were the heads of various departments, the technical advisers, doctors, pharmacists, chemists . . .

'This world was divided into two main camps which could roughly be called the old guard and the new, the former considering that only drugs sold on prescription should be made there, the latter preferring products giving a high profit margin, drugs of the kind launched with publicity campaigns in the papers and on the wireless.'

Pardon murmured:

'I know a little about that.'

'It seems that Josset was basically inclined to the old guard, but he let himself be pushed, under pressure, into the second group.

'Still, he did resist . . .'

'And his wife?'

'She was the leader of the moderns. She had been instrumental in the dismissal of an advertising director two months previously. He had been a good man who had the medical clientele well in hand and was the avowed enemy of cheap drugs.

'Both in the Avenue Marceau and at Saint-Mandé that made for an undercurrent of intrigue, suspicion and probably hatred. . . . But that didn't get me anywhere.

'We couldn't dig deeply into everything at once. Normal day-to-day work takes up the time of most of the men even when a sensational case breaks.

'I have rarely felt our shortcomings so much. At a time when we needed to know the life history of ten, maybe even of thirty people who hadn't even been heard of the previous day, I only had a handful of men at my disposal.

'They are expected to penetrate worlds they don't know and to form an opinion in a ridiculously short time.

'Now in a trial, the word of a witness, a concierge, a taxi-driver, a neighbour, a chance passer-by, can have more weight than the denials and statements made under oath of the accused.

'Adrien Josset kept on denying everything, in spite of stronger and stronger evidence. His lawyer kept on making unfortunate statements to the press.

'I had fifty-three anonymous letters which led us to every part of Paris and the suburbs and we had, besides, to send to the provinces to ask their forces to collect evidence.

'Some people believed they had seen Martin Duché in Auteuil that night, and there was even a tramp near the Pont Mirabeau who claimed that Annette's father, blind drunk, had propositioned him.

'Others told us the names of young men who had been Christine Josset's protégés.

'We followed up every lead, even the most unlikely, and I sent a fresh report to Coméliau every evening. He would read it and shrug his shoulders.

'One of the young men brought to our notice in this way was a chap called Popaul. The anonymous letter said:

' "You will find him at the Bar de la Lune in the Rue de

Charonne. Everyone there knows him, but they won't say anything because they've all got something to hide."

'The author gave details and said that Christine Josset liked low types and that she had met Popaul several times in a boarding house near the Saint-Martin canal.

' "She bought him a little car, a *quatre-chevaux*. That didn't stop Popaul beating her up more than once and making her scream." '

Maigret himself went to the Rue de Charonne, and the bar in question was indeed a meeting-place for young delinquents who vanished when he appeared. He questioned the landlord and the barmaid and, in the days following, regular customers, whom he had some difficulty in finding.

'Popaul? Who's that?'

They said that too innocently. If one were to believe them, no one had ever heard of Popaul, and the inspector could get no more satisfaction in the boarding houses near the canal.

At the motor taxation office, and in the driving-licence offices, there was no useful information. Several owners of new *quatre-chevaux* were named Paul. They had even found some of them, but four or five had left Paris.

As for Christine's friends of both sexes, they kept the same polite silence. Christine was a charming woman, a 'darling', a 'pet', an 'exceptional creature'.

Madame Maigret had taken Madame Pardon into the kitchen to show her something, and then, so as to leave the men in peace, the two women settled down in the dining-room. Maigret had taken off his jacket and was smoking a meerschaum pipe which he only used at home.

'The Grand Jury was named, and we at the Quai were effectively put out of commission. Other cases kept us busy all summer. The papers announced that Josset, after a nervous depression, had been moved to the infirmary at the Santé, where he was being treated for a stomach ulcer.

'Some people sneered, because it has become almost a tradition for a certain class of person to pretend that they are ill when they are put in prison.

'When the new law term opened, and he was seen at the trial, in the dock, one could see that he had lost more than three stones and that he wasn't the same man. His clothes flapped on his thin body, his eyes were sunken, and, although his counsel challenged the public and the witnesses with his manner, he himself seemed indifferent to what was going on around him.

'I didn't hear the judge's questioning of the accused, or the statements of Coméliau and the inspector of the Auteuil police, who were the first witnesses, because I was in the witnesses' waiting-room. Among others, I was rubbing shoulders with the concierge from the Rue Caulaincourt, who was wearing a red hat and seemed very pleased with herself, and with Monsieur Lalinde, the former colonial administrator, whose testimony was the most damning, and who seemed to be in a very bad state. I thought he too had grown thinner. You would have said he was in the grip of an obsession, and I wondered if he was going to change his original statement in public.

'Whether I liked it or not I had to add my brick to the case so carefully built up by the prosecution.

'I was only an instrument. I could only say what I had seen, what I had heard, and no one asked me what I thought.

'I spent the remainder of the two days in court, and Lalinde didn't retract; he didn't change one word of his previous statement.

'As I walked along the corridors during adjournments, I heard what the public thought, and it was obvious that no one at all doubted Josset's guilt.

'Annette too appeared in the witness box, causing a disturbance in court, with whole rows of people standing up to see her. The judge threatened to clear the court.

'She was asked detailed questions – leading questions, really, particularly about the abortion.

' "Was it indeed Josset who took you to see Madame Malletier in the Rue Lepic?"

' "Yes, sir."

' "Face the jury, please."

'She wanted to add something else, but she was already being asked another question . . .'

*

Several times Maigret had the impression that she was trying to explain details that no one was worrying about. For example, hadn't it been she who, when she told her lover that she was pregnant, had asked him if he knew an abortionist?

'It went on like that,' the inspector said to Pardon.

Sitting in the public gallery, he could hardly keep still. He continually wanted to raise his hand, to interrupt.

'In two days, in barely a dozen hours, and including the reading of the charge, the case for the prosecution and that for the defence, they had tried to sum up, for people who had known nothing about it before, a whole way of life; to describe not only one character but several, for Christine, Annette, her father, and others who came into the case marginally, were brought into it one by one.

'It was hot in the courtroom, for that year we were having a wonderful Indian summer. Josset kept looking at me. Several times I caught his eye, but it was only at the end of the first day that he seemed to recognize me and smiled slightly at me.

'Had he understood that I had doubts, that this case left me feeling uncomfortable, that I was annoyed with myself and with others, and that because of him I had come to hate my profession?

'I don't know. Most of the time he was sunk in a kind of indifference which several reporters took to be scorn. Since he had taken care with his appearance, they spoke of his vanity and tried to find proofs of it in his career and even in his childhood and young manhood.

'The Attorney-General, who was himself acting as Public Prosecutor, also stressed this vanity:

' "A vain weakling . . ."

'Maître Lenain's aggressive remarks didn't change the atmosphere in the court – quite the opposite!

'When the jury retired I was sure what their anwer to the first question would be: "Yes!", and probably unanimously –

'Josset had killed his wife.

'I expected a "No", in all justice, to the second question, which was about premeditation. As for extenuating circumstances . . .

'Some people were eating sandwiches, there were women

passing sweets around, the reporters had calculated that they had time to run to the bar in the Palais de Justice for a drink.

'It was late when the foreman of the jury, an ironmonger from the VIth *arrondissement*, was called upon to speak. He held a slip of paper in his trembling hand.

' "To the first question: *yes*.

' "To the second question: *yes*.

' "To the third question: *no*."

'Josset had been found guilty of killing his wife, of having done so with premeditation, and he was not allowed the benefit of extenuating circumstances.

'I saw him take the blow. He grew pale, he was shocked, he couldn't believe his ears at first. He began to wave his arms as if struggling, then he suddenly grew calm and, turning one of the most tragic looks I have ever seen towards the public gallery, he said in a clear voice:

' "I am innocent!"

'There were some jeers. A woman fainted. Police rushed into the courtroom.

'In no time at all Josset had suddenly been whisked away, and a month later the press announced that the President of the Republic had turned down his appeal.

'No one thought about him any more. A new trial caught hold of people's imaginations, a vice case which brought forth juicy disclosures every day, so that Josset's execution only took up a few lines on the fifth page of most papers.'

There was silence. Pardon stubbed out his cigar in the ashtray while the inspector filled his pipe again. The women were still talking in the next room.

'Do you think he was innocent?'

'Twenty years ago, when I was a newcomer to the profession, I would perhaps have said "Yes" without hesitating. Since then I've learned that anything, even the improbable, is possible.

'Two years after the trial I had in my office a wide boy suspected of dealings in the white slave trade. It wasn't the first time we had seen him. He was part of our regular clientele.

'His identity card said he was a sailor, and in fact he did sail a lot to South and Central America on cargo boats, though he spent most of his time in Paris.

'With that kind of person things are different, for we're on familiar ground.

'And sometimes we can work out a compromise.

'At one point, looking at me out of the corner of his eye, he muttered;

' "Suppose I had something to sell?"

' "What, then?"

' "Some information you'd be very interested in . . ."

' "What about?"

' "The Josset case."

' "That's been over for a long time."

' "That's no reason not to . . ."

'In exchange, he wanted me to keep his girl-friend out of it. He really seemed to be in love with her. I promised to go easy on her.

' "On my last trip I met a chap called Popaul. . . . A character who used to hang around the Bastille district . . .'

' "In the Rue de Charonne?"

' "Could be. . . . He hadn't been doing very well over there and I bought him a few drinks. . . . Round about three or four in the morning, when he'd had half a bottle of tequila and was good and drunk, he began to talk:

' " 'The bosses here don't think I'm tough. . . . They don't believe me when I tell them I chopped a woman in Paris. . . . Even less when I tell them she was a rich woman and nuts about me. . . . But it's true, and I'll always be sorry I did such a mad thing. . . . But I never could stand being treated in a certain way, and it was her fault for going too far. . . . Haven't you ever heard of the Josset case?' " '

Maigret stopped speaking. He took his pipe out of his mouth.

'My man couldn't tell me any more. Popaul, if there was any Popaul – some people have wild imaginations – went on drinking and fell asleep. . . . The next day he said he didn't remember a thing . . .'

'Didn't you go to the Venezuelan police?'

'Unofficially, for there were things to be taken into account. Over there are several Frenchmen who have good reason not to come back to France, some old lags amongst them. In answer to

117

my question I had an official letter asking me to give fuller details of identity.

'Is there any such person as Popaul? Was he, proud of his virility and his toughness, angry at being treated by Christine Josset in the way that men treat a prostitute, and did he take his revenge on her?

'I have no way of knowing.'

He got up and stood in front of the window, as if to clear his mind.

While Pardon kept an eye on the telephone out of habit, Maigret asked him, a little later:

'By the way, what happened to the Polish tailor's family?'

It was the doctor's turn to shrug his shoulders.

'Three days ago I was called in to the Rue Popincourt because one of the children has measles. I found a North African there, already living with the mother. She looked a bit embarrassed and said:

' "It's for the children's sake, you see . . ." '

The Old Man Dies

Translated from the French
by Bernard Frechtman

Chapter One

From the cashier's desk where she was sitting and smiling vaguely, Fernande saw the couple enter and realized at once that they were newcomers. They were both very young and were wearing new clothes from head to foot, like newly-weds, which they no doubt were. As soon as they crossed the threshold, they tried to conceal their surprise and hesitation.

Antoine had also spotted them from the back room but had not bothered, and it was François, the red-headed waiter, who had gone to welcome them.

'This way, please . . .'

He gave them a bad table, in the middle of the restaurant, and the young people glanced at a corner table without daring to say anything. In any case, if they had asked for it, François would have said that it was reserved.

The buxom Liselotte went to take their coats and, as she passed the cashier's desk, winked at the boss's wife.

The Ambassador and his guests had not yet arrived, but their table for eight was set in the back room, which the staff called 'the Senate' because it was reserved for good customers and prominent persons.

The couple, who were from the provinces, had probably been living in Paris only a short time. While strolling about the Central Market, they had noticed a restaurant that looked more or less like the others, though a bit more attractive because of the hams and salamis that hung in the window.

The sign, Chez l'Auvergnat, was also modest, and the young people were taken a little aback when François handed them the menu on elegant paper and as big as a folio.

Yet the tables in the front room were old marble-topped cast-iron tables, the bar was a standard tin bar, and in the black frame on the faded green wall above it was the 'Law regarding Drunkenness in Public'.

'I suggest that you start with beef broth or *cochonnades*.'

From her post between the two rooms and facing the cloak-room, Fernande was in the habit of taking everything in. She saw her husband, who was wearing a dark blue suit, bend forward over two newspapermen who were accompanied by young women whose pictures had been in the papers and magazines.

Behind the glass partition she could also see the chef bustling about his electric stoves.

The British Embassy had rung up to reserve a table for eight, which had created a certain nervousness in the establishment. Antoine had sent out for flowers. Although he had shaved at eleven in the morning, he had gone upstairs a little before seven to run his electric razor over his cheeks a second time.

Almost all the tables were occupied. The two youngsters had decided on the *cochonnades* and were astounded to see so many different kinds of pork delicacies on the trolley that was rolled up to their table. The block of country butter that sat enthroned in the middle amazed the woman in particular.

Where was Auguste at the time? No doubt, as usual, at one of the tables of what was called 'the bistro'. The restaurant was his. He had bought it in 1913 with his savings and a little money that his brother had lent him. He had never dreamed that he would be sent to the front the following year.

At that time, what was now the Senate was occupied by the kitchen, and the present kitchen, which was spick and span behind its glass partition, was the bedroom.

Two Rolls-Royces stopped at the kerb. Antoine hurried to the door. The Ambassador and his guests were not wearing evening clothes and walked to their table unostentatiously, though everybody watched them.

It was not the first time that important persons had come to dine. The guest of honour, on the Ambassador's right, was a middle-aged woman who must have had her face lifted, for her features were completely immobile. She gazed idly and as if condescendingly at the curiosities the diplomat pointed out to her.

Fernande recognized him. He had lunched there two or three

times without saying who he was. He brought to his guest's attention, with the pride of someone who had discovered an extraordinary place, the glass partition that made it possible for diners to follow the preparing of the dishes. Then he pointed to the paintings on the walls, among which were three Utrillos.

Old Auguste had got them for almost nothing. A friend from Riom, with whom he had gone to school, ran a restaurant at the time in Montmartre, at the very top of the Rue du Mont-Cenis. Auguste had lent him some money and, as his old schoolmate was unable to repay it, had accepted the pictures in return.

Antoine was taking the order and discreetly advising his guests. To begin with, galantine of suckling pig, a few slices of Auvergne sausage, and a Saint-Flour delicacy. Then, leg of lamb from Brayaude, accompanied by a red Chanturgue wine that had a slight taste of violets.

Everything was going well. Everything was running smoothly. It was half past nine, and two tables had already asked for the bill.

Auguste had taken down from the wall a faded photograph of the restaurant as it had been in 1920, with himself at the bar, in shirt sleeves, and his wife a bit off to the side. He was showing it to two out-of-town customers who had dined too well and whom he had just given a glass of brandy on the house.

Of course, he had poured a drink for himself too, after a furtive glance in the direction of the cashier's desk and of his son, for he was not supposed to drink. He always took advantage of a busy moment to sit down at a table and help himself to a glass of wine or spirits. Whenever his eye caught his daughter-in-law, he would smile at her with a look of complicity.

Antoine was strict. Fernande was not. Why deprive a man close to eighty of his little pleasures?

As always, there was the hum of conversation in both rooms and the clink of glasses and clatter of plates. One no longer noticed the noise, just as one no longer noticed the smell of cooking and of wine.

Outside, vegetables were being piled up all over the Market, and the sheds were already lit up.

Fernande's eyes followed her husband, the waiters, and the customers who were putting on their coats and moving towards the door. Nobody on the staff slept enough, and towards the middle of the evening everyone began to feel pleasantly drowsy.

The two provincials had left, and Auguste was now standing near the newly-weds, to whom he was showing the photograph.

She could not hear what he was saying. Always the same story. How he had left Riom for Paris at the age of fifteen; how in those days throats were slit in the dark streets around Les Halles; how he sent for specialities from Auvergne, his birthplace, including the big loaves of greyish bread that were in the window.

She had to take her eyes off him for a few seconds. Her husband had nodded to her on his way to the kitchen to let her know that everything was all right and that the English party was pleased.

When she looked around again, Auguste was swaying. He was holding on to a chair, which was toppling under the pressure. Clinging to the red and white checked tablecloth, he dragged with him the plates and food of the young couple.

There was a crash, but no actual confusion. François, the red-headed waiter, was the first to get to the old man and was about to grab his shoulders when Antoine pushed him aside and lifted up his father, whom François took by the feet.

It had happened so quickly that one would have thought the scene had been rehearsed. Joseph, who had been working in the restaurant for thirty years, was already picking up the dishes and apologizing. The young people, upset and bewildered, were staring at the old man who was being helped to a door near the desk that opened on the hallway of the building. Fernande had had time enough to see that her father-in-law's face was purple, that one of his eyes was shut, and that the other had a fixed look.

She did not leave her post, from where she heard footsteps on the narrow, ill-lit staircase.

Antoine and François were puffing when they got to the first floor where they entered the low-ceilinged apartment of the two old people.

Eugénie had been put to bed at eight o'clock, as every evening. She was seventy-nine years old, a year older than her husband, and was no longer in her right mind.

During the day, she was put into a chair near the window. The servant, Madame Ledru, fed her as one does a child.

Being half asleep, she did not realize what was going on. Perhaps she was merely surprised to see the lamps.

'Go and get Madame Ledru,' ordered Antoine.

The servant occupied a small room facing the court. She arrived in a purple bathrobe.

'Help me undress him and put him to bed. . . . François you can go down now. . . . Tell my wife I'll be back in a minute.'

He could not leave the restaurant in the lurch. Downstairs, the rhythm must not be broken or changed.

Auguste was still breathing, but with a wheeze that distorted his mouth, as if he had no control of the movement of his lips. What was most impressive was his open eye that looked off into space.

'Phone Dr Patin. . . . Tell him it's urgent. . . . Call me as soon as he comes.'

Antoine walked away reluctantly from the bed where his mother and father were lying side by side. At the threshold, he hesitated. What could he do? He hadn't the slightest notion. The doctor who lived two streets away in the Rue Pierre-Lescot, would be there in a few minutes. Downstairs, it was a little like going on stage from the wings. Antoine went through the dark hallway of the building and, by pushing the door near Fernande's cash desk, returned to the light and warmth of the restaurant. He saw the flowers on the Ambassador's table, and the kitchen, where things were in full swing.

The newly-weds, who had not left, had lost their appetite and were pale. They were eating a dish of veal tripe that had just been served. Other customers watched Antoine as he walked to the desk.

'He's breathing,' he whispered to his wife, whose only reaction was to flutter her eyelids.

Some tiny bits of glass on the floor indicated where old Auguste had fallen. On one of the greenish walls a brighter rectangle showed where the photograph of the father and mother in 1920 belonged. Joseph had picked it up and, since the

125

frame was broken, had handed it, as if it were a relic, to Fernande, who had slipped it under the cashbox.

The dishes kept coming from the kitchen. The diners were now up to the cheese and dessert. The smell of cigar smoke began to mingle with that of cooking.

Antoine continued to keep an eye on everything, particularly in the Senate. He played the role of both proprietor and headwaiter, but because of the style of the establishment he wore a dark blue suit instead of the customary evening clothes.

'My father had a dizzy spell,' he said to the Ambassador.

The woman in the party was looking at him with limpid, impassive eyes. Who was she? The others treated her with marked respect. Wasn't she more or less related to the royal family?

A minor king from the Near East had once come for dinner with a vivacious party and two bodyguards. He had been hard to please because he did not eat pork, which was the restaurant's speciality.

Had Patin arrived? He had been the family doctor for almost forty years. He had treated Antoine and his two brothers when all three children had come down with scarlet fever at the same time. The family did not yet have the rooms on the first floor, and the children slept in cots on the top floor, in a maid's room with a sloping ceiling and window.

His wife's eyes seemed to be asking him a question. He looked around to be sure that things were going right, then disappeared again and went up the stairs three at a time.

As soon as one left the warm odours of cooking, one entered a domain that smelled of poverty, for most of the tenants were people who lived from hand to mouth.

Madame Ledru had put out the ceiling light and left on only a bedside lamp. She was sitting by the head of the bed and holding the old man's wrist while looking at her watch.

His breathing seemed weaker. From time to time, Auguste would make two or three convulsive movements, as if his whole body were protesting against what was happening to it.

'How many?'

'His pulse keeps changing all the time. . . . Just a moment ago it was a hundred and forty . . . and now I hardly feel it.'

'What about the doctor?'

'He's out seeing a patient. . . . An accident in a butcher's shop.
. . . His wife's trying to reach him. . . . She gave me the name of
another doctor who lives in the Rue Étienne-Marcel. I telephoned. He promised to come right away.'

The mother was sleeping, unconscious of what was going on
around her.

Antoine went downstairs again. It was his duty to be there –
at least for the big table – when brandy was served. As for
Fernande, she could not go up because it was the time when
more and more customers asked for the bill.

Antoine managed to smile. He had adopted that smile years
before, and he automatically hurried over as soon as anyone
raised his hand a few inches.

The English party seemed satisfied, except the princess or
duchess, who was still frozen and impenetrable. She refused the
marc brandy but accepted the old Armagnac in a large liqueur
glass. Three minutes later the glass was empty.

A car stopped. Antoine waited a few minutes. When he went
upstairs, he found a man whom he did not know, a man of
uncertain age and with thinning hair.

It was the doctor from the Rue Étienne-Marcel. No sooner
did he open his mouth than old Dr Patin arrived panting and
puffing. The two men shook hands and exchanged a questioning look.

There was no need for them to use a stethoscope on the
patient. Auguste's face was growing more and more purple, and
when one of the doctors passed his hand in front of the one
open eye, the pupil did not react.

'No point in taking him to the hospital,' muttered Patin as he
shook hands with Antoine.

'Can anything be done?'

'The end may come at any moment. . . . On the other hand,
he may hold out for hours . . .'

The doctors withdrew to a corner of the room and conversed
in a low tone, while Antoine who felt hesitant and useless, remained standing near the bed.

He was about to go down again. He could hardly bear the
sight of that eye which looked nowhere, of that twisted mouth.

127

He did not recognize his father. It was not a man who was lying on the bed but an unconscious thing that would soon be stark and stiff.

Just as he was about to step back, he thought he caught a kind of slight gleam in the staring eye. It resembled a look of surprise, and at the same moment the sound of breathing stopped.

'Doctor!' he called.

Patin rushed over, touched the eyelids, leaned forward, and pressed his cheek against Auguste's chest.

When he straightened up, he murmured, 'It's over, Antoine. . . . Have you been in touch with your brothers?'

'Not yet.'

'How's the judge getting along?'

'He's all right. He's the one who's handling the Mauvis affair.'

'And Bernard?'

Antoine's face clouded over.

'I haven't heard from him for months.'

Patin understood. He had known them as little children and as teenagers. He had attended the marriages of Antoine and of Ferdinand. He knew the family history by heart.

'Convey my condolences to your wife.'

The two doctors left together by the steep, narrow staircase.

'Can I call in old Marinette to lay him out?' asked Madame Ledru.

He nodded, went downstairs, opened the small door, and, as he went by, whispered to his wife, 'It's over.'

He got caught up in his work again, in the evening routine, until the last customer would have left and the iron shutters would be closed.

To Joseph too, who was sixty-eight and walked with his toes turned out, then to François, then to Jules, who stood behind the bar and was in charge of the wines, Antoine repeated, in a more and more natural voice, 'It's over.'

Then to Julien Bernu, the chef, 'It's over.'

Liselotte, who was very buxom and appetizing in her black

128

silk uniform, had no need to make an effort to smile at the customers when she helped them on with their coats. She was too young, too full of vitality.

*

The last customers had left shortly after eleven, and Antoine was now waiting to close the shutters. His father always waited with him to shut up shop, and for the two of them it was a kind of rite.

When Fernande had finished her accounts, she left by the small door and went up to the second floor, where the couple had a flat directly above that of the old people. She took with her the green metal box that contained the receipts.

Jules, who got dressed more quickly than the others, went off with his hands in his pockets and his coat collar turned up for it was a cold March evening.

Behind the bar was a trap-door that opened on to a staircase leading to the cellar, and Antoine went, as he did every night, to insert the iron bar that closed it and put on the padlock.

The two women dish-washers left by the door of the building. The staff hardly knew them, for such help never stayed long. At times one of the waiters had to hunt for men in the street to do the dishes.

Julien Bernu, the chef, was wearing an elegant camel-hair coat, and a sports car was waiting for him at the corner.

'See you tomorrow, boss.'

He hesitated, wondering whether he ought to add something, and finally shook Antoine's hand with a firmer grip than usual.

The rest of the staff did the same. They trickled out one after the other and went on with their personal lives.

Only two lights were left on. There was smoke around them, rather like a fog, and the smell of food had ceased to be appetizing.

The shutters were closed from the outside by means of a crank that was kept behind the bar. Les Halles was in full swing, and trucks were invading all the neighbouring streets.

Fifty years before, and even after the First World War, the

bar stayed open until dawn. It was frequented in those days by all kinds of people, including tramps and prostitutes who dozed with their backs against the wall.

Antoine went outside. The night before, his father had followed him. They had both been silent. They had heard the rattle of the big shutter as it descended jerkily and then the noise of the narrower one that protected the door.

He had to go back by way of the corridor and then put away the crank. Antoine remained standing behind the bar for a moment, looking at the bottles on the shelves. He finally chose a marc brandy and poured himself a glass, which was unusual, for all he ever drank was a bit of wine with his meals.

Then he put out the lights, walked to the corridor, and closed the small door. He had checked to see that everything was in order in the kitchen and at the sink. He trudged up the stairs with his shoulders bowed. When he entered his parents' bedroom, he was surprised to find an old woman whom he did not know.

'I've done the best I could, sir. I thought you'd be pleased if I brought four candles and some holy water. You can give me whatever you like . . .'

It was the old maid whom he had heard about, the one who looked after all the dead bodies in the neighbourhood. She had a round, gaping face with big blue innocent eyes, and she wore black clothes that must have dated from twenty years before.

He opened his wallet and handed her a few notes, while she pointed to his mother, who was still sleeping in the wooden bed.

'How is she?'

'She didn't bat an eyelash when we took the body away.'

Antoine did not know where they had put his father. He crossed the old-fashioned living-room where he had done his homework when he was a child and had played with his two brothers. The kitchen had served as a storeroom, since the family ate in the restaurant before the customers came.

Auguste's body was stretched out on Madame Ledru's bed in the servant's bedroom. A towel was wrapped around the head to keep the jaw from dropping. Both eyes were closed, and the face had lost the weird look it had had earlier.

130

The hands were clasped over a rosary that did not belong to anyone in the family.

Fernande stood and watched her husband, waiting to see his reactions. As he remained motionless and silent, she murmured, 'It seems that it's Marinette who . . .'

Two of the candles were lit, and a sprig of holly was lying in a finger bowl that probably contained holy water.

Antoine did not pray. They had not been taught to pray. He felt very tired, and he remembered that he still had to inform his brothers.

Madame Ledru made a suggestion: 'It would be better if I sat up with him, because I don't mind not sleeping. . . . If necessary, I can lie down for a while on the couch in the living-room.'

Everything suddenly looked so old, so decrepit! Auguste had always been against any change whatever in the flat where his wife herself had become a kind of object that was moved about from time to time in the course of the day.

'Come along . . .'

They went up to the second floor. The room was laid out in the same way, but the colours were brighter, the furniture was modern, and there was light.

He took off his jacket while his wife unhooked her black dress and then shook her brown hair.

'Are you going to ring Ferdinand first?'

He nodded, picked up the telephone, and dialled the number. While waiting for an answer, he loosened his tie a little.

At Parc-de-Sceaux, where Ferdinand lived with his wife and son in a modern block of flats, the bell seemed to be ringing in empty space.

'Maybe you dialled the wrong number.'

He went on listening. He seemed bored rather than sad.

'Hello. . . . Is that you, Véronique?'

His sister-in-law spoke in a hushed voice.

'Is Ferdinand in?'

'He's sleeping, poor thing. . . . I had to give him a sleeping-pill because the Mauvis affair is getting him down. . . . What's the matter, Antoine? . . . Why are you ringing so late? . . . Has anything happened to your mother?'

'To my father ...'

'Is he ill?'

'He's dead.'

'From what?'

'The doctor didn't tell me. ... I didn't even think of asking. ... I suppose it was a stroke. ... He was all blue ...'

'Is he at the hospital?'

'No. At home, in the maid's room.'

'Do you think I should wake Ferdinand? Is there anything he can do?'

'I think he'll be angry if we don't inform him.'

'I don't know. ... You might be right. ... Hold the line.'

More than two minutes went by, during which time there were several clicks. At one point, a choked voice kept repeating, 'Arthur. ... Arthur. ... Are you still there? ... Do you hear me?'

It was a woman's voice and sounded far away. A moment later it gave way to Ferdinand's.

'Hello. ... That you Antoine?'

'Yes. ... Excuse me for waking you ...'

'You did the right thing. ... My wife's been plying me with medicines. ... I've been running a temperature the last three days with a sore throat, but the investigation has reached such a point that I can't stay at home. ... The reporters are after me from morning to night. I half expect them to camp on my doorstep. ... So Papa's dead? ... What time did it happen?'

'I didn't notice ... around ten o'clock ...'

'What time is it now?'

'Ten past twelve.'

'Why didn't you call me earlier?'

'The restaurant was jammed, and there was a party of eight with the British Ambassador.'

'A stroke?'

'Patin didn't tell me.'

He repeated, 'He was all purple.'

'Did he know he was dying?'

'I don't think so.'

'Where did it happen?'

'He was chatting with some customers, in the restaurant. ...

132

Suddenly he fell down, dragging the table-cloth and everything on the table . . .'

'Did he say anything?'

'Nothing.'

'Have you rung Bernard?'

'Not yet.'

'Have you seen him recently?'

'No. Have you?'

'I caught sight of him in a taxi about a month ago. Luckily he didn't see me. . . . I think I'd better drop by. . . . What do you think?'

'There's nothing more one can do.'

'I know. But if Bernard comes, there'll surely be a discussion, and it would be better if I were there.'

'As you like.'

Fernande asked him, 'Is he coming?'

Her husband nodded and then looked up Bernard's number in an address book. When last heard from, he was living in the Boulevard Rochechouart. Things were no doubt going to start getting complicated.

The telephone rang in a flat that Antoine had never seen, and a man's voice, which was unfamiliar, answered: 'Who's speaking?'

Antoine could hear the sound of music and voices and the clinking of glasses.

'I think I've got the wrong number.'

'Who do you want to talk to?'

'To Bernard Mature.'

'Bernard, eh! . . . Good old Bernard. . . . Well, old boy, Bernard's not here.'

The man was drunk, and someone was taking the phone from him. This time it was a woman's voice at the other end.

'Hello. This is Nicole.'

'It's me, Nicole.'

'Antoine? What's happened? Why are you phoning at this hour?'

'Isn't Bernard there?'

Even if she had been drinking, she had her wits about her.

'He's away for the moment,' she answered cautiously, as if on the defensive.

'Out of town?'

'Why do you ask?'

'Because I have a piece of bad news for him.'

'What is it?'

'Father's dead.'

He was the only one who treated her like a sister-in-law, though she had been living with his brother for five years. They had both thought there was no point in marrying.

'That's terrible,' she murmured, then added, in another tone, 'Be quiet, all of you! There's been a death in the family.' She continued, 'Excuse me. . . . Some friends of Bernard dropped in. They thought he was here and brought a few bottles. I don't know how to get rid of them. They think they're at home. . . . Listen, Antoine, I'm really upset. . . . Today's Friday, isn't it? . . . That's right, Saturday, since it's past midnight. . . . Bernard drove south on Thursday with a friend. They may be in on a big property deal.'

Bernard was always expecting to be in on big deals whether property or not, on the Riviera or elsewhere.

'I know they had an appointment tonight at the Carlton Bar, but I don't know where they're staying.'

'When is he due back?'

'He didn't say. It depends on the deal. But all the same he has to be informed, doesn't he? How did it happen?'

'He suddenly collapsed in the restaurant.'

'A heart attack?'

'I don't know. . . . Half an hour later, he was dead.'

'Is Ferdinand with you?'

'I'm expecting him.'

'I'll do my best to find him. . . . If I phone all the hotels I may get the right one.'

Fernande questioned him again: 'Where is he?'

'In Cannes, so she says. It's not necessarily true. There are several people at Nicole's place drinking and playing music.'

'You think she'll come?'

'Her? What for?'

'I don't know. . . . Are you getting undressed?'

134

'Not before I see Ferdinand.'

'Véronique'll come with him.'

It was inevitable, for Ferdinand was so short-sighted that he had never driven a car, and now that he had one his wife acted as chauffeur. She drove him to court every morning and picked him up in the evening. At noon he lunched frugally at the snack bar at the courts or in a little restaurant near by.

'What do you think's going to happen?'

'I have no idea. It'll depend on Bernard.'

'And Véronique.'

'You think Véronique will make difficulties?'

'Perhaps more than Bernard. . . . How about some coffee.'

'Not a bad idea.'

He smoked little, for he could not allow himself to smoke in the restaurant. He contented himself with an occasional cigarette, which he seldom had time to finish.

In five hours he would be up and about, to do his shopping, as he did every morning. Of course, he did not have far to go.

It was Jules who ran the bar in the morning and served the customers.

At noon Antoine would put on his blue suit, and the two rooms would gradually fill up. By three o'clock they would be empty again. That enabled him to sleep a little, until about half past six, at which time he had a shower and dressed again.

Someone knocked at the door of the flat below. The floors were so worm-eaten that one could hear what went on all through the house, Madame Ledru must have answered that Antoine and his wife were upstairs. Fernande went to open the door just as Ferdinand and Véronique reached the landing.

The two brothers did not kiss. They had never in their life kissed each other. They shook hands and looked at each other with a grave expression. Véronique, however, kissed both Antoine and Fernande.

'What a misfortune . . .'

And her husband retorted with his usual commonsense, 'At his age it was to be expected. The important thing is that he didn't suffer. . . . What's surprising is that Mama wasn't the first to go. . . . Incidentally, how is she?'

'She wasn't aware of anything. She was sleeping.'

135

'Do you think she still recognizes what goes on around her?'

'It's hard to say.... At times one has the impression that she comes to herself, that she's trying to say something.... When that happens you'd swear she was fighting against a kind of fog, but it doesn't last and she falls back into her state of torpor.'

'It seems that Father's been put into the maid's room.'

'That was done so as not to move Mama.... I suppose that tomorrow we'll have to set up a private chapel in the living-room.... There'll be quite a crowd. All his friends from Riom and the Auvergnats in Paris.'

For Auguste had been president of the Association of Auvergnats in Paris.

Ferdinand was fifty-three. He wore thick glasses and was almost completely bald. Véronique, though she had become stout, did not look her age.

'Won't that be troublesome?'

'I hesitate to close the restaurant until the funeral. That's not how things are done in the business. Usually one closes only on the day of the funeral.'

'By the way, has the priest come?'

'No. I didn't think of sending for him.'

'Father was a choirboy when he was a child. Of course, he stopped going to church, but all the same it would be a good thing if you informed the parish. People wouldn't understand your not letting the church know.'

Fernande came in with coffee and cups. The armchairs and couch were covered with blue leather, and a red wall-to-wall carpet concealed the defects in the flooring.

'Someone rang the bell downstairs.'

'Who could it be?'

They all stood still and listened. Madame Ledru opened the door, spoke in a low voice, and then shut the door.

Light footsteps were heard on the stairs.

'I bet it's Nicole,' said Fernande as she stood up.

And when she opened the door, it was indeed Nicole whom they saw in the doorway.

She looked at them, one after the other, as if her visit were the most natural thing in the world, and took off her leopard-skin coat as she walked in.

'I thought it would be better if I came.'

Fernande, who was in her dressing-gown, went off to get another cup.

'Where is he?'

'On the first floor, in Madame Ledru's room.'

'Why isn't he in his bed?'

'Because my mother was already in it,' replied Antoine irritably.

Chapter Two

There was an embarrassing silence. No one knew where to look. Ferdinand was only three years older than Antoine, but one would have thought that the difference in age, instead of ceasing to matter, had increased as time went by. Perhaps it was because of Ferdinand's profession. To the family he was the judge, someone important, a person who knew things of which the others were completely ignorant.

There had been a period, during their adolescence, when the two brothers were real friends. In those days Ferdinand took Antoine more or less under his wing. Neither of them bothered about Bernard, whom they regarded as a child.

Each had lived his life in his own way. Each of them had married. Ferdinand had lived in La Rochelle at first. Then he had been assigned to Poitiers, where he had remained for eight years before getting a post in Paris. He had aged more rapidly than the others, so much so that it was hard to imagine that he had ever been young.

One felt that he took life seriously, that he gave every problem the same scrupulous attention, whether it had to do with his professional duties, his family, or himself.

Antoine, who was a head taller and whose brown hair was not even thinning, seemed to be of another breed.

What were the two brothers thinking about as Nicole observed first one and then the other? Had they not been expecting this confrontation for a long time? Nevertheless, it had taken them unawares, in the middle of the night, with Ferdinand fighting against a sore throat and Antoine hardly able to keep his eyes open.

'Tell me, Ferdinand . . .'

Nicole's tone was always slightly formal when she spoke to the judge or his wife, whereas she felt completely at ease with Antoine. She was only twenty-eight and was pretty, chic, and vivacious. She came from another world.

Ferdinand looked at her with his short-sighted eyes, and she continued without the slightest embarrassment, 'I know that it's none of my business, but, since Bernard is away, I'm obliged to speak for him. . . . You know about such things – don't you think that seals should have been affixed?'

'To what?'

'I don't know . . . to the dead man's rooms . . . to the safe . . .'

'What safe?'

Antoine felt more ill at ease than his brother, for he knew that the question had been directed at him, and he suspected that Ferdinand would not completely side with him.

'I don't think,' said the examining magistrate, 'that my father ever had a safe. . . . Is that right, Antoine?'

'There's none in the house.'

Nicole was nevertheless determined.

'All the same, he must have put his will somewhere.'

There was an almost oppressive silence. Fernande brought a cup, filled it with coffee, then looked for a place to sit down. She had heard everything from the kitchen. Everyone was looking at Antoine.

'Father never mentioned a will to me.'

'Didn't he have a notary?'

'It wasn't like him to put his affairs into the hands of a notary.'

'He had a bank account, didn't he?'

'If he did, he didn't tell anyone.'

Old Auguste was born in Saint-Hippolyte, a village near Riom with a population of three hundred. His father, who was a day-labourer, could neither read nor write.

At the age of twelve, Auguste was already working in a fruitshop, near the Law Court, and slept in the back room with his clothes on. At fifteen, he took a train and went to Paris alone.

'Ferdinand ought to know better than I what's to be done in such a case.'

Ferdinand was embarrassed and looked at his wife as if to ask her for advice.

'It depends. . . . There was once a written agreement between Father and Antoine.'

It had been drawn up after the war, in 1945. Antoine had come back from Germany, where he had been a prisoner for more than four years. He hesitated about going back to his job of cook at the Brasserie de Strasbourg, where he had been working in 1939.

He was twenty-seven years old and unmarried. At the time, there was only a small restaurant on the ground floor. In the window were hams and sausages and big loaves of dark bread from Auvergne that were delivered three times a week.

Their mother did the cooking, and there was only one waiter.

Auguste was not yet an old man. During the war he had made a lot of money, thanks to the food he managed to bring in from Auvergne.

A new clientele had begun to frequent the restaurant. Newspapermen and theatre people had discovered what they called Mère Mature's cooking.

'My boy, why not stay with me instead of going off and working for someone else? We could set up another room, a bigger kitchen . . .'

Ferdinand, who was still in La Rochelle, already had a child. Bernard, who had not finished school, worked vaguely in the film industry and came to see their father only when he needed money.

Antoine finally let himself be talked into joining his father, and as the plan for enlarging the establishment grew more and more definite, he became enthusiastic. It was he who had had the idea of a glass-enclosed kitchen that made it possible for the customers to see the food being prepared.

For twenty-five years his mother had been satisfied with cooking four or five dishes, each on a given day.

She, too, was from Saint-Hippolyte, where her father had a small farm. She had gone to school with Auguste, who ran into her again when he went back to see his brother. She was twenty at the time.

Thereafter, their history was that of most of the shopkeepers in the neighbourhood. After stinting for years, they were able to buy a business which it took them a long time to finish paying for. Then, long years without a day's rest and without the idea of a holiday ever occurring to them.

They were both on the floor below, Auguste with two candles burning at his side, and his wife, who had been unconscious for about a year of what went on around her.

They had once been young. At night, before going to sleep in the wooden bed which they had bought second-hand two days before their marriage, they would reckon up the day's takings together, delighting in the money that came in and in being able to pay off their debts, one after the other.

'When we no longer owe anything . . .'

For a long time that was their sole aim. Then there had been Ferdinand, who had crawled about on all fours in the sawdust of the restaurant and on the tiles in the kitchen.

They knew little of Paris other than the neighbourhood of Les Halles and the few streets in the vicinity.

Auguste had a big bluish-black moustache. Standing behind his bar with his sleeves rolled up, he was proud of his bulging muscles.

Then Antoine was born. The two children slept in their parents' bedroom, and Antoine remembered certain evenings when his mother peeled vegetables in the kitchen while his father arranged his bottles.

Between Ferdinand and Bernard there was a difference in age of six years. The bedroom was no longer big enough for all of them, and, since there was no other solution, they rented a garret on the sixth floor for the two older boys.

At first, the youngsters were frightened. They were afraid of being alone at the top of the house, which seemed to them enormous and which swarmed with people they did not know.

140

They slept in the same bed so as to comfort each other. In winter it was very cold, and they wore long cotton-flannel night-shirts.

Ferdinand was sent to school. Then it was Antoine's turn. They played in the street with other children.

In those days it seemed to Antoine and Ferdinand that they would never separate.

They were now looking at each other sheepishly. Although their father's body was still warm, a stranger had just put her finger on the sore spot.

'Has anyone looked in the drawers?' she asked.

Both brothers were shocked, but they knew the question was valid, and they realized what it implied.

'No one has looked for anything in the flat,' said Antoine, who felt that the question had been aimed at him.

'When Father collapsed, I carried him up to the first floor, and I had to go down while Madame Ledru phoned the doctor. I couldn't stay away from the restaurant, which was full . . .'

It was impossible to read anything into Ferdinand's expression, though he seemed ill at ease.

'Don't you know where Bernard is?' he asked, turning to Nicole.

'He'll surely phone me tomorrow morning, and when I tell him what's happened he'll take the first plane . . .'

'What would you like us to do meanwhile?'

'I don't know. . . . It's you who ought to make the necessary arrangements.'

'What arrangements?'

'Your father was rich. . . . First of all, there's the business, which is worth a lot of money.'

Antoine turned red. Although the remark was meant for him personally, he did not want to answer.

'Half of the business belongs to Antoine, who was our father's partner for twenty years,' declared Ferdinand.

'Are there any papers that were signed in the presence of a notary?'

'Not in the presence of a notary. . . . They signed an agreement between themselves.'

'And your father received half the profits every year?'

This time the judge did not answer for his brother.

'I paid him his share regularly.'

'That means a big sum?'

'A certain sum, yes . . .'

'How much, for example?'

'One would have to look at the books.'

'And where are the books?'

Antoine pointed to a modern chest of drawers with three doors.

'They're here.'

But he did not offer to show them to her.

'What did he do with the money?'

'That was his own affair. He didn't talk about it to anyone.'

'All the same, he didn't keep it in his room?'

'I suppose not.'

'Haven't you tried to find out?'

'No . . .'

He looked at Fernande, who was boiling inwardly and biting her nails so as not to lose her temper.

Why didn't Ferdinand say something to defend his brother? Both he and his wife had become speechless. Their father had died at about ten o'clock, and at one in the morning, there they were, above his head, involved in a discussion about his money.

Antoine stood up and, mastering himself, declared in a trembling voice, 'I prefer that you come and see . . .'

Ferdinand made a gesture of protest, though without conviction. His wife stood up before he did. Nicole first finished her cup of coffee and then walked to the door.

'Aren't you coming with us?' Antoine asked Fernande.

'I don't have the heart to.'

Yet Fernande had been a street-walker who wandered at night from bar to bar and whom Antoine had literally picked up in the street.

It was three years before he dared introduce her to his father. Then, after his marriage, although they had rented the flat on the second floor, it was two years before his mother had said a word to her and allowed her to show her face on the ground floor.

They went down the ill-lit staircase in Indian file. The worn steps creaked beneath their feet. The door was not locked. In the living-room, Madame Ledru, whom they had never called by her first name because, being the widow of a surveyor, she stood on her dignity, hastily got up from the couch on which she had been dozing.

The door of the bedroom was open, and one could see the quivering flames of the candles. They walked in without a word. Véronique crossed herself. Nicole merely gazed silently at the dead man's face.

'I don't know whether you want to look round in this room,' said Antoine in a low voice.

Nicole's answer was to withdraw to the living-room. Ferdinand and his wife followed her. The room gave one the feeling that the clock had been turned back forty years. In a gilded frame above the fringed couch, an enlarged photograph of Hector Mature, the day-labourer of Saint-Hippolyte, looked at them with expressionless eyes. A green plant – which one would have sworn was the same that had been there when the brothers were children – loomed above a copper jardinière.

'I suppose these are the drawers that interest you.'

'I haven't asked for anything,' replied Nicole. 'I merely think it's better all around that things be done properly.'

There was an old dining-room sideboard, the upper doors of which were fitted with leaded glass. Antoine opened its two drawers, revealing a jumble of small objects that had accumulated over the years.

A cardboard box contained photographs of the three brothers at different ages, a silver thimble, and a lock of hair that meant nothing to anyone there. Was it the hair of one of the children that the mother had wrapped in a piece of tissue paper? Was it a lock of her own hair that Auguste had cut off when they were engaged or in the early days of their marriage?

Two marbles, an agate, and a whistle. Newspaper articles praising the restaurant. Letters. Ferdinand recognized his own handwriting and Bernard's. There were also letters that Véronique had written from La Rochelle and later from Poitiers when her husband was too busy, some of which contained photos of their two children, Marie-Laure and Jean-Loup.

Marie-Laure was now living with a girl friend in the Avenue Victor Hugo, where the two young women ran a women's boutique, and Jean-Loup was a houseman at the Salpêtrière hospital.

Old bills for pieces of furniture and for objects that no longer existed, and also Ferdinand's first report-card from the Lyceé Voltaire.

'You see . . . no will . . . no money either in this drawer . . .'

He opened the one on the left. It was fuller than the first and overflowing with photos and letters. The photos were of people they hardly knew or did not know at all, of their mother's cousins, of childhood friends, of a class in a school playground. And then some little sachets containing hair and with the name of each of the brothers written in pencil.

In the bottom of the sideboard were a few books, some balls of wool, and, on the lowest shelf, odds and ends of cloth of various colours that Eugénie Mature had carefully saved.

The top of the sideboard contained glasses and a few bottles of spirits.

There was no desk in the flat.

'There's still my parents' bedroom . . .'

They hesitated as he walked ahead, but they finally followed him. He opened the tall wardrobe and its drawers, and then a chest of drawers, which contained only linen.

There was no point in staying there. When they were on the landing, crowded together, they did not know whether they ought to go up or down.

'I've got to get my coat,' said Nicole.

They went upstairs in silence. The visitors put on their hats and coats. Ferdinand would have liked to stay behind so as to dissociate himself from Bernard's common-law wife, but he was not asked to.

'I hope Bernard will be here tomorrow. . . . I apologize for this visit. . . . I was obliged to come . . .'

She was not asked why she was obliged, and she walked to the landing.

'See you tomorrow, Antoine,' said Ferdinand. 'I don't know

at what time I'll be able to drop by. Ring me up at my office if you need me. I'll be there almost all day.'

Véronique made an effort to kiss Fernande, something she had not done more than three or four times in her life.

'Ferdinand worries me. He overworks. He takes his profession so much to heart . . .'

When the door was finally closed and there was the sound of footsteps going down the stairs, Antoine and Fernande found themselves face to face. A long time went by without their saying a word. Antoine went into the bedroom and undressed. His wife picked up the cups and put them into the kitchen sink.

As she walked by the bathroom, she saw him, in his pyjamas, brushing his teeth. She merely sighed, 'We're in for something!'

He made no comment but simply asked, 'Have you wound the clock?'

It was she who attended to the matter every day. The alarm rang at five in the morning. He would immediately turn it off, with a gesture that had become mechanical, and would get out of bed noiselessly, for Fernande still had two hours to sleep.

'The thing that disappoints me is Ferdinand's behaviour. . . . I didn't expect him to side with her.'

Antoine did not answer. His brother had not sided outright with Nicole. Rather, he had remained neutral. It was because of his wife. If Véronique had said nothing, it was because she knew what attitude her husband would adopt.

'Good night,' he sighed.

'Good night, Antoine.'

There was an empty space in the bed between them. Now there was emptiness everywhere.

*

'Do you think Antoine knows where your father put his money?'

Ferdinand did not answer immediately. Settled in the seat beside his wife, who was driving, he stared blankly at the empty streets on the way to the Porte d'Orléans. He was glum and ill at ease.

He was upset by what had just happened, and he foresaw other difficulties.

'My father never talked about such things,' he finally murmured.

Véronique was his wife, but she was not a Mature who had been born and bred in the old house in the Rue de la Grande-Truanderie.

All his life, Auguste had been a jovial man with a hearty voice and ready wit, but he had also been a shrewd and secretive peasant who kept certain things to himself.

Did his wife herself know how much they made when the two of them ran the business?

He was the man, the head of the family. He could just as well have been the chief of a tribe who was surrounded by his children, daughters-in-law, and grandchildren.

If he had not tried to keep Ferdinand at home, it was because he had realized that his son would not stay. From the time he started going to school, the boy was ashamed of the restaurant and of his father, and when he was asked what his father did for a living, he would answer, 'He's in business.'

It was the same when he was at the Lycée. Ferdinand did not have the build of the Matures either. He was the puniest of the three sons, a dreamy, introspective boy.

He had never really been involved in the family life, and his youth had been a period of marking time until he left home.

He had not felt that he had a definite vocation. He had chosen law because two of his friends were at law school, but he soon realized that he was not meant for pleading, that his shyness was a handicap at the bar.

It was not exactly shyness. He looked at everything with a desire to understand, as if seeking his rightful place among men.

'After all, he must have put his money somewhere.'

'I know . . .'

'What amazes me is that none of you ever dared to ask him. . . . You're his sons . . .'

Obviously! Antoine, perhaps, might have been able to. Ferdinand felt a certain affection for Antoine, who nevertheless resembled him so little. With Antoine, old Auguste had succeeded. Instead of going on with his studies, Antoine learned

146

the business, while Bernard took advantage, as it were, of the war and enlisted in the army when he was eighteen.

He served only six months, the time it took the Germans to reach Paris, and thereafter he never lived in the family home.

'You think he put a lot of money aside?'

'He must have made quite a pile, and he spent hardly anything.'

'Antoine was his favourite, wasn't he?'

'He's the one who stayed with him.'

The others had urged him to sell his business, either to Antoine or someone else, and to retire to Auvergne with his wife. The old man would not hear of it. He needed his tin bar, his marble-topped tables, the coming and going that began in the early hours of the morning. He needed coffee and croissants, bottles of wine, the smell of cooking.

'Wasn't he capable of leaving his nest-egg to Antoine without saying anything to anyone?'

'I don't think so.'

'What's to be done if nothing is found?'

'I don't know yet.'

Ferdinand was not rich. He had only his salary to live on. Five years before, his wife and he had done something rash. Was it she who was the more guilty of the two? Although the idea had been hers, he had not resisted, at any rate not enough.

Ever since their marriage, they had lived in old houses, at first in La Rochelle, then in Poitiers, and after that in Paris, where they had a third-floor flat in a house without a lift in the Rue Saint-Louis-en-l'Ile.

The two children were still living with them. Marie-Laure was taking courses in art history, and Jean-Loup had begun to study medicine.

The flat had become too small for four adults, and there was only one bathroom for the whole family, a bathroom with an ancient hot-water tank.

Garden cities were beginning to be built on the outskirts of Paris, modern blocks of flats that were called *Résidences*, and almost every week Véronique showed her husband pictures of the new flats that appeared in the newspapers.

'There's even a swimming pool!' exclaimed Jean-Loup.

The flats were not to let but for sale.

'After the first payment and the ten annual payments, there's no more rent to pay.'

They had visited several of them on Sundays. What they saw did not always correspond to the description in the advertisement, but Véronique got enthusiastic over the *Résidence* of Parc-de-Sceaux.

They had waited six months for the house to be finished. Finally, each of them had his own bathroom. A terrace looked out on the park, and a swimming pool was at the disposal of the residents of the five buildings.

Ferdinand had swum in it only twice, for he felt self-conscious about his poor build and did not have full control of his body. He could hardly swim, and it made him feel ashamed. Véronique, who thought she was too stout, did not bathe in the pool either.

'We'll be able to do without a maid,' she had said. 'Every thing works by electricity.'

They had actually done without a maid for seven or eight months, but as Véronique had to act as chauffeur, they ended by engaging one.

Marie-Laure, at the age of twenty-two, was the first to leave. The reason she gave was that she wanted to earn her living. She had become infatuated with a girl friend, and they had opened a shop together. Her parents hardly ever saw her. She lived in another world and no longer had anything in common with them.

Thus, a room remained unoccupied, although her parents kept Marie-Laure's furniture in it, out of a kind of superstition, as if she were going to come back.

When she did set foot in the flat, it was almost always to get things that belonged to her. Little by little she emptied the room, and Ferdinand resigned himself to using it as a study.

And now a second room was empty, for Jean-Loup lived almost entirely at the Salpêtrière, where he was a houseman.

He was an odd boy, unobtrusive and timid, like his father, and perhaps a bit moody. He had decided to specialize in child psychiatry. He, too, wore glasses. His fellow students regarded him as an ambitious young man who was interested only in his studies.

Studies that were expensive. Marie-Laure had also needed a lot of money when she set up her shop.

Instalments had to be paid on the flat, and interest accumulated.

The situation was not tragic. Other families had the same difficulties. Ferdinand could not claim that he was unwell. He was never really ill. It was a matter of twinges, sore throats, pains in the joints, stomach-aches, ailments which without worrying him, made him anxious, and Véronique, who was going through her menopause, was not very helpful.

With their father's money, they would be saved. Their share would be enough to pay what they owed on the flat, and they would no longer have to bother about instalments.

They would be able to buy a new car, for theirs had already done more than sixty thousand miles, and to travel when they were on holiday instead of spending two or three weeks at a second-class hotel in Brittany.

'I don't know whether you feel as I do. . . . Antoine didn't seem to me to be acting naturally. He was ill at ease, as if he were hiding something from us.'

When Ferdinand was fifteen and Antoine twelve, they got on very well, and Antoine would confide in Ferdinand, whom he admired very much.

'You have an easier time of it at school than I! You're lucky to be clever.'

Ferdinand would encourage him.

'You're clever too. Maybe it's another kind of cleverness.'

It was odd to think that there had been real intimacy between them and that for years they had slept in the same bed.

Yet that evening they had hardly dared look each other in the face.

'I mistrust Fernande too. In the first place, why did they wait two hours before phoning us? He was your father, wasn't he? You're the oldest. You're the one who should have taken things in hand.'

They had arrived. The building had a garage in which there were smarter and more powerful cars than theirs.

They went up in the lift. There, too, they lived on the third floor. Véronique, who had the key in her bag, opened the door and put on the light.

The house in the Les Halles area had a smell that one recognized immediately after being away for months. But there was nothing of the sort here. Everything was clean and orderly. They had had to buy new furniture, for the old things, which had followed them through their various homes, clashed with the setting.

'Is your throat still sore?'

'A little.'

They went straight to the bedroom, where once again they were going to undress in each other's presence.

The two brothers had also undressed in each other's presence when they were young, and yet they now felt like strangers.

Wasn't Véronique a stranger to him? Their common memories dated only from their first meeting at the home of a fellow student. She was the daughter of an important commercial lawyer, and her family had lived in the Boulevard Haussmann at a time when the neighbourhood was one of the smartest in Paris.

The husband and wife did not have the same past, and words conjured up different images for them.

They had been in love. They had thought so. They had certainly been in love, for they had got married and had lived together ever since.

It had never occurred to Ferdinand to deceive his wife or, with all the more reason, to leave her.

They had had two children. They had known happy hours, particularly when Jean-Loup and then Marie-Laure were born. The christenings and first communions had been occasions for lively gatherings.

When they had moved into the new flat, the four of them had walked all around it with delight. They had drunk champagne, convinced that cares and troubles were gone forever.

Ferdinand worked very hard. He was scrupulously thorough, a perfectionist. The file of a judicial inquiry had almost to be wrested from his hands because it was never complete enough for him.

Only in his office did he feel a certain superiority. Men and women, all of whom were more or less 'cases', marched in and out.

He would observe them with his short-sighted eyes and ask them questions in an effort to understand. Unlike certain colleagues, he did not regard them as enemies of society, and some of them intimidated him because they had a strength of character which he knew that he himself lacked.

In a few hours, tired after an almost sleepless night, he would again be face to face with René Mauvis, who would be handcuffed. The corridor would be full of reporters and photographers, as it had been every day for two weeks.

In the late afternoon he could not even send Mauvis back to the Santé prison in case the crowd attacked him, and he therefore kept him in a cell in the basement of the courts.

What did he know about Mauvis? Until the age of thirty-two he had been a model and unassuming clerk in a bank on the Grands Boulevards and had lived alone in a three-room flat in the Rue de Turenne, near the Place des Vosges.

Mauvis was a bachelor. His concierge had never seen him come home with a woman, and as far as his colleagues knew, he had no girl friends.

His only passion seemed to be billiards, which he played two or three evenings a week in a café in the Boulevard Beaumarchais. He was accused of having strangled two little boys, within a period of six months, in the forest of Saint-Germain, where he claimed he had never been in his life.

'Can't you take a day off and rest? You're practically alone in court on Saturday.'

It was true. He was allowed to carry on the investigation in his own way and at times of his own choice. He was tempted. It was essential that he have a talk with Antoine the next day, or rather that same day, and perhaps with Bernard too, if he came back from the Riviera.

'Are you hungry?'

'No.'

'Do you want a pill?'

She was referring to the sleeping-pills that he took.

'I don't think I need it. . . . Good night.'

151

They kissed. It was a ritual gesture before turning over and going to sleep. Each was used to the other's smell, to the smell of the couple, and they had reached the point of breathing in the same rhythm.

His father was dead. Ferdinand used to see him not more than once a month, when he dropped in, on his way past, to drink a cup of coffee at the bar.

'Won't you have lunch with us?'

He would sometimes let himself be tempted, would recapture the taste of the cooking of former days, but he usually refused because he was not allowed to pay.

His father was dead, and there was suddenly a great void.

Chapter Three

Antoine dressed quietly in the semi-darkness. He knew that Fernande heard him anyway, but he did not speak to her so as not to wake her completely.

In another month it would be broad daylight when he began his marketing. In the heart of Paris, he followed the succession of the seasons by the hour of sunrise, just as one did in the country.

He put on a turtleneck sweater and an old black leather jacket. On the first floor, he opened the door of his parents' flat. Madame Ledru was sleeping on the couch in the living-room. The light of the candles was dancing in the room where Auguste was alone with eternity.

There had been no vigil. Nobody had kept the dead man company, and Antoine felt somewhat guilty about it.

In the Rue Pierre-Lescot, the air was already heavy with the smell of vegetables, and a special light shone on the dark little men who were moving busily about heaps of food in the iron sheds.

Most of them had been there since the night before. The dawn was cool, and women were slapping their arms in order to warm themselves. In the bars, coffee, white wine, and brandy were being served without let-up, as they had been in his restaurant in the old days.

'Hello,' he called out as he went by.

He did not know all the names, but the faces were familiar to him.

'Hello, Antoine,' people would answer, especially the old ones who had known him as a child, when he went with his father. There were also some from the neighbourhood who had played with him in the street.

The others would say, more respectfully, 'Hello, Monsieur Antoine.'

A toothless vegetable woman, who was wearing a man's jacket over two or three sweaters, asked, 'Is it true?'

'It's true, Berthe.'

'He always used to say to me that he'd die behind his bar.'

He saw the first strawberries in pretty baskets of woven shavings, and he discussed the price before buying twenty baskets of them.

'I'll send them over in a little while with Nestor. I also have peaches, but of course they're not from Auvergne.'

He continued on his way, at first among the pyramids of fruit and vegetables that rose up in the streets, and then in the passage-ways of the sheds.

He had his dealers. He needed flowers for the tables and chose anemones. Then he went back and bought several bunches of chrysanthemums for the death-chamber.

The darkness was fading, and the big lamps were getting paler above people's heads. As he walked along, the menus took shape in his mind, almost mechanically.

'I was told about your poor father . . .'

Or else it was:

'Who'd have thought that old Auguste would go off so suddenly! . . . Still, it's better that way. . . . He was so proud of his strength that he'd have been ashamed of being ill.'

The whole little world of Les Halles had heard the news, and even those who said nothing to Antoine looked at him more solemnly than usual.

He was going to have to attend to the funeral, but he did not

153

want to do anything before consulting his two brothers. In the past they had been relieved by Antoine's staying with their parents, because it had spared them a responsibility.

Now that Auguste was dead, they would not at all relish their brother's behaving as if he were specially privileged.

It had already started the night before. Even Nicole, who was not really a member of the family, had come running to defend Bernard's rights.

As for Ferdinand, his attitude had not been clear, and probably he would not side with Antoine when the time came.

Yet, of the three, Antoine had been the least lucky, for he had wasted four long years in a camp in Pomerania.

Ferdinand had not been called up because of his short-sightedness. He had spent the war years in La Rochelle, where he had just received an appointment.

As for Bernard, he had regained his freedom after spending six months in uniform far from the front.

It was not Antoine who had proposed to their father that he stay with him. He could have worked a few years more at the Brasserie de Strasbourg or elsewhere and have put aside enough money to set up on his own in any neighbourhood. He was hard-working and knew his job.

If he had been willing to stay, perhaps it was so that there would always be a Mature in the Rue de la Grande-Truanderie. Even when they were very young, the two others had wanted to get away from home, but not he, and it was not, as one might have thought, because he was worried about the future.

He felt at home in the little restaurant with its good smells. He had thought about it constantly when he was in Germany and wondered whether he would live to see the end of the war.

His father sent him packages, and his mother postcards, which were full of mistakes and which he answered without ever admitting that he was depressed or that he suffered periodically from dysentery.

'Well, are you staying?'

'I am,' he answered with a smile.

What happened that day was quite unexpected. They were

both standing on the threshold at about seven in the morning. It was May. The spring was particularly lovely.

The moment before, they were still a father and son standing next to each other and watching the traffic in the street.

But the moment Antoine gave his answer, the relationship between the two men changed. As naturally as can be, they became partners, accomplices of a sort, and the difference in age ceased to exist.

'Do you agree that this is the right time to expand?'

'We ought to take advantage of the new clientele as soon as possible.'

'The flat on the second floor is going to be free. The Meyers are going back to Alsace.'

The Meyers, the Chaves, little Madame Brossier, the Maniages, the Gagneaus, the Allards, Justine and Berthe, and hundreds of others were not only names to them but faces, real persons who had entered their lives at one time or another.

Some had gone away, leaving only a faint trace. Others were still around and had greeted Auguste's son solemnly that morning.

To them he was the old man's heir. To them, but not to his brothers, nor to his sister-in-law, nor to Nicole.

The father and son did not even realize how it had happened. At first, while they were discussing plans for enlarging the restaurant, Antoine had replaced his mother at the stove and had added new dishes to the restaurant's specialities.

The customers got used to him. Wearing his white chef's hat, he would come and shake hands with them when his father asked him to.

'Come in for a minute. Monsieur Bicard wants to meet you.'

He would dry his hands on his apron, and Auguste was proud to say, as he turned to the tall, broad-shouldered young man, 'This is my son Antoine. He's now my partner.'

Actually, it was not yet a real partnership. His father would give him whatever money he needed, as when he was still growing up.

'What did you make at the Brasserie de Strasbourg? I'll give you twice as much.'

155

The old man made the offer several months later, and at that time the other brothers saw no objection.

The idea of the glass partition between the inner room and the kitchen was Antoine's. A friend had spoken to him about the same kind of thing in a Milanese restaurant.

Joseph, who had already been working in the restaurant before the war, had joked, 'The clients'll look as if they were at a side-show.'

That was why the back room had since been called the Side-show, when it was not the Senate. As for the first room, with its tin bar and old-fashioned marble-topped tables, they eventually christened it, because of its past, the Flea Market.

'Attend to the Fleas. I'll wait on the Side-show.'

The customers, of course, suspected nothing, just as they did not know the nicknames by which old Joseph referred to some of them.

A cabinet minister who came for lunch at least once a week would have been surprised to learn that he was referred to as the Mug, and one of the leading society women in Paris would have had a stroke if she had known that in the Rue de la Grande-Truanderie she was vulgarly called the Hag.

When Antoine met Fernande, he was still living with his parents and was on a salary. His mother kept house. He slept in the bedroom which was later given to Madame Ledru.

Fernande was very young and delicate-looking and was lost in a world of which she understood nothing. She had left her Breton village a few months before, and after a few evenings in a dance hall in the Rue de Lappe found herself walking the streets.

It took him some time to realize that he loved her, and only then did he make her change her way of life. He rented a room for her in a hotel in the Rue Étienne-Marcel where he joined her every night.

Because he was the only one of the sons who still lived with his parents, his mother could not get used to the idea that he had become a man, and she was upset about his sleeping away from home.

'You ought to get married, Antoine. There are lots of nice

girls in the neighbourhood. You'd have no trouble finding one. I'm sure that Marie Chaussard . . .'

The Chaussards were their neighbours. They were butchers. The father had come to Paris at about the same time as Auguste, and the two of them had set up in business within a year of each other.

Marie was plump and rosy, like most women who live in a butcher's shop, a fact that Antoine had often noticed, though without knowing how to explain it.

She was a little younger than he. Her brother Léon worked with his father and at six in the morning was already cutting up animals behind the closed grating of the shop.

Antoine did not marry Marie Chaussard but, three years later, Fernande, and his mother had cried. Then he waited for the flat on the second floor to be free so that he could move into it.

His brothers knew almost nothing about their life, which they had seen only from the outside. As far as they were concerned, Antoine had married a trollop who led him by the nose.

Later, they were obliged to recognize that the trollop wasn't such a bad wife after all.

As for Antoine, he regretted only one thing: that he did not have children. The reason was that Fernande had contracted a venereal disease a few weeks after coming to Paris and had had to have an operation.

He could not forgive the doctors for having literally butchered her. As for her, after so many years she was still ashamed to let him see her naked belly.

'That's life,' as François, the red-headed waiter, would say, he who at the age of thirty-five had five children and whose wife was expecting a sixth.

François would have been satisfied with one or two, at most three.

He had been obliged to move to Romainville, near a quarry, so as to have room enough for his kids.

'That's life.'

At present, the one-time trollop would go upstairs several times a day to take care of her mother-in-law, who was no longer aware of what was going on. Sunk in her bed or armchair, the old lady lived in a kind of dream world, and God knows what the life around her meant to her.

She would sometimes smile vaguely, the way babies do, or clutch hold of Madame Ledru's arm when she was seized with an indefinable fear.

She had become so thin that she seemed unearthly. She did not suffer. She lived in a world of her own and recognized none of the people around her.

In a little while, Jojo, the Les Halles idiot, who had inordinately large hands, would be bringing to the restaurant the crates and bags he had picked up in the sheds of Antoine's various dealers.

Antoine, who had come back to the Rue de la Grande-Truanderie, entered Léon Chaussard's butcher's shop by the small door.

Léon was two years older than he and had four butcher's shops in Paris. He, too, had stayed at home with his father. At the age of eighty-three the old man still made his round of the sheds every morning.

In the afternoon, when a ray of sun brightened the pavement in front of the shop, the old man would install himself on a chair and sit there an hour or two smoking his pipe slowly and watching people go by.

'What do you advise today?'

'I have some nice sweetbreads, not too expensive.'

'Let me have fifteen portions. ... Have you any lamb chops?'

'Not the kind you like.'

Antoine fingered the meats, made his choice, and changed his menus accordingly.

'Is it true that it happened right in the restaurant?'

'Yes.'

'Did he realize he was dying?'

'I don't know. He fell to the floor and seemed to have lost consciousness immediately. One of his eyes was shut. He had trouble breathing. I wonder whether, in cases like that, the mind keeps working. Dr Patin claims it doesn't.'

'Does your mother know?'

Antoine shrugged.

'You know how she is.'

'Still, it's better for her.'

Perhaps for Auguste too, since he would not have to bury his wife. He had not spent a single night away from her ever since they had been married, and even in recent times, when she looked at him as if he were a stranger or pet dog, he would often sit down in front of her in the hope that they might pick up the thread of God knows what conversation.

'Have your brothers come?'

'Only Ferdinand. We weren't able to notify Bernard. He's away.'

Léon had two sisters, one of whom was the Marie whom the family had wanted to marry off to Antoine. Both girls were married, Marie to someone who worked in the Tax Department. Léon had had trouble with his two brothers-in-law when he had taken over the father's business.

'Did Ferdinand say anything?'

They understood each other without having to go into detail.

'Nicole was the one who talked most.'

'Did Bernard finally marry her?'

'No, but it's as if he did. Last night you'd have thought she was demanding on behalf of the family that I give a reckoning.'

'Do you have things in writing?'

'Only a letter from my father in which he recognizes that I'm half-owner of the business.'

'Signed before a notary?'

'Not at all. My father consulted what he called his business adviser, a kind of consultant who had a small office in the Rue Coquillière.'

'Do you know him?'

'I saw him two or three times, when he came to eat in the restaurant. That was long ago. A dirty, sloppy-looking fellow who was always carrying a black leather briefcase ... Jason, I think ... yes, Ernest Jason.'

'Is he a lawyer?'

'No. ... As far as I know, he's a former business agent who got into trouble. My father had complete confidence in him because his family was from Riom.'

'Do you think your brothers'll make you sell or buy up their share?'

'Anything can happen. . . . Especially as far as the two wives are concerned. . . . Last night, my sister-in-law, who'd always refused to speak to Nicole, sided with her.'

'You'd better not do anything without seeing a lawyer, someone serious, who knows about business.'

They did not shake hands. They had known each other too long.

'So long, Léon.'

'Good luck.'

It was after seven. The shutters of the restaurant were raised, and Jules, who was wearing a blue apron and whose sleeves were rolled up, had started the coffee.

On the counter was a basket of warm croissants and near it a pyramid of hard-boiled eggs in a wire container.

'Morning, boss.'

Antoine went behind the counter to get a cup of coffee. He ate three croissants, then, after hesitating briefly, a hard-boiled egg. At a table were two market-gardeners who had taken thick slices of buttered bread out of their pockets and were drinking white wine.

'Has my wife come down?'

'Not yet.'

'Has anyone phoned?'

That was the hour when he went up to wash and change. Then, when the chef arrived, the two of them would draw up the menus for lunch and dinner.

Only two or three dishes ever changed, and the day's specials were written in red on the big bill of fare.

The other dishes, from the *cochonnades* to the *flangarde*, a kind of cold flan, remained unchanged.

'Has the bread been delivered?'

He had just noticed that only three loaves were left in the window.

'If my brother comes, let me know.'

'The judge?'

To everyone, including the family, Ferdinand was the judge.

'My son, the judge,' as Auguste had said only the night before.

He had been proud of him. There had been, as it were, no bonds between them, but Ferdinand was nevertheless a son of his who had become a magistrate.

Antoine was a man like himself. They understood each other. They shared the same kind of life, had the same way of thinking, lived among the same people.

At times, when Auguste had taken a little drink at the table of an old customer, his son would whisper, 'Remember what the doctor told you.'

'I only wet my lips. After all, I can't refuse to have a drink with friends.'

He had been a little afraid of Antoine. The way his son looked at him from a distance when he had a glass in his hand made him feel uncomfortable. He would sometimes cheat, would pour himself a glass of wine at the bar when Jules was elsewhere for a moment. He imagined that no one would know.

Antoine had not been urged by Fernande to speak to his father. It had been his own idea. He had had to brace himself, as if he were doing something wrong.

'Papa, we've got to have a serious talk.'

Words like that were almost unimaginable in a home where life seemed to follow the rhythm of nature, to unfold without complications, without real problems.

'About what, my boy?'

It was about 11 a.m., a time of day when things were slack. They had sat down in the Side-show. Behind the partition Julien Bernu was bustling about with his assistant, Arthur's predecessor, for Arthur was only seventeen at the time. Nor had they yet taken on Big Louise to peel the vegetables.

'I'm now thirty. . . . I'm married. . . . I could be a father.'

'Is your wife pregnant?'

'No. The doctor says she can't have children.'

'Is that what you want to talk to me about?'

'I want to talk to you about my situation in the restaurant.'

'I understand,' said Auguste, whose face clouded over.

And silencing his son with a gesture, he added, 'If I were in your place, I'd do the very same thing. It's natural for you to think of the future.'

'I enjoy working with you,' mumbled Antoine, lowering his head. 'But what if . . .'

'Yes, what if I should die. Your two brothers would demand their share of the restaurant, where they've never done anything.'

Auguste had lit one of the small, very dark cigars that he smoked from time to time.

'You're right. We ought to straighten that out. I'll have to take it up with my adviser.'

He had not proposed that he discuss the matter with Ferdinand. Yet in his mind, the word 'adviser' covered lawyers, judges, and notaries as well as business agents and attorneys.

It was the first time in the seventeen years since that conversation had taken place that Antoine realized the full consequences of it.

The two men had let weeks go by without referring to the matter again. Then, one afternoon, when Antoine returned to the restaurant after his nap, his father handed him an envelope.

'Read this agreement and tell me whether it'll do.'

Antoine went upstairs again, almost furtively, to read it.

'What is it?' asked Fernande.

'A business matter.'

'Anything wrong?'

The paper began as follows: 'I the undersigned, Auguste Victor André Mature, born in Saint-Hippolyte, Puy-de-Dôme, on 25 July 1887 . . .'

Antoine reread the date twice. It seemed to him so long ago!

'. . . owner of a business establishment known as Chez l'Auvergnat, in the Rue de la Grande-Truanderie . . .'

His father had diligently copied a text that had been written for him and by virtue of which he recognized that in exchange for his son's investing a certain amount in the business and of his working in it, the restaurant henceforth belonged to the two men. The net profits, after the annual inventory, were to be shared equally.

Antoine had shown the paper to Ferdinand a few days later.

'What do you think of it?'

'Who drafted the agreement?'

'Someone Papa knows and whom he trusts. Why do you ask? Anything wrong with it?'

'It's no great shakes, but, all in all, it'll do. Have you really put money into the business?'

'All my savings.'

Ferdinand had looked at him ironically.

'You're lucky to have been able to save. It's obvious you don't have children.'

'I'll have to tell Bernard about it.'

'That'll encourage him to drop in and touch you for a loan more often.'

Time had flown by! Those conversations seemed to have taken place only yesterday, and yet the restaurant had had time to win its two-star rating in the Michelin Guide; Marie-Laure, who could have been married and a mother, had declared her independence and was running a shop; Auguste had just died; and their mother was practically no longer in the world of the living.

Had Antoine done the right thing in countersigning the paper that his father had handed him one afternoon with a serious look, and perhaps reluctantly?

*

When Antoine came down again an hour later, half a dozen customers were standing at the bar and others were sitting at tables. It was the morning clientele, people from Les Halles and from the neighbourhood. They were all talking about what had happened the night before, and when Antoine entered there was a sudden silence.

'Hasn't my brother come?' he asked Jules in a tone of surprise.

'He went up to the first floor,' answered Jules, who was rinsing glasses at the bar.

Antoine was freshly shaven and was wearing a dark suit, as he usually did. He went up to the first floor and opened the door, which was never locked so that Madame Ledru would not be needlessly disturbed. Besides, what was the use of locking it?

His mother was already settled in her armchair near the window, the muslin curtain of which was drawn so that she could see what was going on in the street.

Madame Ledru, who had found time to wash and dress, was giving her lunch. She kept dipping little pieces of buttered bread into a soft-boiled egg and then putting the edge of the spoon to the old woman's lips.

'Are you looking for Monsieur Ferdinand? He's at the back.'

Antoine found him standing at the foot of the bed in which their father was lying and on both sides of which fresh candles were burning.

Ferdinand, who was standing and staring at the dead man's face, from which the towel had been removed, looked as if he were praying. Was he really praying? Had Véronique, who attended mass every Sunday and abstained from meat on Friday, converted him?

The two brothers remained standing in silence for several moments. Their eyes were looking in the same direction, and perhaps they felt again, during those few seconds, the bonds that had existed between them when they were children.

Ferdinand was the first to move towards the door. Antoine followed him. Neither of them stopped in the dark living-room, where they did not feel they belonged. They went downstairs and sat down at a table in the second room, which was empty.

'Didn't Véronique come with you?'

'She dropped me off at the door. She took advantage of being in the neighbourhood to buy a few things at Les Halles.'

She had obviously wanted to leave the two brothers together – or perhaps it was Ferdinand's idea.

'Have you heard from Bernard?'

'Not yet.'

'Do you really think Nicole doesn't know where he is?'

'It's hard to tell with her.'

Bernard was one of Ferdinand's big worries, for he had the unfortunate habit of getting involved in rather shady affairs, and several times he had signed cheques that were not covered. Their father or one of the brothers had always fixed things up, but there was a limit to what could be done, and Ferdinand's professional situation might one day become delicate.

'What was he like the last time you saw him?'

'He was wearing a new suit and had a broad smile. He was setting up a company to sell television programmes in foreign countries.'

Bernard had spells of euphoria during which he dressed smartly and assumed the manner of an important businessman. He would refer to well-known people, saying that they were his partners, and listening to him, one got the impression that they were on intimate terms.

'I had dinner yesterday with the Minister who told . . .'

The astonishing thing was that it was not always false. He was sometimes seen at Fouquet's, Maxim's, the Berkeley, and, in the evening, in the fashionable night-clubs.

On Sundays he managed to get himself invited to private estates in the outlying suburbs, and usually he had a car. Did it belong to him or had he borrowed it from a friend?

'Do you believe it, about that deal?' asked Antoine, who had a certain respect for his elder brother's opinions.

'Same as the others.'

After a few weeks, there would be no further mention of the matter. Bernard would turn up in low spirits with his features drawn and a shifty look in his eyes:

'Listen, Ferdinand, you simply must help me out. It'll be the last time. If you let me have five thousand, I'll be able to wait for a big sum of money that's coming in, and I'll pay you back. Besides, there's always my share of the inheritance as a guarantee.'

Was it entirely his fault? When he was discharged from the army, immediately after the invasion, the black market was beginning and Bernard found a way of making money.

He would get a barrel of nails for a provincial hardware dealer, who would give him in exchange a number of whole hams, which he then sold at a high price. Everything was scarce. Anything could be turned to account. It was simply a matter of knowing where to get merchandise, which became a medium of exchange.

He kept his ears open in the bars he frequented, and this enabled him to act as intermediary in important deals.

'What of it?' he would say. 'What's wrong with what I'm doing? Isn't my father involved in deals too? If it weren't for the black market, Paris would have died of hunger long ago.'

It was precisely about Bernard that Ferdinand wanted to talk.

'It would surprise me very much if Bernard didn't show up today. Nicole must have spoken to him by now about the inheritance.'

'I am not to blame if Father didn't leave a will.'

'Bernard won't think so.'

'Do you?'

'Maybe we haven't searched carefully enough. He may also have left it with a notary, or in a vault in some bank. You who lived with him ought to know whether he went to a bank from time to time, in which case it's probably one in the neighbourhood.'

Antoine made no comment. He was incapable of answering and looked guilty, although he felt innocent.

'When did you give him his share of the profits?'

'Around the end of January, after the inventory.'

'Was it a big sum?'

'Rather big.'

'Did you pay by cheque?'

'No. In cash. Everything here in Les Halles is paid for in cash. The agents, the market-gardeners, the middlemen always have big wads of notes on them.'

'Did he get his share at the end of January?'

'At the beginning of February . . . 3 February, to be exact.'

'What did he do with it?'

'I have no idea. . . . He went upstairs.'

'We haven't found any money there.'

'Maybe because we didn't look thoroughly enough, as you said. It's now March. He had time to take the money elsewhere.'

'Did he ever tell you whether he bought property?'

'He didn't talk to me about his personal affairs. It wasn't for me to ask. Would *you* have dared ask him for an account?'

Ferdinand was forced to admit that he would not. Despite the fact that their father had aged and had sometimes been touchingly naïve, he nevertheless had remained head of the family, and he made a point of letting everyone feel it.

'An idea occurred to me a little while ago, when I was talking to Léon.'

'The butcher?'

'That's right. . . . I was telling him about the paper that father and I once signed. It wasn't he who drew it up. He merely copied what someone had drafted for him. I think I know who. A certain Jason, Ernest Jason, who had an office in the Rue Coquillière. He had lunch here two or three times. He was middle-aged at the time, with a yellow, bilious complexion. I don't know what's become of him, but I'll try to find out.'

'It would be a good thing if we could talk to him before Bernard gets back.'

It was odd the way both of them, especially Ferdinand, feared the youngest brother, the one who had almost gone to the bad.

'When is the funeral taking place?'

'I haven't thought about it yet. . . . Tuesday?'

'Make it early, because I have a big day in court.'

'It can't be earlier than nine o'clock.'

'I suppose there'll be a prayer at the end?'

'I plan to attend to it this morning. First I have to see the undertaker.'

'Are you going to send out announcements?'

Ferdinand quite naturally shifted the responsibility for these details on to his brother.

'You won't be able to mention Nicole's name . . .'

'Of course not.'

'One more question. . . . Don't think I'm asking it out of personal interest. . . . How much do you think the business is worth?'

'It depends. . . . The government has definitely decided to transfer Les Halles to Rungis. Most of the old houses will be torn down, including this one and probably the whole street.

Things'll drag on for a while, but it's obvious that in three years, at the most, the new owner would have to break even. That being so, we'd be lucky to get more than a hundred thousand francs.'

To Antoine, who handled big notes all day long, the figure seemed very low. But Ferdinand's involuntary reaction made him realize that his brother didn't think so.

'Judging from what you tell me, I suppose that during the last few years you must have given Father more than five hundred thousands francs. Is that right?'

'He certainly didn't have much less than a million.'

'Bernard'll want to see the books.'

'I'll show them to him.'

'He'll go mad when he sees those figures.'

'What can I do?'

Ferdinand looked at his watch and stood up.

'My wife must be waiting for me in the car. .... I'll let you attend to the funeral.' And pointing to the ceiling, he added, 'I'm planning to come to see him tomorrow, Sunday, with the children.'

Just as he was leaving, he could not prevent himself from looking at Antoine admiringly and exclaiming, as if he were joking, 'You're certainly rich!'

'I work ...'

'So do I.'

The old car was by the kerb down the street, and Véronique was at the wheel.

'Has he found the will?'

'No. I don't think he spent much time looking for it. He mentioned a business agent with whom my father used to deal long ago. All he knows is that he had an office in the Rue Coquillière.'

She threaded her way between the trucks. The car was permeated with the smell of the vegetables and flowers she had bought.

Ferdinand realized that it would be wiser not to mention any figures to his wife, but he could not resist.

'Guess how much Antoine gave our father since they became partners.'

'I have no idea. . . . A lot?'

'Close to a million.'

'Which means that Antoine too has a million. Is that right?'

'So it seems.'

'We therefore ought to inherit more than three hundred thousand francs . . . not counting our share of the restaurant.'

They looked at each other unbelievingly, torn between joy and fear. To them, who had to be careful about every expense, the figures were staggering.

They would have been ashamed to live in the Rue de la Grande-Truanderie, which in the morning smelled of Les Halles and in the afternoon of poverty. Nor would they have been willing to go up and down the dark, worm-eaten staircase several times a day and to live in rooms which, even if they had been modernized, smacked of small shopkeepers. A butcher's shop on one side, a narrow haberdashery on the other, and the hubbub of Les Halles all night long.

But Antoine had made a million!

'Do you think the money'll turn up?'

'It's bound to be somewhere.'

'You know your father, you ought to have some idea of what he might have done with it.'

'During the war, he bought gold, he admitted it to me. I know he kept it in the house, but he never told me where. I don't know whether he continued. . . . It's possible. . . . It's also possible that he bought property. . . . That's the kind of investment that tempts people like him.'

They had reached the courts, and Ferdinand became the judge again. Briefcase in hand, he rushed to the main staircase, looking very preoccupied.

'My father died,' he rapped out to the clerk of the court, who had been surprised to see him arrive late.

And the clerk did not know whether he ought to put out his hand to express his condolence.

'Send for Mauvis.'

He really had to stop thinking about that million. The mention of it affected him almost like a blow in the solar plexus. He had never envied anyone, particularly not his brother, although Antoine was taller, younger, and better built than he.

A simple figure, mentioned in a very natural tone, had suddenly made him see Antoine in a different light.

Until that morning, Ferdinand, being the eldest, had somehow considered himself head of the family. He was the most intelligent and best educated, and it seemed obvious to him that he had been more of a success than the others.

Of course, Antoine drove a more luxurious car than his, and every August, when the restaurant was closed, he and Fernande would travel to Venice, Greece, Spain, or elsewhere.

A thick folder had been prepared for him and was lying on his desk. In a few minutes the police would bring to his office a small, quiet-looking man who earned, at the most, a thousand francs a month working all day in a bank.

Ferdinand suddenly felt inferior, Antoine had summoned up the image of wads of bank notes that were passed from hand to hand like ordinary merchandise. He remembered his amazement when, as a child, he had seen the business agents take similar rolls from their pockets while drinking their spiked coffee at the bar.

It had never occurred to him that Antoine was now in the same class.

'Has Brabrant called from the police station?'

'He's following up on a new witness, but he doesn't think he can get hold of him today because of the week-end.'

Would he resign if his father's million was found? He was thinking about it seriously, in spite of himself, while sharpening his pencil.

No! In the first place, his share wouldn't be enough to live on. It was better to wait until retirement age and get his full pension.

Besides what would he do all day in his flat in Parc-de-Sceaux? He had no hobbies. He didn't potter around. He had never collected anything. He didn't go fishing or hunting.

Almost every evening he took files home to study while Véronique read or watched television in the next room.

As a matter of fact, what would he do with his time when he retired? Would they sell the flat, which had already become too big and which was so expensive?

To go where? To the country? Neither Véronique nor he

cared for the country. A wasp was enough to frighten his wife, who had never wanted to go picnicking with the children because she loathed sitting on the grass.

He would read, well and good. He would go walking.

He suddenly felt as if he were naked, vulnerable. He had thought his life was normal, satisfactory, even enviable, and all at once he realized that there was nothing at the end of it.

Except, perhaps, if the million was found, a million which he had not earned, which came from elsewhere, from the patient work of first his father and mother in the restaurant of which he was ashamed, then of the old man and Antoine.

They, too, would travel, Véronique and he. They would spend part of the winter in the South, which they hardly knew. They had been there for short stays, but without enough money to live there as one should.

He was not accusing Antoine of cheating them. His brother had nevertheless profited from the family business. And he had been careful to get their father to sign an agreement.

Of course, it had not been proved that the document was enough to establish his rights. Ferdinand had hardly ever bothered about common law, and even less about commercial law.

He looked at the first typewritten page of the file without seeing it. He heard someone coughing in front of him. It was one of the two policemen who had brought René Mauvis.

The round-shouldered, blank-looking prisoner was standing between the two men in uniform. Nothing in his attitude betrayed his impatience.

'Sit down.'

He sat down on a chair, while the policemen installed themselves on a bench against the wall.

Ferdinand looked at his watch, as he had done when he was with his brother.

'Hasn't your lawyer come? Dubois, are you sure you sent for him?'

The clerk nodded. He, too, was a poor man. So were the policemen. They were waiting. Half an hour later they would still be waiting, with the impersonal air of people who stand in line in front of a cinema, of those who stood in line in front of shops during the war.

Their father had indirectly benefited from the war. Thanks to the food he had managed to obtain, his clientele had changed. As a matter of fact, Antoine had benefited from the war too.

Bernard had never lived so well as at that time – which must have got him into bad habits. He was not unhappy. When he had money he spent it without compunction, and when he had none he borrowed shamelessly from his father or brothers.

'Ring up his lawyer.'

The clerk obeyed. A moment later his voice expressed surprise.

'Are you sure, Mademoiselle? Didn't he leave a message?'

The poor man was flabbergasted and hardly dared repeat to the judge what he had just learned.

'Monsieur Gerbois and his wife left last night for their country home near Dreux.'

The others had come for nothing.

'Take him back.'

Mauvis who was still handcuffed, stood up docilely and walked out between the two policemen.

'You may go too, Dubois.'

'Are you staying, sir?'

'I don't know. . . . I'll see.'

He had nothing to do and was not tempted to go home, where he had nothing to do either.

Finally, he took down his hat and coat and then turned around in the empty corridor to lock the door.

Chapter Four

It was half past twelve. The slanting sunlight lit up the front room, the Flea Market, as old Joseph called it, although the clientele had become much the same as in the Side-show. The old tin counter now looked more like a stage prop than a real bar.

Fernande, who was wearing a black dress, had just lifted

172

herself on to her high chair behind the cashier's desk, while Liselotte, who was in the cloakroom, pulled her skirt half-way up her thighs to readjust her garters.

There were still only ten customers. Julien Bernu and his helpers were at their posts. Everyone was ready, as if in the theatre. It was somewhat like a play, with afternoon and evening performances. All the actors, major and minor, knew their roles by heart.

Antoine, in a dazzling shirt, was holding a parchment-like menu that Joseph – as usual – called the programme. Antoine went over to a couple who were waiting to give their order.

Saturday had become a quiet day ever since important people had got into the habit of beginning the week-end on Friday. Even the streets of Paris had a different look.

When the front door opened, it was not a customer who came in, but Bernard Mature. He was wearing a camel-hair coat and a beige hat.

He took two or three steps and remained standing in the middle of the floor. Without even glancing at his sister-in-law, he stared at Antoine, waiting for his brother to notice him.

Antoine first went to the service window of the glass partition to give the chef the order he had just taken. When he turned around and saw his brother, he frowned and then went up to him.

'Hello, Bernard. Did Nicole finally manage to contact you?'

'I've just got off the plane. She was waiting for me at the airport and had time to tell me what happened.'

His breath smelled of alcohol. He could not be called a drunkard, but every day he drank his few glasses of whisky, like most Parisians who live a certain kind of life and frequent fashionable bars.

In his good periods, when things were bright, he kept to his ration, but when trouble began, he drank more.

His features then became blurred, his flesh grew flabby, and his eyes watered. That was his way of bucking himself up, of giving himself confidence. At bottom, he was weak, and it was too easy to blame the war for his shortcomings.

Antoine looked at him with a feeling of uneasiness. It was the wrong moment. A batch of customers entered, and they hesitated about choosing a free table. Antoine signalled to Joseph with a glance that he was to take over.

'Come . . .'

He led Bernard to the small door that opened on to the passage and the staircase. Bernard did not greet Fernande as he went by, which was a bad sign.

He was the only stout one in the family. He had been quite plump even as a child, and the others had made fun of his big behind. His mouth was as fleshy as a woman's, and he was almost chinless. In fact, when he was about twenty, he wore a beard for several months to hide the defect.

'Do you want to see him?'

Bernard did not answer. He could not refuse to see his father, but Antoine could feel that he had not come for that. Still wearing his overcoat, he stood for a moment in sullen silence at the foot of the bed.

'Has Mama noticed anything?'

'No. She's still the same.'

'I want to talk to you.'

Antoine preferred their conversation to take place elsewhere than in the first-floor living-room, between the bedroom where their father was lying and the one where their mother was dozing.

'Come upstairs.'

No sooner did they get to the second floor than Bernard became aggressive. He had started preparing for the meeting not only when he reached the airport but immediately after the telephone call he had received from Nicole on the Riviera.

'Has the money been found?'

'Take off your coat. Sit down.'

'I asked you a question.'

'Nothing has been found yet, but we haven't had much time to look. You'll admit that it's not the right moment to search every corner of our parents' flat.'

'That's too easy an answer!' sneered Bernard, who nevertheless took off his coat.

'What do you mean?'

'In the twenty years since you've been back home, Ferdinand

174

and I have hardly ever been here. You lived here with our father. You were together from morning to night. You knew his ways and habits. I hope you don't mind if I find it odd that you don't know what he did with his money.'

'You know what he was like.'

'I beg your pardon! I knew him the way a child knows its parents. I rang up Ferdinand. He'd just got home. I got the impression that he has the same doubts as I.'

He lit a cigarette, looked around for an ashtray, and also looked, so it seemed, for something to drink. His hands were trembling.

'Admit that it's convenient. Papa suddenly dies when Fernande and you are alone in the house.'

Antoine corrected him gently. 'It happened in front of more than thirty people. And Madame Ledru hasn't left the flat since.'

'Who engaged her?'

'I did.'

'You see! You wait two hours to phone Ferdinand and to try to contact me.'

'I couldn't leave the restaurant.'

'Couldn't Joseph replace you?'

'It was hard that evening. I had important customers.'

'The fact remains that when Ferdinand arrived, our father was already in a shroud, with a candle at each side.'

The alcohol he had drunk was beginning to have its effect. Antoine felt that his brother was wavering, that he was trying hard to continue his offensive. Without saying a word, Antoine went to get a bottle of whisky from a small piece of furniture full of bottles. He put a glass and a jug of water on a small table.

'Aren't you having any?'

'Never during working hours. You know that.'

Bernard had reached the point where he was mistrustful of everything. Nevertheless, he poured himself a glass of whisky and took a big swallow without water.

'I hardly got a wink of sleep last night. Some people with whom I'm doing business kept me at the casino. Did you look again this morning?'

'I haven't had time. I had to attend to the restaurant, and then the funeral. Fernande addressed the announcements.'

'Is it on Tuesday?'

'I asked Ferdinand what he thought. A date had to be set. It was urgent. He preferred it to be at nine in the morning.'

'Who's attending to the inheritance?'

'What do you mean?'

'It seems there's a million involved, to say nothing of the business. There are three of us. Matters like that aren't to be treated lightly. Usually a notary takes care of the interests of each party and sees to it that everything goes off properly.'

'I don't know whether Father had a notary.'

'Do you find it normal that he didn't draw up a will?'

'He didn't expect to come down suddenly with a stroke. Besides, people like him seldom leave a will. He must have imagined that his three sons . . .'

He bit his tongue.

'Go on,' said Bernard challengingly.

'I too expected you to trust me.'

'Well, I'll be damned! Papa dies, and there's no trace of the million he made over the last twenty years. *Your* million is in a safe place. His has evaporated, as if by a miracle.'

He stamped out his half-smoked cigarette on the carpet, though an ashtray was within arm's reach.

'It's less than twenty-four hours since Father died,' explained Antoine patiently. 'I found time this morning to go looking for a man named Jason in the Rue Coquillière. Papa had dealings with him. I found an old building full of more or less shady-looking offices with enamelled plaques on all the doors. Jason moved out three years ago. He didn't leave an address, though he told the concierge that he was retiring to a place near Ville-neuve-Saint-Georges, where he had a little house.'

Antoine was unable to resent his brother's behaviour, and as he watched Bernard, who had stiffened in his aggressive attitude, he felt that he was making a discovery. Bernard was ageless, or rather he was every age at once. His irresolute face revealed the child of long ago, the young man who was at ease nowhere, the maturing man who had not managed to find his place in the world.

176

Would he grow old? Was his health good enough for that? If so, he would be one of those old men who have learned nothing and continue to talk about their dreams as if they were realities.

Hadn't there been something childish about their father too, to the very end? At the moment of his collapse, he was showing a young couple a picture of what he had been, a picture of a young man with a bristling moustache, standing on the threshold of his domain, flexing his muscles and full of self-assurance.

'When will Ferdinand be here again?'

'What do you mean?'

'I suppose the three of us are going to get together. . . . We don't even know when he's going to be put into the coffin. One would think he was no one else's father but yours.'

Antoine could feel that his attitude and tone and the look on his face were expressions, not of a momentary bitterness, but of a hatred that had matured over the years.

There was a difference of nearly four years between them. Ferdinand and Antoine had been real brothers for a certain time. But Bernard had never played with the others, had never confided in them.

He would use the slightest pretext to complain about them to their mother, who defended him.

'Both of you, let your little brother alone. Aren't you ashamed to pick on him?'

The little brother! That was what he had always been. And what he still was. He was capable now of bursting into a fit of rage and of stamping his feet and crying as when he had been a child.

'I'm warning you, Antoine, that I won't let myself be bamboozled. I have friends who are lawyers. I'm going to consult them this very afternoon. As for Nicole, when she comes here again, I'd like her to be treated like a member of the family and not like an undesirable stranger. If you must know, I've decided to marry her.'

'Do you have anything else to say to me?'

'I advise you to find the will and the money. It's advisable that you do. Do you know the legal term that might be applied to your case before long? Captation of inheritance. I may seem like a nobody, but I know a thing or two about the law.'

He looked at the bottle hesitantly, then poured himself another drink and gulped it down.

'Don't think I'm drunk. I'm perfectly aware of what I'm saying and doing, and I'm telling you now that Ferdinand'll side with me.'

He had some trouble finding the sleeves of his coat, and he put on his hat as he walked to the stairs.

'A word to the wise!'

It was grotesque, theatrical, Antoine was nonetheless overwhelmed, and he almost took a drink to buck himself up before going downstairs.

But he didn't. He waited long enough for Bernard to leave the building and then slowly returned to the Senate. Fernande glanced at him anxiously. To reassure her, he simply shrugged his shoulders before going to shake hands with an old customer.

The restaurant business was really odd! They were like actors on a stage. For hours every day his wife and he could exchange only hurried glances, at times a few words in a whisper. He had to smile, to listen to funny stories or to confidences.

At the age of forty-nine, he was beginning to walk like old Joseph. Most waiters and restaurant owners end up with flat feet. The world around them is no longer the world that others see, but numbered tables, familiar or unfamiliar faces, menus, dishes, bills.

For twenty years he had been serving the same delicacies in the same order on the same trolley. The gesture with which he offered the menu never varied, nor did the one with which he poured solemnly the first drops of Gamay d'Auvergne, Chanturgues, Blanc Rosé de Corent or Sauvagnat. The customer would examine the liquid as if he were a connoisseur, would smack his lips and glance at him as if they were both in on a secret.

Auguste had a brother, three years older than he, who still lived in Saint-Hippolyte. Fernande had tried to reach him all day, but in vain, for the old man had always refused to have a telephone installed.

As for his two or three children, one of whom was a girl

whom Antoine remembered vaguely, he had no idea of what had become of them.

Fernande had sent a telegram. The brother's name was Hector. Antoine had been a child the last time he had seen him. He had been struck by the resemblance to his father, although his uncle's features were more weather-beaten and his skin was the colour of baked clay.

There was also a Bourdin, a sister of his mother whom they had not been able to inform. She had married a Riom grocer, who was probably dead as his name was no longer in the telephone book.

While brooding over these wisps of thought, which he was unable to get out of his mind, Antoine went back and forth from the tables to the service window, sometimes going into the kitchen to explain to the chef the particular wishes of a customer.

'Above all, no garlic. No onions either.'

He would sometimes look into the first room, as if expecting to see his father offer a drink on the house.

Then he would again see him lying stretched out upstairs, with his hands together, and truly dead, that his mind was no longer working behind his icy forehead.

A little while before, when he had entered the bedroom with Bernard, he had felt like apologizing, like mumbling 'Excuse me, Papa.'

In his mind's eye he saw them all again, Ferdinand, Véronique, Nicole, Bernard, each going up to the foot of the bed and standing motionless for a moment, as in church. The dead man lay there like an object, and they did not seem surprised to see him suddenly inert.

Antoine himself expected his father to start talking again. He almost felt like saying to him, 'Do you see the situation they're putting me in. I don't hold it against them, but I'd really like to avoid all this mess.'

He, too, was surprised. He knew that when it came to money his father had always been reticent, mysterious, in the manner of peasants. The old man never got used to the fact that the government assumed it had the right to ask him what he earned.

It was the fruit of his labour, of his, the labour of Auguste, who had begun to earn his living at an age when others were still playing marbles. The idea of a holiday had never occurred to him. At the most, he had gone back to his home-town once in a blue moon, and for years he had not even done that.

The last time he returned to Paris, he was gloomy. Shaking his head, he said. 'They're almost all dead, or they'll be dead before long. It's now full of strangers, both in Riom and Saint-Hippolyte.'

To him, a stranger was someone who was not from his village, from his street.

'In Riom they have stores just like those in Paris, and the women show their knees when they walk in the street.'

He and Chaussard, the old butcher next door, could talk for hours on end about people who no longer existed, except in their memories and in family albums. At times, one would have thought they were sitting on a bench in school. . .

'Alfred, do you remember when I told him . . .'

'No, no, Auguste, it wasn't you who told him to go to hell. It was little Arthur, whose father was a blacksmith. . . . Wait, his name's on the tip of my tongue. . . . He was an awful pest.'

Come to think of it, didn't the two men talk about other personal matters? Both of them had succeeded in business. Chaussard, with his four butcher's shops in Paris, was the richer of the two.

Hadn't they been tempted at times to compare their success? Antoine made up his mind to question old Alfred, who would be wary, for he had a tendency, like Auguste, to trust the younger generation only so far and no further.

To them, Antoine was a youngster. They probably still regarded him as if he were wearing shorts.

He was in a hurry to discuss things with Fernande. They had hardly seen each other all morning, had hardly been together except when the undertaker called.

Then his wife had come over to show him the list of people to whom she was sending the announcements.

'What do I do with the Auvergnats in Paris?'

'There must be thousands of them. We can't inform everyone. Ring up and ask for a list of the members of the committee.'

'Do you think they'll come with their flag and band? Your father was president of the association. I remember a funeral to which some of them even came in costume.'

Meanwhile, Auguste was lying upstairs motionless, with his hands crossed on his stomach and with a rosary between his fingers as in the days when he served at mass.

'I don't know whether Riom has a local newspaper. But there must be one at Clermont-Ferrand. You ought to telephone and get them to insert an obituary.'

They would surely forget to send announcements to cousins and second cousins, who were going to be offended.

The telephone rang near the cashier's desk. Fernande answered.

'One moment.'

She glanced at her husband who came over.

'Ferdinand,' she whispered.

His brother's voice was curt.

'I've just rung up Bernard. . . . Hello! . . . Do you hear me?'

'Yes . . .'

'Are you in the restaurant?'

'It's mealtime, isn't it?'

'We've decided to get everyone together tomorrow. I suppose you close on Sunday, don't you?'

'That's right.'

'Which do you prefer, the morning or the afternoon?'

'It doesn't matter to me.'

'I couldn't be there before eleven in the morning, because of mass, and since we have a lot to say to each other, it's better to meet early in the afternoon.'

'What time?'

'Two o'clock?'

'All right.'

'You still haven't found anything?'

'No.'

'I've tried to calm Bernard down.'

'Thank you.'

'I'll probably bring Jean-Loup and my daughter. In the long run, it concerns them too.'

'See you tomorrow.'

He had not taken his eyes off his wife, to whom he merely whispered before giving the bill to a table, 'Tomorrow at two . . . big family meeting.'

*

He had spent almost an hour waiting on the benches of the local municipal office and being sent from one clerk to another before getting to Ernest Jason's address. As soon as lunch was over, and without waiting for all the customers to leave, he had gone to get his car in the Rue des Halles and had driven to Villeneuve-Saint-Georges.

He still had to find the Rue des Ajoncs, and he asked several people where it was, but none of them knew. Finally, someone directed him to an outlying neighbourhood, near a spot where several railway tracks ended, and after driving in and out of streets full of little old houses and shacks, he finally saw a plaque with the name of the street he was looking for.

The street was rather short. At one time it must have bordered on the countryside, and there were still a few trees in the little gardens. The corner house was a small empty café. He went in to ask for information and ordered a glass of beer.

'Jason? . . . No, I don't know anyone by that name in the neighbourhood. Are you sure he lives in the Rue des Ajoncs? You know, we've been here only two years.'

She was wearing red slippers and a knitted garment that hung down over her hips. A cat was lying on a cane-bottomed chair near the cylindrical stove, the pipe of which went up to the ceiling.

The place did not look like a real café, and Antoine wondered who could be tempted to sit down in it.

A round-shouldered man holding a pair of pincers came in from the garden.

'Joseph, do you know anyone named Jason?'

'It's higher up, on the left side. He's not there any more. In fact, I think he died, but his daughter still lives in the house. It's called "The Linnets".'

The street seemed to have been forgotten by the expanding

city. Grass was growing between the paving stones. The houses, with their wooden balconies and ill-proportioned roofs were much alike. The only real difference was the colour of the shutters. Those of 'The Linnets' were yellow and had not been repainted for years.

The gate, which was also yellow, stood between two hedges. He opened it and crossed a small, weedy garden. When he reached the door, he rang the bell.

Nothing was stirring in the street. Nothing stirred in the house either. All he heard was trains coming and going and goods-waggons hitting against each other in the siding. Then a big plane turned in the bright blue sky before heading for the airport.

He rang again, then knocked at the door. Stepping back, he glanced at the windows. On the left side, he saw a face behind the net curtains.

Whereupon he knocked at the window, and the woman decided to go to the door, which she opened slightly.

'What do you want?'

He hardly saw anything of her, just about half of her head, a single eye, uncombed hair, and a dirty apron.

'Monsieur Ernest Jason lives here, doesn't he?'

'Do you know him?'

'No I don't.'

'Then what does it matter to you whether he lives here or not?'

She was crabbed. Crabbed and stupid. Needlessly aggressive. There was a mistrustful look in the one eye which he saw.

'I have an important question to ask him.'

'What question?'

'It's a personal matter. At least tell me when he'll be in.'

'He won't be in. He died.'

'How long ago?'

'Is it any business of yours?'

'I wouldn't have asked otherwise.'

'It'll be six months next week.'

'Did you know him well? Was it from him that you rented the house?'

'I didn't have to rent it from him. He was my father.'

He had put his foot against the door to prevent her from slamming it in his face, and he pressed slowly.

'Could I have a talk with you?'

He now saw all of her. She was fat, ill-looking, with swollen legs and a big, unhealthily pink face in which blue eyes expressed instinctive fear.

She resigned herself to letting him come in. The entrance was tiled with little squares of all colours. The room on the left was a combination living- and dining-room, but a dining-room in which nobody ate, except a canary which was hopping about in a cage. Everything was congealed, was outside time, like the clock, which probably had not worked for years.

'People are constantly coming to plague me,' she said warily. 'I can't tell them anything because I knew nothing about his business.'

'Did your father live here?'

'Don't you know?'

There was something disquieting about the conversation, about the atmosphere of the house, about the woman's attitude and expression.

'Don't I know what?'

'He died at Fresnes.'

'In the prison?'

'Yes. They gave him a two-year sentence, and he died in the infirmary three months later. He'd said as much in court. He swore to them that he was innocent and that they were committing murder.'

It was more and more difficult to ask questions.

'On what grounds was your father sentenced?'

'Fraud, according to them.'

'What exactly was his profession? He had an office in Paris, didn't he?'

'Yes. He was an educated and intelligent man. He'd been a business agent. You haven't come to ask me for money?'

'No.'

'Lots of them take advantage, because they read in the papers that my father was sentenced. So they ring the bell, and they claim they entrusted my father with their savings. So they tell me, but I knew nothing about his business.'

'Isn't it true?'

'I don't know . . . He helped people when he was a business agent. It was his job to attach their property or to evict them. He didn't want to continue. It's because he was too kind that they put him in gaol.'

She finally sat down on the edge of a chair on which there were a piece of knitting and ball of wool with two needles stuck in it. Antoine hesitated for a moment, and then he too sat down.

'Do you know when he was sentenced?'

'On 11 September.'

'In Paris? Were you there?'

'He didn't want me to go. When I got married, he kept his room here, but most of the time he slept in a small room behind his office. He'd been a widower for ten years. My mother suffered for a long time, and I know I'll end up as she did. My husband works on the railways.'

Reassured by the visitor's attitude, she went on talking for the sake of talking.

'Two years ago, he told me . . .'

'Are you referring to your father?'

'To whom else would I be referring? He told me he was retiring, and he came to live with us. I realized at once that he was having trouble.'

'Did he tell you what it was?'

'People who had a grudge against him. Because, since he was no longer a business agent . . .'

She was losing the thread of her ideas, and Antoine could see that she was trying to remember what she meant to say.

'Wait. . . . Oh, yes. . . . He wanted to help people. He knew the laws, you realize? The shopkeepers, the people who work around Les Halles, where my father had his office, don't know them. For them he was a kind of bone-setter.'

One had to enter her universe, which, as a matter of fact, began to seem rather coherent.

'Take me, for example, I'm treated by a bone-setter. The doctors are unable to find out what's wrong with me. So when my sister-in-law talked to me about the healer in Lagny . . .'

She knitted her brow. Her head felt heavy, and she was over-taxing herself. It was all too complicated for her.

'You were saying that he helped them.'

'Yes. ... With all the papers one has to fill out nowadays. People don't even understand what's being asked of them. It's like with the Welfare State. There are questions in small print and you have to write the answer in a box or on a dotted line. So, if you make a mistake, there's trouble, and someone comes to attach your belongings.'

'I understand.'

'In the banks, they take your money, make you sign papers, and give you a book. It's your hard luck if they attach you too. They claim there's nothing left in our account. But what's there to prove they haven't made a mistake, with the thousands and thousands of accounts they have?'

It was almost the way old Auguste would have spoken. He belonged to a time when there weren't banks on every street corner, when identity cards didn't exist, nor passports either, and when two envelopes were enough to prove who you were.

'Who took action against him?'

'I don't know. There were several of them. First there was one, then others, then still others. The one I heard about most was a locksmith named Bougerol who came here several times to make a row. I didn't see him because my father locked me up in the kitchen, but I heard his voice and the insulting things he said. He once threatened my father that he'd settle his hash.'

'Did your father ever talk to you about Auguste?'

'Auguste who?'

'Mature . . . a friend of his.'

'In the end, he no longer had any friends. They all turned against him when they realized that there was no hope for him. . . . Who are you?'

'Auguste's son.'

'Why didn't he come himself?'

'Because he's dead.'

'What exactly do you want?'

'I'm trying to find out.'

'To find out what?'

'My father's will hasn't turned up.'

'Are you sure he made one? My father didn't leave any. It's true that he didn't leave any money either. Only this house, which he put in my name and my husband's.'

'If he entrusted anyone with it, it was probably your father.'

'Why?'

'Because he trusted him. It was your father who drew up all his papers.'

'Have you come to ask me for money, you too?'

'No. But I suppose your father kept books, that he had documents in his office and that he brought them here when he came to live with you.'

'He had a trunk full of papers that he put in the attic. He said they were of no interest.'

'Are they still here?'

'The police came to get them. To turn them over to the judge.'

'Didn't your father also have an address book?'

'He did.'

'Are you the one who has it now?'

'Who, what?'

'Are you the one who has it?'

'No, the judge.'

Beads of perspiration stood out on Antoine's forehead. He could think of no other questions to ask. He felt awkward. He had done his best not to alarm the poor woman, who, when she saw him stand up, was immediately frightened.

'Do you think there's a will?'

She, too, was now standing. She had asked the question in order to keep them talking. Then she looked at the canary tenderly.

'Thank you very much. I apologize for having disturbed you.'

'If only the others were as polite. ... Even women come knocking ...'

When the door shut behind him, he breathed with relief. He walked to the corner, where he had left his car in front of the little café. The man who had informed him was in the process of putting wires between pegs.

'Did you find it?'

'Yes, I did, thank you.'

The car was a pale grey Mercedes with a noiseless engine. His brothers resented that too. How had he been able to live all those years without realizing it?

Until the night before, his brothers had been his brothers. He did not see them often because each of them lived a different kind of life.

He was the only one who had remained at home, and no doubt that was why he had never been aware of their problems.

When Bernard turned up in the Rue de la Grande-Truanderie, it was almost always because he needed money. He would rarely ask their father. After spending a few minutes with the two old people, which he did because he was unable to avoid it, he would take Antoine into a corner or else go outside with him, and they would walk for a while without speaking.

'I could have asked Ferdinand, but you know that they have a hard time making ends meet, especially since they bought the flat. I was supposed to get a rather big cheque on the 15th, but I learned yesterday that payment has been postponed until next month.'

'How much?'

'Five thousand. . . . Is that too much?'

He was very casual about it and wasted no time with thanks. To him the restaurant was a property that belonged more or less to the whole family.

If he preferred not to ask his father for money, it was because the old man regarded all figures as enormous.

As Bernard saw it, his brother had only to dip into the cash-box. Antoine was a shrewd man. He had the best of it. Did he deprive himself of anything? And didn't Fernande have a mink coat?

Ferdinand was a different case. He was no longer a Mature. When he was at the university, he had begun to look at his home as if he were a stranger. The ways of the family became more and more foreign to him.

In addition, Véronique had had a greater influence on him than he on her. When her father and mother were still alive, the couple wrote to them regularly, and her mother often went to see them in La Rochelle and then in Poitiers.

188

The grandchildren were members of his in-laws' family and were hardly ever seen in the Rue de la Grande-Truanderie.

Now and then, Ferdinand and Véronique would come for lunch or dinner, but they came when the customers did, and so they didn't sit down with the members of the family, who ate at a marble-topped table near the bar.

'What do you suggest we have, Antoine?'

Antoine would jot down their order, pass it on to the chef, and then sit down beside them for a few minutes.

'How's Mama?'

She had been better, then worse, then a little better again, until there was no further question about her condition.

'Does Father drink much?'

'He has a little drink now and then. I keep an eye on him. One can't deprive him of his last pleasure.'

It had always been hard for old Auguste to call his daughter-in-law by her first name.

'You're very pretty, Véronique . . .'

He would awkwardly bring her a flower, as if to tame her, though he knew very well that he never would.

'How are the children?'

Their names stuck in his throat, and besides, the names were a bit fancy.

Antoine, however, kept thinking of the old days when each in turn had crawled about on the floor, which was covered with sawdust at the time.

When he got back, he saw that Fernande was worried. She was staying upstairs, on the first floor, in his mother's bedroom, because she had given Madame Ledru the day off so that she could rest in her son's flat.

'Did you learn anything?'

'I'm not sure. . . . I've got to have a talk with Ferdinand.'

He felt the need to exchange a few words with his father. The idea of the candles had not been his but Marinette's. He blew them out and parted the curtains of the window that looked out on the yard. However, he did not dare remove the rosary or the sprig of holly that was soaking in the holy water.

Chapter Five

That evening, after closing the shutters of the restaurant, putting out the lights, checking the equipment, and putting the padlock on the trap door, Antoine did not go up to his own flat on the second floor, but to his parents'.

Fernande, wearing a dressing-gown, was in the dimly lit living-room.

'Is she sleeping?'

'For the past hour. She's been quiet.'

He went to the back room, where he switched on the ceiling light. He hesitated to sit up with the dead body. People still did that kind of thing in the country, though fewer and fewer did in the cities. He finally went over to his father and kissed him lightly on the forehead, saying inwardly, 'Good evening, Father.'

He walked to the door backwards, turned off the light, and went back to his wife.

'Go upstairs and sleep. I'll stay here with Mama.'

'No, I'll stay. You can't look after her. A man can't give her the chamber-pot if she needs it, or change her clothes.'

The house had become so different in twenty-four hours! He finally went upstairs alone, undressed in the empty flat, and went to bed.

On other Sundays, they slept late, and then they would dawdle about for the pleasure of having nothing to do. The closed shutters gave the restaurant a special atmosphere, and it was odd to go into the glass-enclosed kitchen around one o'clock and take from the refrigerator the meal that Julien Bernu had prepared for them the night before.

They would eat near the bar. In the afternoon, they would sometimes go to the cinema or drive out into the country. Occasionally Auguste went with them.

But this Sunday was not like the others. When Antoine went down to the first floor in his dressing-gown, his wife was giving the old lady her breakfast.

'Were you able to sleep?'

'Very well. She woke up only once.'

They did not hear the familiar din of Les Halles. The street was empty, and all the shutters were closed. At nine o'clock, the undertaker's little truck stopped in front of the house, and a few passers-by lingered to watch his assistants carry in the heavy black hangings and then the empty coffin.

There was a sound of hammering. The men were transforming Madame Ledru's room into a private chapel. Antoine had brought them a bottle of white wine and glasses, and they drank as they worked around the body.

Antoine and then his wife went up to dress. When they were together again on the first floor, Auguste was in his coffin, which was to remain open until the following evening.

Men and women from the neighbourhood who were on their way to mass or simply out for a breath of air paused for a moment in front of the house and looked up at the windows, for everybody now knew that Auguste had died.

The doorbell rang five or six times in the course of the morning. Each time it was a delivery boy bringing flowers.

Antoine did not have lunch. He took a slice of ham from the refrigerator and ate it with a piece of bread. A little later, Fernande did the same. She was disturbed by the thought of the family meeting that was to take place.

Ferdinand and his wife had lunch together after mass and hardly said a word to each other. The night before, in bed, they had discussed for almost an hour Auguste's death and the questions it raised.

'I hope you'll stick up for your rights,' Véronique had concluded. 'In any case, I'll be there.'

Bernard had had a bad night, and Nicole had had to take care of him, for he had kept drinking until he went to bed. In the morning, he was no better. He had a hangover. Sitting up in bed, where he had perspired a great deal, he asked for a drink to set himself up.

'Don't forget that you've got to have your wits about you this afternoon.'

Nicole gave him a tiny glass of whisky.

'I don't mind your drinking it. In an hour, you'll eat something. I'll let you have another drink before you leave, but that'll be all.'

His head ached, and from time to time he had twinges that made him think his heart was going to stop beating.

'You'd better call the doctor. I don't feel well, Nicole.'

'You'll feel better later.'

'Do you think you ought to come with me?'

'I won't let you go alone.'

They lived in a four-room flat, above the shop of a picture-framer, in the Boulevard Rochechouart. They were six months behind with the rent.

She did not ask him why he had gone to Cannes. He had left without saying anything. She knew that it was enough for some vague friend to suggest in a bar at two in the morning that he come along.

Nicole had been a saleswoman in a smart shop in the Rue Saint-Honoré and, after that, had worked as a model for two years. She still posed occasionally for women's magazines, though less and less often.

Marie-Laure and her friend Françoise were sleeping in their flat in the Avenue Victor Hugo after getting home at three in the morning. They had twin beds, like a husband and wife. Françoise wore severely tailored, rather masculine suits, but actually the two women were playing a kind of game, for there was nothing dubious in their relationship.

Françoise was the first one up. She went to prepare the coffee.

'What time is it?'

'Noon. Don't forget that you have to be at your grandfather's at two.'

'You think it's necessary?'

'You promised your mother . . .'

They shared a car, a small, milky-white English convertible, which they took turns driving.

'May I have the car?'

'No. I need it to go to Louveciennes. I'll drop you off at Les Halles, and you'll join me at the Lemerciers'.'

Jean-Loup, in a white smock and with a stethoscope around

his neck, was slowly making his rounds in the children's wards, and a nurse, who took notes, was following him.

He had arranged with a colleague to replace him that afternoon. At one o'clock, he entered the housemen's dining-room.

It was at least three years since he had seen his grandparents. At home, when he was a child, his parents hardly ever spoke of the Matures. He did not quite understand why his parents insisted on his attending a meeting that didn't concern him.

He too had a car, a small, cheap one, which was all he needed. He arrived early. The shutters of the restaurant were closed. He entered the hallway of the building, knocked at a door on the right, then, getting no answer, went up to the first floor.

There he found Antoine, who had not yet put on his tie and jacket.

'Hello, Uncle Antoine.'

His eyes looked larger because of his glasses, and he seemed quite lost.

'Haven't my parents arrived?'

The flowers had begun to fill the flat with a sweetish smell.

'They won't be long. It's only ten to two. . . . Do you want to see him?'

Jean-Loup stood in front of the corpse for a moment, as the others had done the night before. Meanwhile, Antoine, who was behind him, finished dressing.

'How's Grandmother?'

'Still the same.'

'Does she suspect anything?'

She had not even noticed that Auguste no longer lay down beside her at night in the bed they had shared for fifty years.

'Where's it taking place?'

'I thought we'd be more comfortable downstairs.'

In the first room or the second, whichever they preferred. Antoine and his nephew went down together.

'Would you like a drink?'

'No, thank you.'

Jean-Loup was the tallest member of the family, and he stood with his body bent slightly forward. His father and mother knocked on the door near the cashier's desk and entered without waiting.

They kissed Jean-Loup.

'Are we late?'

'No, I came early.'

'Have you see him?'

'I went upstairs for a moment.'

They barely greeted Antoine. The lights were on because of the shutters, and the two rooms looked unreal. The unlit kitchen behind the enormous sheet of glass gave the impression of being an aquarium.

A few moments later, Bernard and Nicole arrived. Véronique winced and pretended not to see Nicole.

'Are we late?'

Bernard was presentable. His eyelids were only slightly red, and he tried to behave properly.

'Isn't Marie-Laure coming?'

'She promised to be here.'

They were standing, not knowing where to sit.

'Has the private chapel been set up?'

'This morning. ... They're coming tomorrow evening to close the coffin.'

'Where's Fernande?'

'With Mama. I told Madame Ledru to take the day off. She was exhausted.'

'Who sat up with Papa?'

'Nobody. Fernande slept on the couch in the living-room.'

A car stopped outside, a door slammed, and a voice said, 'I hope it won't be too lugubrious.'

A moment later, there were hesitant steps in the hallway. Antoine went to open the door.

'Hello, everybody! Why are you all standing and looking at each other?'

'We were waiting for you.'

Antoine did not know how to get the meeting started. On the one hand, he was the host and it was he who was receiving them, but, on the other, they were in their father's home, and they all had the same rights.

'Where do we sit?'

Ferdinand sat down on the banquette to the left of the bar, and everyone else finally settled around two marble-topped tables. Jean-Loup, who had crossed his long legs, looked at the others, each in turn, as if they were strangers.

Their hats and coats were lying helter-skelter on another table.

Ferdinand, after clearing his throat, was the first to speak.

'Who decided about the cemetery?'

Everyone looked at Antoine.

'As I told you yesterday on the phone, I first thought that our father would have wanted to be buried in Saint-Hippolyte, near his parents' grave. ... He never talked about it. ... Almost everyone he knew there is dead.'

He added hesitantly, 'His real family is now in Paris. There's no room in the Père-Lachaise Cemetery, except for those who have a vault. The only solution is to bury him in Ivry.'

There was a silence. Perhaps they saw in their mind's eye an enormous modern cemetery, which was still too new and in which Auguste would have felt out of place.

'Do you think there'll be a lot of people?'

'There certainly will, when the funeral leaves the house. All the neighbours and local shopkeepers. I think that some distant relatives from Riom and Saint-Hippolyte are coming too.'

'What have you arranged?'

'I've asked for twenty cars. There'll be a luncheon here for those who come from Auvergne.'

The others neither approved nor disapproved. The matter did not interest them. They had mentioned the subject in order to warm up, so as not to tackle the real question immediately.

'Did you ask for prayers?'

Bernard was wriggling on his chair. He was ill at ease and kept looking at the bottles lined up behind the bar. Nicole, knowing what state he was in, was urging him to hold out a little while. It was better for him not to start drinking too soon lest he cause a fight. The night before, in his drunkenness, he had been bitter and violent and had threatened to take steps with his brothers. She had locked the drawer containing his revolver. Before leaving, she had opened it, just to be sure that he hadn't touched it.

Once again Ferdinand spoke up.

'You still haven't found the will?' he asked in a calm but cutting voice.

'I haven't looked. I prefer that you do it yourself. You know the flat. You knew our father.'

The silence that followed became menacing.

'Is there anything new about the money?'

They were all expecting Antoine to reply in the negative.

'There is.'

Everyone sat up in his chair.

'Have you found it?'

'No.'

'Explain what you mean.'

Until then, everyone present had lived his life without great hopes of its ever changing. They knew, of course, that they would inherit something and that they were entitled to a greater or lesser share of the restaurant in which they had become strangers.

Ferdinand for example, expected at most to be able to buy a new car, to pay off some of the debts with which he had been saddled since buying the new flat, and even perhaps, to spend a holiday in Italy with Véronique.

For Bernard, it would mean gaining a few months. Perhaps it would be the long-awaited opportunity of working out a deal that would materialize.

But everything had changed since the night before. Antoine had mentioned a magical figure, a figure that made people dream, on which the government had built its national lottery. A million!

It was not an abstract figure. It summoned up the idea of wealth, of a different kind of life, a life from which anxiety would disappear for ever. The fact that they might have to share the money hardly mattered. No one even thought about it. Nor did anyone remember that their mother was also one of the heirs, or that Auguste had had income tax to pay every year, or that there would be death duties.

'I first went to the Rue Coquillière.'

And, turning to Jean-Loup, who was looking at him with great interest, he continued:

'When my father and I drew up an agreement about the restaurant, he asked a business adviser in the Rue Coquillière to draft the text. The adviser was a man named Jason. I know that my father saw him again. Jason came here several times, though I didn't take much notice of him.'

'Did you find him?' asked Bernard. Nicole laid her hand on his.

'I found a trace of him. His office no longer exists. The concierge mentioned a house that Jason had in Villeneuve-Saint-Georges. I went there. I finally managed to get his address through the district office.'

'What did he say?'

'Nothing. He's dead.'

One would have thought that he had purposely kept them in suspense. For a moment they had sat there breathless, with their jaws practically hanging. Now they were looking at him angrily, furiously.

'So you know nothing?'

'I haven't finished. I had a talk with his daughter, who's not in her right mind. Jason died in Fresnes Prison a few weeks after getting a two-year sentence for fraud.'

Ferdinand was getting paler, and his right hand, in which he was holding his glasses, kept opening and closing nervously.

'If I understand correctly,' he broke in, 'you claim that Papa entrusted Jason with his money, that Jason was a swindler, and that, since he died in prison, we have no further recourse.'

'I don't claim anything.'

'Don't you find that explanation too easy? Papa is dead. Jason is dead. His daughter is mad. And the money has disappeared without a trace.'

Despite Nicole's making signs to him, Bernard got up and went behind the bar to pour himself a drink.

'It's a lousy trick!' he called out.

Everyone turned to him.

'The day Antoine came back home, we should have been wary. Especially since he shacked up with that woman.'

All eyes now shifted to Antoine, who managed, with a very great effort, to remain in his chair. His fists were so tightly clenched that the knuckles were livid.

To everyone's surprise, it was Jean-Loup who broke the silence. He was very calm, as if he were speaking with the voice of reason.

'If I understand correctly, no paper has been found indicating what my grandfather did with his money.'

The others nodded.

'Has anyone looked in his wallet?'

They sat there stupefied. No one else had thought of it. It was Madame Ledru who had undressed Auguste, and it had not occurred to anyone to ask what she had done with his clothes. What they were looking for was papers, documents, cheque-books, in any case something voluminous enough to correspond to the old man's investments over a period of twenty years or so.

Antoine stood up.

'If anyone wants to come with me, I'll go and look for it.'

Jean-Loup got to his feet.

'I think it would be better if I went,' he said.

*

Jean-Loup was so tall that at one point on the way upstairs he had to lower his head so as not to knock it against the low ceiling. There had just been talk of millions, and now they were opening an old brown door entering a flat of another age where he had been only two or three times when he was a child.

He caught a glimpse, at the far end of the living-room, of part of the private chapel. Flowers were lying at the foot of the coffin.

'Do you want to see her?'

Antoine felt strange in the presence of the young man who was already treating patients in hospitals and who was going to be a doctor.

Jean-Loup followed his uncle into the room which had been his grandparents' bedroom and which was still his grand-mother's.

The old lady was sitting in her armchair, near the window, with a red blanket on her knees. Fernande, who had been sitting opposite her, stood up when her nephew entered.

'Hello, Jean-Loup.'

'Hello, Aunt.'

He went up to his grandmother and kissed her on the forehead, as he had done in the past. She drew back and rolled her eyes in search of someone she could ask for help.

'She doesn't recognize anyone.'

'I know,' he answered, looking at the old woman with a professional eye.

'Do you remember what was done with my father's things when he was undressed?'

'You know very well that I was downstairs. I didn't think of asking Madame Ledru.'

'He must have been wearing his black suit.'

Auguste had always dressed in black. His wife had always had a hard time getting him to buy a new suit. When Antoine opened the huge oak wardrobe, it was clear that his father had not given up his old things easily, even when they were threadbare, for about ten shapeless jackets were lined up on hangers.

In the same wardrobe there were also dresses, all of them black or purple, which Eugénie had not worn since she had been confined to the bedroom. On a shelf were her straw and felt hats and her husband's grey caps and round, black felt hat.

Everything in the wardrobe had been worn for years, had been part, as it were, of each one's personal role. Looking at the various objects, Antoine had the impression that each of them retained the odour of the owner's body.

He ran his hands over one of the jackets, felt something, put his hand into an inner pocket, and took out a greyish wallet.

He handed it to his nephew, who understood the gesture. Jean-Loup was embarrassed and mumbled very quickly, 'You mustn't hold it against them.'

It was a way of letting Antoine know that he was not necessarily with the others, that he did not belong to a clan.

'Is there anything else?' he asked.

In one of the pockets Antoine found a handkerchief and in another a short amber cigar holder that the old man had hardly ever used and a big peasant's knife.

Auguste had continued to use the knife to cut his food long

after his arrival in Paris. When he opened it, he did so with an almost ritual gesture.

Fernande did not dare ask whether things were going all right. She contented herself with smiling vaguely at her husband before sitting down again near the invalid.

Bernard had taken advantage of their absence to help himself to a second drink. He had offered one to the others, but only Marie-Laure had accepted.

Jean-Loup handed the wallet to his father without opening it. Ferdinand began by feeling it.

'It contains something hard,' he mumbled.

On both sides of it were pockets from which he removed papers. In order to get to the hard object he had to slide his hand to the very bottom, into what leather dealers call the secret pocket, the one that runs the whole length of the wallet.

He took out a flat, shiny key and showed it to the others, particularly to Antoine.

'Do you know what it's for?'

'I've never seen it. I'm sure it doesn't open any door or piece of furniture in the house.'

He took it in his hand and saw a figure, 113, which was engraved on the key ring.

'It's a key to a safe-deposit box in a bank vault.'

'How do you know?'

'Because I have almost the same kind for my box.'

A sense of relief could be felt around the two marble-topped tables.

'We now have to find out which bank it is,' murmured Ferdinand.

'That won't be hard. Father never went very far. Outside the neighbourhood he felt as if he were in a foreign country.'

He laid the key on the table, and they all stared at it, fascinated, for a question suddenly arose, one which had just occurred to all of them at the same time.

It was Sunday. The banks did not open until nine o'clock the following morning. At that time, Ferdinand would be in court, Jean-Loup at the hospital, Marie-Laure in her shop, and Antoine in the restaurant.

Whom were they going to entrust with the key that probably gave access to the old man's fortune?

They looked up and glanced at each other. Perhaps they were a little ashamed of their thoughts?

'I'm against Antoine's going.'

It was Bernard who had spoken. He was standing in the background, with a glass in his hand, and staring sternly at his brother as if challenging him again.

'You really don't know what there could be in the vault?'

'I've told you that Father never mentioned it to me.'

Bernard attacked again.

'I demand that we all go together.'

His statement revealed the ridiculousness, if not the odiousness, of the situation. They were all hypnotized by a shiny key that nobody wanted to touch but that nobody was willing to let anyone else take.

In what bank vault did the key open box 113? They might have to try six or seven before finding the right one. Could they go there in a crowd? And should Ferdinand, who had been unable to question Mauvis the day before because the lawyer had not shown up, put off the questioning a second time?

It was Marie-Laure who started the conversation going again.

'To whom do the three Utrillos belong?'

'To Father,' replied Antoine.

'Is each of you going to take one?'

'I'll do what the others decide. I'm ready to buy them at a price set by an expert.'

Ferdinand looked at his wife, and then at his daughter, whom he asked, 'Do you have any idea what they're worth?'

'Anywhere between fifty and a hundred thousand francs apiece. It depends on when they were painted.'

They belonged to the period when women wore long skirts and had big behinds.

'Why are you so eager to buy them?' asked Ferdinand, who was still mistrustful.

'So that they remain where they've been for such a long time. They used to be in the bedroom upstairs. When I first saw them, as when you did, they were in the back room. ... You really won't have anything to drink? Fernande apologizes for not being here, but she has to stay with Mama. If you leave her alone for a moment, she imagines she's been abandoned.'

It was not an ordinary family meeting. There should have been coffee cups or wine glasses on the tables. There should also have been a relaxed atmosphere.

It was as if each of them were trying to find something to say to break the silence, especially Ferdinand, who liked playing the role of eldest brother and who, as such, was supposed to be acting as chairman.

'The most urgent thing is obviously find the bank.'

They were going around in a vicious circle. What was to be done with the key until then?

Again it was Jean-Loup who found the solution.

'All you have to do is put it in an envelope and seal it. The three brothers can initial the seals.'

'I wonder whether there's any wax in the house. I saw a piece not long ago in one of the drawers in my bedroom.'

As Antoine closed the door behind him, Bernard growled, '*He's* not worried. He already has his share.'

Although Nicole looked at him beseechingly, he went behind the counter again to fill his glass. Marie-Laure eased his conscience by calling out to him, 'May I have one too, Uncle Bernard?'

Her mother looked at her in amazement.

'Have you started drinking whisky?'

'I've been drinking it for a long time, you know. Even when I was still living at home. Only I didn't dare do it in front of you. Would you like a drink, Papa? You don't mind a drop of whisky from time to time either.'

'Whisky for everybody?'

With Antoine out of sight, they relaxed, as if on holiday.

'Not for me,' snapped Véronique.

Bernard, delighted with his role, was filling the glasses.

'Ice?'

'Just plain water.'

Antoine stayed away for quite a while. He gave himself time enough to exchange a few words with Fernande.

'How's it going?'

'Better than at the beginning, thanks to Jean-Loup.'

'What are you going to do with that candle and the wax?'

'We found a key to a vault in Father's wallet. Nobody wants to trust anyone else with it. We're going to seal it.'

He had also found a brown envelope. When he returned to the restaurant, he looked at the glasses on the table without saying a word, lit the candle, and handed the wax and the envelope to his brother.

'You're used to this kind of thing, Ferdinand.'

The judge felt a little ashamed. In the greyness of his office or in the course of visits to the scene of a crime, he had often had to deal with sordid affairs. And now he and his family were involved.

He put the key into the envelope, pasted down the flap, and melted the wax.

'What are we going to sign with?'

As if ironically, though unintentionally so, Antoine handed him a silver toothpick. Each of the brothers then initialled the five wax seals with it.

'What do we do with it now?'

'I suggest . . .'

Antoine and Bernard, who had spoken at the same time, stopped at the same time.

'Say it.'

'I suggest that Ferdinand keep the envelope.'

'That's exactly what I was going to say.'

'For once we agree.'

As if to celebrate the easing of the tension, Antoine went to the bar to get the bottle and a glass, poured himself a few drops, and put the bottle on the table.

'Help yourselves.'

Jean-Loup, who was sitting with his legs crossed, was watching the scene as if he were a stranger. The death of Auguste was forcing him to examine the family background, and he was observing things coolly and objectively. Perhaps he was more aware than his father of the distance between Ferdinand and himself.

In the flat, too, he was less at ease than in his pigeon-hole at the hospital. And when he looked at his sister from time to time, he felt no emotional tie.

'I think you're losing sight of an important point,' he finally declared in a neutral tone.

Everybody turned to him.

'Uncle Antoine spoke to us earlier about a certain Jason who was sentenced a few months ago to two years in prison for fraud.'

He turned to his father.

'It ought to be easy for you to find out which examining magistrate handled the affair.'

'That's no problem, because each of us more or less specializes. Probably Pénaillon or Mourine. They deal with such matters by the dozen.'

'Are you friendly with them?'

'I know them. We shake hands when we meet in the corridor.'

'I wonder whether, among the papers that were found at Villeneuve-Saint-Georges, of which there seems to have been a trunkful, he found any concerning my grandfather.'

The finding of the key had made them forget the shady adviser and had restored their optimism.

'What else is there in the wallet?'

The question was addressed to Ferdinand, and it was with great reluctance that he searched in his father's wallet. He first pulled out an identity card that had been renewed ten years before and a prescription for glasses signed by an oculist in the Rue du Temple.

'Did Father wear glasses?'

Antoine was the most surprised of all.

'I never saw him with them.'

'Do you know about such things?' asked Ferdinand, handing the paper to his son.

'Not much. It's for reading glasses, rather strong ones, it seems to me.'

The prescription, which was three years old, illustrated the old man's secrecy or sense of shame. His eyes had been getting weaker. He had had difficulty reading the newspaper. He had no doubt waited a long time before consulting an oculist in the neighbourhood.

The prescription reminded Antoine of what his father had been doing a few minutes before he collapsed. The old man was proudly showing a young couple a photograph of himself standing in front of his restaurant in 1920, when he was in the prime of life. He had continued to hold himself erect and to throw out his chest. He was proud of his vitality and laughed at Dr Patin, who prescribed medicines for him.

He had never ordered the glasses, but he had nevertheless kept the prescription in case they became absolutely necessary.

'Who is it?' asked Marie-Laure, who was leaning over her father.

He had taken from the wallet a faded photo with broken corners in which a two- or three-year-old boy was looking straight ahead as if he were very sure of himself and was defying the future.

'It's me. I didn't remember the picture.'

'I wasn't born yet,' said Antoine.

Ferdinand had been an only child at the time. Auguste had a bluish-black moustache that he set every night with a transparent gadget. His wife did the cooking for twenty-five or thirty people, and the menu was written in chalk on a slate.

There was also a photograph of Bernard on the day of his first communion and one of Antoine as a soldier.

They were all surprised. It had never occurred to them that Auguste might be sentimental, and yet he had kept the photos of his three sons in his old wallet.

The last photo, which was tiny and crackled, was protected by a plastic case. It had been cut out of a group picture, and if they had not found it in their father's wallet, the sons would never have recognized it.

It was their mother when she was very young, perhaps sixteen. She was wearing two braids, and the hair over her forehead was tousled. The collar of her dark dress, which covered her neck, had a lace collaret.

They found nothing else, except a copy of a birth certificate, also yellowed and crackled, which dated from the time of

Auguste's arrival in Paris. Was it a precautionary measure that his parents had taken, at a time when identity cards did not exist, in case he got lost or was injured in an accident?

'Ferdinand . . .'

Véronique was showing him her wrist-watch.

'Keep the wallet until we meet again so that we can each choose a few souvenirs.'

'Don't forget the envelope,' said Bernard.

Ferdinand put it gravely into his pocket and stood up.

'If Antoine has time tomorrow to go to the banks in the neighbourhood, which he knows better than we do, he might ask whether Father had an account or a vault in one of them. Will you have time, Antoine?'

'I may. I expect that as soon as people receive the announcement, they'll start dropping in.'

'Aren't you closing the restaurant?'

'It's not the custom to. Only on Tuesday.'

'If anything turns up, call me in court. Bernard, will you be at home?'

He would be there, in bed. Nicole foresaw it, for she had been unable to keep him from drinking, and he had reached the point where he was going to continue.

The meeting was ending better than it had begun. They looked at each other without quite knowing how to break up.

Ferdinand was putting on his grey overcoat, Nicole her leopard-skin coat, and Bernard his camel-hair, though he was having trouble finding the armholes.

Jean-Loup, who was coatless, was the only one who shook hands with Antoine.

'See you on Tuesday,' he said.

They all walked to the hallway, where they passed two children from the third floor who were dressed up in their Sunday best. They were followed by their parents.

'Pierre and Lina, let the people go by.'

And the parents nodded respectfully.

Chapter Six

Véronique, who was in her dressing-gown, had just finished putting her hair up in curlers. She called out from the bathroom, 'Aren't you undressing?'

It was ten in the evening. Ferdinand, who had not taken off his grey suit, which was a kind of uniform for him, was in the living-room. He was reading a magazine article, though his mind was elsewhere.

Upon leaving Antoine's place – the others were already saying and thinking 'Antoine's place' and not 'Father's place' – Jean-Loup had rushed off to the hospital and Marie-Laure had asked her parents, 'Could you drive me to Louveciennes?'

During the drive, they had been silent and preoccupied almost all the time, as if they all had a guilty conscience. About twenty cars, including two Rolls-Royces and a number of very smart sports cars, were parked in front of the villa to which the daughter was going.

'Whose house is it?'

'A fellow who runs a big advertising firm.'

Ferdinand and his wife had had dinner in a small restaurant in Versailles before going home, where they did not know what to do and where there was no television programme that interested them. Véronique had filed her nails. Her husband had read. They had fallen into the habit, without any particular reason, of going to bed earlier on Sunday than on other days. Besides, Ferdinand went to bed earlier and earlier, perhaps because he and his wife had nothing to say to each other.

The doorbell rang, and they both started.

'Do you mind going?'

He stood up, feeling intrigued and at the same time vaguely uneasy. Nobody ever rang their bell so late. When he opened the door, he saw Bernard, who was very excited, and Nicole, who was resigned and watchful.

'Excuse me, Ferdinand. . . . I can imagine what you're probably thinking, and I admit straight off that you're right: I'm drunk.'

He staggered towards the living-room and let his coat fall on the carpet without bothering to pick it up.

'Isn't your wife here? Véronique's a marvellous girl, and I'd like her to know that I think so.'

Nicole had been driving ever since they had left the restaurant. She knew that there was no point in going home. It was too late. Bernard had got under way. All she could do was hope for the best.

'One more, just one, Nicole. I absolutely must find that man. I've forgotten his name. It's not because I'm drunk. There are people like that, I can't manage to remember their names.'

'What does he do?'

'He's a lawyer. He's always being mentioned in the papers. We had a drink together a week ago. No, it was two weeks ago. It doesn't matter. Anyway, it's absolutely essential that I talk to him, you realize, because I'm the only one who smelled a rat, though I didn't let on. . . . Ferdinand's a judge, eh? Well, Ferdinand's a half-wit, he didn't understand a thing, or else he's in on it and if so he's a son of a bitch.'

They had wandered from bar to bar. She had signalled to the successive barmen, who knew her, to pour as little whisky as possible into their glasses. He had refused to have dinner and contented himself with nibbling peanuts.

He had finally found the man he was looking for, who really was a lawyer. The man was in a not much better state than he. Bernard had then prevailed upon Nicole to drive him to his brother's place.

'Is it any of my business or not? Am I a Mature or not, eh?'

Véronique, who was anxious, emerged from the bathroom with a towel tied around her head to hide the curlers.

'Don't be afraid, Véronique. . . . I know you're ashamed of Nicole because we live in sin. I swear to you that we'll be married in a month, and, if you really want us to, we'll even have a church wedding. . . . I was saying to my brother that you're a marvellous girl. Nicole thinks so too. She's furious because I've had one too many and because I'm disturbing you, but it was ab-so-lute-ly necessary.'

He was rarely in such a state. Oddly enough, he seemed

younger when he let himself go. One had the feeling that he was defenceless. He gave the impression of wanting to be taken for a man at any cost.

'In the first place,' he began, with a broad gesture, 'everything we said this afternoon is a lot of rubbish.'

He turned to Ferdinand with a look of distrust.

'Am I right, yes or no?'

'I don't know what you mean.'

'The key, for example, that was a lot of rubbish, right?'

'Sit down.'

He dropped into a chair, which he had not realized was so low, and for a moment he was surprised.

'Neither you nor I nor Antoine nor anyone has the right to go and open the vault, even with the key. . . . What do you have to say?'

'It's true that there are a certain number of formalities.'

'Formalities my eye!'

He was proud of himself. It was he, the youngest, the one who was regarded as a poor fool, who had discovered the truth of the matter.

Despite the fact that Ferdinand was a judge, he had let himself be taken in, unless it was he who had taken them all in.

'What does it say, Article . . . Article what, Nicole?'

'Which one?'

'The first one I asked you to write down.'

She took from her bag a red diary in which she had taken notes so as not to irritate him.

'774 . . .'

'Good! Have you got a statute book, Ferdinand?'

He was triumphing.

'I know the article you refer to.'

'Go and get your statute book.'

His brother came back with the book.

'An estate may be accepted unreservedly or without liability to debts beyond its assets.'

'Well and good! And who has the right to accept it only without liability to debts beyond its assets? Ha! Ha! Ha! Any one of the heirs . . . you see? . . . Véronique, if you want to be an angel, let me have something to drink.'

She looked at Nicole, who shrugged.

'Don't be afraid. . . . I know how to behave, and I won't soil your carpet.'

He laughed. He was master of the situation.

'I'm clear-headed, you understand? I'm drunk but clear-headed.'

He repeated the last word three or four times with great delight.

'It's because I'm clear-headed that I understood. . . . My friend . . . what's his name, Nicole?'

'Liotard.'

'Liotard . . . a great lawyer. . . . Do you know Liotard, Ferdinand?'

'I've heard of him.'

'We had a drink together, and I told him what was bothering me, because he's like a brother. . . . Excuse me! Not a real brother like you, you understood what I mean. . . . Now look at the article whose number Nicole is going to give you.'

'Article 793.'

Ferdinand read it in order to keep him quiet:

'The statement by an heir that he wishes to be considered as such only without liability to debts beyond its assets must be filed in the record office of the local court which . . .'

'Good! The local court. . . . Do you see what I'm getting at? In the next article the statute states that the declaration is followed by a faithful and exact inventory of the estate. . . . Am I clear-headed or not? . . . Thanks Véronique. . . . Here's to everyone's health. . . . To the health of our poor father. . . . They have three months in which to start the inventory, which may go on for a long time. . . . What's the upshot? . . . That Antoine can keep us waiting as long as he likes and during that time can fiddle the accounts.'

His mind dashed off in another direction.

'You see, Ferdinand, Antoine and we two aren't on an equal footing. You and I are poor idiots. . . . Yes we are! Yes we are! . . . I know what I'm saying. . . . You musn't be ashamed of it.

210

... Villains are never poor idiots. ... You may be a judge, but you earn hardly enough to live on, and me, I've never had any luck. ... I'm just as intelligent as Antoine ... even more ... only, I ...'

Words failed him. He took a swallow and frowned. His face was all red. He was pathetic. He looked at his brother with his big moist eyes.

'Nicole, what's his name again?'

'Liotard.'

'Right. ... Do you know him?'

'I've already told you.'

'I beg your pardon. ... He gave me his legal opinion at Jean's, a bar where you can find him almost any evening. ... Have you ever been to Jean's?'

'No.'

Never mind! He dropped the matter. He was searching his memory, anxious not to lose the thread. It was very hard, all the more so because he realized the importance of what he had to say.

'You were about to go to bed. ... I beg your pardon, Véronique. ... Only, tomorrow. ... To begin with ...'

To begin with what? In the car, he had planned what he was going to say. Standing at Jean's mahogany bar, Liotard had delivered a lecture on the laws governing inheritance. He knew the articles in the statute book by heart and reeled them off, giving the exact number of each and every one, like a juggler tossing balls into the air.

'I need money. I'm not trying to hide the fact, and I'm not ashamed of it. ... Honest people spend their time running after money. ... You need money too, Ferdinand. I dare you to say you don't.'

It was better to agree with him in order to avoid an outburst, for in that state he was capable of losing his temper, of stamping like a child, of saying what he thought about everyone. Nicole, who realized the danger, looked at Ferdinand and his wife beseechingly, as if pleading with them to be patient.

'All right! What was I saying?'

'That we needed money.'

'Now supposing Antoine accepts the inheritance only without
... how does it go?'

'Without liability to debts ...'

'That gimmick allows him to keep us waiting for months, for
years. ... That's not all. ... There's another article about joint
... joint ...'

'Joint property ...'

'If he wants to, Antoine has the right to run the restaurant
without selling it and without giving us anything. Is that fair?'

'Not completely ... more or less ...'

'Well? ... Are you beginning to understand? ... Who has the
upper hand? ... Did our father ever keep books? Did he know
anything about book-keeping? Who's been attending to money
matters for the last twenty years? ... We found a key, well and
good. ... But we don't have the right to use it before everyone
agrees to accept the inheritance without further discussion. ...
Without liability to debts. You get it?'

No. Ferdinand did not see what his brother was driving at.

'Either we accept and we get the money right away or we
accept only without liability to debts and we can wait for years,
until the restaurant's not worth a damn. ... What was it that
Antoine said? ... That it would probably be demolished in
three years. ... You know what Liotard ...'

He smiled, proud of having thought of the lawyer's name all
by himself.

'You know what Liotard called our affair? A hornet's nest.
... Without an inventory. Antoine tells us what he wants and
gives us whatever figures happen to suit him. ... With an inventory, he has all the time in the world. ... Correct?'

It was correct. Ferdinand, who had thought about the matter,
had deliberately avoided raising the question that afternoon.
Two days earlier, he had not been expecting that there would be
any change in his material situation, but ever since there had
been talk of millions, he had been as impatient as Bernard and
was making an effort to avoid complications.

He wasn't proud of himself. He kept telling himself that he
was acting in the way he was for Véronique's sake, so that she
would have a better life.

He, too, was jealous of Antoine, who had just proved to be

the rich member of the family. He was the least educated of the three, most probably the least intelligent. Fernande had been a street-walker, and yet the two of them were a real couple. There was a deep understanding between them.

'Let me have another drink Véronique. I swear it'll be the last. Don't worry, Nicole. As soon as I finish what I have to say, we'll go. Tomorrow I'll be ill, yes, I know ... I apologize. ... You'll have to take care of me. ... Ferdinand, don't you ever drink?'

'Very seldom.'

'You're lucky. When I get going, I make Nicole unhappy and I get angry with myself. You don't know Nicole. She's the one who refused to get married, because she was afraid it would damage my reputation. ... I did my best to explain to her that ...'

He stood up and, at the last second, avoided falling head-first on to the little table where he had put his glass. Regaining his balance, he went over to the young woman and kissed her hand.

'To begin with, all three of us are Father's sons, right? And the three photos were in his wallet, right or wrong? That's proof, and Antoine can say what he likes. ... If you and I can't come to an agreement, Antoine'll trick us. ... There's something else the lawyer said to me ... Liotard. ... You see that I remember everything, that I'm clear-headed. ... It's about our mother. ... Under what system were they married?'

'Joint estate ...'

'Consequently, she's entitled to half. ... If we go to the conciliation magistrate, she'll have to come along or she'll have to sign papers ...'

Véronique was looking at her husband in amazement, even with reproach in her eyes. Why hadn't he spoken to her about these possible complications?

'Could *you* drag Mama to the magistrate's office?'

'No.'

'Do you think she's still capable of signing her name? Someone has to hold her hand. ... Dr Patin knows very well that she's no longer in her right mind. In which case, as Liotard says, a guardian or family council has to be appointed.'

Again he was deep in his chair, with his head down. He kept running his hand over his forehead.

'We'll be taken in, Ferdinand. ... That's why I came. ... That's why I disturbed you. ... We musn't be taken in. ... We've been taken in all our life. ... You know me ... I'm a good chap. ... I trust people. ... It's because I trust them. ... I've drunk too much. ... When this is all over, I'll stop drinking. ... If I drink, it's because. ... Nicole?'

'What?'

'You remember what he said at the end? ... Excuse me ... I'm beginning to get mixed up. ... One more drink, Véronique, a tiny little one.'

'No!' exclaimed Nicole. 'If you let him have it, he'll fall asleep and I won't be able to take him home.'

'I'm clear-headed.'

'I know.'

'So, tell them ...'

Nicole was embarrassed. She looked at them hesitantly, one after the other.

'It's no business of mine. ... I didn't even know Liotard. ... He was tight and was listening to the sound of his own voice. His advice may be worthless. According to him, you must absolutely avoid getting involved with judges and you must get as much money from Antoine as possible. ... That's exactly how he put it. As for the conciliation magistrate and permission to open the vault, he claims that it's a trivial formality and that your mother's signature is enough, even if someone has to help her write her name.'

She was dizzy with confusion. It made her uncomfortable to see Véronique, who had always given her the cold shoulder, watching her with curiosity and even with budding sympathy.

'What do you think, Ferdinand?'

'I've got to think it over. I've got to reread the statute, because I've never dealt with common law and I have to refresh my memory.'

'A pig in a poke!' exclaimed Bernard, who had remained silent for some moments.

Since he did not explain what he meant but just sat there sleepily with a smug smile on his face, Nicole spoke up.

'Liotard said that it amounted to buying a pig in a poke. In order to be able to open the vault, you first have to accept the inheritance. But nobody knows what the vault contains.'

'We could also inherit debts,' mumbled Bernard, who tried to laugh and at the same time reached for his empty glass.

Véronique started.

'He was obviously joking. I think he was teasing Bernard. . . . All the same, he was bothered by the Jason matter.'

'I'll look into it tomorrow morning. Even if I have to postpone my interrogation until Tuesday – no, Wednesday.'

He was forgetting about his father's funeral.

'Come, Bernard. . . . Now that you've said what you had to say. . . . You're sleepy. . . . And so are Ferdinand and Véronique.'

'Do you agree, Ferdinand?'

'Of course.'

Neither of them made clear what it was that they agreed to, Bernard because he was incapable of doing so and Ferdinand because he had forced himself to say 'Of course' in order to get rid of his brother.

'Stand up.'

She helped him to get to his feet, picked up his coat from the floor, and handed it to him.

'You know, Ferdinand, it did something to me to see that photo of you when you were little. After all, we're brothers. Right? We ought to defend each other like brothers. That's what I said to Nicole, who didn't want me to come.'

It took several minutes to get him to the lift. Ferdinand and his wife leaned over the shaft and waited until they heard the front door close and the noise of a car going off.

*

The alarm rang at 5 a.m., as usual, and Antoine reached out in the darkness and turned it off before Fernande awoke. He groped his way through the bedroom, put the light on in the bathroom, and began to shave with the anxious look of a man who has a hard day ahead of him.

It was still dawn when he began his rounds of the vegetables, which smelled of damp earth, and then of the fish and shellfish sections.

He did not hurry. Plodding along, he shook the hands that were offered him here and there and said 'Thank you' when anyone mumbled 'My condolences, Antoine'.

He arrived at Léon's place and for a few moments silently watched the butcher cut up and dress meat. It was Léon who spoke first.

'My father won't admit it, but he had an awful shock. Yesterday I saw him walk up and down in front of the restaurant four or five times and look up at the windows on the first floor. He and Auguste were very fond of each other. They were the last two. And now my old man is waiting for his turn.'

A little later, after Antoine had given his order, Léon asked, 'Can I go and see him today?'

'Of course. . . . By the way, thanks for the flowers.'

'That's the least I could do.'

Jules had had time to open the shutters and start the coffee. There were more people than usual in the first room. People from Les Halles, as always at that time of day. The room smelled of spiked coffee and warm croissants. Antoine had the feeling that the people were not looking at him in quite the way they usually did. He was no longer Auguste's son. He had taken the old man's place and had become the boss.

'Jules, let me have a cup of coffee.'

Jules whispered in his ear, 'Some of them have asked whether they can go up and see him.'

'I'll tell you when I come down.'

Fernande had already thought about it. She was wearing a very simple black dress, the one she wore when she sat at the cashier's desk. She was helping Madame Ledru tidy up the flat and install the old lady in her chair.

'I suppose they'll be coming by?'

'Yes. Some of them downstairs have already asked.'

'They can come up. Liselotte will have to take my place at the desk at lunchtime. I've just received a phone call from Riom, from someone named Gabriel Mature, who, if I understood correctly, is a distant cousin of yours. He's an assistant stationmaster. He said that since he doesn't have to pay his fare, he'll be glad to come to the funeral if you find a room for him in the neighbourhood.'

'What did you say to him?'

'That we'd find one. I'll attend to it in a little while.'

He went downstairs.

'They can go up,' he said to Jules.

Then he went to the kitchen to work with Julien Bernu. As Fernande was too busy in the flat, it was he who wrote the names of the day's specials on the menus.

When he went out, flowers were being delivered. There would be other deliveries throughout the day. Because of the black hangings, they could not open the casement window in the room where the coffin was, and the smell was getting sickening. It had already begun to spread through the house.

At about nine-thirty he entered the Crédit Lyonnais, the bank in the Rue Saint-Honoré where he had an account. He knew the assistant manager, Monsieur Grangier, who attended to his affairs when necessary.

'My condolences, Monsieur Mature. I heard about what happened to your father. As a matter of fact, when does the funeral start from the house?'

'Tomorrow morning, at nine.'

'I'll be there, of course. Is there anything I can do for you?'

'My brothers and I are rather puzzled. My father didn't leave any papers, but we found a key in his wallet.'

He took his bunch of keys from his pocket and separated the vault key from the others.

'It's about an eighth of an inch longer than this one, and shinier. The ring is round instead of oval, and the number 113 is engraved on it.'

'Have you got it with you?'

Antoine blushed before answering.

'No. . . . I gave it to my elder brother.'

'If it's a vault key, as I have every reason to think, it's probably from the Comptoir d'Escompte, because their keys resemble your description. Do you suppose your father banked with a local branch?'

'He seldom left the neighbourhood.'

'Would you like me to ring up my colleague? There's a branch in the Boulevard de Sébastopol. One moment . . .'

217

Among the several telephones on his desk he chose the one that was an outside line. He dialled the number.

'May I please speak to Monsieur Favret. . . . Tell him that Monsieur Grangier would like to speak to him. . . . Have a seat, Monsieur Mature. . . . Hello! . . . Favret? . . . Very well, thanks. . . . Yours too? . . . Give her my regards. . . . I'm calling for a bit of information. . . . The father of one of our good clients has just died . . . Mature, yes. . . . What? . . . That's exactly why I rang you. . . . His son is in my office. . . . They found a key with the number 113. . . . No paper, no. . . . It's in your bank? . . . One moment, I'll ask him. . . . There are several heirs, aren't there? Three brothers, if I'm not mistaken. . . . Is your mother still alive? . . . Favret? The mother and three sons. . . . They're all over twenty-one. . . . The conciliation magistrate. . . . Thank you very much. . . . I'll tell him . . .'

He was somewhat like a magician who has just performed a trick.

'As you see, it wasn't complicated. It was at the Comptoir d'Escompte in the Boulevard de Sébastopol that your father had a safe-deposit box. . . . On the other hand he never opened an actual account. I suppose it was because you looked after his affairs. . . . All that's necessary is for you and your brothers to appear before the district magistrate in the Rue du Louvre, or even, I think, his clerk.'

'What about my mother?'

'Can't she go with you?'

'She no longer leaves her bedroom.'

'You'll be given a form for her to sign. . . . I'm delighted to have been able to help, especially since you probably have your hands full.'

Antoine hardly noticed that spring was in the air, that women were wearing light-coloured dresses, and that men, including himself, were not wearing coats for the first time that year.

At home, there was a continuous stream of people going up and down the old staircase, and every fifteen minutes a messenger boy arrived with flowers or a wreath.

He rang up the court and had to wait quite a while before getting Ferdinand at the other end.

'This is Antoine.'

'As a matter of fact, I expect to come and see you in an hour. Will you be there?'

'I will. . . . I found the bank.'

'How did you manage?'

'I asked the assistant manager of mine. I described the key to him, and he rang up the Comptoir d'Escompte in the Boulevard de Sébastopol. Papa had a box, but not an account.'

'I'll be over.'

Too bad for René Mauvis. He could wait till Wednesday. He was a nobody, the kind of person who was shoved about and squeezed in crowded Métros at 6 p.m., and no one would ever have talked about him but for the fact that he was suspected of two murders. As for the lawyer, Ferdinand had already rung him up.

'I'm terribly sorry about upsetting your schedule. The questioning could have taken place on Saturday, and it's not my fault if I'm obliged to put it off until Wednesday. . . . No! Absolutely impossible. . . . Tomorrow's my father's funeral.'

At the same time, Antoine was relieving Fernande for a little while so that she could go out for a breath of air. The flat on the first floor was suffocating. There were flowers everywhere. They overflowed the chapel and invaded the living-room, where the couch was covered with them.

Fernande had placed a silver tray on a small table, and on it lay about twenty visiting cards, some with the corner turned down.

It was all new to Antoine. There had never been a death in the family, and he felt bewildered. He did not recognize the two undertaker's assistants who came to shut the coffin.

He stood in the living-room, not far from the open door, as Fernande had done. The visitors hesitated for a moment and then went up to him and shook hands, while muttering something more or less unintelligible.

'Thank you.'

He did not know all of them, for there were many who were not from Les Halles. Workmen who had done a job for them looked completely different because they were wearing suits, whereas Antoine had always seen them in their working clothes.

It took old Hector, Léon's father, a long time to climb the stairs, and when he arrived, the coffin was shut. He remained standing, very erect, looking at it a long time, without paying any attention to the people who came and went.

Then he dipped the sprig of holly in the holy water and solemnly made a cross in the air above his friend's body.

He would live another year or two, perhaps only until the following winter. Then it would be Antoine's turn to greet him one last time in the nearby flat.

When Fernande returned, she whispered to him, 'Your brother's upstairs. I thought it was better to ask him to come up because they've started to set the tables downstairs and it won't be long before the staff has lunch.'

He went up to the second floor and found Ferdinand standing in the middle of the living-room.

'Not too tired?' asked the judge. 'I didn't expect such a crowd.'

'Neither did I.'

'Unfortunately, we can't help you. It's so long since I left the neighbourhood that I no longer know anyone. And obviously Véronique can't help either.'

'Obviously.'

'I thought it would be better if you and I had a personal talk. Bernard and Nicole came to see us last evening.'

Antoine looked at him, but with hardly any surprise. He felt he had no contact with reality that morning, and he caught himself wondering what his brother did at home in the evening.

There were people in the restaurant, people on the first floor, and Ferdinand in his own flat. And in an hour, immediately after the staff had lunch, he would have to take up his post in the Side-show and hand the menu to his customers.

'Bernard had been drinking and was rather far gone. . . . You know what he's like. . . . Now that he's caught a glimpse of a fortune, he wants it right away and is scared stiff of not getting his hands on it.'

'What's on his mind?'

'The opening of the safe-deposit box, naturally. But first of all, I have a question to ask you. I suppose, of course, that you are going to declare that you're an heir.'

'What do you mean? Do you mean I'm not if I don't?'

'Of course you are. There are certain legal details. Now listen to me. . . . I've given the matter a great deal of thought. We have two ways of settling the inheritance. Each of us can declare that he's an heir without liability to debts, in which case it's the local court that deals with the matter and that appoints the experts . . .'

Antoine, who only a few minutes before had been in the dead man's bedroom, looked at his brother and frowned.

'Is there anyone who's asking for an inventory?'

'Not I. . . . Nor Bernard either. . . . We both trust you, and as for Mama, poor thing, it's self-evident . . .'

Then why did Ferdinand look so embarrassed and anxious? He was rubbing and twisting his hands the way he did when he was a child and had to show his father a report card that he wasn't proud of.

'I don't see what can complicate things. My books are at your disposal. They can be examined by any accountant you like. As for the business, it's easy to tell approximately what it's worth.'

'You're right. Or rather, you'd be right if there weren't that vault. We have no idea how much money our father left. In order to open the box, we have to get permission from the judge.'

'I know.'

'I rang him up a little while ago. . . . All three of us the sons, will have to sign, in his presence, a statement that we accept the inheritance.'

'What about Mama?'

Ferdinand avoided looking at him.

'If we admit that she's not in her right mind, there'll be complications. . . . I've brought a form for her to sign.'

'She's incapable of writing.'

'Not if your wife holds her hand.'

Antoine almost jumped to his feet with indignation.

'What's going on anyway?' he exclaimed, trying not to lose

his self control. The blood had rushed to his head, and he looked at his brother grimly.

'Nothing's going on. I'm trying to explain things as simply as possible. The law provides that, if there are no minors, the rightful heirs can divide the inheritance without formalities. I've come to ask you, in Bernard's name and my own, if that's all right with you.'

'But what about Mama?'

'I don't think we're wronging anyone by helping her sign a paper of which she would approve if she were in her right mind. The vault has to be opened, right or wrong?'

'Yes, it has to be, but . . .'

Antoine was about to say, 'But we might wait until Father was buried.'

He was being rushed, he was being hounded. He began to wonder why his brothers were in such a hurry and whether they were setting a trap.

'In that case, the box will be opened at two-thirty this afternoon. I've made an appointment with the judge for two o'clock. Each of us will sign the same paper that Mama signs. Here, this one's for Mama. Ask your wife to . . .'

Antoine took it from his hands and left. He was no longer red, but pale. He pushed aside, almost roughly, some strangers who were barring his way on the landing. He motioned to Fernande, who was receiving condolences, to follow him for a moment, and he took her into the mother's bedroom.

'It seems that it's necessary that she sign. . . Can you hold her hand?'

She looked at him in surprise.

'Did Ferdinand . . . ?'

He nodded.

'Mightn't we have trouble?'

'He claims we won't. If we don't have her signature, we'll have to declare that she's insane and we'll be involved in court action.'

She was more wary than he.

'Antoine, have you thought it over?'

He was so disgusted that he would have done anything at that moment, would have signed anything in order to have peace.

'Do it. . . . I'll take your place meanwhile.'

He went into the living-room and stood in the middle of the floor. His face was frozen, and he kept mumbling mechanically to those who came up to him and put out their hand, 'Thank you. . . . It's kind of you. . . . Thank you. . . . Yes, tomorrow at nine. . . . Thank you . . .'

It seemed to him an eternity before Fernande returned and slipped the paper into his hand.

'Did you do it?'

'It wasn't easy.'

Then he went up to join his brother.

Chapter Seven

'Did your wife manage it?'

Antoine handed him the paper without saying anything, without even having glanced at it. Ferdinand put it into his wallet, but there was no sign of his leaving.

'I've got to talk to you about this Jason. . . . I'd rather that Bernard weren't present, because he'd start worrying again.'

Antoine looked at him with indifference.

'It was my colleague Mourine who dealt with the affair, just as I thought. I had a short talk with him this morning. Jason was one of those shady business advisers of which there are still quite a number around the Porte Saint-Martin, the Porte Saint-Denis, and Les Halles. Some of them specialize in buying and selling businesses. Others make loans at high interest. Still others help the workmen and shopkeepers draw up their income-tax declaration and keep their account books. . . . Jason did all those things. In recent years, the public prosecutor's office stuck its nose into his affairs two or three times, but without ever finding anything objectionable. . . . His clients had confidence in him, and he acted as their accountant, notary, lawyer, and banker. . . . Do you see what I mean? . . . He was what simple people, especially in the country and small towns, call a business adviser. . . . People like him are wily. . . . From what I gather, because it's not my field, he sometimes bought annuities. . . . He also began – and even reputable notaries are sometimes tempted to do the same thing – to speculate with his clients' money. . . . One fine day he found himself in a tight spot. He was unable to pay certain sums that he owed. The news spread like wildfire in the neighbourhood, and his clients got panicky and turned against him. . . . To my colleague Mourine, it's a common affair. . . . There were about thirty plaintiffs in all. . . . An examination of the books and papers that were seized at Villeneuve-Saint-Georges revealed, as he expected, that the book-keeping was falsified. . . . I wanted to know whether Father was one of those who filed a complaint. It seems he wasn't. . . . Mourine has entrusted me, as a friend, with this memorandum book, which was seized with the rest of the documents. It's a personal favour.'

He took from his pocket a black, rather large memorandum book covered with oilcloth. There was a rubber band around it.

'Jason wrote down the names and addresses of his clients and crossed out, in red ink, the names of those who died, because he worked mainly with old people. . . . Father's name is in the book. Here's the page. . . . As you can see, under the name and address there are only dates, without any other statement. . . . It starts in September 1947 . . .'

'When Father signed our partnership agreement.'

'After that he wrote down other dates, in a column: March 1948, February 1949, March 1950, and so on. Occasionally, though rarely, there's a mention of other times of the year, August, November, and once December.'

Antoine handed the book back to his brother.

'I'm afraid,' sighed Ferdinand, 'that we're in for some unpleasant surprises. The thing that reassures me is that Father wasn't one of the plaintiffs. . . . It's time for me to be going. . . . I still have to let Bernard know about our appointment. Two o'clock in the office of the conciliation magistrate of the first arrondissement, in the Rue du Louvre.'

'I'll go down with you.'

Antoine did not offer him his hand, nor did he go and see Fernande. He went straight to the kitchen and then took up his post in the second room to receive and place the customers who were beginning to arrive.

He had pasted a notice on the glass door: *The Restaurant will be closed on Tuesday.*

The odour of the flowers had spread to the ground floor, where it mingled with the smells from the kitchen. He made the same gestures he made every day, uttered the same words, but he did so mechanically. Liselotte was attending to both the cloakroom and the cashier's desk.

He had not had lunch. He contented himself with eating a cold chicken leg during one of his visits to the kitchen.

François, the red-headed waiter, had taken up lunch for Fernande and the old woman. The first room was flooded with sunlight, which was reflected by the tin bar and the bottles. That morning the sun had also bathed the vegetables, fruits, and flowers in Les Halles, but Antoine had not particularly noticed it.

Usually, the first thing he did when he left the house in the morning was to look at the sky. Like a peasant, he could almost tell what time it was from the position of the sun, from the angle of the rays in the restaurant or the flat.

But he had been insensitive to it since Saturday, and the day before, he had hardly realized that spring had suddenly arrived.

When he went upstairs, his mother was in bed and Fernande was tidying up the room. A glance at her husband was enough for her to see that he was out of sorts.

'Are you upset? Is anything wrong? Was it Ferdinand's visit?'

'Not only that,' he replied, waving his hand as if he were shooing off something impalpable.

'Are you going out?'

'I'm going with them to the magistrate's office. And from there we'll all go to the bank.'

When he got to the Rue du Louvre, he found Ferdinand waiting in the street.

'Bernard hasn't arrived yet,' said his brother, looking at his watch. 'He's late.'

At that very moment, a car stopped at the kerb. Nicole was at the wheel. Bernard seemed to be all right, though he had a faraway look in his eyes, as if he were elsewhere.

'Hello!' he called out.

And Nicole said very quickly to Ferdinand, 'Don't worry. I have no intention of going with you. I wanted to be sure he'd keep his appointment. He didn't feel well this morning, and I had to give him an injection.'

The magistrate handled the matter with great dispatch.

'Antoine Mature? . . . Please sign here. . . . And then here. . . . Thank you. . . . I suppose that you are Bernard Mature and that you've been informed . . .'

'Where do I sign?'

'Here. . . . And here again.'

Less than ten minutes after entering the office, they received permission to open the box. Nicole and the car were no longer there.

The three brothers started walking to the Boulevard de Sébastopol. They had nothing to say to each other. Each was preoccupied with his own thoughts. They walked along the streets where they had played as children, and Antoine remembered in particular the way they had played when the street cleaners, who were armed with water hoses as powerful as those of firemen, washed away the odds and ends of vegetables and other refuse. The great sport, in the summer, was to run through the jet. Ferdinand had done it too, and then Bernard. Did his brothers remember?

The manager of the Comptoir d'Escompte, a lean, dapper-looking man with greyish hair, was waiting for them. He shook hands with them when they arrived.

'This way, gentlemen.'

He led them to the basement, where a uniformed guard opened a grille and then a huge iron-clad door.

'Do you have the permit from the magistrate?'

Ferdinand handed it to him.

'Excellent. Who has the key?'

'Here it is.'

It was embarrassing for Ferdinand to open the envelope with the five seals. The manager raised his eyebrows when he saw it.

The manager opened a first lock with a key of his own and then a second with the one that had just been given to him.

There was a moment of almost agonizing silence. The three brothers were watching as if they were in suspense, as if they half expected to find the box empty.

'If you need me, please send for me. I'm entirely at your disposal.'

He walked away briskly. His new shoes squeaked. Behind the brothers were tables and chairs. In a corner, near the grille, the impassive guard pretended to be looking elsewhere.

Ferdinand looked as if he were asking his brothers what he should do. Then he reached into the box, took out a pile of documents, and laid them on the table. They were stocks and bonds, and the text of most of them was in English. They were arranged in packets, each of which was held together by a rubber band.

Neither of the brothers knew English. Some of the texts were in Spanish, but the brothers did not know Spanish either.

'We'll have to send for him,' suggested Bernard.

'Unless one of you two knows what they're about.'

'Would you like me to inform the manager?' asked the guard.

'Please.'

They were underground, surrounded by thick cement that deadened all sounds. At a nearby table a woman of about forty, who was slowly clipping coupons from a pile of documents in front of her, occasionally glanced quizzically at the three brothers.

What was one to make of them? They hardly dared look at each other. The fluorescent lights made them look paler than they were, almost greenish. They sat there as if they were suspended in time, in space, with their eyes fixed on the grille, the staircase, waiting for the little man who was going to deliver his verdict.

'Did you send for me, gentlemen?'

As the two others remained silent, Ferdinand again spoke up.

'We'd like to know the approximate value of these stocks.'

The manager glanced at the first packet.

'Canadian gold mines . . .'

Then at the second.

'Colombian mines . . .'

A third, a fourth. When he came to the last packet, he looked at them in surprise.

'I suppose it was your father who bought these stocks. May I ask you whether you expect them to be worth a large sum?'

'Our father had close on a hundred thousand francs to invest every year.'

'Do you know who advised him?'

'Probably a business adviser in the neighbourhood.'

Bernard, whose patience was exhausted, was biting his nails, as when he was a child.

'Can you take action against him?'

'He died in prison.'

'That doesn't surprise me. . . . I regret very much to inform you, gentlemen, that you won't get ten thousand francs for all these stocks, provided you find a buyer, which I doubt you will.'

There remained in the vault a bulky manila envelope with a rubber band around it. Ferdinand's fingers trembled as he opened it.

The envelope contained four packets of notes adding up to ten thousand francs each and two thousand eight hundred and fifty francs in small notes.

The two others seemed puzzled, but Antoine had already recognized the envelope he had given his father.

'It's Papa's share of last year's profits,' he explained. 'I paid him that sum on 3 February, the day after the inventory.'

'Do you still need me, gentlemen?'

Bernard broke in.

'Is there any chance of these stocks going up?'

'They're not even quoted any more. Some of them never were. As for the South American stocks, they have to do with mines that were nationalized without compensation.'

'What are we to do with them?'

'Whatever you like. . . . Do you want to keep the box?'

The end of the conversation was pitiful. Antoine's two

brothers looked to him like ghosts that were tossing about in an unreal universe.

The trim little man took on the bearing of a kind of god who had just issued his verdict, and they almost expected to see him snigger.

What memory would he retain of his meeting with the Mature brothers?

'Where are you going?' called Ferdinand to Antoine, who had started to leave.

'Home.'

'One moment. . . . We'd better leave together.'

He turned to the manager.

'May we keep the vault a few days?'

'In what name?'

'In the names of the three of us.'

'All you need do is give a specimen signature at the desk. . . . I'll prepare the forms.'

Ferdinand put the stocks back into the vault. He was unable to carry them under his arm because he had no paper in which to wrap them.

'What am I to do with the money?'

'Let's go somewhere else and talk about it.'

'Shall I take it?'

'I ask that we take it,' said Bernard, who looked as though he were about to cry.

When they got upstairs, each of them signed a form without seeing the manager again. Outside, the sun was shining brightly. A department store was having a sale, and women were fingering linens that were being displayed on stands which were set up on the pavement.

'What about having a drink somewhere?'

Antoine preferred not to go back to the restaurant with them. They entered the cool shade of a big café and walked to a corner where there was hardly anyone.

Bernard ordered a cognac and his two brothers a glass of beer.

'I wonder whether Father went mad?'

'It was Jason . . .' began Ferdinand.

He broke off, waiting for the drinks to be served. Bernard gulped down his cognac and ordered another.

'Be careful. Don't forget that tomorrow's the funeral.'

'I don't give a damn about the funeral.'

He checked his sobs.

'You two aren't short of money . . . but if I don't shell out ten thousand francs before the end of the week, God knows where I'll be. . . . Maybe in your office!' he snapped bitterly at Ferdinand. 'And all because our father thought he was cleverer than other people, whereas he was just an old idiot.'

'It was Jason . . .'

'What do you mean, Jason?'

'We talked about it yesterday. Father trusted him.'

'And Jason sold him those stocks?'

'Probably. . . . Father imagined that in that way he'd be leaving us a fantastic fortune. . . . That's one of the reasons why he never talked to us about money. He wanted to surprise us.'

'Why didn't he lodge a complaint when Jason was arrested?'

Antoine, who was lost in a kind of reverie, was asking himself the same question. He barely heard what his brothers were saying. He was the one who had known their father best, and he imagined how terrible a blow it must have been to the old man when he learned that the man he had trusted was nothing but a swindler.

To have lodged a complaint along with the others would have been to admit he had been naïve. It would also have been to admit to his sons that he was not leaving them the inheritance they were expecting.

He had worked all his life, ever since the age of twelve, to accumulate a fortune, counting every sou, and all that remained of it was the restaurant, which was really run by Antoine.

He had lived for months with a sense of shame, knowing that when he was gone he would leave behind him bitterness instead of regret.

Antoine had the feeling that he had never understood his father so well, his peasant character, his humbleness and pride.

'What do we do with the money?' asked Bernard at last. He was so impatient and so filled with anguish that he could no longer bear it.

For him it was exactly as when he went to see one of his brothers about a loan. He would start by asking for thousands of francs for a terrific deal. Little by little he would reach the point of being satisfied with two or three hundred francs, mere pocket money.

He had just lost a fortune. The future had collapsed in a few minutes. There nevertheless were bank notes in Ferdinand's pocket, notes that he could feel, that would enable him to deal with what was most urgent, to delude himself for a few weeks, to feel that he was on the crest of a wave.

'What do you think, Antoine?'

'You can divide it between you, as a partial payment of what I owe you for the restaurant.'

'Don't you want us to sign a receipt?'

'I don't need a receipt.'

He stood up.

'If you don't mind, Fernande's waiting for me.'

He had no desire to be present when the money was divided amidst the glasses on the table, beneath the eyes of the indifferent waiter.

Chapter Eight

One would have thought that the whole little world of Les Halles, all the shopkeepers in the neighbourhood, were meeting in the Rue de la Grande-Truanderie. Old Chaussard, dressed up in his Sunday best, was standing very erect on the pavement opposite the restaurant. Beside him was his son, who was wearing a black suit and black tie.

Women had come as they were, in their old working clothes, abandoning their stalls for a moment, and there were some who were drying their eyes with the corner of an apron.

Gabriel, the second cousin from Riom, had brought his wife and three children, and they were standing in the private chapel, where there was no longer room enough for those who walked by the coffin at the last minute.

Fernande, Véronique, and Nicole remained behind, while the

three brothers walked side by side behind the hearse, which was moving slowly in the direction of the Church of Saint-Eustache.

The air was mild. The sun was shining again. Behind the brothers, the dark crowd wound its way over three hundred yards, and the bells were tolling in a cloudless sky.

The brothers did not say a word. Nor did they look at each other. The master of ceremonies, who was wearing a two-pointed hat, led them to their places in the first row, in the semi-darkness of the church, and they remained standing while the chairs grated behind them on the stone floor.

The rear door remained open, for the crowd overflowed into the street. A big diamond-shaped patch of sunlight stood out in the dimness.

At the offertory, everyone put his hand into his pocket mechanically.

'*Pater Noster . . .*'

The priest, who was wearing a black chasuble, walked around the catafalque and swung the censer. A young choirboy trotted behind him and knelt in front of the tabernacle as he went by.

'*Et ne nos inducas in tentationem . . .*'

The voices of the choirboys in the rood-loft flooded every nook and corner of the huge nave.

'Amen . . .'

Antoine's face was flushed, and he could feel that his ears were red. The following day, he would find all the men and women who filled the church back at their posts in Les Halles and around it, as if nothing had happened. About 7 a.m., after talking with Léon behind the red iron bars of the butcher's shop, he would ask Jules to give him his morning cup of coffee. In a few years Les Halles would disappear. The sheds would be dismantled as if they were children's toys. The façades of the houses would come down first, then the floors and staircases, revealing wallpaper with marks of furniture.

The man in the two-pointed hat touched Antoine's sleeve. Antoine followed him. Or rather he followed Ferdinand, who, as eldest brother, led the procession.

Outside, people were jostling each other. Not only was the

hearse loaded with flowers, but two cars were needed to transport all the other wreaths and bouquets.

All one could see was heads, hundreds of heads, and, somewhere above them, the stiff banner of the Auvergnats of Paris.

As Antoine went by, someone – he didn't know who – shook his hand furtively. A moment later he was in one of the cars with his brothers.

It took another ten minutes for the funeral procession to get under way. In the car in front of them Antoine could see the priest's white surplice and the blond hair of the choirboy.

They drove slowly through Les Halles between two hedges of silent spectators. When they reached the quais of the Seine, the cars began to speed up.

The three brothers sat quietly, without speaking, as if each were ignoring the other's presence. They were now riding between rows of houses. There were balconies, with clothes drying on the railings. Then they came to the suburbs, with their cheap housing projects and empty lots.

Cars passed them. The passengers turned around to see the hearse and tried to make out the faces of the people in the cars that were following it.

Flowers were budding, and little tufts of delicate green grass were sprouting. Trees were flowering here and there. Powerful jets were watering the land around the walls of a market-garden, and a woman was bending over and picking leeks.

In a little while they would be back in the restaurant, in the Side-show, where tables had been set up side by side, as for a wedding.

They would again see Gabriel, the stationmaster, and his wife, and the old woman who lived in Saint-Hippolyte and of whom they had caught only a glimpse, and others too who were more or less related to the family, people who for a brief spell had played a part in their father's life.

Was it really Auguste who was in the hearse which they saw from time to time when it rounded a corner?

To Antoine, perhaps to others too, he was not only dead. He no longer existed. Nothing of him remained. Nor had he left anything behind.

There had once been the sixteen-year-old blonde girl with tousled hair whose photograph he had kept in his wallet all his life. There had been the restaurant in Les Halles, with its sausages and hams and huge loaves of bread, the restaurant in the photograph which he had been proudly showing to a couple a moment before being struck down and dragging the tablecloth and dishes along with him.

There had been children, first Ferdinand, then Antoine, then Bernard, all of whom had crawled at one time or another in the sawdust.

They had been a family. Auguste had had a wife and three sons.

A wife who now had to be spoon-fed and whose signature had been stolen the night before so that it could be transformed into money as fast as possible.

Three sons who had been brothers, who had slept together, who had all been afraid of the dark, who had all known the same joy of romping in the sun.

All three of them were now sitting in the car, all of them silent, without anything to say to each other, without daring to speak, because old Auguste was dead and they had become strangers.

All that remained in Les Halles was the tin bar and the hams and sausages in the window. When the house itself disappeared, Antoine and Fernande would probably build a hotel somewhere, preferably by the sea, and they would grow old together without leaving anything behind, except money that would be squabbled over by Jean-Loup's children, perhaps by those of Marie-Laure too if she ever married, and by Bernard grown old and still in quest of a fortune.

Antoine looked at the two faces in front of him.

They were as empty as his.

Épalinges
17 March, 1966

Maigret and the Minister

Translated from the French
by Moura Budberg

Chapter One

Every evening when he came home Maigret stopped at the same spot on the pavement, just after the gas-lamp, and raised his eyes to the lighted windows of his flat. It was an automatic movement. Probably if he had been asked point-blank whether there was a light there or not he would have hesitated before replying. In the same way, almost as if it were a superstition with him, he began unbuttoning his coat between the second and third floors and searching for the key in the pocket of his trousers, though invariably the door opened as soon as he stepped on the door-mat.

These were rites that had taken years to become established and on which he depended more than he would have cared to admit. It was not raining tonight, so it did not apply, but his wife, for instance, had a special way of taking his wet umbrella from his hand at the same time as she bent to kiss him on the cheek.

He brought out the traditional question:

'No telephone calls?'

She replied, closing the door:

'Yes, there was one. I'm afraid it's hardly worth while taking off your coat.'

The day had been grey, neither hot nor cold, with a sudden shower towards two o'clock in the afternoon. At the Quai des Orfèvres, Maigret had attended only to routine business.

'Did you have a good dinner?'

The light in their flat was warmer, more intimate than at the office. He could see the newspapers and his slippers waiting for him beside his armchair.

'I dined with the Chief, Lucas and Janvier at the Brasserie Dauphine.'

Afterwards the four of them had gone to a meeting of the

237

Police Provident Fund of which, for three years running and much against his will, Maigret had been elected vice-president.

'You've got time for a cup of coffee. Take your coat off for a minute. I said you wouldn't be back before eleven.'

It was half past ten. The meeting had not lasted long. There had been time for some of them to have a half pint in a bar and Maigret had come home on the Métro.

'Who was it that telephoned?'

'A minister.'

Standing in the middle of the sitting-room, he frowned at her.

'What Minister?'

'The Minister of Public Works. Point, I think he said.'

'That's right, Auguste Point. He telephoned here? In person?'

'Yes.'

'You didn't tell him to ring the Quai des Orfèvres?'

'He wanted to speak to you personally. He has to see you very urgently. When I said you weren't in, he wanted to know if I was the servant. He sounded upset. I told him I was Madame Maigret. He apologized, wanted to know where you were and when you would be back. He gave me the impression of being a timid man.'

'That's not his reputation.'

'He even wanted to know if I was alone or not. And then he explained that his call was to be kept secret, that he wasn't calling from the Ministry but from a public booth and that it was important for him to be in touch with you as quickly as possible.'

While she was speaking, Maigret watched her, still frowning, with a look that proclaimed his distrust of politics. It had happened several times in the course of his career that he had been approached by a statesman, a deputy or senator or some high official, but it had always been through the proper channels. He would be summoned to the Chief's office and the conversation would always begin: 'I'm sorry, my dear Maigret, to put you in charge of a business you won't like.'

And indeed they invariably turned out to be pretty unsavoury affairs.

He was not personally acquainted with Auguste Point; had

never seen him in the flesh. He was not the kind of man to be often quoted in the newspapers.

'Why didn't he ring up the Quai?'

He was really talking to himself. But Madame Maigret replied even so:

'How do I know? I'm only repeating what he said to me. First of all, that he was speaking from a public box . . .'

This detail had particularly impressed Madame Maigret to whom a Minister of the Republic was an individual of some importance, not to be imagined creeping in the dark into a public telephone box at the corner of some street.

'. . . Then he said that you were not to go to the Ministry, but to his private apartment which he keeps . . .'

She consulted a scrap of paper on which she had made some notes:

'. . . at 27 Boulevard Pasteur. You don't need to wake the concierge, it's on the fourth floor, on the left.'

'He's waiting there for me?'

'He'll wait as long as he can. He has to be back at the Ministry before midnight.'

Then, in a different tone, she asked:

'Do you think it's a hoax?'

He shook his head. It was certainly unusual, bizarre, but it didn't sound like a hoax.

'Will you have some coffee?'

'No thanks, not after the beer.'

Still standing, he poured himself a drop of sloe gin, took a fresh pipe from the mantlepiece and moved towards the door.

'See you soon.'

Back in the Boulevard Richard-Lenoir, the humidity that had hung in the air all day had changed to a dust-like fog that threw a halo round the street lamps. He did not take a taxi, for it was as quick to reach the Boulevard Pasteur by Métro; besides, he did not feel he was on official business.

All the way, as he stared mechanically at the moustachioed gentleman reading the newspaper opposite him, he was wondering what it could possibly be that Auguste Point wanted of him and why he had arranged for them to meet so urgently and so mysteriously.

All he knew of Auguste Point was that he was a lawyer from the Vendée, as far as he could remember from La Roche-sur-Yon, and that he had come into politics late in life. He was one of those deputies elected after the war for their personal qualities and their conduct during the occupation.

What that conduct had been exactly Maigret did not know. Yet, while others of his colleagues had come and gone and left no trace behind them, Auguste Point had been re-elected time after time, and three months ago, when the last Cabinet was formed, he had been given the Public Works portfolio.

The Superintendent had heard no scandal about him of the kind that circulate around most politicians. Nor was there any gossip about his wife or his children, if he had any.

By the time he left the Métro at the Pasteur station, the fog had grown thick and yellow and Maigret could taste its dusty flavour on his lips. He saw no one in the boulevard; heard only some steps in the distance, towards Montparnasse, and in the same direction a train that whistled as it left the station.

A few windows were still lit and gave an impression of peace and security in the fog. These houses, neither rich nor poor, neither old nor new and divided into flats all very similar to one another, were inhabited mainly by people of the middle class, teachers, civil servants, employees who took the Métro or the bus to work at the same time every morning.

He pressed the street button and, when the door opened, muttered an indistinct name at the concierge as he moved towards the lift. It was a very narrow lift, designed for two. Smoothly and noiselessly, it began its slow ascent past a dimly lit staircase. The doors on all floors were of an identical dark brown; even the door-mats were alike.

He rang the bell on the left, and the door opened immediately as if someone had been waiting inside with a hand on the knob.

Auguste Point stepped outside and sent the lift down again; Maigret had not thought of doing that.

'I'm sorry to disturb you at such a late hour,' he murmured, 'Will you come in, please?'

Madame Maigret would have been disappointed, for he resembled as little as possible her idea of a minister. He was about

240

the same build and height as the Superintendent, though squarer and tougher looking, one might say more of true peasant stock. His roughly chiselled features, the large nose and mouth, put one in mind of a bust carved out of horse-chestnut.

He wore a plain grey suit with a ready-made tie. Two things about him were striking – the bushy eyebrows, as wide and thick as a moustache, and the almost as long hairs that covered his hands.

He was studying Maigret, without attempting to conceal it, without even a polite smile.

'Sit down, Superintendent.'

The flat, smaller than the one in the Boulevard Richard-Lenoir, probably consisted of only two, perhaps three rooms and the tiniest of kitchens. They had moved from the hall, where some clothes were hanging, to the study that was typical of a bachelor's lodgings. A few pipes were standing in a rack on the wall, ten or twelve of them, some of clay, one a beauty of a meerschaum. An old-fashioned desk, like the one Maigret's father had had long ago, was covered with papers and tobacco ash; it had a set of pigeonholes and small drawers. He did not yet dare examine the photographs on the wall of Auguste Point's father and mother in the same black and gold frames which he might have found in any farm in the Vendée.

Sitting in his swivel-chair, again so similar to that of Maigret's father, Auguste Point was playing with a box of cigars.

'I wonder would you care . . .' he began.

The Superintendent murmured, smiling:

'I prefer my pipe.'

'Some of this?'

The Minister offered him an open packet of grey tobacco and lit his own pipe which he had allowed to go out.

'You must have been surprised, when your wife told you . . .'

He was trying to open the conversation but was not pleased with his attempt. Something curious was taking place.

They sat there in the warm, peaceful study, both of the same build and of about the same age, unashamedly studying one another. It was as if they had discovered the resemblance and were intrigued by it but were not quite ready yet to admit its existence.

'Look, Maigret, between men like us, there's no point in the usual formalities. I only know you from the newspapers and from what I've heard about you.'

'As with me, Your Excellency.'

With a slight gesture, Auguste Point gave Maigret to understand that at this moment the use of the title was inappropriate.

'I'm in terrible trouble. Nobody knows it yet, nobody even suspects it, neither the President of the Council nor even my wife and she normally knows my every movement. You're the only one I've turned to.'

For a moment he looked away and pulled at his pipe, as if embarrassed by what could be mistaken for vulgar calculated flattery.

'I didn't want to do the conventional thing and go straight to the police. What I'm doing is irregular. You were under no obligation to come here, just as you are under no obligation to help me.' He rose, sighing.

'Will you have a drink?'

And with what could be taken as a smile:

'Don't worry. I'm not trying to bribe you. It's just that tonight I really need something to drink.'

He went into the next room and came back with a half-finished bottle and two thick glasses of the kind used in country inns.

'It's only some home-made spirits that my father distils every autumn. This one is about twenty years old.'

They looked at each other, each holding a glass.

'Your health!'

'And yours, Your Excellency.'

This time Auguste Point seemed not to hear the last words.

'If I don't know how to begin, it isn't because I'm embarrassed, but because the story is difficult to tell with any degree of clarity. You read the newspapers?'

'I do, on the evenings when the world of crime allows me some peace.'

'You follow political events?'

'Not much.'

'You know that I'm not what is called a politician?'

Maigret nodded.

'Very well. You're probably aware of the Clairfond disaster?'

This time Maigret could not help giving a start and a certain anxiety, a certain caution must have shown in his expression, because the other man bent his head and added in a low voice:

'Unhappily this is what it's all about!'

A short time ago in the Métro, Maigret had tried to puzzle out why the Minister had arranged to meet him in secret. The Clairfond affair had never entered his mind, though recently all the newspapers had been full of it.

The Sanatorium of Clairfond, in Haute Savoie, between Ugines and Mégève, at a height of more than fourteen hundred metres, was one of the most spectacular post-war achievements. It was some years ago now and Maigret had no idea whose was the original idea of establishing a home for abandoned children comparable to the modern privately owned sanatoria. At the time it had been much in the news. Some people had seen in it a purely political enterprise and there had been violent debates in the Chamber of Deputies. A commission had been selected to study the project and eventually, after much discussion, it had materialized.

A month later came the disaster, one of the most distressing in history. Snow had begun to melt at a time when it hadn't happened in human memory. The mountain streams had swelled, as did a subterranean river, the Lize, so unimportant, that it is not even marked on the map. It had undermined the foundations of a whole wing at Clairfond.

The inquest, opened on the day after the disaster, had not yet been completed. The experts could not come to an agreement. Neither could the newspapers which, according to their political persuasion, propounded different theories.

One hundred and twenty-eight children had died when one of the buildings collapsed; the others were urgently evacuated.

After a moment of silence Maigret murmured:

'You were not in the Cabinet at the time of the construction, were you?'

'No. I wasn't even a member of the parliamentary commission that allocated the funds. To tell you the truth, up to a day or so ago I only knew what everyone knows of the business from the newspapers.'

He paused.

'Have you heard anything about the Calame report, Superintendent?'

Maigret looked at him, in surprise, and shook his head.

'You will be hearing about it soon. I'm afraid you'll be hearing too much about it. I suppose you don't read the weekly papers, the *Rumeur*, for instance?'

'Never.'

'Do you know Henri Tabard?'

'By name and reputation only. My colleagues of the Rue des Saussaies would know him better than I do.'

He was referring to the Department of Security which came under the Ministry of the Interior, and was often asked to deal with cases connected in some way with politics.

Tabard was a carping journalist whose gossip-filled weekly had the reputation of a cheap black-mailing rag.

'Read this – it appeared six days after the disaster.'

It was short, and sinister.

' "Will someone one day decide under pressure of public opinion to reveal the contents of the Calame Report?" Is that all?' The Superintendent was surprised.

' "Contrary to popular belief, it won't be because of foreign policy, nor because of events in North Africa that the present government will fall at the end of the spring, but because of the Calame report. Who is keeping back the Calame report?" '

There was an almost comic sound to the words and Maigret smiled as he asked:

'Who is Calame?'

But Auguste Point was not smiling. He was emptying his pipe into a large copper ashtray while he explained:

'He was a professor in the National School of Civil Engineering. He died two years ago of cancer, I believe. His name is not widely known, but it is famous in the world of engineering, and public works. Calame was called in as consultant for large undertakings in countries as different as Japan and South America and he was an indisputable authority on everything concerning the resistance of material, particularly concrete. He wrote a book, which neither you nor I have read, but which every architect knows, called "The Diseases of Concrete".'

'Was Calame involved in the building of Clairfond?'

'Only indirectly. Let me tell you the story in a different way, more from my own standpoint. At the time of the disaster, as I told you, I knew nothing of the sanatorium, that was not in the newspapers. I couldn't even remember if I had voted for or against the project five years ago. I had to look up the records to find out that I had voted for it. Like you, I don't read the *Rumeur*. It was only after the second paragraph appeared that the President of the Council called me in and asked me:

' "You know the Calame report?"

'I replied candidly that I did not. He seemed surprised and I'm not sure that he didn't glance at me with a certain suspicion.

' "It should be among your archives," he said to me.

'It was then that he told me the whole story. During the debate on the subject of Clairfond, five years ago, as the parliamentary commission was divided, one of the deputies, I don't know who, had suggested consulting the opinion of an engineer of unquestioned standing. He put forward the name of Professor Julien Calame, of the National School of Civil Engineering, and the latter spent some time studying the project, and even went to the site in Haute Savoie. He then made a report which normally should have been sent to the commission.'

Maigret began to understand.

'This report was an unfavourable one?'

'Wait a moment. When the President talked to me about it, he had already ordered a search in the archives of the Chamber of Deputies. The report should have been found in the files of the commission. It turned out that not only was it not there, but that part of the accounts had also disappeared. You see what it all means?'

'That there were people interested in keeping the report unpublished?'

'Read this.'

It was another paragraph from the *Rumeur*, again short, but no less menacing.

'Is M. Arthur Nicoud powerful enough to prevent the Calame report from seeing the light of day?'

Maigret knew that name as he knew hundreds of others. He had heard of the firm Nicoud and Sauvegrain because it was mentioned almost everywhere where there were public works, whether roads, bridges or locks.

'It was the firm Nicoud and Sauvegrain who built Clairfond.'

Maigret was beginning to regret that he had come. Though he felt drawn to Auguste Point, what he had heard made him as uneasy as when an unsavoury story was told in the presence of a woman.

He could not help wondering what part Auguste Point could have played in the tragedy that had cost the lives of one hundred and twenty-eight children. He was almost on the brink of asking straight out:

'And where do you come into all this?'

He could imagine that some people had taken bribes, politicians, perhaps persons in high office.

'I'll try to finish quickly. The President asked me to have a thorough search made in the archives of my Ministry. The National School of Civil Engineering comes under the Ministry of Public Works, so that, logically, we should have had somewhere in our files, at least a copy of the Calame report.'

The words 'Calame report' recurred.

'You found nothing?'

'Nothing. We searched through tons of dusty paper in the attic and we found nothing.'

Maigret was beginning to feel restless, uneasy in his chair and the other man noticed it.

'You don't like politics?'

'I confess I don't.'

'Neither do I. Strange as it may seem it was to fight against politics that twelve years ago I agreed to stand at the election. And when, three months ago, I was asked to join the Cabinet, it was again with the idea of bringing a little cleanliness into public affairs that I allowed myself to be persuaded. My wife and I are simple people. You can see the sort of flat we occupy in Paris, during the parliamentary sessions, since I became a deputy. It is more like a bachelor's rooms. My wife could have remained in La Roche-sur-Yon where we have a house, but we are not in the habit of living apart.'

He was speaking quite naturally, without any hint of sentimentality in his voice.

'Since I have been a Minister, we live officially in the Ministry, Boulevard Saint-Germain, but we come to seek refuge here as often as we can, particularly on Sundays. But all that's beside the point. If I rang you from a public box, as your wife no doubt told you – for if I'm not mistaken you have the same kind of wife as I have – if I did that, it's because I'm suspicious of being overheard. I'm convinced, rightly or wrongly, that all my calls from the Ministry, maybe even from here are recorded somewhere, I prefer not to know where. I might add, to my shame, that this evening I walked in one door of a cinema on the boulevard and out of the other and twice changed taxis. I can't even be sure this house is not being watched.'

'I saw no one as I arrived.'

Maigret was feeling a sort of compassion for Auguste Point. Up to now Point had tried to talk in a detached fashion. But when he came to the essential point of their meeting, he became evasive and went round in circles, as though he feared that Maigret would get a wrong impression of him.

'The Ministry's archives have been turned upside down and God alone knows how many papers there are there which no human being can remember. During this time, I had telephone calls from the President at least twice a day and I'm not at all sure that he trusts me. Searches have been made also in the School of Civil Engineering without any result until yesterday morning.'

Maigret couldn't help asking, as one does at the end of a novel:

'The Calame report has been found?'

'Something, anyway, that appears to be the Calame report.'

'Where?'

'In the attic of the school.'

'A professor?'

'A supervisor. Yesterday morning I was given a note from a certain Piquemal, of whom I'd never heard. On it someone had written in pencil: "With reference to the Calame report". I asked him in at once. I took care to send my secretary, Mlle Blanche, from the room, though I've had her with me for twenty years as she comes from La Roche-sur-Yon and worked in my chambers there. You'll see that this is important. My parliamentary private secretary was not in the room either. I was left alone with a man of middle age who stood staring at me, saying nothing, with a grey paper parcel under his arm.

' "M. Piquemal?" I asked, a little anxiously, since, for a moment, I thought that I was facing a maniac.

'He nodded.

' "Sit down."

' "It's not worth while."

'I had the impression that his eyes weren't friendly. He asked me, almost impertinently:

' "Are you the Minister?"

' "Yes."

' "I'm a supervisor at the School of Civil Engineering."

'He stepped forward, handed me the parcel and uttered in the same tone:

' "Open it and give me a receipt."

'The parcel contained a document of about forty pages, obviously a carbon copy:

' "Report concerning the construction of a sanatorium at Clairfond in Haute Savoie." The document was not signed by hand but the name of Julien Calame with his qualifications, was typed on the last page, as well as the date.

'Still standing, Piquemal repeated:

' "I want a receipt."

'I wrote one out for him. He folded it, slipped it into a worn brief case and moved to the door. I called him back.

' "Where did you find these papers?"

' "In the attic."

' "You will probably be called upon to make a written declaration."

' "You know where to find me."

' "Have you shown this document to anyone?"

'He looked me straight in the eye, contemptuously.

' "No one."

' "Were there no other copies?"

' "Not so far as I know."

' "Thank you." '

Auguste Point looked at Maigret in embarrassment.

'That's where I made a mistake,' he went on. 'I think it was because of Piquemal's bizarre behaviour, for he looked like an anarchist about to throw his bomb.'

'How old was he?' asked Maigret.

'Forty-five perhaps. Neither smartly nor badly dressed. His eyes were the eyes of a fanatic or a madman.'

'Did you gather any information about him?'

'Not straight away. It was five o'clock. There were still four or five people in my waiting-room and I had to preside at an engineers' dinner in the evening. When my visitor left, my secretary came in and I slipped the Calame report into my personal briefcase. I should have telephoned the President of the Council. If I didn't do so, I swear to you that it was again because I was wondering if Piquemal was mad. There was nothing to prove that the document wasn't a false one. Almost every day we are visited by some lunatic or other.'

'So are we.'

'In that case you can understand me. My appointments lasted until seven o'clock. I just had time to go to my flat and change.'

'Did you talk to your wife about it?'

'No. I took my briefcase with me. I told her I'd come to the Boulevard Pasteur after dinner. This kind of thing often happens. We come here together on Sunday for a little meal that she cooks up, and I also come here alone when I have something important to do and want peace and quiet.'

'Where was the banquet?'

'At the Palais d'Orsay.'

'You took your briefcase with you?'

'It remained locked in the care of my driver, whom I trust absolutely.'

'You came back here directly after?'

'About half past ten. Ministers have the privilege of not having to stay after the speeches.'

'You were in evening dress?'

'I took it off before I settled down at this desk.'

'You read the report?'

'Yes.'

'Did it seem authentic to you?'

The Minister nodded.

'It would cause an explosion if it were published?'

'Without any doubt.'

'Why?'

'Because Professor Calame practically prophesied the disaster. Though I'm in charge of Public Works I'm incapable of giving you chapter and verse of all his arguments and particularly of the technical details he provides to support his opinion. At any rate, he quite clearly pronounced himself against the entire project and said it was the duty of every person who read the report to vote against the construction of Clairfond as it was planned or at least to demand a further inquiry. Do you understand?'

'I begin to.'

'How the *Rumeur* got wind of this document I don't know. Have they got another copy? Again I don't know. As far as one can judge the only person in possession of a copy of the Calame report last night was myself.'

'What happened then?'

'Towards midnight, I telephoned the President of the Council, but I was told that he was at a political meeting in Rouen. I almost called him there.'

'You didn't do so?'

'No. Because I was afraid of the lines being tapped. I felt that I was in possession of a case of dynamite which might not only overthrow the government, but also ruin the reputations of a number of my colleagues. It is unbelievable that those who had read the report should have been capable of allowing . . .'

Maigret thought he could guess the rest.

'You left the report here in this flat?'

'Yes.'

'In your desk?'

'Yes, it has a lock. I considered that it was safer here than in the Ministry where there are people coming and going all the time.'

'Your driver remained at the door all the time while you studied the file?'

'I sent him away and took a taxi at the corner of the Boulevard.'

'Did you talk to your wife when you got home?'

'Not about the report. I didn't mention it to anybody until the next day, at one o'clock in the afternoon, when I met the President in the Chamber of Deputies. I put him in the picture; we were standing by the window.'

'Was he upset?'

'I think so. Any head of government would have been upset in his place. He asked me to fetch the report and to bring it personally to his study.'

'The report was no longer in your desk?'

'No.'

'And the lock had been tampered with?'

'I don't think so.'

'Did you see the President again?'

'No. I felt quite ill. I drove to the Boulevard Saint-Germain and cancelled all my appointments. My wife telephoned to the President and said that I was unwell, that I had collapsed and would go and see him tomorrow morning.'

'Does your wife know?'

'For the first time in my life I lied to her. I can't remember what I said to her exactly and several times I must have broken off.'

'Does she know you are here?'

'She believes I am at a meeting. I wonder if you quite understand my situation: I find myself suddenly alone, with the feeling that as soon as I open my mouth, I'll be attacked. Nobody would believe my story. I held the Calame report in my hands. I am the only one, beside Piquemal, to have had it. *And at least three times in the course of the last years I have been invited by Arthur Nicoud, the builder in question, to his place in Samois.*'

Suddenly he slumped. His shoulders seemed narrower, his chin softer. He seemed to be saying:

'Do whatever you like. I have nothing more to say.'

Maigret, without asking permission, poured himself some

spirits and only after drinking himself remembered to fill the Minister's glass.

Chapter Two

Probably, at some stage in his own career, Maigret had had a similar experience, but never, he thought, of such intensity. The smallness of the room, its warmth and intimacy, heightened the atmosphere of drama which the smell of the rustic alcohol, the desk like his father's, the enlarged photographs of the old people on the walls made Maigret feel like a doctor who has been summoned with great urgency and into whose hands the patient has placed his life.

The most surprising thing of all was that the man who was sitting opposite him, as if waiting for the diagnosis, resembled him if not exactly like a brother, certainly like a cousin. And not only physically. A glance at the family portraits told the Superintendent that his and Auguste Point's origins were very close. Both were born in the country of enlightened peasant stock. Probably the Minister's parents had had the ambition ever since he was born for him to become a doctor or a lawyer, just as Maigret's had done.

August Point had gone beyond their wildest dreams. Were they still alive to know it?

He didn't dare to ask these questions yet. The man opposite him had gone to pieces and he knew it wasn't because of weakness of character. Looking at him, Maigret was overcome by a complex mixture of emotions; he was angry and disgusted and profoundly discouraged. There had been a time in his own life when he had found himself in a similar situation, though less dramatic one, and that, too, had had a political background. He wasn't to blame. He had acted as it was his duty to act, had behaved, not only as an honest man, but strictly according to his obligations as an official. Nevertheless, in the eyes of almost everyone he had done wrong. He had had to go before a disciplinary council and as everything was against him, had been blamed. It was at this time that he had momentarily left the

P.J.* and become an exile in the Mobile Brigade of Luçon, in the Vendée, the very department that Auguste Point represented in the Chamber of Deputies. His wife and his friends had told him over and over again that his own conscience was what mattered but often he seemed to behave, without realizing it, like a guilty man. On those last days at the P.J. for instance, while his case was being discussed in high places, he didn't dare to give any orders to his subordinates, not even to Lucas or to Janvier and when he came down the main staircase, he had kept close to the wall.

Auguste Point too was no longer capable of thinking with any lucidity about his own case. He had just said all that he had to say. During the last hours he had acted as a man who is drowning and who only hopes for a miracle to save him. Wasn't it strange that he had appealed to Maigret, a man whom he did not know, whom he had never seen?

Without realizing it, Maigret had taken on the case and his questions were those of the doctor who tries to establish a diagnosis.

'Have you inquired into the identity of Piquemal?'

'I asked my secretary to telephone the School of Civil Engineering and she was told that Jules Piquemal had been working there for fifteen years as a supervisor.'

'Isn't it peculiar that he didn't hand the document to the School Director but brought it to you himself?'

'I don't know. I didn't think about it.'

'It seems to indicate that he realized its importance, doesn't it?'

'I think so. Yes.'

'In fact, since the Calame report has been rediscovered, Piquemal is the only person, besides yourself, who has had the opportunity of reading it?'

'Not counting the people or person in whose hands it is now.'

'We can leave that at the moment. If I'm not mistaken, only one person, beside Piquemal, has known since Tuesday at one o'clock, that you were in possession of the document?'

* Police Judiciaire. Something equivalent to the C.I.D., with a seat in the Quai des Orfèvres, whereas Security Police has its seat in the Rue des Saussaies.

'You mean the President of the Council?'

Auguste Point looked at Maigret in dismay. The present head of the government, Oscar Malterre, was a man of sixty-five who, since he was forty, had in one capacity or another, been a member of successive Cabinets. His father had been a mayor, one of his brothers was a deputy and the other a Colonial governor.

'I hope that you are not suggesting . . .'

'I suggest nothing, Your Excellency. I'm trying to understand. The Calame report was in this desk last night. This afternoon, it was no longer there. Are you certain that the door hadn't been forced?'

'You can see for yourself. There is no mark on the wood or on the metal of the keyhole. Could they have used a master key?'

'And the lock of your desk?'

'Have a look. It is not a complicated one. I have often forgotten my key and opened it with a piece of wire.'

'Excuse me, if I ask you all the usual routine questions, just to clear the air. Who besides yourself has the key to the flat?'

'My wife, of course.'

'You told me that she knows nothing of the Calame affair.'

'I didn't talk to her about it. She doesn't even know that I've been here yesterday and today.'

'Does she follow politics at all closely?'

'She reads the papers, keeps enough in touch to enable us to talk together about my work. When it was suggested that I should put myself forward as a deputy, she tried to dissuade me. She didn't want me to become a Cabinet Minister, either. She has no ambition.'

'Does she come from La Roche-sur-Yon?'

'Her father was a solicitor there.'

'Let's come back to the keys. Who else has them?'

'My secretary, Mlle Blanche.'

'Blanche, who?'

Maigret was making notes in his black notebook.

'Blanche Lamotte. She must be . . . wait a moment . . . forty-one . . . no, forty-two years old.'

'You have known her for a long time?'

'She started to work for me as a typist when she was barely

seventeen, just out of the Pigier school. She has been with me ever since.'

'Also from La Roche?'

'From a neighbouring village. Her father was a butcher.'

'Pretty?'

Auguste Point seemed to ponder over this as though he had never asked himself the question.

'No. I don't think you could say that.'

'In love with you?'

Maigret smiled to see the Minister blush.

'How did you know that? Let us say that she's in love in her own way. I don't think there's been a man in her life.'

'Jealous of your wife?'

'Not in the usual sense of the word. You might say she's possessive of what she considers to be her field.'

'That means that in the office it is she who is the boss.'

Auguste Point, who was no child, seemed surprised at Maigret discovering such a simple truth.

'She was in your office, you told me, when Piquemal was announced, and you asked her to leave the room. When you called her back, did you still have the report in your hand?'

'I think so. . . . But I can assure you . . .'

'Your Excellency, please try to understand, I'm blaming nobody, suspecting nobody. Like yourself, I'm trying to find my way. Has anyone else got keys to the flat?'

'My daughter has one.'

'What age is she?'

'Anne-Marie? Twenty-four.'

'Married?'

'Well, she was going to get married next month. With all this storm ahead, I simply don't know. Do you know the Courmont family?'

'Only by name.'

If the Malterres were famous in politics, the Courmonts were equally so in diplomacy and had been, for at least three generations. Robert Courmont who had a house in the Rue de la Faisanderie and was one of the last Frenchmen to wear a monocle, had been an ambassador for more than thirty years, in Tokyo and in London, and was a member of the Institute.

'His son?'

'Yes, Alain Courmont. He's thirty-two years old and he has already been attached to three or four embassies and now he's head of an important department in the Foreign Office. He has been appointed to Buenos Aires; he was to go there three weeks after his marriage. So you can see that the situation is even more tragic than it seems at first glance. A scandal of these dimensions . . . awaiting me at any moment . . .'

'Did your daughter often come here?'

'Not since we took up residence in the Ministry.'

'You mean she's never been here since then?'

'I would prefer to tell you everything, Superintendent. If I don't, it would be pointless to have turned to you. Anne-Marie has graduated in philosophy and literature. She's not a blue stocking, but neither is she like the usual run of young girls today. One day, about a month ago, I found some cigarette ash here. Mlle Blanche doesn't smoke, neither does my wife. I asked Anne-Marie and she admitted that occasionally she came to the flat with Alain. I didn't try to find out any more. I remember what she said to me, without blushing, looking me straight in the eye: "One must be realistic, father. I'm twenty-four and Alain's thirty-two." Have you any children, Maigret?'

The Superintendent shook his head.

'I suppose there was no cigarette ash anywhere today?'

'No.'

Now that he had only to answer questions Auguste Point was beginning to look less depressed, like a patient who answers a doctor, knowing that the doctor will provide him with some relief in the end. Could Maigret be lingering on this question of the keys on purpose?

'Nobody else?'

'My parliamentary private secretary.'

'Who is he?'

'Jacques Fleury.'

'You've known him for a long time?'

'I was at the Lycée with him, then at the University.'

'Also from the Vendée?'

'No, he comes from Niort. It isn't far away. He's about my age.'

'Lawyer?'

'He never read for the bar.'

'Why?'

'He's an odd character. His parents were rich. When he was young, he never wanted regular work. He had a passion for something new every six months. For example, once he took it into his head to run a fishery and he had a few boats. He was also involved in some colonial enterprise that failed. I lost sight of him. When I was elected as deputy, I used to see him now and then in Paris.'

'Ruined?'

'Completely. He always kept up appearances. He never ceased to do so, nor to be extremely amiable. He is the typical amiable failure.'

'Did he ever ask you any favours?'

'I suppose so but nothing important. A short time before I became Cabinet Minister, it just happened that I bumped into him more often and when I found myself in need of a private secretary he was there, at my disposal.'

Auguste Point frowned.

'Since we are on the subject, there is something I'd better explain. You probably cannot imagine what it is like to become a Cabinet Minister from one moment to the next. Take my case. I'm a lawyer, a small provincial lawyer, of course, but this doesn't minimize my knowledge of the Law. Then I was appointed Minister of Public Works. I became, overnight and without any apprenticeship, the head of a Ministry, that was full of competent executives, even such illustrious men as Calame. I did what the others do. I assumed an air of confidence. I behaved as if I knew it all. This didn't stop me feeling a certain irony and hostility around me and I was also conscious of a number of intrigues of which I understood nothing. Even at the head of the Ministry, I'm an outsider, for even there, I'm among people who are aware and have been aware for a long time of what goes on behind the scenes. To have beside me a man like Fleury, with whom I can relax . . .'

'I can understand. When you chose him as your assistant, was he already in touch with the political world?'

'Only through casual encounters in bars and restaurants.'

'Married?'

'He has been married. He must still be, for I don't think he ever divorced and he had two children by his wife. They don't live together any longer. He has at least one other entanglement in Paris, maybe two, for he has the gift of complicating his existence.'

'You're sure he didn't know you were in possession of the Calame report?'

'He didn't even see Piquemal in the Ministry. I didn't mention anything to him.'

'What is the relationship between Fleury and Mlle Blanche?'

'Outwardly cordial. Deep in her heart, Mlle Blanche cannot stand him, because she is a bourgeoise through and through and Fleury's sentimental life exasperates and upsets her. . . . You see – we are getting nowhere.'

'You are quite certain that your wife doesn't suspect that you are here?'

'She noticed, this evening, that I was worried. She wanted to profit from the fact that for once I had no important engagement in the evening and put me to bed. I talked to her about a meeting . . .'

'Did she believe you?'

'I don't know.'

'Are you in the habit of lying to her?'

'No.'

It was almost midnight. This time it was the Minister who filled the little stemless glasses and moved, sighing, to the rack to choose a curved pipe with a silver ring.

As if confirming Maigret's intuition, the telephone rang. Auguste Point glanced at the superintendent, wondering if he should answer.

'It's probably your wife. When you get home, you'll be forced to tell her the whole story.'

The Minister lifted the receiver.

'Hallo! Yes, it's me.'

He looked guilty.

'No. I've got someone with me. . . . We had to discuss a very important matter. . . . I'll tell you all about it when I see you. I don't know. . . . It won't be very long. . . . Very well. . . . I assure

you I'm perfectly well. . . . What? . . . From the President? . . .
He wants me to what? . . . Very well. . . . Yes, I'll do it straight
away . . . see you soon.'

With beads of sweat on his forehead he turned again to Maigret like a man who does not know to which saint to pray.

'The President's house has rung three times. . . . The President
has asked me to ring him at any time . . .'

He wiped his brow. He even forgot to light his pipe.

'What do I do now?'

'I suggest you telephone him. In any case you'll have to admit
to him tomorrow morning that you no longer have the report.
And there's not a chance that we lay our hands on it overnight.'

Point's next remark was almost comical, it showed his confusion and the instinctive confidence some people have in the
power of the police. For he said, almost mechanically:

'You think so?'

Then, sinking heavily into his chair, he dialled a number that
he knew by heart.

'Hallo! This is the Minister of Public Works. I'd like to speak
to the President. . . . Forgive me, Madame. . . . It's Auguste
Point speaking. . . . I believe your husband is expecting. . . . Yes.
. . . I'll wait . . .'

He gulped down his glass of spirits, his eyes fixed on Maigret's waistcoat buttons.

'Yes, my dear President. . . . Please forgive me for not calling
you earlier. . . . I'm better. . . . Yes. . . . It was nothing. . . .
Perhaps I was a little tired, yes. . . Also. . . . I was going to tell
you . . .'

Maigret could hear a voice at the other end of the line that
was in no way reassuring. Auguste Point looked like a child
who is being scolded and who tries vainly to justify himself.

'Yes, I know. . . . Believe me . . .'

At last, he was allowed to speak and was searching for the
right words.

'You see, something, well, something quite extraordinary has
happened. . . . I beg your pardon? . . . It's about the report, yes.
. . . I took it yesterday to my private flat. . . . Yes, in the Boulevard Pasteur . . .'

If only he could have been allowed to tell the story as he wanted to tell it. But he was continually interrupted. He was becoming confused.

'Well, yes. . . . I often come here to work when. . . . I can't hear you. Yes, I'm here at the moment. . . . No, no, my wife did not know I was here, or she would have passed on your message. . . . No! I've no longer got the Calame report. . . . This is what I've been trying to tell you all the time. I left it here, believing it would be much safer than in the Ministry and when I came to collect it this afternoon, after our conversation . . .'

Maigret turned his head away when he saw tears of humiliation or perhaps irritation drop from the heavy eyelids. 'I spent some time searching for it. No, certainly not, I didn't do that!'

With his hand on the receiver, he whispered to Maigret:

'He is asking whether I alerted the police . . .'

He was listening again – resigned, occasionally muttering a word or two.

'Yes, yes. . . . I understand . . .'

His face was bathed in sweat and Maigret was tempted to go and open the window.

'You have my word, my dear President . . .'

The top light was not lit. The two men and the corner of the study were lit only by a lamp with a green shade which left the rest of the room in darkness. From time to time a taxi was heard hooting in the fog on the Boulevard Pasteur and more rarely a train whistled in the distance.

The father's photograph on the wall was that of a man in his middle sixties, taken probably about ten years earlier, judging by Auguste Point's age. The mother's photograph, on the other hand, was of a woman of barely thirty, wearing a dress and hair style dating back to the beginning of the century and Maigret surmised from this that Madame Point, like his own mother, had died when her son was quite small.

There were possibilities which he hadn't mentioned yet to the Minister and which he was beginning to turn over automatically in his mind. Because of the telephone call, of which he had been the accidental witness, he was thinking of Malterre, the President of the Council, who was also Minister of the

Interior and, it followed, had the National Security Department in the palm of his hand.

What if Malterre had got wind of Piquemal's visit to the Boulevard Saint-Germain and had had Auguste Point followed. ... Or even if after his conversation with Point. ... Anything might be possible – he might have wanted to get hold of the document to destroy it at the same time keeping it as his trump card.

The journalistic slang in this case was to the point, the Calame report was a bomb which brought its possessor unbelievable power.

'Yes, my dear President. ... Not the police, I swear to you ...'

The other man was probably badgering him with questions that pushed him farther and farther out of his depth. His eyes called for Maigret's help, but there was no help forthcoming. He was already giving in ...

'The person who is in my study is not here in the capacity of ...'

After all, he was a strong man, both physically and morally. Maigret, too, knew his own strength and he, too, in the past, had given in when he had been caught in a much less powerful trap. What had crushed him – he remembered it and would remember it all his life – was the impression of being up against an anonymous force, without name or face, impossible to get hold of. And this force had been no ordinary force, it had been the Law.

Auguste Point was dropping the receiver.

'It's Superintendent Maigret. ... I asked him to come and see me privately, I'm certain that he ...'

He was interrupted. The receiver seemed to vibrate.

'No trail, no. Nobody. ... No, my wife knows nothing, either. ... Nor my secretary. I swear to you, Your Excellency.'

He forgot about the traditional 'dear President' and became humble.

'Yes. ... At 9 a.m. ... I promise. You want to speak to him? ... One moment ...' Humiliated, he glanced at Maigret.

'The President wishes to ...'

The superintendent seized the instrument.

'I'm here, Your Excellency.'

'I hear that my colleague of Public Works has told you of the incident?'

'Yes, Your Excellency.'

'I needn't underline that the matter must remain rigorously secret. There is no question of holding a regular inquiry. Nor will National Security be informed.'

'I understand, Your Excellency.'

'It is obvious that if you, personally, without any official involvement, without appearing to be interested, should discover anything concerning the Calame report, you'll let me . . .'

He hesitated. He didn't want to be personally implicated.

'. . . You'll let my colleague Point know about it?'

'Yes, Your Excellency.'

'That's all.'

Maigret wanted to hand the receiver over to the Minister but the line had gone dead.

'I'm sorry, Maigret. He forced me to give your name. It's said that he was a famous assize lawyer before entering politics and I can well believe it. . . . I apologize for putting you into such a position . . .'

'You're seeing him tomorrow morning?'

'At 9 a.m. He doesn't want the other members of the Cabinet to be informed. What distresses him most is whether Piquemal has talked, or will talk, as he is the only one, beside the three of us, who knows that the document has been discovered.'

'I'll try to find out what kind of a man he is.'

'Without disclosing your identity?'

'In all fairness I must warn you that I am bound to talk about it to my chief. I needn't go into any details, by which I mean I needn't mention the Calame report. But it is necessary that he should know that I'm working for you. If it only concerned myself I could tackle the business outside my work. But no doubt I shall need some of my colleagues . . .'

'Would they have to know everything?'

'They'll know nothing about the report, I promise you.'

'I was ready to offer him my resignation but he took the words out of my mouth. He said that he was not even in a position to dissociate me from the Cabinet because that might, if not reveal the truth, at least arouse suspicions in those who had followed the last political events. From now on I'm the black sheep and my colleagues . . .'

'Are you quite certain that the report you had in your hands was in fact a copy of the Calame report?'

Auguste Point raised his head in surprise.

'Do you suggest that it might not have been genuine?'

'I'm suggesting nothing. I am only considering all the hypotheses. If you are presented with the Calame report, genuine or not, and it disappears immediately afterwards, you are automatically discredited (and in fact so is the whole government) because you'll be accused of having suppressed it.'

'In that case, everyone will be talking about it tomorrow.'

'Not necessarily so soon. I would like to know where and in what circumstances it was found.'

'Do you think you can do that without anyone knowing?'

'I'll try. I presume, Your Excellency, that you have concealed nothing from me? If I go so far as to ask the question, it is because, in present circumstances, it is essential that . . .'

'I know. There is one detail that I haven't mentioned before. I spoke to you, at the beginning, of Arthur Nicoud. When I first met him, I don't remember at what dinner, I was a simple deputy and the idea never crossed my mind that I would find myself one day at the head of Public Works. I knew he was a member of the firm Nicoud and Sauvegrain, the contractors of the Avenue de la République. Arthur Nicoud doesn't live the life of a business man, but of a man of the world. Contrary to what one may think you couldn't call him a *nouveau riche*, nor is he a typical tycoon. He is well-educated. He knows how to live. He goes to the best restaurants in Paris, always surrounded by pretty women, mostly actresses or cinema stars.

'I believe that everybody of any importance in the world of letters, arts, politics has been invited at least once to his Sundays in Samois. I have met many of my colleagues from the Chamber, some press barons and scientists, people whose integrity I'd swear to. Nicoud himself, in his country mansion gives the impression of a man whose main concern is to offer his guests the finest food in an elegant background. My wife has never liked him. We have been there about half a dozen times, never alone, never on an intimate footing. On some Sundays there were about thirty of us lunching at little tables and then we foregathered in the library afterwards or round the swimming-pool.

'What I didn't tell you was that once, I think it was two years ago, yes, two years ago, at Christmas time my daughter received a tiny gold fountain pen with her initials on it, accompanied by Arthur Nicoud's card. I almost made her send the present back. I don't remember now to whom I spoke about it, to one of my colleagues, I think, and I was rather angry. He told me that Nicoud's gesture had no significance, that it was a mania of his, at the end of every year, to send little presents to the daughters or wives of his guests. That year it was fountain-pens which he must have ordered by the dozen. Another year it had been compacts, always in gold, because apparently he has a passion for gold. My daughter kept the fountain pen. I believe she still uses it.

'If the story of the Calame report hits the headlines tomorrow and they print that Auguste Point's daughter had received and accepted . . .'

Maigret nodded slowly. He did not minimize the importance of such a detail.

'Nothing else? He never lent you money?'

Auguste Point blushed to the roots of his hair. Maigret could well understand why. It was not because he had something to reproach himself with, but because from now on, anyone might put the question to him.

'Never! I swear to you . . .'

'I believe you. You haven't any shares in the company?'

The Minister said no, with a bitter smile.

'I'll do everything I can, starting from tomorrow morning,' Maigret promised. 'You realize that I know less than you do and that I'm completely unfamiliar with the political world. I also doubt if we would be able to discover the report before the man who has it now makes use of it. You yourself – would you have suppressed it to save your colleagues if it compromised them?'

'Certainly not.'

'What if the head of your Party had asked you to?'

'Not even if the President of the Council himself had put it to me.'

'I was more or less certain that that is what you would say. I'm sorry to have asked the question. I'll be going now, Your Excellency.'

The two men rose and Auguste Point stretched out his large, hairy hand.

'I apologize for involving you in all this. I was so discouraged and confused.'

Now that his fate was in another man's hands, his heart was lighter. He spoke in his normal voice, switched on the top light and opened the door.

'You can't come to see me at the Ministry without arousing curiosity, because you're too well-known. And you can't telephone because, as I told you before, I suspect my line is tapped. This flat is known to everybody. How are we going to keep in touch?'

'I will find some way of communicating with you as soon as it's necessary. You can always telephone me in the evening from a public box as you did today and if I'm not there, leave a message with my wife.'

They both thought of the same thing, at the same moment, and could not help smiling. Standing by the door they looked so like conspirators!

'Good night, Your Excellency.'

'Thank you, Maigret. Good night.'

The Superintendent did not bother to take the lift. He walked down the four flights, rang for the night door to be opened and found himself back in the street fog that had become thicker and colder. To find a taxi he had to walk to the Boulevard Montparnasse. He turned to the right, his pipe between his teeth, his hands in his pockets and after walking about sixty feet two large lights appeared in front of him and he could hear the engine of a car being started. The fog prevented him from judging the distance. For a moment Maigret got the impression that the car was coming straight at him, but it only passed by, enveloping him for a few seconds in a yellow glow. He did not have time to raise his hand to hide his face. Besides, he felt sure it would have been useless. No doubt somebody was interested in the person who had paid such a long visit that evening to the Minister's flat, whose windows above, were still lit up.

With a shrug Maigret went on his way and met only a couple walking slowly, arm in arm, mouth to mouth, who just missed bumping into him.

Eventually he found a taxi. There was still a light in his flat on Boulevard Richard-Lenoir. He pulled out his key, as always, and as always his wife opened the door before he had time to find the lock. She was in her nightdress, and bare-footed; her eyes were swollen with sleep and she returned at once to the hollow she had made in the bed.

'What is the time?' she asked in a distant voice.

'Ten minutes past one.'

He smiled as he thought that in another, more sumptuous but anonymous flat another couple was going through the same motions. Auguste Point and his wife were not in their own home. It was not their own home, nor their own bed. They were strangers in the large official building they lived in which must have seemed to them full of traps.

'What did he want you for?'

'To tell the truth, I don't quite know.'

She was only half-awake and trying to come to her senses while he was undressing.

'You don't know why he wanted to see you?'

'I should say to seek my advice.'

He did not want to use the word consolation, which would have been more precise. It was funny. It seemed to him that if he were to utter the words 'Calame report' here, in the familiar, almost tangible intimacy of his own flat – he would have burst into laughter. At the Boulevard Pasteur half an hour ago, the words had been charged with meaning. A Cabinet Minister, with his back to the wall, had spoken them with something like awe. The President of the Council had talked of the Report as of a State matter of the utmost importance. It was a question of some thirty pages that had lain about for years apparently in an attic without anyone bothering about them until a school supervisor had discovered them perhaps by accident.

'What are you thinking about?'

'About a certain Piquemal.'

'Who is that?'

'I don't really know.'

It was true that he was thinking of Piquemal, or rather repeating the three syllables of his name and finding them comical.

'Sleep well.'

'You too. Oh, and please wake me at 7 a.m.'

'Why so early?'

'I have to telephone someone.'

Madame Maigret's hand was already on the switch to put out the light which was on her side of the bed.

Chapter Three

A hand gently touched his shoulder and a voice whispered in his ear:

'Maigret! It's seven o'clock.'

The smell of the coffee in the cup that his wife was handing to him rose to his nostrils. His senses and his brain were beginning to function rather in the same way as an orchestra when the musicians try out their instruments in the pit. As yet there was no coordination. Seven o'clock; therefore it was a different day from the others, for usually he got up at eight. Without raising his eyelids he discovered that the day was sunny, whereas the day before had been cloudy. Even before the idea of fog reminded him of the Boulevard Pasteur, he felt a bad taste in his mouth, which had not happened to him for a long time on waking up. He wondered if he was going to have a hangover and thought of the little stemless glasses and the rustic alcohol from the Minister's village.

Gloomy, he opened his eyes and sat up in bed, reassured to find he had no headache. He had not realized, last night, that they had both of them drunk a considerable amount.

'Tired?' his wife asked him.

'No. I'll be all right.'

His eyes swollen, he sipped his coffee, looking around and muttering in a voice still full of sleep.

'It's a fine day.'

'Yes. There's some hoar-frost.'

The sun had the acidity and freshness of a rustic white wine. Paris life was starting in the Boulevard Richard-Lenoir, with certain familiar noises.

'Must you go out so early?'

'No. But I have to telephone Chabot and after eight I risk not finding him at home. If it's market-day at Fontenay-Le-Comte, he may have been out since half past seven.'

Julien Chabot who had become magistrate at Fontenay-Le-Comte where he lived with his mother in the large house where he was born, had been one of his friends from his student days at Nantes and two years ago, coming back from a congress in Bordeaux, he had dropped in to see him. Old Madame Chabot attended the first Mass, at six in the morning, at seven the house was already humming with life, and at eight, Julien went out, not to the Palace of Justice, where he was by no means burdened with work, but to stroll in the streets of the town or along the Vendée.

'Please, may I have another cup?'

He drew the telephone to his side and dialled the operator. At the moment when the operator was repeating the number he suddenly thought that if one of his hypotheses of the night before were correct his telephone must already be tapped. This irritated him. He suddenly experienced once again the distaste that had overcome him when much against his will he had himself become involved in a political intrigue. And alongside this feeling came a sense of grievance against Auguste Point, whom he did not know from Adam, whom he had not previously met and who had found it necessary to appeal to Maigret to get him out of a mess.

'Madame Chabot? ... Hallo! ... Is it Madame Chabot speaking? ... It's Maigret here. ... No! Maigret ...'

She was somewhat deaf. He had to repeat his name five or six times and explain:

'Jules Maigret, in the Police ...'

Then she exclaimed:

'You're in Fontenay?'

'No, I'm calling from Paris. Is your son there?'

She spoke too loud, too close to the instrument. He didn't hear what she was saying. More than a minute passed before he recognized his friend's voice.

'Julien?'

'Yes.'

'You can hear me?'

'As clearly as if you were speaking from the station. How are you?'

'Very well. Listen to me. I'm disturbing you because I need some information. Were you having your breakfast?'

'Yes. But it doesn't matter.'

'You know Auguste Point?'

'You mean the Cabinet Minister?'

'Yes.'

'I used to see him often when he was a lawyer at La Roche-sur-Yon.'

'What do you think of him?'

'He is a remarkable man.'

'Give me some details. Anything that comes into your mind.'

'His father, Evariste Point, owns a well-known hotel at Sainte-Hermine, Clemenceau's town; famous not for its rooms, but for its good cuisine. Real lovers of good food came from all over the place to eat there. He must be almost ninety. Several years ago he made over the business to his son-in-law and to his daughter, but he still keeps an eye on it. Auguste Point, his only son graduated at about the same time as we did, but at Poitiers, and then at Paris. Are you still there?'

'Yes.'

'Shall I go on? He was a prodigious worker, a swotter. He opened a solicitor's office, in Town Hall Square, at La Roche-sur-Yon. You know the town. He was there for years, mostly doing litigation work between farmers and landowners. He married the daughter of a solicitor, Arthur Beloin, who died two or three years ago and whose widow still lives at La Roche. I think, if there hadn't been a war, Auguste Point would have continued peacefully to practise as a solicitor in the Vendée and in Poitiers. During the years of occupation one heard very little about him; his life went on as if nothing unusual was happening. Everybody was surprised when a few weeks before they retreated, the Germans arrested him and took him to Niort, and then to somewhere in Alsace. They caught three or four other people at the same time, one of them a surgeon from Bressuires and it was then that we learnt that throughout the war, Auguste Point had hidden British agents and pilots escaped from German camps in the farm he owns near La Roche.

'He came back, thin and a sick man, a few days after the liberation. He did not try to push himself, or worm his way on to committees, nor did he march in any procession. You remember the chaos there was at the time. Politics got mixed up in it, too. Nobody could tell the saints from the sinners. And it was to him they finally turned when they were no longer certain of anything. He did some good work and always with no fuss, without getting a swollen head and we sent him to Paris as deputy. That's more or less the entire story. The Points have kept their house in the town. They live in Paris when the Chamber is in session, then come back as soon as possible and Auguste has retained many of his clients. I believe that his wife helps him a lot. They have a daughter.'

'I know.'

'Well, then you know as much as I do.'

'Do you know his secretary?'

'Mlle Blanche? I often saw her in his office. We call her the Dragon because of the ferocity with which she protects her employer.'

'Nothing more about her?'

'I presume she's in love with him, in the manner of ageing spinsters.'

'She worked for him before she was an ageing spinster.'

'I know. But that's another matter and I can't help you there. What's up?'

'Nothing yet. Do you know a man called Jacques Fleury?'

'Slightly. I met him two or three times but it must be twenty years ago, at least. He must be living in Paris. I don't know what he is doing.'

'Thank you and forgive me again for taking you away from your breakfast.'

'My mother's keeping it warm.'

Not knowing what more to say, Maigret added: 'Is the weather fine, with you?'

'There's some sun, but there's frost on the roofs.'

'It's cold here, too. See you soon, old chap. Give my regards to your mother.'

For Julien Chabot, this telephone call was an event and he was going to ponder over it on his stroll in the streets of the town, wondering why Maigret was so interested in the comings and goings of the Minister of Public Works.

The superintendent's breakfast was accompanied by a lingering after-taste of alcohol and when he went out, he decided to walk, and stopped at a bar in the Place de la République in order to clean out his stomach with a glass of white wine.

He bought all the morning papers, which he was not in the habit of doing, and arrived at the Quai des Orfèvres just in time for the daily report. While his colleagues were gathered in the boss's office, he said nothing, did not really listen, but idly contemplated the Seine and the passers-by on the Pont Saint Michel. He alone remained behind when the others left. The boss knew what that meant.

'What is it, Maigret?'

'Trouble.'

'In the Department?'

'No. Paris has never been so calm as it's been these last five days. But last night, I was summoned in person by a Cabinet Minister and he's asked me to take on an affair I don't like. There was nothing I could do but accept. I warned him I would talk to you about it, but without giving you any details.'

The Director of the P.J. frowned.

'It stinks?'

'Yes, very much so.'

'Connected with the Clairfond disaster?'

'Yes.'

'And a Cabinet Minister has personally entrusted you . . .'

'The President of the Council has been informed.'

'I don't want to know any more. Get on with it, old chap, if you have to. Be careful.'

'I'll try to.'

'Do you need any men?'

'Yes, definitely, three or four. They won't know precisely what it is about.'

'Why didn't he get in touch with Security?'

'You don't understand?'

'I do. That's why I'm not happy about you. Well . . .'

Maigret went to his office and opened the door leading into the inspectors' room.

'Will you come in for a moment, Janvier?'

Then seeing Lapointe on the point of leaving the room:

'Have you got anything important on?'

'No, sir. Just routine jobs.'

'Pass them on to someone else and wait for me. You, too, Lucas.'

Back in his office with Janvier, he closed the door.

'I'm going to give you a hell of a difficult assignment, old boy. There won't be any written report to edit, nor any account to give to anyone but myself. If you make a blunder it may cost you quite a bit.'

Janvier smiled, pleased to be put in charge of a delicate matter.

'The Minister of Public Works has a secretary called Blanche Lamotte, aged about forty-three.'

He had pulled his black notebook out of his pocket.

'I don't know where she lives or what her working hours are. I want to know all about her, the kind of life she leads outside the Ministry and the people she meets. Neither she, nor anyone else, must suspect that the P.J. is interested in her. Perhaps if you watch the staff leaving the building, at noon, you'll be able to discover where she lunches. See what you can do. If she notices you're taking an interest, you'll have to play up to her, if necessary.'

Janvier, who was married and had just had his fourth child, pulled a face.

'Very well, sir. I'll do my best. There's nothing specific that you want me to find out?'

'I want everything you can find and then I'll see what I can make use of.'

'Is it urgent?'

'Very urgent. You won't mention it to anyone, not even to Lapointe or Lucas. Understood?'

He went to the communicating door and opened it again.

'Lapointe! Come here.'

Little Lapointe, as everyone called him because he was the last to join the staff and looked more like a student than a policeman, had already gathered that this was to be a confidential mission and was clearly excited about it.

'You know the School of Civil Engineering?'

'Yes, Rue des Saints-Pères. I used to lunch in a small restaurant almost opposite for a long time.'

'Very well. There is a supervisor there, called Piquemal. His first name is Jules, like mine. I don't know whether he lives in the school or not. I know nothing about him, and I want to know as much as possible.'

He repeated more or less the same as he had said to Janvier.

'For some reason, from the description I've had of him, he gives me the impression of being unmarried. Perhaps he lives in a small hotel. In that case, take a room in the hotel and pretend you're a student.'

Then it was Lucas' turn and there were similar instructions, except that Lucas was assigned to Jacques Fleury, the Minister's parliamentary secretary.

The three inspectors rarely had their photographs in the paper. The general public did not know them, or more precisely, of the three, it knew Lucas and him only by name.

Of course if National Security had had a hand in the business, they would be immediately recognized but that was inevitable. Besides, in that case, as Maigret had already decided that morning, his telephone conversations, whether from his home or from the Quai des Orfèvres, were being listened to by the Rue des Saussaies.

Somebody, the night before, had deliberately shone their lights on him, as much as was possible in such a fog, and if this someone knew Auguste Point's refuge, knew that he was there that night and had a visitor, he was also bound to be able to recognize Maigret at first sight.

Alone in his office he opened the window as if being involved in this business had given him a longing for a breath of fresh air. The papers were on the table. He was on the point of looking at them, then decided to deal first with current affairs, sign reports and summonses.

This almost made him feel a tenderness for the petty thieves, the maniacs, the swindlers, the felons of every variety with whom he usually had to deal.

He made several calls, went back to the inspectors' room to give instructions which had no connection with Point or the wretched Calame report.

By now, Auguste Point must have already gone to the President. Had he told his wife the whole story before he went, as the superintendent had advised him to do?

It was cooler than he had expected and he had to shut the window. He installed himself in his chair and opened the first newspaper in the pile. They were all still full of the Clairfond disaster and all, whatever party they belonged to, were forced, because of public opinion, to clamour for an inquiry.

The majority blamed Arthur Nicoud. One of the articles had the title:

THE MONOPOLY NICOUD-SAUVEGRAIN.

It published the list of works entrusted to the firm in the Avenue de la République over recent years by the government and by certain municipalities. The cost of the works was given in columns on the opposite page and the total reached several billions.

Then in conclusion:

'It would be interesting to establish the list of officials, ministers, deputies, senators, municipal counsellors of the city of Paris and others who have been Arthur Nicoud's guests in his luxurious property in Samois.

'Perhaps a careful study of the counterfoils of Mr Nicoud's cheque book would be revealing.'

One paper, the *Globe*, of which the deputy Mascoulin was, if not the owner, certainly the inspiration, had a headline in the style of Zola's famous 'J'accuse'.

IS IT TRUE THAT ...?

And a number of questions followed, in larger print than usual, in a lay-out that emphasized the text.

274

'Is it true that the idea of the Clairfond Sanatorium was not born in the minds of legislators desperately concerned with children's health, but in the mind of a dealer in concrete?

'Is it true that this idea had been introduced five years previously to a number of high-placed officials over luxurious lunches given by that dealer in concrete at his property in Samois?

'Is it true that not only did they find there excellent food and wine, but that the guests emerged from their host's private study with fat cheques in their pockets?

'Is it true that when the project took shape, all those who knew the site chosen for the miraculous sanatorium realized the folly and the danger of the enterprise?

'Is it true that the parliamentary commission entrusted with recommendations to the Chamber and presided over by the brother of the present President of the Council found itself obliged to appeal to the experienced opinion of an expert of untarnished reputation?

'Is it true that that specialist, Julien Calame, professor of applied mechanics and civil architecture at the National School of Civil Engineering went to spend three weeks on the spot with the plans ... and that on his return he handed over to the proper quarter a report catastrophic for the supporters of the project ... that nevertheless the funds were allocated and the construction of Clairfond started a few weeks later?

'Is it true that up to his death, two years ago, Julien Calame, according to all who saw him, gave the impression of a man with a load on his conscience?

'Is it true that in his report he foresaw the Clairfond disaster almost exactly as it happened?

'Is it true that the Calame report, which must have existed in a number of copies, has disappeared from the archives of the Chamber of Deputies as well as from those of several interested ministries?

'Is it true that at least thirty government employees have lived in terror since the disaster lest a copy of the report should be found?

'Is it true that in spite of all precautions, it has been found at a very recent date?

'. . . and that this resurrected copy has been handed over to the proper quarters.'

Then, in a further headline across the page:

WE WANT TO KNOW

'Is the Calame report still in the hands of the person to whom it was given? Or has it been destroyed to save the gang of compromised politicians? If it is not so – where is it at the moment of writing and why has it not yet been published, when public opinion justifiably demands the punishment of those guilty of a disaster that has cost the lives of one hundred and twenty-eight young Frenchmen?'

And at the end of the page, in the same print as the two preceding titles:

WHERE IS THE CALAME REPORT?

Maigret found himself wiping his forehead. It was not difficult to imagine Auguste Point's reaction on reading the article.

The *Globe* did not have a large circulation. It was an independent paper. Nor did it represent any of the big parties; only a small faction, of which Joseph Mascoulin was the leader.

But the other papers would certainly set in motion their own independent inquiries, to discover the truth. And this truth Maigret, too, wished to discover, provided it was discovered in its entirety.

He had, however, the impression that it was not what they were searching for. If Mascoulin, for instance, was the man in whose hands the report was at the moment, why did he not publish it in letters as large as his article? He would have immediately provoked a ministerial crisis, a radical sweep of the parliamentarian ranks and he would have appeared to the public as the defender of the people's interests and of political morality.

For a man who had always worked in the background this was a unique opportunity to achieve great prominence and probably play a tremendous part in the years to come. If he was in possession of the document, why did he not publish it?

It was Maigret's turn to put the questions.

If Mascoulin did not have it, how did he know that the report had been found?

How had he learnt that Piquemal had handed it over to an official person?

And why did he suspect that Auguste Point had not transmitted it higher up?

Maigret had no desire to penetrate or to have knowledge of the shady side of politics. But he did not have to know much about the intrigues that simmer behind the scenes to be aware:

1. That it was in a dubious if not blackmailing paper like the *Rumeur* owned by Hector Tabard that the Calame report had been mentioned three times after the Clairfond disaster.

2. That the discovery of this report had followed this publication in rather strange circumstances.

3. That Piquemal, a simple supervisor at the National School of Engineering had gone direct to the Minister instead of following the old established rule, in this case, of approaching the director of the school.

4. That Joseph Mascoulin had become aware of this operation.

5. That he seemed equally aware of the disappearance of the report.

Were Mascoulin and Tabard playing the same game? Were they playing it together or each on his own account?

Maigret went to open the window again and stood for a long time looking at the Seine, smoking his pipe. Never had he had to deal with such a complicated case, with so little evidence at his disposal.

When the crime was a burglary or a murder he was at once on familiar ground. Here, on the contrary, it was a question of people whose names and reputations he knew only vaguely from the newspapers. He knew, for instance, that Mascoulin lunched every day at the same table in a restaurant in the Place de la Victoire called 'Filet de Sole' where a constant stream of people came to shake his hand and whisper him some information. Mascoulin was believed to know all there was to know about the private life of all the politicians. His interpellations were rare, his name appeared in the papers only on the eve of an important issue. Then one might read:

'The deputy Mascoulin foretells that the project will be adopted by three hundred and forty-two votes.'

Professionals took these prognostications as they would the Bible, for Mascoulin was rarely mistaken, and then never by more than two or three votes.

He did not take part in any commissions, did not preside over any committee, nevertheless he was more feared than the leader of a big party.

Maigret decided he would go at noon to the 'Filet de Sole' and lunch there, if only to see at closer quarters the man of whom he had only had a glimpse on official occasions.

Mascoulin was a bachelor, though he was over forty. No mistresses were connected with his name. He was never seen at receptions, theatres or night clubs. He had a long, bony head and already at noon, he seemed to need a shave. He dressed badly, that is to say, he paid no attention to his clothes; they were never pressed and gave an impression of doubtful cleanliness.

Why was it that from the description that Auguste Point had given him of Piquemal, Maigret formed the opinion that this man was rather of the same type?

He suspected solitary men, people without an acknowledged passion.

Finally he decided against lunching at the 'Filet de Sole', because that would have seemed a declaration of war, and instead made his way to the Brasserie Dauphine. He found there two colleagues with whom for an hour he succeeded in talking of things other than the Calame report.

One of the afternoon papers had taken up the theme of the *Globe* in a much more prudent manner, with veiled insinuations, demanding only the truth on the subject of the Calame report. One of the editors had tried to interview the President of the Council himself on the subject but did not succeed in approaching him. Auguste Point was not mentioned, for the building of the sanatorium was in fact the business of the Ministry of Public Health.

At three o'clock there was a knock on Maigret's door. He growled and immediately it was opened, and Lapointe came in, with a worried expression on his face.

278

'You've got news?'

'Nothing definite, sir. Up to now, everything has been a matter of chance.'

'Give me all the details.'

'I tried to follow your instructions. You'll tell me if I made mistakes. First I telephoned the National School of Civil Engineering pretending that I was a cousin of Piquemal's and that I had just arrived in Paris and wanted to see him but didn't have his address.'

'Did they give it to you?'

'Without the slightest hesitation. He lives at the Hôtel du Berry, Rue Jacob. It's a modest hotel, with about thirty rooms and the owner herself does most of the cleaning, while her husband does the accounts. I went back home to fetch a suitcase and presented myself at the Rue Jacob as a student, as you suggested. I was lucky, there was a free room and I took it for a week. It was about half past ten when I came down and stopped at the office to have a chat with the proprietor.'

'Did you mention Piquemal?'

'Yes, I told him that I had seen him in the holidays and remembered that he lived here.'

'What did he tell you?'

'That he was out. He leaves the hotel every morning at eight o'clock and goes to a small bar to have his coffee and croissants. He has to be in the school at half past eight.'

'Does he return to the hotel during the day?'

'No. He comes back regularly round about half past seven, goes to his room and goes out again only a couple of times a week. It seems he is the most regular man in the world, never entertains anyone, sees no women, doesn't smoke or drink and spends his evenings and sometimes part of the night reading.'

Maigret sensed that Lapointe had more to say and waited patiently.

'Perhaps I did wrong? But I thought I was doing the right thing. When I discovered that his room was on the same floor as mine and got the number, I thought you would like to know what was inside it. During the day the hotel is almost always empty. There was only someone playing the saxophone on the third floor, probably a musician practising, and I could hear the servant on the floor above me. I tried my key. They are simple keys, an old-fashioned type. It didn't work at first, but I fiddled about a bit and managed to open the door.'

'I hope Piquemal didn't happen to be at home?'

'No. If they search for my fingerprints they'll find them everywhere, because I didn't wear gloves. I opened the drawers, the cupboard, and an unlocked suitcase as well, hidden in a corner. Piquemal has only one extra suit, dark grey, and a pair of black shoes. His comb has got half its teeth missing and his toothbrush is ancient. He doesn't use cream to shave himself, only a brush. The proprietor is right when he says that he spends his evenings reading. There are books all over the place, particularly books on philosophy, political economy and history. Most of them have been bought second-hand on the quais. Three or four of them come from public libraries. I copied a few of the authors' names. Engels, Spinoza, Kirkegaard, St Augustin, Karl Marx, Father Sertillange, St Simon.... Does it make any sense to you?'

'It does. Go on.'

'There was a cardboard box in one of the drawers containing membership cards, old and new, some from twenty years back, some only three. The oldest is the Association of the Cross of Fire. There is another one dated 1937, belonging to the Action Française. Immediately after the war, Piquemal joined a branch of the Communist party. The card was renewed for three years.'

Lapointe was consulting his notes.

'He has also belonged to the International League of Theosophy, based in Switzerland. You've heard of it?'

'Yes.'

'I forgot to tell you two of the books were about Yoga and there was a practical text-book of Judo as well.'

Judging by all this Piquemal had tried all manner of philosophical and social theories. All extremist parties have men like him who march behind the banners staring fixedly ahead.

'That's all?'

'So far as his room is concerned, yes. No letters. When I came down, I asked the proprietor whether he ever got any mail and he replied that he'd never seen anything except prospectuses and circulars. I went to the bistro at the corner. Unfortunately, it was the aperitif hour. The counter was crowded. I had to wait for a long time and have two drinks before I could speak to the owner without appearing to be leading an inquiry, I told him the same story: that I came from the provinces and was anxious to see Piquemal.

' "The professor?" he asked.'

Which seemed to indicate that in certain circles Piquemal assumed the rank of a professor.

' "If you had come at eight o'clock. . . . By now he must be busy teaching. . . . I don't know where he lunches."

' "Did he come this morning?"

' "I saw him picking out his croissants, as usual. He always eats three. But today somebody I don't know, and who had arrived before him, came up to him and engaged him in conversation. Generally speaking Piquemal is not forthcoming. He must have too many things on his mind to waste his time in idle talk. He's polite, but cold – you know the kind – 'Good morning. How much is that? Goodbye.' It doesn't bother me because I have other clients like him, people who work with their minds and I can imagine how it is with them. But what surprised me was to see M. Piquemal leave with the stranger and instead of going to the left, as he usually does, they turned right." '

'What was the other man like, did they describe him?'

'Not very well. A man about forty, looking like a minor official or a commercial traveller. He walked in without saying anything, a little before eight, went to the counter and ordered a coffee with milk. No beard or moustache. On the corpulent side.'

Maigret could not help thinking that this could be the description of some dozen inspectors from the Rue des Saussaies.

'That's all you know?'

'Yes. After lunch I rang up the National School of Civil Engineering again and asked for Piquemal. This time I didn't tell them who I was and they didn't ask me. But they replied that he hadn't been seen all day.'

'Is he on holiday?'

'No. He just didn't turn up. What is more astonishing is that he didn't telephone to say he would be absent. It's the first time it's ever happened. I went back to my room in the Hôtel de Berry. Then I went and knocked at Piquemal's door. I opened it. There was nobody there. Nothing had been moved since my first visit. You've asked me for all the details. I went to the school, and pretended to be the friend from the provinces. I learnt where he lunches – about a hundred yards away, Rue des Saints-Pères, in a Norman restaurant. I went there. Piquemal hadn't lunched today. I saw his napkin with a numbered ring on it and a half-finished bottle of mineral water on his usual table. That's all, sir. Did I do anything wrong?'

What prompted him to ask the last question, in some anxiety, was that Maigret's forehead had a frown on it and his face was troubled. Was this affair going to end like the other political affair with which Maigret had had to deal and which had disgraced him at Luçon? That other time, too, it had all come about because of a certain rivalry between the Rue des Saussaies and the Quai des Orfèvres, each of the police departments receiving different directives, each defending opposing interests whether they liked it or not because of a struggle in high places.

At midnight, the President of the Council had learnt that Auguste Point had approached Maigret.

At 8 a.m. Piquemal, the man who had discovered the Calame report, had been approached by a stranger in the little bar where he was peacefully drinking his coffee and he had followed the man without hesitation, without argument.

'You've done good work, my boy.'

'No spelling mistakes?'

'I don't think so.'

'And now?'

'I don't know. Perhaps you'd better stay on in the Hôtel de Berry in case Piquemal returns.'

'In that case, I'll telephone you.'

'Yes, here or at home.'

One of the men who had read the Calame report had disappeared.

Auguste Point who had also read it was still there, but he was a Cabinet Minister and therefore more difficult to conjure away.

At the very thought of it, Maigret seemed to taste again the drink he'd had the night before and all he wanted was a glass of beer somewhere cheek by jowl with ordinary people with ordinary little problems.

Chapter Four

Maigret was on his way back from the 'Brasserie Dauphine' where he had gone to have a pint of beer, when he saw Janvier proceeding rapidly towards Police Headquarters.

It was almost hot, in the middle of the afternoon. The sun had lost its dimness and for the first time this year, Maigret had left his coat in the office. He called 'Hey!' two or three times. Janvier stopped, saw him and walked back to him.

'Do you want a drink?'

Without any particular reason the superintendent was reluctant to go straight back to the Quai des Orfèvres. The spring, probably, had something to do with it, adding to the atmosphere of tension which had surrounded him since the day before.

Janvier had a comic look on his face, the look of a man who is not quite sure whether he is going to get a scolding or be patted on the back. Instead of staying by the counter, they went to the back room, which at this time of day was empty.

'A beer?'

'If I may . . .'

They stayed silent, waiting to be served.

'We aren't the only ones trailing the little lady, boss,' Janvier murmured. 'I get the impression that there are quite a few of us interested in her movements.'

'Tell me the whole thing.'

'I made it my first business, this morning, to go and have a look round near the Ministry, in the Boulevard Saint-Germain. I got to about twenty feet of it when I saw Rougier standing on the opposite pavement, and apparently taking a keen interest in the sparrows.'

Both men knew Gaston Rougier, an inspector from the Rue

des Saussaies with whom they were, as a matter of fact, on the best of terms. He was a decent sort, who lived in the suburbs and always had his pockets full of photographs of his seven or eight children.

'Did he see you?'

'Yes.'

'Did he speak to you?'

'The street was almost empty. I couldn't possibly avoid him. When I got up to him, he asked me:

' "You, too?"

'I acted the fool and asked:

' "Me, too, what?"

'Then he winked at me.

' "Nothing. I'm not asking you to let the cat out of the bag. I'm surprised to see so many familiar faces about, this morning, that's all. It's just bad luck that there's not even a bistro opposite this blasted Ministry."

'From where we were standing, we could see into the inner yard and I recognized Ramire of General Information, who seemed to be getting on like a house on fire with the concierge.

'I kept up the acting and went on my way. I didn't stop till I got to a café in the Rue Solferino and tried my luck with the telephone directory. I found Blanche Lamotte's name and her address, 63 Rue Vaneau. It was only a stone's throw away.'

'And there again you bumped into Security?'

'Not quite. You know the Rue Vaneau. It's quiet, almost provincial, even has a few trees in the gardens. No. 63 is an unpretentious block of flats, but quite comfortable. The concierge was in her room, peeling potatoes.

' "Is Mlle Lamotte at home?" I asked.

'I could tell at once she was looking at me somewhat ironically. However, I ignored this.

' "I'm an inspector from an insurance company," I said.

' "Mlle Lamotte has applied for a life insurance and I'm just making the usual inquiries." She didn't actually burst out laughing, but very nearly. And then she asked me:

' "How many different branches of the Police are there in Paris?"

' "I don't know what you mean."

284

' "As far as you're concerned, I've seen you before with a fat superintendent, whose name I've forgotten, when the little lady in 57 took an overdose of sleeping pills two years ago. This time all your colleagues have been at it."

' "How many of them have been here, then?" I asked.

' "There was one yesterday morning."

' "Did he show you his badge?"

' "I didn't ask him for it. I'm not asking for yours, either. I'm quite capable of recognizing a policeman when I see one."

' "Did he ask you a lot of questions?"

' "Four or five: if she lived alone, if she was visited sometimes by a man about fifty, on the fat side. . . . I said no."

' "Is that the truth?"

' "It is. Also if she often had a briefcase when she came home. I told him she did sometimes, that she also has a typewriter upstairs in her flat and that she often brings work back in the evening. I suppose that you know as well as I do that she's a Cabinet Minister's secretary."

' "I'm aware of it, yes."

' "He also wanted to know if she had had her briefcase with her last night. I had to admit that I hadn't noticed. Then he pretended to be going away. I went up to the first floor where I go every day, to oblige an old lady. I heard him on the stairs a little later on, but I didn't let on I was there. But I do know that he stopped at the third floor, where Mlle Blanche lives and that he got into her flat."

' "You allowed him to do that?"

' "I've been a concierge long enough to have learnt not to be on bad terms with the police."

' "Did he stay there for a long time?"

' "About ten minutes."

' "Did you see him again?"

' "Not that one."

' "Did you speak to the lady about it?" '

Maigret was listening, staring hard at his glass, trying to fit the incident in with the events that he already knew. Janvier went on:

'She hesitated. She felt she was blushing and decided to tell me the truth.

' "I told her that someone had been here asking questions about her and had gone up to her floor. I didn't mention the police."

' "Did she seem surprised?"

' "At first – yes. Then she murmured: 'I think I know what it's about.' "

' "As for the ones that came this morning, a few moments after she had gone to work – there were two of them. They told me as well that they were from the police. The smaller went to show me his badge but I didn't look at it."

' "Did they go up too?"

' "No. They asked me the same questions and some others as well."

' "What others?"

' "Whether she goes out a lot, who with, who her friends are, male and female, whether she does a lot of telephoning, whether . . ." '

Maigret interrupted the inspector:

'What did she tell you about her?'

'She gave me the names of her friends, of a certain Lucile Cristin who lives in the neighbourhood, who most likely works in an office and has a squint. Mlle Blanche lunches in the Boulevard Saint-Germain, in a restaurant called "The Three Ministries". In the evening she cooks her own dinner. This Lucile Cristin often comes to eat with her. I've not been able to find her address. The concierge also told me about another friend, who doesn't often come to the Rue Vaneau, but whom Mlle Blanche goes to dine with every Sunday. She's married to an agent in the Halles called Hariel and lives in the Rue de Courcelles. The concierge believes she comes from La Roche-sur-Yon, like Mlle Blanche.'

'Did you go to the Rue de Courcelles?'

'I gathered from you I was to leave no stone unturned. As I don't even know what it is all about . . .'

'Go on.'

'Her information was correct. I went to Mme Hariel's flat; she leads a comfortable life, has three children; the youngest is eight. I put on the insurance agent act again. She was perfectly calm and I took it from that that I was the first to come and see

286

her. She knew Blanche Lamotte in La Roche, where they went to school together. They had lost sight of one another and met accidentally in Paris three years ago. Mme Hariel invited her friend to her home and she got the habit of coming to dine every Sunday. Nothing of any interest besides that. Blanche Lamotte leads a regular life, entirely devoted to her work and talks enthusiastically about her boss for whom she would gladly die.'

'That's all?'

'No. About a year ago, Blanche asked Hariel if she knew of any vacant job for a friend of hers, who was in difficulties. It was Fleury. Hariel, who seems to be a kind-hearted man, gave him some work in his office. Fleury had to go there every day at 6 a.m.'

'What happened?'

'He worked for three days, and after that they never saw him again and he never even apologized. Mlle Blanche was very embarrassed by the whole thing and apologized profusely for him. I went back to the Boulevard Saint Germain with the idea of calling at "The Three Ministries". I could see, long before I got there, not only Gaston Rougier on the old spot but one of his colleagues as well, I've forgotten his name.'

Maigret was trying hard to put all this information into some kind of order. On Monday evening Auguste Point had gone to his flat in the Boulevard Pasteur and had left the Calame report there, believing it to be safer there than elsewhere.

On Tuesday morning, someone who pretended to be from the police, had presented himself at the Rue Vaneau, the residence of Mlle Blanche, and after asking the concierge some questions of no importance had managed to get himself into her flat. Was he really from the police? If he was, the whole business had an even more unpleasant twist to it than the superintendent imagined. However, he had a feeling that this first visit had nothing to do with the Rue des Saussaies. Was it the same man who, finding nothing in the secretary's flat, had gone on to the Boulevard Pasteur and taken the document from there?

'She didn't describe him to you?'

'Only vaguely. An ordinary party – neither young nor old,

rather stout, with enough experience in questioning for her to take him for a policeman.'

This was almost the same description that the owner of the bar in the Rue Jacob had given of the man who had approached Piquemal and had left with him. As for this morning's little lot – the ones who had not gone to the secretary's flat – it seemed likely they would be from the Security Department.

'What am I to do now?'

'I don't know.'

'Oh, I forgot, as I recrossed the Boulevard Saint-Germain I thought I caught a glimpse of Lucas in a bar.'

'It could have been him . . .'

'Is he on the same case?'

'More or less.'

'Am I to go on taking an interest in the lady?'

'We'll see after I've talked to Lucas. Wait here for a moment.'

Maigret went to the telephone and called the P.J.

'Is Lucas back?'

'Not yet.'

'Is it you, Torrence? As soon as he turns up, please send him to the Brasserie Dauphine.'

A boy was passing in the street with the latest edition of the afternoon papers bearing large headlines and Maigret walked to the door searching for some change in his pocket. When he came back and sat down beside Janvier he spread out the paper. The headline running across the entire page said:

HAS ARTHUR NICOUD ESCAPED?

The news was sensational enough for the paper to have altered its front page.

'The Clairfond case has reopened in an unexpected manner, though there are those who ought to have foreseen it. It is known that the day after the disaster public opinion was greatly upset and demanded a thorough examination of the people responsible. The Nicoud and Sauvegrain enterprise, which five years ago built the now all too famous sanatorium should have been, according to those in the know, made the object of a strict and immediate inquiry. Why has nothing been done? This is what we hope will be explained to us in the next few days. However, Arthur Nicoud, afraid of appearing in public, has considered it safer to seek refuge in a hunting lodge he owns in Sologne. The police were apparently aware of it. We have even been assured that it was, in fact, the police who suggested to the contractor that he should disappear for a time from circulation, in order to avoid trouble. Only this morning, four weeks after the disaster, has it been decided in high places to summon Arthur Nicoud and question him on matters that are of burning interest to everyone. Early this morning two inspectors from the Security Department went to the lodge where they found no one but the game-keeper. He told the officers that his master had left the night before for an unknown destination. But it did not remain unknown for long. Two hours ago, in fact, our special correspondent in Brussels telephoned to say that Arthur Nicoud had arrived in the town later this morning and occupies a luxurious suite in the Hôtel Metropole. Our correspondent succeeded in approaching him and put to him the following questions which we reproduce verbatim together with the replies.

' "Is it true that you left your lodge in Sologne so abruptly because you were warned that the police were coming to visit you?"

' "It is completely untrue. I knew and know nothing about the police's intentions; for the last month they have known perfectly well where to find me."

' "Did you leave France, because you could foresee fresh developments?"

' "I came to Brussels because I have some building plans here that necessitated my presence."

' "What building plans?"

' "The construction of an aerodrome for which I have put in a tender."

' "Do you intend to go back to France and place yourself at the disposal of the authorities?"

' "I have no intention of altering anything in my plans."

' "Do you mean to say that you will remain in Brussels until the Clairfond case is forgotten?"

' "I repeat that I'm staying here as long as my business keeps me."

' "Even if an order were issued for you to return?"

' "The police had a whole month in which to question me. It isn't my fault if they haven't done so!"

' "You have heard about the Calame report?"

' "I don't know what you are talking about."

'At this point Arthur Nicoud put an end to the conversation, which our correspondent immediately telephoned to us. It seems – though we were unable to get a confirmation – that an elegant, fair-haired young woman arrived an hour after Nicoud and was shown immediately to his apartment where she probably is at the moment. In the Rue des Saussaies, it has been confirmed that two inspectors went to Sologne to question the contractor on several matters. When we mentioned an order to return, we were told that there could be no question of that for the moment.'

'Is that the case we're working on?' Janvier muttered with a wry expression.

'It is.'

He opened his mouth, probably to ask how it had happened that Maigret had agreed to have anything to do with such an unsavoury political case. But he said nothing. Lucas could be seen crossing the square, slightly dragging his left leg as usual. He did not stop at the bar, but came and sat opposite the two men, wiping the sweat from his face and looking gloomy.

Pointing to the paper, he uttered in a reproachful voice which he never used in Maigret's presence:

'I've just read it.'

And the superintendent felt a little guilty as he faced his colleagues. Lapointe had probably also discovered by now what it was all about.

'A pint?' offered Maigret.

'No. A Pernod.'

And this, too, was not characteristic of Lucas. They waited to be served before they began to talk in an undertone.

'I suppose you bumped into the man from the Big House everywhere you went?' It was their way of describing Security.

'You might have warned me to be discreet,' grumbled Lucas. 'If it is a question of getting ahead of them, I can tell you straight away they're way up in front.'

'Tell us.'

'Tell you what?'

'What you've been up to.'

'I started to stroll up and down in the Boulevard Saint-Germain, having got there a few minutes after Janvier.'

'And Rougier?' asked the latter, unable to keep from smiling at the comical side of it.

'He was standing in the middle of the pavement and saw me arrive. I pretended to be going somewhere in a hurry. He laughed at me and greeted me with: "You searching for Janvier? He has just turned the corner of the Rue Solferino." It is always a pleasure to be made to feel a fool by someone from the Rue de Saussaies. As it was impossible to get any information on Jacques Fleury in the neighbourhood of the Ministry, I . . .'

'You looked for a telephone directory?' asked Janvier.

'I didn't think of it. I knew that he frequented the bars in the Champs-Elysées, so I went to Fouquet's.'

'I bet he's in the directory.'

'Possibly. Will you let me say what I've got to say.'

Janvier, by this time, was in a light-headed teasing mood like someone who has just had a good scolding and watches someone else being scolded in his turn.

In fact, all three of them, Maigret included, felt on foreign ground, each as clumsy as the other and each could imagine their colleagues at Security enjoying the joke behind their backs.

'I had a chat with the barman. Fleury is notorious in a way. Most of the time he lives on credit as long as he can and when he owes too much they don't allow him to be served any more. Then he disappears for a few days, until he has exhausted his credit in all the other bars and restaurants.'

'Does he pay in the end?'

'He turns up eventually, full of the joys of spring and settles his account.'

'And then it starts all over again?'

'Yes. It's been going on for years.'

'Even since he's been in the Ministry?'

'With the difference that now he is Private Secretary and people think he has some influence, more of them supply him with food and drink. Before that he used to disappear for months on end. One day he was seen working in the Halles, counting the cabbages coming off a lorry.'

Janvier darted a significant glance at Maigret.

'He has a wife and two children, somewhere in the direction of Vanves. He is supposed to be supporting them. Luckily his wife has a job, something like housekeeping for an elderly gentleman. The children work, too.'

'Who does he go to the bars with?'

'For a long time it was with a woman of about forty, a stout woman with dark hair, they tell me, known as Marcelle; he seemed to be in love with her. Some say that he took her away from the cashier's desk of a Brasserie at the Porte Saint Martin. Nobody knows what became of her. For more than a year, he has been seen with a Jacqueline Page and lives with her in a flat in the Rue Washington, above an Italian grocer's. Jacqueline Page is twenty-three years old and sometimes works as an extra in films. She cultivates all the producers, directors and actors who come to Fouquet's and is as accommodating as they could wish.'

'Is Fleury in love with her?'

'Apparently.'

'Is he jealous?'

'So they say. But he doesn't dare protest and pretends not to notice anything.'

'Have you seen her?'

'I thought I ought to go to the Rue Washington.'

'What sort of a story did you tell her?'

'There was no need of a story. As soon as she opened her door, she exclaimed: "What, another of you?" '

Janvier and Maigret could not help exchanging a smile.

'Another what?' asked Maigret, knowing perfectly well what the reply would be.

'Another policeman, you know what I mean. Two of them had been there before me.'

'Separately?'

'No, together.'

'Did they question her about Fleury?'

'They asked her if he worked in the evenings and brought documents home from the Ministry.'

'What did she tell them?'

'That they had other things to do with their evenings. That girl doesn't mince her words. Curiously enough her mother looks after the pews in the church at Picpus.'

'Did they search the flat?'

'No, they just looked round the rooms. It isn't really a flat. It's more a sort of camping site. The kitchen is just large enough to prepare breakfast in. The other rooms, a living-room, a bedroom and what could be called a dining-room were in complete chaos, with shoes and a woman's underclothes all over the place and records and coloured magazines, paper-backs, not counting the bottles and glasses.'

'Does he come home to lunch?'

'Rarely. Usually she keeps to her bed until the middle of the afternoon. Now and then he rings her up in the morning suggesting she should meet him in a restaurant.'

'Have they got many friends?'

'Just people who go to the same dives as they do.'

'Is that all?'

For the first time, Lucas's voice rang with an almost pathetic reproach as he answered:

'No, it isn't! Your instructions were to provide you with as much information as possible. In the first place I have here a list of about a dozen of Jacqueline's former lovers, including some that she still goes on seeing.'

With an expression of disgust, he threw a paper with pencilled names on it on the table.

'You'll see that it contains the names of two politicians. Another thing: I almost found the girl Marcelle again.'

'How did you do that?'

'On my two legs. I toured the bars of the main boulevards, beginning with the one by the Opéra. As usual it was the last one I came to, in the Place de la République, that was the right one.'

'Marcelle has gone back to being a cashier?'

'No, but they remember her and have seen her in the neighbourhood. The owner of the bar believes that she lives nearby, in the direction of the Rue Blondel. He has met her often in the Rue de Croissant, so he gathers that she works in a newspaper office or a printers.'

'Did you check?'

'Not yet. Must I?'

The tone was such that Maigret murmured:

'Angry?'

Lucas forced himself to smile.

'No. But you must admit it's a rum sort of job. Especially when one learns afterwards from the paper that it's this miserable business we're on to! If I must go on, I'll go on. But I can tell you frankly . . .'

'Don't you think I'm not as fed up as you are?'

'No. I know you are.'

'The Rue de Croissant is not as long as all that. Everyone knows everyone else in that part of the world.'

'And I suppose I'll get there just after the boys of the Rue des Saussaies, like last time!'

'It's very probable.'

'All right, I'll go. May I have another?' He was pointing to his glass which he had just emptied. Maigret gave a sign to the waiter to repeat the order and at the last moment ordered himself a Pernod instead of a beer.

Inspectors from other departments had forgathered to have a drink at the bar at the end of the day and waved their hands in greeting. Maigret was frowning, thinking of Auguste Point who must have read the article and must be expecting to see his own name in equally large letters in the papers any minute now. His wife, whom he must have informed of the whole business was probably as anxious as he was. Had he spoken to Mlle Blanche? Did they realize, the three of them, just how much activity was going on around them?

'What am I to do now?' asked Janvier in the tone of one repelled by his assignment, but resigned to seeing it through.

'Are you brave enough to keep watch in the Rue Vaneau?'

'For the whole night?'

'No. I'll send Torrence to relieve you about eleven, let's say.'

'You think something will happen there?'

Maigret admitted:

'No.'

He had not the vaguest idea. Or rather he had so many and such muddled ideas that he could not make head or tail of them. One had to come back to the simpler facts, those one could check. It was certain that on Monday afternoon, the man Piquemal had come to see the Minister of Public Works. He must have approached the porter, filled in a form. Maigret had not seen it, but it must have been put on record and Auguste Point would not have invented such a visit.

At least two persons from the adjoining offices were likely to have heard the conversation: Mlle Blanche and Jacques Fleury.

Security had thought of that, too, as they had made inquiries at their lodgings.

Had Piquemal really handed the Calame report to Auguste Point? It seemed improbable to Maigret that the latter should have conjured up all this comedy which, then, would seem to make no sense at all.

Auguste Point had gone to his private house, on the Boulevard Pasteur. He had left the document in his desk again. The superintendent believed that this was true. Therefore, the person who had come to see Mlle Blanche the next morning and searched her flat, was not certain exactly where the report was to be found.

And in the afternoon the document had disappeared.

Wednesday morning Piquemal also disappeared.

On the same day Joseph Mascoulin's paper first mentioned the Calame report and demanded publicly to know where the document was hidden.

Maigret's lips were moving, he spoke in a low voice, as though to himself.

'It's either one thing or the other – they may have stolen the report to destroy it, or stolen it to use it. Up to now it seems that no one has used it.'

Lucas and Janvier listened without interrupting him.

'Unless . . .'

He slowly drank half his glass, and wiped his mouth.

'It seems complicated, but when it is a question of politics, things are rarely simple. Only one or two people involved in the Clairfond case have any reason to destroy the document. If we learn that it has disappeared after having surfaced for a few hours, suspicion will automatically fall on them.'

'I think I begin to understand,' murmured Janvier.

'In this case, about thirty politicians at least, without counting Nicoud himself, are faced with a scandal and worse. If one succeeds in throwing suspicion on one individual, and if one can produce evidence against him, and this individual is vulnerable – one has the ideal scapegoat. Auguste Point's position is indefensible.'

His two colleagues glanced at him in surprise. Maigret had forgotten that they knew only a part of the case. The point when it was possible to keep things secret from them had been passed.

'He is on the list of Nicoud's guests at Samois,' he told them. 'The contractor made his daughter a present of a gold fountain-pen.'

'You saw it?'

He nodded.

'And it was he who . . .?'

Lucas did not finish his question. Maigret had understood it. The inspector had wanted to say:

'It was he who asked you to help him?'

This at last dissipated the embarrassment that had weighed on the three men.

'Yes, it was. By now, I would be surprised if others didn't know it, too.'

'We needn't be secretive any more?'

'Certainly not as far as Security is concerned.'

They lingered over their glasses another quarter of an hour. Maigret was the first to rise, to wish them good night and go to his office in case he was wanted. There was no message for him. Point had not telephoned nor had anyone connected with the Clairfond case.

At dinner, Mme Maigret saw by his face that he had better not be questioned. He spent the evening reading an international police magazine and went to bed at ten.

'You have a lot of work on your plate?'

They were on the point of going to sleep. She had kept the question for a long time on the tip of her tongue.

'Not much, but what there is is nasty.'

Twice, before falling asleep, he was tempted to ring up

Auguste Point. He did not know what he would have said to him, but he would have liked to establish contact.

At eight o'clock he was up. Behind the curtains, a light mist clung to the windowpanes and seemed to have hushed the noise of the street. He walked to the corner of the Boulevard Richard-Lenoir to take the bus and stopped to buy the newspapers.

The bomb had exploded. The papers asked no more questions, but announced in headlines:

THE CLAIRFOND CASE

Disappearance of Jules Piquemal, who found the Calame Report

'The report which was handed in at a very high level is understood to have also disappeared.'

His newspapers under his arm, he got into the bus and did not read any more before arriving at the Quai des Orfèvres.

As he walked down the passage he heard the telephone ringing in his office, and hurried to lift the receiver.

'Superintendent Maigret?' the telephonist asked. 'It's the third time in a quarter of an hour that you have been called from the Ministry of Public Works. I'm putting you through now.'

He still had his hat on his head and was still wearing his coat, slightly damp from the morning fog.

Chapter Five

The voice was that of a man who had not slept the night before, nor on the preceding nights either and who made no effort to choose his words because he had passed the stage of worrying what he sounded like. It was that flat, lifeless disheartened tone that indicates in a man rather the same symptom as when a woman weeps in a particular dreary way, her mouth wide open, and looks ugly without minding it.

'Can you come and see me at once, Maigret? Unless it embarrasses you personally, there is no reason now to avoid the Boulevard Saint-Germain. I warn you that the waiting room is full of journalists and the telephone never stops. I have promised them a press conference at 11 a.m.'

Maigret glanced at his watch.

'I'll come straight away.'

There was a knock at the door. Little Lapointe walked in as Maigret was still holding the receiver, frowning deeply.

'You've got something to tell me?'

'Yes, some fresh news.'

'Important?'

'I think so.'

'Put on your hat and come with me. We can talk on the way.'

He stopped for a moment at the door to ask the doorman to warn the chief that he would not be at the morning briefing. In the car park he went to one of the small black cars of the P.J.

'You drive.'

And as they were driving along the embankment:

'What have you got to tell me?'

'I spent the night at the Hôtel de Berry in the room I rented.'

'Piquemal hasn't reappeared?'

'No. A man from Security kept watch all night in the street.'

Maigret was prepared for this. It was not disturbing.

'I didn't want to go to Piquemal's room while it was dark, for I'd have had to switch on the light and it would have been seen from the street. I waited till it was light and then gave it a more thorough search than I did the first time. I went through all the books one after the other and searched between the pages. In a treatise on political economy I found this letter, which had been slipped in as a book-mark.'

Driving with one hand, he pulled his wallet out of his pocket with the other and passed it to Maigret.

'On the left side. The letter that's headed the Chamber of Deputies.'

It was a small note, like those the Deputies use for short memoranda. It was dated the previous Thursday. The writing was small, uneven, with letters climbing one on top of the other and the ends of the words almost indecipherable.

Dear Sir,

I thank you for your communication. I am greatly interested in what you tell me and will be glad to see you tomorrow, towards 8 p.m. at the Brasserie du Croissant, Rue Montmartre. I beg you not to mention the matter in question to anybody until then.

Yours

There was no real signature, simply a scrawl that might have meant anything.

'I expect it's Joseph Mascoulin,' growled the superintendent.

'Yes, it's him. I went earlier to a friend who is a stenographer in the Chamber and knows most of the deputies' handwriting. I had only to show him the first line and the scrawl at the end.'

They were already in the Boulevard Saint-Germain, opposite the Ministry of Public Works. Maigret could recognize several cars belonging to the Press. He glanced at the opposite pavement, but saw no one from the Rue des Saussaies. Now that the bomb had actually exploded, had they called off the watch?

'Do I wait for you?'

'Yes, it would be better that way.'

He crossed the yard, went up the main stairs and found himself in a waiting-room with a dark-red carpet and yellow pillars. He recognized a few faces here and there. Two or three journalists were on the point of approaching him but an usher forestalled them.

'Will you come this way, Superintendent. The Minister is expecting you.'

Auguste Point was standing in the huge dark study, with all its lamps lit, and seemed to him stouter and more massive than at the Boulevard Pasteur flat. He shook Maigret's hand, held it for an instant in his own, with the pressure of one who has just sustained a great shock and is grateful for the slightest display of sympathy.

'Thank you for coming, Maigret. I cannot help reproaching myself now for involving you in all this. You can see that I was right to be anxious!'

He turned to a middle-aged woman who had been telephoning and had put down the receiver.

'May I introduce Mlle Blanche, my secretary, whom I mentioned to you.'

Mlle Blanche glanced suspiciously at Maigret, very much on the defensive. She did not stretch out her hand, but merely nodded in his direction.

Her face was insignificant, not attractive, but under her simple black dress, brightened only by a narrow strip of white lace at the neck, Maigret was aware with surprise of a body still young and rounded and very desirable.

'If you don't mind, we'll go to my flat. I've never been able to get used to this office; I never feel at ease in it. You'll take all the calls, Blanche, won't you?'

'Yes, Your Excellency.'

Auguste Point opened the door at the back and murmured, in the same flat voice:

'I'll go first. It's rather complicated getting there.'

He was not quite familiar himself with the surroundings and seemed lost in the deserted corridors, hesitating before several doors.

They came to a narrow staircase, went up and walked through two large empty rooms. The sight of a servant in a white apron, carrying a broom, indicated that they had reached the private apartments.

'I meant to introduce Fleury to you. He was in the office next door. At the last moment I forgot about it.'

Now they could hear the sound of a woman's voice. Point pushed open another door and they found themselves in a small sitting-room where a woman was sitting by the window with a young girl beside her.

'My wife and daughter. I thought it best to talk in their presence.'

Madame Point could have been any little middle-aged bourgeoise whom one meets shopping in the street. Her face too looked tense, her eyes a little vacant.

'I must tell you straight away how grateful I am to you, Superintendent. My husband has told me everything and I know how much the conversation you had with him has helped him.'

Newspapers, with sensational headlines, were spread out on the table.

At first Maigret paid slight attention to the young girl who seemed calmer, more controlled than either of her parents.

'Would you like a cup of coffee?'

It all reminded him a little of a house where someone has just died, the daily routine suddenly interrupted, people coming and going and bustling about without knowing where to settle or what to do. He still wore his overcoat. Anne-Marie asked him to take it off and hung it over an armchair.

'Have you read this morning's papers?' the Minister asked at last, still standing.

'I only had the time to see the headlines.'

'They don't mention my name yet, but everyone in the Press knows about it. They must have got their information in the middle of the night. I was told so by a typesetter in the Rue du Croissant. I immediately telephoned the President.'

'What was his reaction?'

'I don't know whether he was surprised or not. I've lost my capacity of judging people's reactions. Obviously I was interrupting his sleep. It seemed to me that he showed some astonishment, but I found as I talked to him on the telephone that he was less disturbed than I had expected him to be.'

He seemed to be talking in a forced manner, without any conviction, as though words had no longer any importance.

'Sit down, Maigret. I apologize for standing all the time, but I haven't been able to make myself sit down since this morning. It's driving me mad. I've got to keep standing and walking up and down. Before you came in I had been pacing my office for an hour while my secretary was answering the telephone. Where was I? Ah, yes. The President said something like: "Well, my friend, we'll have to face the music!" I believe those were his exact words. I asked him if it was his men who were detaining Piquemal. Instead of answering me directly he muttered something like: "What makes you think that?" Then he explained to me that he couldn't swear to what was going on in his departments any more than I or any other Minister could. He gave me a lecture on the subject: "We are made responsible for everything" – he was saying – "though, in fact, we're only passing through and the people we give orders to know perfectly well they had a different boss yesterday and may well have a different one tomorrow!" I suggested that the best I could do was to offer him my resignation the next morning.

' "You're too hasty, Point," he said. "You're taking me unawares. In politics, things don't happen as they're expected to happen. I'll think your suggestion over and ring you up shortly."

'I suppose that he telephoned some of our colleagues. Perhaps they met to discuss the matter. I don't know. At the moment they have no reason to keep me informed.

'I spent the rest of the night pacing up and down my room while my wife tried to reason with me.'

Point's wife looked at Maigret as if to say: 'Help me! You see what a state he is in!'

It was true. That earlier evening, in the Boulevard Pasteur, Point had seemed to Maigret like a man staggering under a sudden blow and incapable of dealing with it but prepared to put up a good fight. Now he spoke as though he was no longer concerned with events, as though he had given up, knowing his destiny had been taken out of his hands.

'Did he call you back?' asked Maigret.

'At about half past five. As you see there were quite a number of us awake last night. He said that my resignation would serve no useful purpose, that it would only be considered an admission of guilt and that all I had to do was to tell the truth.'

'Including the contents of the Calame report?' asked the superintendent.

Point managed a smile.

'No. Not exactly. Just when I believed the conversation had come to an end he added: "I daresay you'll be asked whether you had read the report." I replied: "I *have* read it."

' "That's what I had understood. It's a very lengthy report, filled, I presume, with technical details on a subject not necessarily familiar to a legal mind. It might be more exact to say that you had skimmed through it. You haven't got it to hand at the moment to refresh your memory. The reason I am saying this, my friend, is to help you avoid more serious difficulties than those you will have to face already. If you speak of the contents of the report and implicate anyone – whoever it may be – it

302

doesn't concern me and I don't care one way or the other – but you'll be accused of making charges which you are unable to support. Do you understand me?" '

For at least the third time since the beginning of the conversation, Point lit his pipe and his wife turned to Maigret.

'Please smoke, if you wish. I'm used to it.'

'From seven o'clock onwards the telephone never stopped ringing – mainly journalists wanting to question me. At first I told them that I had no announcement to make. Then they almost seemed to be threatening me. Two newspaper editors rang me personally. In the end I asked everybody to come to my office at eleven o'clock today, for a press conference. I had to see you beforehand. I suppose that . . .'

He had had the courage, perhaps through tact, or fear or even superstition, to wait until now to put the question.

'I suppose you haven't discovered anything?'

Perhaps it was on purpose, to make the gesture more significant and thus inspire confidence in the Minister, but when he pulled the letter from his pocket and handed it to Auguste Point he did it in complete silence. There was something theatrical about it, that was out of character.

Madame Point did not move from the sofa where she was sitting, but Anne-Marie came up to her father and read over his shoulder.

'Who is it from?' she asked.

Maigret in his turn was asking Point:

'Do you recognize the handwriting?'

'It means something to me, but I can't quite place it.'

'This letter was sent last Thursday by Joseph Mascoulin.'

'To whom?'

'To Julien Piquemal.'

There was a silence. Point, without a word, handed the note to his wife. Each of them was trying to assess the importance of this discovery.

When Maigret began to speak again it was, as at the Boulevard Pasteur, in the form of an interrogation.

'What sort of terms are you on with Mascoulin?'

'No terms at all.'

'Have you quarrelled?'

'No.'

Point looked grave, anxious. Maigret although he never meddled in politics, was not quite ignorant of parliamentary custom. In a general way, the deputies, even though belonging to different parties, and even though attacking one another ferociously on the political platform, could still maintain friendly relations with one another, reminiscent, in their familiarity, of relations in schools and barracks.

'You are not on speaking terms?' Maigret insisted.

Point drew his hand across his forehead.

'All this goes back a few years, to my first days in the Chamber. A bright new Chamber, as you probably remember, and we all swore we would keep out anyone whose hands weren't clean. It was immediately after the war and the country was swept by a wave of idealism, a thirst for decency. The majority of my colleagues, at any rate a large number of them, were as new to politics as I was.'

'Not Mascoulin.'

'No. There were a few left from the old Chamber, but everyone was convinced that the newcomers would create the right atmosphere. After a few months, I was not quite so confident. After two years, I was discouraged. You remember, Henriette?'

He turned to his wife.

'It got to the point,' she said, 'where he had decided not to stand for Parliament again.'

'I had to speak at a dinner and I expressed my misgivings in so many words, and the press was there to put it all on record. I should be very surprised, if they don't remind me of some parts of my speech any day now. The subject of it was, dirty hands. I tried to explain that basically it was not our political machine that was deficient, but the climate in which politicians have to live, whether they like it or not. I needn't repeat it all now. You remember the famous slogan: "The Republic of Comrades". We meet every day. We shake hands like old friends. After a few weeks everybody is on familiar terms and each man tries to help the next. As the days go by, you shake more and more hands and if these are not quite clean, you shrug your shoulders tolerantly, and say: "Oh, well, he's not a bad chap," or "He has to do it to keep his votes." You follow me? I had stated publicly that if each of us refused once and for all to shake dirty hands, the hands of any individual not quite straight, the political atmosphere would be purified immediately.'

He added bitterly, after a few moments:

'I practised what I preached. I avoided certain journalists and certain unsavoury business men who haunt the corridors of the Palais Bourbon. I refused certain services which I believed I ought to refuse to some influential electors. And one day in the Hall of Lost Steps Mascoulin came up to me, his hand outstretched. I pretended not to see him and turned very ostentatiously towards another colleague. I know he went scarlet in the face and has never forgiven me. He is the type of man who doesn't forgive.'

'You did something similar with Hector Tabard, the editor of *Rumeur*?'

'I refused to see him a couple of times and he didn't insist.'

He glanced at his watch.

'I have one hour left at my disposal, Maigret. At eleven o'clock, I'll have to face the journalists and answer their questions. I had thought of presenting them with a statement, but it wouldn't satisfy them. I've got to tell them that Piquemal came to me with the Calame report and that I went to my flat in the Boulevard Pasteur to read it.'

'And you didn't do so?'

'I will try to be less explicit. The most difficult, the most impossible part will be to get them to accept that I left the famous report in a flat without any supervision and that when the next day I wanted to pick it up to take it to the President of the Council – it had disappeared. Nobody will believe me. Piquemal's disappearance doesn't simplify anything, on the contrary. They will say that it was one way of shutting up an embarrassing witness. The only thing that could have saved me would have been to present them with the thief.'

He added, as though apologizing for his resentment:

'I couldn't have expected that in forty-eight hours, even from you. What do you think I should do?'

Mme Point interrupted with determination.

'Hand in your resignation and we'll go back to La Roche-sur-

Yon. The people who know you will know you're not guilty. You don't have to worry about the others. Your conscience is clear, isn't it?'

Maigret's eyes turned to Anne-Marie and he saw her draw her lips together. He saw that the young woman did not share her mother's views and that as far as she was concerned such a retreat on her father's part would mean that she would have to give up all her hopes.

'What is your opinion?' Point murmured, hesitantly.

This was a responsibility the superintendent could not accept.

'And what is yours?'

'I feel I ought to hold out. At least, if there's even the slightest hope of finding the thief.'

It was once again an indirect question.

'I keep on hoping, right to the last minute,' muttered Maigret, 'otherwise I would never take on a case in the first place. Because I'm on foreign ground with politics, I wasted time in activities which may appear useless. But I'm not at all sure that they are as useless as they seem.'

Maigret had to instil some assurance in Point, if not a certain confidence, before he met the journalists, so he began to go over the situation, clarifying it.

'Don't you see, Your Excellency, we have arrived at a point where I feel more at home. Until now I've had to work by stealth as it were, though in fact we've bumped into the men from the Rue des Saussaies all the way along the line. No matter where we went, the men from Security were always there – at the door of your Ministry, at your secretary's lodgings, at Piquemal's or at your Parliamentary Private Secretary's place. At one moment I wondered what they were looking for, and whether the two departments weren't perhaps pursuing parallel inquiries. Now I am inclined to believe that all they wanted was to see what we discovered. It wasn't you, or your secretary, nor Piquemal or Fleury that was being watched, it was me and my men. Once Piquemal's disappearance and the disappearance of the documents became official, then Security could call off their watch as it automatically became the P.J.'s business anyway, being on Paris territory. A man doesn't disappear without leaving a trace. And a thief is always caught in the end.'

'Some time or other . . .' murmured Point with a sad smile.

And Maigret, rising and looking him straight in the eyes:

'It's your job to hold out until then.'

'It doesn't only depend on me.'

'It depends mostly on you.'

'If Mascoulin is behind this manoeuvre he will challenge the government quite soon.'

'Unless he prefers to profit from what he knows to increase his influence.'

Point glanced at him with surprise.

'You know so much? I thought you knew very little of politics.'

'This kind of thing doesn't only happen in politics; there are Mascoulins in every walk of life. I believe – tell me if I'm wrong – that he has one passion only, a passion for power, but he is a cold-blooded animal who knows how to bide his time. Every now and then he opens fire in the Chamber or in the Press by uncovering some kind of scandal or misuse of authority.'

Point was listening with renewed interest.

'Little by little, in this way, he has created a reputation for himself of a merciless crusader. So that all the embittered and the rebels of Piquemal's type go to him as soon as they think they have uncovered something dubious. I expect he receives the same sort of letters as we do when some mysterious crime is committed. We get letters from madmen, cranks and maniacs, and people who snatch the opportunity of satisfying their hatred for a relative or some old friend or neighbour. Among them there are always some that provide us with real evidence, without which a good number of murderers would still be scouring the streets. Piquemal – the Hermit, the searcher after truth in all extremist parties, in religion, in philosophy – he's precisely the type of man who, when he found the Calame report would never for a moment have considered handing it over to his immediate supervisors, whom he doesn't trust. He turned to the professional crusader, convinced that by doing so, the report would escape God knows what secret conspiracy.'

'If Mascoulin has the report in his hands, why hasn't he used it yet?'

'For the reason I have just given you. He must, periodically,

307

launch a scandal in order to keep up his reputation. But the blackmailing newspapers like *Rumeur* don't publish all the information they get either. On the contrary it's the things they keep silent about which are the most profitable. The Calame report is too precious a morsel to throw as food to the common herd. If Mascoulin has it in his possession, how many top people do you reckon he has at his mercy, including Arthur Nicoud?'

'Quite a number. Several dozen.'

'We don't know how many Calame reports he holds, which he can use at any moment and which will allow him to do his worst, when he feels in a strong enough position.'

'I had thought of that,' Point admitted. 'And it's that that frightens me. If it's Mascoulin who is keeping the report back, it's in perfect safety and I would be surprised if we ever found it. And if we don't produce it or if we have no actual proof that a certain person has destroyed it, I will be disgraced, because it is I who will be accused of its disappearance.'

Maigret saw Mme Point turn her head away because a tear was running down her cheek. Point saw it, and for a moment, was almost overcome himself, while Anne-Marie was saying:

'Maman!'

Mme Point shook her head as if to indicate that it was nothing and left the room abruptly.

'You see!' her husband said, as if there were no need for further comment.

Did Maigret do wrong, when he allowed himself to be impressed by the dramatic atmosphere that surrounded him and declared with complete assurance:

'I can't promise you to find the report, but I'll be damned if I don't put my hand on the man or woman who got into your flat and stole it. That at least is my profession.'

'You think you can?'

'I'm certain.'

He had risen from his chair. Point murmured:

'I'm coming down with you.'

And turning to his daughter:

'Run and tell your mother what the superintendent has just said to me. It will do her good.'

They went back the same way as they had come through the corridors of the Ministry and found themselves once again in Point's office where a tall, slender individual, with grey hair, was opening the mail, while Mlle Blanche answered the telephone.

'I would like to introduce Jaques Fleury, my Parliamentary Private Secretary. . . . Superintendent Maigret.'

The latter had the impression that he had seen the man somewhere before, probably in a bar or a restaurant. He carried himself well, was dressed with a certain elegance in direct contrast to the careless attire of the Minister. He was the type one frequently meets in the bars of the Champs Elysées in the company of pretty women.

His hand was dry, his handshake firm. He looked younger, more energetic, from a distance; close to, one saw the weary pouches under the eyes, the slight droop of the lips which he concealed by a nervous smile.

'How many are there in there?' Point asked him, pointing to the waiting-room.

'A good thirty. There are some correspondents from foreign papers as well. I don't know how many cameramen, they're still coming in.'

Maigret and the Minister exchanged glances. Maigret seemed to be saying with an encouraging wink:

'Keep your chin up!'

Point asked him:

'Will you go out through the waiting-room?'

'As you will be telling them that I'm in charge of the inquiry, it no longer matters. On the contrary.'

He was aware all the time of the suspicious eyes of Mlle Blanche on him; he had not had time to win her over. She seemed to be still hesitating about the opinion she should be forming of him. Maybe the composure of her employer convinced her, however, that Maigret's intervention was a good thing.

When the Superintendent crossed the room the photographers were the first to rush towards him and he did nothing to avoid them. The reporters, too, showered him with questions.

'Are you in charge of the Calame report?'

He waved them away with a smile.

'In a few minutes, the Minister himself will answer your questions.'

'You're not denying that you are connected with it?'

'I deny nothing.'

Some of them followed him to the marble staircase, hoping to force a declaration out of him.

'Ask the Minister,' he repeated. One of them asked:

'D'you believe that Piquemal has been murdered?'

It was the first time that this hypothesis had been clearly stated.

'You know my favourite answer,' he replied, 'I believe nothing.'

A few moments later, after some more camera clicks he got into the car of the P.J. where Lapointe had been spending his time reading the newspapers.

'Where are we going? To the Quai?'

'No. Boulevard Pasteur. What are the papers saying?'

'They are chiefly concerned with Piquemal's disappearance. One of them, I don't remember which, went to interview Mme Calame, who is still in the flat where she lived with her husband, Boulevard Raspail. She appears to be an energetic little woman who doesn't mince her words and didn't try to avoid questions. She hadn't read the report, but remembers well that her husband went to spend a few weeks in the Haute Savoie, about five years ago. On his return, he was very busy and it often happened that he worked till late at night.

' "Never before had he had so many telephone calls," she said. "Crowds of people whom we didn't know from Adam came to see him. He was anxious and worried. When I asked him what was bothering him, he told me it was his work and responsibilities. He often spoke of responsibilities at that time. I had the impression that something was gnawing at him. I knew he was ill. Over a year before the doctor had told me that he was suffering from cancer. I remember that once he sighed: 'Heavens, how difficult it is for a man to know where his duty lies!' " '

They were driving down the Rue Vaugirard and a bus was making them slow down.

'There's a whole column about it,' added Lapointe.

'What did she do with her husband's papers?'

'She left them all as they were in his study which she cleans regularly, just as she did when he was alive.'

'Had anybody come to see her recently?'

'Two people,' replied Lapointe, with an admiring glance at his boss.

'Piquemal?'

'Yes. That was the first visit, about a week ago.'

'Did she know him?'

'Fairly well. While Calame was alive, he often came to get advice from him. She thinks he was studying mathematics. He explained that he wanted to find one of his papers he had once given to his teacher.'

'Did he find it?'

'He had a briefcase with him. She left him in the study, where he remained about an hour. When he came out, she asked him if he had found what he wanted and he said no, that unfortunately his papers must have been lost. She didn't look in his briefcase. She had no suspicion. It was only two days after . . .'

'Who was the second visitor?'

'It was a man about forty, who pretended to be a former pupil of Calame and asked her if she had kept his files. He, too, talked of some work which they had done together.'

'Did she allow him into the study?'

'No. She thought the coincidence was too strange and replied that all her husband's papers had been left in the School of Engineering.'

'Did she describe her second visitor?'

'The paper doesn't mention it. If she did the reporter is keeping it to himself and is probably pursuing his own little inquiry.'

'Park here, by this pavement. It's here.'

By day the boulevard was as peaceful as by night with its own particular reassuring character of middle-class life.

'Do I wait for you?'

'You come with me. We'll probably have some work to do.'

The concierge's glass door was on the left of the hall. She was an elderly, rather dignified woman, who looked tired.

'What is it?' she asked the two men, without getting out of

her armchair, while a marmalade cat jumped from her lap and came to rub itself against Maigret's legs. He gave his name, and was careful to take off his hat and adopt a respectful tone.

'M. Point has asked me to make inquiries about a robbery of which he was a victim two days ago.'

'A robbery? In the house? He never said anything to me about it!'

'He will confirm it to you, when he sees you and if you have any doubts about it, all you have to do is to telephone him.'

'That's all right. If you're the superintendent, I've got to believe what you say, haven't I? But how could it have happened? This is a quiet house. The police haven't had to set foot in it for the thirty-five years I've been here.'

'I would like you to try and remember what happened on Tuesday, particularly in the morning.'

'Tuesday. . . . Wait a moment. . . . That was the day before yesterday.'

'Yes. The Minister came to his flat that evening.'

'Did he tell you that?'

'He not only told me, but I met him there. You opened the door for me a little after ten o'clock.'

'I believe I remember, yes.'

'He must have left a short time after me.'

'Yes.'

'Did you open the door to anyone else that night?'

'Certainly not. The tenants seldom come home later than midnight. They are all quiet people. I would have remembered if I had.'

'When do you open the door in the morning?'

'At half past six, sometimes seven.'

'After that you remain in the lodge?'

It consisted of one room, with a gas cooker, a round table, a sink, and behind the curtain, a bed with a dark red cover.

'Except when I sweep the stairs.'

'What time is that?'

'Not before nine. After I've taken round the post that comes at half past eight.'

'The lift has glass windows, so I suppose that you can see who goes up and down?'

'Yes. I always watch it, it's a habit.'

'That morning did you see someone going up to the fourth floor?'

'I'm certain I didn't.'

'Nobody asked you if the Minister was at home that morning or even early in the afternoon?'

'Nobody. There was only a telephone call.'

'To you?'

'No, to the flat.'

'How do you happen to know?'

'Because I was on the stairs between the fourth and the fifth floors.'

'What time was it?'

'Perhaps ten o'clock. Perhaps a little earlier. My feet don't allow me to work quickly any more. I heard the telephone behind the door. It rang for a long time. Then, a quarter of an hour later, when I'd finished cleaning and came down there was the telephone again, and I remember I said to myself: "You can ring as long as you like." '

'And then?'

'Nothing.'

'You went back to the lodge?'

'To tidy myself up a bit.'

'You didn't leave the house?'

'For about a quarter of an hour or twenty minutes, as I do every morning, just for my shopping. The grocer is next door, the butcher's at the corner. From the grocer's I can see who comes and goes. I always keep an eye on the house.'

'And from the butcher's?'

'I can't see, but I'm never there long. I live alone with my cat and buy the same thing almost every day. At my age, you don't have much of an appetite.'

'You don't know exactly what time it was when you were at the butcher's?'

'Not precisely. There is one of those great big clocks over the cashier's desk, but I never look at it.'

'When you got back, you saw no one leave that you hadn't seen come in?'

'I don't remember. No. I'm more concerned with the ones

that come in, than with the ones that go out, apart from the tenants that is, because with them I have to be able to answer whether they're in or not. There are always the tradesmen, the gas-men, and the vacuum cleaner salesmen.'

He knew that he would get nothing from her and that, if, later on, she remembered some detail, she would be sure to let him know.

'The inspector and I are going to question your tenants,' said Maigret.

'Go ahead. You'll see they're all good people, except perhaps the old woman on the third, who . . .'

Maigret felt much more himself now he was back on a routine job again.

'We'll come to see you before we leave,' he promised.

And he took care to stroke the cat before he left.

'You take the flats on the left,' he said to Lapointe, 'and I'll tackle the ones on the right. You understand what I'm looking for?'

And he added, familiarly:

'Go to it, old chap!'

Chapter Six

Before ringing at the first door Maigret hesitated, turned to Lapointe who on his side was about to ring the bell.

'You're not thirsty?'

'No, boss.'

'You start. I'll be back in a moment.'

At a pinch he might have made the telephone call he had suddenly thought of from the concierge's lodge. But apart from the fact that he preferred to talk without witnesses, he felt it would be good to have a drink, a glass of white wine, for instance. He had to walk about a hundred yards before he found a small bar where there was not a soul besides the owner.

'A glass of white,' he ordered.

He changed his mind.

314

'No, I'll have a Pernod.'

It was more in harmony with his mood and with the time of day, also with this tidy little bar that seemed permanently empty. He waited to be served and had drunk half of his glass before he went to the telephone.

When the newspapers report the story of an inquiry, one gets the impression that the police follow a straight line, that they know where they are going from the start. Events follow one another logically, like the entries and exits of characters in a well-directed play.

Unnecessary comings and goings are rarely mentioned; neither are tedious searches in various directions that come to nothing and the haphazard soundings to right and left.

Maigret could not have mentioned a single inquiry during which at one moment or the other, he had not floundered. This morning he had not had the time, at the P.J., to inquire after Lucas, Janvier and Torrence who had all been given instructions the day before, all of which this morning seemed of no importance.

'The P.J.? Will you call Lucas, please. If he isn't there, get me Janvier.'

He heard Lucas' voice at the other end.

'Is that you, boss?'

'It is. First of all will you make a note of something very urgent. I want you to get hold of a photograph of Piquemal, the chap from the School of Engineering. It's useless to look for one in his hotel room. He hasn't one there. I'd be surprised if they haven't one of those group-photos at the school, the kind they take usually at the end of the year. The men at the Identity Department may be able to make some use of it. I want them to get on to it as quickly as possible. There's still time to get the photo in the afternoon papers. It is to be transmitted to all police-stations too. To be sure to miss nothing, I want inquiries made at the Legal Medical Institute.'

'O.K., boss.'

'Any news?'

'I've found the woman called Marcelle; her name is Marcelle Luquet.'

In his own mind, Maigret had already abandoned this line of

inquiry, but he did not want to make Lucas feel he had worked for nothing.

'And? . . .'

'She works as a proof-reader at the "Imprimerie du Croissant"; she's a member of the night-team there. It isn't where they print the *Rumeur* or the *Globe*. She's heard Tabard mentioned, but doesn't know him personally. She has never met Mascoulin.'

'Did you talk to her?'

'I gave her a cup of coffee and cream at the Rue Montmartre. She's a nice woman. She lived alone until she met Fleury and fell in love with him. She still loves him. She bears him no grudge for leaving her and if he'd have her back tomorrow, she'd go back to him like a shot. According to her he's just a great child who needs understanding and affection. She insists that though he may be capable of childish manoeuvring, he is incapable of real dishonesty.'

'Is Janvier with you?'

'Yes.'

'Put him on, will you.'

Janvier had nothing to say. He had walked the street in front of the block in the Rue Vaneau, until Torrence came to relieve him.

'Blanche Lamotte came home on foot, alone, about 11 p.m. and went up to her room, where the light was on for about half an hour.'

'There was no one about from the Rue des Saussaies?'

'No one. I was able to count the people in the street, coming back from the cinema or the theatre.'

Torrence had had an even less eventful time. He had only seen seven people in the Rue Vaneau the whole night.

'The light went on at 6 a.m. I suppose she gets up early to do her chores. She went out at ten minutes past eight and walked in the direction of the Boulevard Saint-Germain.'

Maigret went back and finished his Pernod at the counter and as it was a small one, he ordered another, while he was filling his pipe.

When he came back to the block in the Boulevard Pasteur, he found that Lapointe was busy at his third flat and he began patiently to do his own stint. Questioning people can be a long drawn out affair. At this hour both men found only women at their chores. Their first reaction was to close the door on them thinking they were peddling some kind of domestic gadget or were insurance agents. At the word police, they all gave a start in exactly the same way. While the men talked to them, their minds were elsewhere, on what was boiling at the time on the stove, or what the baby was up to on the floor, or on the vacuum cleaner they had left running. Some of them were embarrassed at being caught in their working clothes and automatically tried to straighten their hair.

'Please try to remember what you did on Tuesday morning. . .'

'Tuesday, yes . . .'

'Did you happen, for instance, to open your door between ten and midday?'

The first woman whom Maigret questioned was not at home at the time but in the hospital where her sister was having an operation. The second, quite a young woman, was holding a child on her arm, supporting it on her hip and was constantly confusing Tuesday and Wednesday.

'I was here, yes. I'm always here in the morning. I do my shopping at the end of the afternoon, after my husband comes back.'

'Did you happen to open your door?'

With infinite patience they had to be gradually led back to the atmosphere of Tuesday morning. Had they been asked point blank: Did you see, in the lift or on the stairs, a stranger to the block going up to the fourth floor . . .? they would have replied confidently 'no' without giving themselves time to think.

At the third floor Maigret caught up with Lapointe, because he had found no one on the left-hand side of the second floor.

The tenants, who resembled the house, lived quite uneventful domestic lives behind their doors. The smells varied from one floor to the other, as did the colours of the wallpaper, but it all belonged to the same honest, laborious class of people, that class which is always slightly intimidated by the police. Maigret was struggling with a deaf old woman, who did not ask him in and made him repeat every question. He could hear Lapointe talking behind the door opposite.

'Why do you want me to open my door?' cried the deaf woman. 'Has that cat of a concierge accused me of spying on the tenants?'

'Certainly not, Madame. You aren't being accused of anything.'

'Then why do the police come and question me?'

'We're trying to establish whether a man . . .'

'What man?'

'A man whom we don't know, but whom we're searching for.'

'What are you searching for?'

'A man.'

'What has he done?'

He was still trying to make her understand when the door opposite opened. Lapointe was signalling to Maigret that he had discovered something and the superintendent abruptly left the irate old woman.

'This is Mme Gaudry, boss. Her husband works in a bank on the Boulevard des Italiens. She has a little boy of five.'

Maigret could see the boy hiding behind his mother, clutching at her skirt.

'She sometimes sends the boy to shop in the neighbourhood in the morning, only if the shop is on this side of the boulevard.'

'I don't allow him to cross the road. And I always keep the door half-open when he is out. That is how on Tuesday . . .'

'You heard someone go up?'

'Yes. I was waiting for Bob. At one moment I thought it was him. Most people take the lift, but I don't allow him to do that yet.'

'I can easily work the lift!' the boy said. 'I've done it already.'

'And you got punished for it! What happened was, I just looked out at the very moment a man was crossing the landing and going up to the fourth floor.'

'What time was it?'

'About half past ten. I had just put my stew into the oven.'

'Did the man speak to you?'

'No. At first I only saw him from the back. He was wearing a light beige overcoat, perhaps it was a raincoat, I didn't look too close, and he had broad shoulders and a thick neck.'

She glanced at Maigret's neck.

'Rather like mine?'

She hesitated, blushing.

'Not quite. He was younger than you are. In the forties, I would say. I could see his face when he got to the turn of the stairs and he looked back at me and seemed upset to find me there.'

'He stopped at the fourth floor?'

'Yes.'

'Did he ring the bell?'

'No. He went into M. Point's flat; it took him quite a time to open the door.'

'As though he were trying several keys?'

'I couldn't swear to that, but it was as if he wasn't familiar with the lock.'

'Did you see him leave?'

'I didn't see him because coming down he took the lift.'

'Was he there for a long time?'

'Less than ten minutes.'

'Did you stay on the landing all that time?'

'No. But Bob wasn't back yet and I left the door half-open. I heard the lift go up, stop at the fourth floor and go down again.'

'Could you describe him, apart from his stoutness?'

'It's not easy. He had a red complexion like a man who likes his food.'

'Spectacles?'

'I don't think so. In fact, I'm certain he hadn't any.'

'Was he smoking a pipe? A cigarette?'

'No. . . . Wait a moment. . . . I'm almost certain he was smoking a cigar. . . . It struck me because my brother-in-law . . .'

It all corresponded, the cigar included, to the description supplied by the bar owner in the Rue Jacob of the man who had approached Piquemal. It could also have corresponded to the description of the stranger who had visited Mlle Blanche in the Rue Vaneau.

A few moments later Maigret and Lapointe met on the pavement.

'Where are we going?'

'Take me to the Embankment. After that, you'll go to the Rue Vaneau and Rue Jacob to find out if, by any chance, the man was smoking a cigar.'

When Maigret got to his office he found that Lucas had already obtained a photograph in which Piquemal appeared, though unfortunately only in the background; it was however clear enough for the specialists of the Identity Department to work with.

He sent in his name to the Director of the P.J. and spent about half an hour there putting him in the picture.

'Well, at least we've got something to go on!' sighed the chief when Maigret had finished.

'Yes, I agree.'

'I shall be even happier when we learn – if we ever do learn – who this man is.'

They both had the same suspicion and preferred not to speak of it. It was not impossible that the individual whose tracks they had discovered three times now, was someone belonging to the other Department, to the Rue des Saussaies. Maigret had good friends there, especially a man called Catroux, to whose son he had been god-father. He hesitated to approach him for if Catroux knew anything, he risked putting him in a false position.

Piquemal's photograph would appear in the afternoon papers. It would be an irony of fate if the man the P.J. were looking for was all the time in the hands of the Security Department. The latter may have withdrawn him temporarily from circulation because he knew too much. Perhaps they had taken him to the Rue des Saussaies to pump him? The papers were going to announce that the P.J. and Maigret in particular were in charge of the case. It would be fair play for Security to let him loose in the country, then a few hours later to announce that they had caught Piquemal.

'You do believe, of course,' insisted the chief, 'that Point is an honest man and is not concealing anything from you?'

'I could swear to it.'

'And the people round him?'

'I think so. I've made inquiries about each one of them. I don't know everything about their lives, of course, but what I do know makes me think that we must look elsewhere. The letter I showed you . . .'

'Mascoulin?'

'He's certainly mixed up in this business. The letter proves it.'

'What are you going to do?'

'Maybe it won't get me very far, but for some reason I'd like to have a closer look at him. All I have to do is go and lunch at the "Filet de Sole", in the Place de la Victoire where he is supposed to hold his meetings.'

'Be careful.'

'I know.'

He went through the inspectors' office to give some instructions. Lapointe had just come back.

'What about the cigars?'

'It's curious that it should have been a women who noticed this detail. The owner of the bistro can't say whether the man smoked a pipe, a cigar or a cigarette, though he stayed at his bar for more than a quarter of an hour. Mlle Blanche's concierge is quite definite.'

'He smoked a cigar?'

'No – a cigarette. He threw the butt on the stairs and put it out with his foot.'

It was one o'clock when Maigret walked into the famous restaurant in the Place de la Victoire, feeling apprehensive, for as a humble official it was hardly prudent to measure oneself against a Mascoulin. He had nothing specific against him except a brief note which the deputy could explain in hundreds of different ways. Here, Mascoulin was on his own ground. Maigret was clearly the intruder and the head waiter watched him come in without rushing to welcome him.

'You have a table?'

'For how many?'

'I'm alone.'

Most of the tables were occupied and there was a continuous hum of conversation, accompanied by the noise of knives and forks and the clinking of glasses. The head waiter looked around and moved towards a table smaller than the others, tucked in behind the door. Finally, in response to a sign, the cloak-room attendant came to take Maigret's coat and hat.

Three other tables were free, but if the superintendent had mentioned them, he would probably have been told that they were reserved, which was quite possible. He had to wait for a long time before his order was taken and had every opportunity of observing everyone in the room.

The restaurant was popular among top people, and at luncheon, they were mostly men, financiers, well known lawyers, journalists and politicians, all belonging more or less to the same circle and making signs of recognition to one another. Some had recognized the superintendent and he was probably talked of in hushed tones at several tables.

Joseph Mascoulin was sitting in the right-hand corner, on a seat against the wall, in the company of Maître Pinard, a lawyer almost as famous as the deputy for the ferocity of his speeches. A third companion had his back to Maigret; he was a middle-aged man with narrow shoulders and sparse grey hair swept over the bald skull. It was only when he turned sideways that the superintendent recognized him to be Sauvegrain, the brother-in-law and associate of Nicoud whose photograph he had seen in the papers.

Mascoulin who was eating a steak, had already spotted Maigret and stared at him as if there was no one else of any interest in the room. At first his eyes lit up with curiosity which was followed by a faint gleam of irony and now he seemed to be waiting with amusement for the superintendent's next move. The latter had at last given his order, added to it half a bottle of Pouilly and gone on smoking his pipe in little puffs, returning the deputy's stare with unconcern. The difference between them was that, as always in such cases, Maigret's eyes appeared vacant. One had the impression that the object he was staring at was as neutral, as uninteresting as a blank wall and that he was thinking of nothing beyond the Sole Dieppoise which he had just ordered.

He was far from knowing the complete history of Nicoud and his enterprise. Popular belief claimed that Sauvegrain, the brother-in-law, who until he married Nicoud's sister about ten years ago, was only an obscure contractor, participated in the business only in name. He had an office in the Avenue de la République, not far from Nicoud. It was a vast, luxurious office, but Sauvegrain spent his days in it waiting for visitors of little importance who were sent to him to pass the time.

Mascoulin must have had his reasons for accepting him openly at his table. Was Maître Pinard there because he looked after Sauvegrain's interests?

A newspaper editor stopped at Maigret's table on his way out and shook his hand.

'On the job?' he asked. And as the superintendent pretended not to understand:

'I don't think I've ever seen you here before.'

His eyes turned in Mascoulin's direction.

'I didn't know that the P.J. took on that kind of case. Have you found Piquemal?'

'Not yet.'

'Still searching for the Calame report?'

This was said in a bantering tone, as though the Calame report had existed only in the imagination of certain people or as though if it did exist, Maigret would never be able to find it.

'We're searching' – was Maigret's evasive reply.

The journalist opened his mouth, didn't say what was on the tip of his tongue, and walked out with a cordial wave of the hand. In the doorway he just avoided bumping into a newcomer whom Maigret probably would not have seen if his eyes hadn't been on the newspaper man.

Just as he was about to push open the second door, the man saw the superintendent through the glass pane and his face expressed alarm. Normally, he would have acknowledged Maigret, whom he had known for many years. He almost did so, then threw a hesitant glance in Mascoulin's direction and hoping perhaps that Maigret hadn't had time to recognize him, made an abrupt about turn and vanished.

Mascoulin, from his corner, had missed nothing of the scene, but his poker face registered nothing.

What was Maurice Labat doing at the 'Filet de Sole' and why

had he beaten a retreat when he saw Maigret in the restaurant?

For about ten years he had been working in a department in the Rue des Saussaies and there had even been a time, true, a very brief one, during which he was believed to have had an influence on the Minister.

Suddenly it was learnt that he had handed in his resignation, then that he had not done so at his own will, but to avoid some more serious unpleasantness. Since then he had continued to be seen on the fringe of circles who frequented places like the 'Filet de Sole'. He had not, as had many others, in the same situation, opened a private investigation agency. No one knew what his profession was, nor what his resources were. Besides having a wife and children he had a mistress in a flat in the Rue de Ponthieu, who was twenty years younger than he and must have cost him a pretty penny.

Maigret was neglecting his Sole Dieppoise and not paying it the attention it deserved, for the Labat incident had given him plenty to think about.

Was it not natural to presume that the person whom the former policeman had come to see at the 'Filet de Sole' was none other than Mascoulin? Labat was that man in a thousand whom one could entrust with the slightly shady jobs and he must have kept some friends in the Rue des Saussaies. Did he hope in beating a hasty retreat that Maigret had not had time to recognize him? Had Mascoulin, whom the superintendent was not able to observe at that moment, given him a sign not to come in? If Labat had been about forty, stout and smoking a cigar, the superintendent would have been certain that he had discovered the man who had gone to the Boulevard Pasteur and the Rue Vaneau and the one who had spirited Piquemal away.

But Labat was barely thirty-six. He was a Corsican and looked like one. Small and slender he wore high heeled shoes in order to appear taller and had a brown moustache like two commas. Last but not least he smoked cigarettes from morning till night and his fingers were yellow with nicotine. But his appearance nevertheless gave Maigret food for thought, and he reproached himself for being so hypnotized by the Rue des Saussaies. Labat had been one of them, but was no longer and there must must have been dozens like him in Paris, whom Security had got rid of for more or less similar reasons. Maigret made a mental note to get hold of a list of these men. He was on the point of telephoning straight away to Lucas to ask him to provide one. The reason why he did not do so, strange as it may seem, was that he hesitated to cross the room under Mascoulin's mocking eyes. The latter, who had not ordered any dessert, was already at the coffee stage. Maigret did not order any dessert either, only some coffee and brandy, and began to fill his pipe, going over faces that he had known in the Rue des Saussaies. He felt like a man searching for a name that is on the tip of his tongue but which keeps eluding him.

From the moment the stout man had been mentioned and particularly since a cigar had been brought into the picture, something had been stirring in his memory. He was so wrapped up in his own thoughts that he hardly noticed that Mascoulin had risen and was wiping his lips with his napkin and exchanging a few words with his companions. More precisely he watched him rise, push the table to make way for himself and finally move quietly across the room towards him, but it was as though all this did not concern him at all.

'May I, superintendent?' Mascoulin was saying, holding the back of the chair facing Maigret.

His face was serious, with a slight, ironical quiver in the corner of his mouth which might have been only a nervous tic.

For a moment, Maigret was taken aback. He had not expected this. He had never heard Mascoulin's voice, which was grave and had a pleasant quality to it. It was said that it was because of his voice that some women, in spite of his unappealing Grand Inquisitor's face, fought for places in the Chamber when he was expected to speak.

'What a curious coincidence that you should have come here today. I was going to telephone you.'

Maigret remained impassive for he was determined to make Mascoulin's task as difficult as possible, but the deputy did not seem to be at all put out of countenance by his silence.

'I've only learnt just now that you are working on Piquemal and the Calame report.' He spoke in an undertone, because of the other people in the room; they were being watched from several tables.

'I've not only got important information to pass on to you, but I believe I ought to make an official announcement. Perhaps you would like to send one of your inspectors to the Chamber a little later, to put it on record? Anyone will tell him where to find me.'

Maigret remained unperturbed.

'It's about this Piquemal with whom it happens I was in contact last week.'

Maigret had Mascoulin's letter in his pocket and began to understand why the man felt it necessary to speak to him.

'I don't remember which day it was, my secretary handed me one of the many letters which I receive every week and which he has to answer. It was signed "Piquemal" and had an address of an hotel in the Rue Jacob, the name of which I have forgotten – the name of some provincial town, I think.'

Without taking his eyes off Mascoulin's face Maigret sipped his coffee and went on puffing at his pipe.

'Every day, as you can imagine, I receive hundreds of letters from every type of person: cranks, semi-lunatics, honest men who point out some violation of rights or other, and it is my secretary's job to separate the sheep from the goats. He's a worthy young man in whom I have full confidence.'

Why did it cross Maigret's mind, as he was studying the other man's face, that Mascoulin was a homosexual? There had never been the slightest hint of anything like that. If he was, he concealed it carefully. It occurred to the superintendent that it might explain certain traits in his character.

'The Piquemal letter seemed sincere to me and I'm certain you'll have the same impression, if I can find it again, for I shall consider it my duty to send it to you. In it he told me that he was the only man in Paris who knew the whereabouts of the Calame report and could lay hands on it. He added that he addressed himself to me rather than to an official body because he knew that too many people were interested in hushing up the story and that I was the only one who inspired him with confidence. I apologize for repeating these words. I sent him a note on the off-chance, giving him an appointment.'

326

Very calmly, Maigret pulled his notebook out of his pocket and took out the letter with the Chamber of Deputies heading, which he merely showed, without handing it across the table in spite of Mascoulin's movement to snatch it.

'Is it this note?'

'I believe so. I seem to recognize my own handwriting.'

He did not ask how it had come to be in Maigret's possession, avoided showing any surprise and said:

'I see you know all about it. I met him at the Brasserie de Croissant which is not far from the printers and where I keep some of my appointments in the evening. He seemed to me a little too excited, too cranky for my taste. I let him speak.'

'He told you he was in possession of the report?'

'Not exactly. Men like him never behave as simply as that. They need an atmosphere of conspiracy. He told me he was working in the School of Engineering, that he had been Professor Calame's assistant and that he believed he knew where to find the report Calame had written on the subject of the Clairfond sanatorium. The conversation didn't last more than ten minutes, as I had some proofs to read.'

'After that Piquemal brought you the report?'

'I never saw him again. He suggested bringing it to me on Monday or Tuesday, at the latest on Wednesday. I replied that I didn't want to touch it – you can understand my reasons. That report is sheer dynamite, as we have seen today.'

'To whom did you advise him to hand it?'

'To his chief.'

'You mean the Director of the School of Engineering?'

'I don't think I was so precise. I may have mentioned the Ministry which naturally came to mind.'

'Did he try to telephone you?'

'Not that I know of.'

'Nor to see you?'

'If he did, he didn't succeed for as I told you before, I had no news of him except from the papers. It seems that he followed my advice, exaggerating it slightly, for he went straight to the Minister. As soon as I heard about his disappearance I told myself I must let you know about the incident. Now it's done. Considering the possible repercussions it might have, I prefer to make a statement and have it properly recorded. So, this after-noon . . . if . . .'

There was nothing else for it. Maigret would have to send someone to him to take his statement. The inspector would find Mascoulin surrounded by his colleagues and journalists. Was it not an excellent way of accusing Auguste Point?

'Thank you,' was all he said. 'I'll give the necessary instructions.'

Mascoulin seemed taken aback, as though he had expected something different. Had he imagined that the superintendent would put embarrassing questions to him or would show in some way that he disbelieved him?

'I'm only doing my duty. If I'd known how things were going to turn out I'd have told you about it before . . .'

He seemed to be playing a part all the time, almost, one would have sworn, without attempting to conceal it. He appeared to be saying: 'I've been smarter than you. Try to find an answer to that one!' Was Maigret wrong? Certainly, from one point of view, because he had nothing to win – on the contrary, he had everything to lose, in measuring himself against a man as powerful and as crafty as Mascoulin.

The latter stood up and stretched out his hand. The super-intendent was suddenly reminded of Point and his story about dirty hands. Without weighing up the pros and cons he picked up his cup of coffee which was empty and carried it to his lips, thus ignoring the hand that was offered to him.

A shadow seemed to flicker in the deputy's eyes. The quiver in the corner of his mouth, far from disappearing, became more accentuated.

But he only murmured:

'Good-bye, Monsieur Maigret.'

Did he intentionally stress the 'Monsieur'? It seemed to Maigret he did. If so it was a barely disguised threat, for it meant that Maigret was not to be allowed to enjoy his title of super-intendent for very long.

He followed him with his eye as he went back to his table and bent over his companions, then called in an absent-minded way:

'Waiter, the bill, please!'

At least a dozen persons who, in one capacity or another, played an important part in the life of the country, had their eyes fixed on him.

Maigret must have drunk his brandy without noticing it; as he went out, he was surprised to find the flavour of it still in his mouth.

Chapter Seven

It was not the first time he had made this kind of entrance, more as a friend than as a boss. He opened the door of the inspectors' office and pushing his hat to the back of his head, went and sat on a corner of a table. He emptied his pipe on the floor by knocking it against his heel and then filled another one. He was watching them as they busied themselves about their different jobs, with the expression of a paterfamilias who comes back home in the evening, pleased to be among his brood and summing them up.

Some time elapsed before he growled:

'Lapointe, my boy, I reckon you're going to have your picture in the papers.'

Lapointe raised his head, trying not to blush, his eyes expressing incredulity. In fact, all of them, with the exception of Maigret, who was much too used to it, were secretly delighted when newspapers published their photographs. But every time it happened, they never failed to protest.

'With such publicity, it'll be easy now to work under cover and not be noticed!'

The others were listening too. If Maigret had come to speak to Lapointe in the general common office, it meant that what he had to say to him was addressed to them all.

'You're going to provide yourself with a shorthand note book and go to the Chamber. You won't have any trouble finding the deputy Mascoulin, I'm sure, and I'll be surprised if you don't find him surrounded by people. He will make a statement to you, which you will carefully take down. Then you'll come here and type it and leave it on my desk.'

The afternoon papers were sticking out of his pocket, with the photograph of Auguste Point and his own on the front page. He had hardly looked at them. He knew almost exactly what was being said.

'Is that all?' asked Lapointe who had gone to fetch his overcoat and hat from the cupboard.

'For the moment.'

Maigret remained where he was, smoking dreamily.

'Listen, my children . . .'

The inspectors raised their heads.

'I want you to think of some of the Rue de Saussaies men, who were either dismissed or obliged to resign . . .'

'You mean recently?' asked Lucas.

'It doesn't matter when. Let's say during the last ten years.'

Torrence exclaimed:

'There must be a whole list of them!'

'Well, give me some names then.'

'Baudelin. The one who is inquiry agent for an insurance company now.'

Maigret tried to recall Baudelin, a tall, pale young man who probably left Security not for dishonesty or indiscreet behaviour, but because he brought more energy and skill to pretending to be ill, than doing his job.

'Anyone else?'

'Falconet.'

This one was over fifty; he had been asked to advance the age of retirement because he had started to drink and had become unreliable.

'Anyone else?'

'Little Valencourt.'

'Too small.'

Contrary to what they had expected at the beginning, they could only think of a few names and each time, after conjuring up the man's appearance, Maigret shook his head.

'It doesn't really fit. I'm looking for a stoutish man, someone like myself.'

'Fischer.'

There was a general burst of laughter, because the man weighed at least eighteen stone.

'Thanks!' growled Maigret.

He stayed a while with them and finally sighed and got to his feet.

'Lucas! Would you please telephone the Rue de Saussaies and ask for Catroux?'

Now that he was only interested in inspectors who had left Security, he no longer felt that he was asking his friend to betray his colleagues. Catroux, who had worked for twenty years in the Rue des Saussaies would be better placed than the P.J. men to answer his question. There was a feeling in the air that the superintendent was on to something, that he was working on an idea; it was still vague, perhaps not quite clear to him yet. His sham gruffness, his eyes that stared at people without seeing them, were a sign that he knew now in which direction to search.

He kept trying to remember a name which he had on the tip of his tongue a moment ago. Lucas was telephoning, talking in a warm, familiar way to the man on the other end of the line who must have been a friend.

'Catroux is not there, boss.'

'You're not going to tell me that he's on some mission at the other end of France?'

'No, he's ill.'

'In hospital?'

'No, at home.'

'Did you ask for his address?'

'No, I thought you had it.'

It is true, they were good friends, Catroux and he. Nevertheless they had never been in each other's homes. Maigret could only remember leaving his colleague one day at his door, at the far end of the Boulevard des Batignolles, on the left, and he remembered a restaurant to the right of the door.

'Has Piquemal's photo appeared in the papers?'

'Yes, on the second page.'

'No one has telephoned about it?'

'Not yet.'

He went to his office, opened a few letters, brought Torrence some papers that concerned him and finally went down to the yard where he hesitated to use one of the P.J. cars. Finally he took a taxi. Though his visit to Catroux was quite innocent, he considered it more prudent not to keep a car from the Quai des Orfèvres waiting at the door.

At first he mistook the house, for there were now two restaurants at fifty yards' distance from one another. He asked the concierge:

'M. Catroux?'

'On the second floor, to the right. The lift is being mended.'

He rang the bell. He did not remember Mme Catroux who opened the door to him and recognized him at once.

'Come in, M. Maigret.'

'Is your husband in bed?'

'No, he's in an armchair. It's only a bad touch of 'flu. Usually he has one at the beginning of every winter. This time it caught up with him at the end.'

On the walls were portraits of two children, a boy and a girl, at every age. Not only were both now married, but photographs of grandchildren were beginning to increase the collection.

'Maigret?' Catroux's delighted voice called out before the superintendent had reached the door of the room where he was sitting.

It was not a sitting-room, but a large room where one felt the greater part of the life of the house was lived. Catroux, wrapped up in a thick dressing-gown, was sitting near the window, newspapers in his lap, more of them on a chair nearby, a bowl of tisane on a small table. He held a cigarette in his hand.

'You're allowed to smoke?'

'Sh . . . sh . . . Don't side with my wife. Only a few puffs now and again, to take away the taste.'

He was hoarse and his eyes were feverish.

'Take off your overcoat. It must be very hot in here. My wife insists that I've got to sweat. Do sit down.'

'Can I give you a drink, M. Maigret?' the wife asked.

She looked like an old woman and the superintendent was surprised by that. He and Catroux were about the same age. It seemed to Maigret that his own wife looked much younger.

'Of course, Isabelle. Whatever he says go and bring the bottle of old calvados.'

There was an embarrassed silence between the two men. Cat-

332

roux obviously knew that his colleague from the P.J. had not come to inquire about his health and he perhaps expected even more embarrassing questions than Maigret had in mind.

'Don't worry, old chap. I have no desire to get you into any trouble.'

At this point, the other man glanced at the front page of the newspaper as though saying: 'This is what it's about, isn't it?'

Maigret waited for his glass of calvados.

'And what about me?' his friend protested.

'You're not supposed to have any.'

'The doctor said nothing about that.'

'I don't need a doctor to tell me what to do.'

'Just a drop, to kid myself!'

She gave him a drop and disappeared discreetly, as Mme Maigret would have done.

'I have an idea at the back of my mind,' admitted Maigret. 'A moment or two ago my inspectors and I tried to draw up a list of people who have worked with you and been chucked out.'

Catroux was looking at the paper, trying to link what Maigret was saying with what he had just read.

'Chucked out, why?'

'Never mind why. You know what I mean. It happens with us too but less often because there are fewer of us.'

Catroux gave a teasing smile.

'Is that why you think so?'

'Perhaps also because we are not involved with so many things. Let's put it this way, the temptation is less strong. We racked our brains just now, but we could only think of a few names.'

'Which names?'

'Baudelin, Falconet, Valencourt, Fischer . . .'

'Is that all?'

'More or less. I thought it would be better to come and see you. They are not what I'm looking for. I want the men who have gone to the bad.'

'Someone like Labat?'

Was it not strange that Catroux should have mentioned this particular name? He could almost have been doing it on purpose as a way of slipping Maigret some information.

'I did think of him. He's probably mixed up in it all right. But he's not the one I'm looking for.'

'You've got a definite name in mind?'

'A name and a face. I started off with a description, and from the beginning it reminded me of someone. Since then . . .'

'What is the description? We'll get on quicker than if I give you a whole list. Particularly as I haven't got all the names in my head either.'

'First of all people took him to be a policeman straight away.'

'This could apply to plenty of people.'

'Middle-aged. Somewhat stouter than average but not as stout as I am.'

Catroux seemed to be estimating his friend's size.

'Either I'm greatly mistaken, or he is making inquiries on his own behalf or for someone else.'

'A private investigator?'

'Perhaps. He needn't necessarily have put his name on an office door, or advertised in the papers.'

'There are plenty of them, including lots of old, honourable men, who have reached the age limit and then opened an agency. Louis Canange, for example. And Cadet, who was my boss.'

'We have some of those, too. I mean the other kind.'

'What else is in your description?'

'He smokes cigars.'

Immediately Maigret realized that his friend had thought of a name. His forehead wrinkled. A disturbed expression crossed his face.

'It means something to you?'

'Yes.'

'Who?'

'A bad one.'

'That's what I'm looking for.'

'A bad one in a small way, but dangerous.'

'Why?'

'Firstly, that kind of person is always dangerous. Furthermore, he's believed to do some politicians' dirty work.'

'It fits perfectly.'

'You think he's mixed up in this business?'

'If he answers to the description I've given you, if he smokes cigars and meddles in politics there's every chance he's my man. You don't want to . . .'

Suddenly Maigret could see a face before him, a rather large face with bags under the eyes, thick lips, deformed by cigar smoking.

'Wait. . . . It's coming back to me. It's . . .'

But he still could not get the name.

'Benoit,' prompted Catroux, 'Eugene Benoit. He's opened a small private office in the Boulevard Saint-Martin, on the ground floor over a watch-maker's. His name is on the window-pane. I think the door is more often closed than open; the whole staff of the agency consists of himself.'

It was the man whom the superintendent had been trying to remember for the past twenty-four hours.

'I don't suppose it would be very easy to get his photo?'

Catroux thought a moment before replying.

'It depends on the exact date when he left the service. It was . . .'

He made some calculations under his breath and then called out:

'Isabelle!'

Isabelle was not far away and came running.

'Look in the lower shelf of the bookcase for a register of the Security Office. There's only one, dating back several years. It contains two or three hundred photos.'

His wife found it at once and he turned the pages, pointed his finger to his own portrait, and found what he was searching for at the back of the book.

'There you are! There he is. He's a few years younger there, but he hasn't changed much. He's always been stout, as far as I can remember.'

Maigret also recognized him, for he had in fact met him in the past.

'Do you mind if I cut out the photo?'

'Of course not. Isabelle, bring some scissors.'

Maigret slipped the bit of shiny paper into his pocket and got to his feet.

'You're in a hurry?'

'Yes, I am rather. And I'm sure you'd rather I didn't tell you too much.'

The other man understood what he meant. Until Maigret knew exactly what Security were doing it was healthier for Catroux that his colleague should tell him as little as possible about it.

'You aren't afraid?'

'Not really.'

'And you believe that Point . . . ?'

'I'm convinced that they are trying to make a scapegoat of him.'

'Another drink.'

'No thank you. Get well soon.'

Mme Catroux saw him to the door and when he got out of the house he took another taxi and told him to go to the Rue Vaneau. He was just trying out his luck. He knocked at the concierge's lodge. She recognised him.

'Forgive me for bothering you again. I would like you to look carefully at a photograph and tell me if this was the man who went up to Mlle Blanche's flat. Take your time.'

It was not necessary. With a moment's hesitation, she shook her head.

'Definitely not.'

'You're certain?'

'Quite certain.'

'Even if the photo dates back a few years and the man has changed?'

'Even if he was wearing a false beard, I'd swear that's not the man.'

He looked at her out of the corner of his eye. For a moment the idea occurred to him that this was something she had been told to say. But no, she looked perfectly sincere!

'Thank you,' he sighed, slipping the photograph back into his pocket.

It was a blow. He had been almost certain that he was on the right track and it had come to nothing at the first testing.

His taxi was waiting and because it was close by he told him to go to the Rue Jacob and walked into the bistro where Piquemal had always had his breakfast. There was hardly anyone there at this time of day.

'Would you care to have a look at this photo?' he asked the owner.

He almost avoided looking at him, for fear of what the reply would be.

'It's certainly the man. Only he seemed to me a little older than that.'

'That's the man who came up to Piquemal and left your place with him?'

'That's him.'

'You are quite certain?'

'Quite.'

'Thank you.'

'You won't have a drink?'

'Not now, thanks. I'll be coming back.'

This changed everything. Until now Maigret had presumed that the same man had visited different places: Mlle Blanche's flat, Piquemal's little bar, the Hôtel de Berry, the professor's widow and the Boulevard Pasteur. Suddenly it turned out that there were at least two men.

His next visit was to Mme Calame, whom he found reading the papers.

'I hope you'll find my husband's report. I can understand now why he was so worried in the last years. I've always had such a horror of these filthy politics.'

She studied him with suspicion, thinking perhaps to herself that it was for the sake of these 'filthy politics' that he had come to see her.

'What is it you want, today?'

He handed her the photograph. She examined it carefully, then raised her head in surprise.

'Ought I to be able to recognize him?'

'Not necessarily. I was wondering if he was the man who visited you two or three days after Piquemal.'

'I've never seen him.'

'You couldn't be mistaken about that?'

'No. It could be the same type of person, but I'm certain it's not the man who came here.'

'Thank you.'

'What happened to Piquemal? Do you think they killed him?'

'Why?'

'I don't know. If they are desperate to hush up the report my husband wrote, then they've got to get rid of everyone who knows about it.'

'They didn't get rid of your husband.'

This reply clearly put her out. She felt herself obliged to protect her husband's memory.

'My husband knew nothing about politics. He was a scientist. He was doing his duty when he wrote the report and when he passed it on to the proper quarters.'

'I'm quite sure that he was doing his duty.'

He decided to go before she started discussing the matter in greater depth. The taxi-driver looked inquiringly at him.

'Where now?'

'To the Hôtel de Berry.'

He found a couple of journalists there looking for information on Piquemal. They rushed up to Maigret, but he shook his head.

'I've nothing to tell you, boys. Just a routine check. I promise you that . . .'

'D'you hope to find Piquemal alive?'

So they were thinking it too?

He left them in the passage while he was showing the photograph to the hotel proprietor.

'What am I supposed to do with this?'

'Tell me if he's the man who came to talk to you about Piquemal.'

'Which one?'

'Not my inspector, who hired a room, but the other one.'

'No.'

He was quite definite. So far, Benoit was the man who had left the bar with Piquemal, but he had not been seen anywhere else.

'Thank you.'

He jumped into the taxi.

'Drive on . . .'

Only when they had started and he had got rid of the journalists, did he give the address of the Boulevard Pasteur. He did not stop at the lodge, but went straight up to the third floor. No one answered the bell, so he had to go down again.

'Mme Gaudry is not at home?'

'She went out half an hour ago with her son.'

'You don't know when she'll be back?'

'She didn't have her hat on. She must be shopping in the neighbourhood. I don't think she'll be long.'

Rather than wait on the pavement he went to the bar where he had been in the morning, and telephoned the P.J. on the off chance. Lucas answered from the inspectors' office.

'Anything fresh?'

'Two telephone calls about Piquemal. The first from a taxi-driver who believes he drove him yesterday to the Gare du Nord. The other from a cinema cashier who thinks she sold him a ticket yesterday evening. I'm going to check.'

'Is Lapointe back?'

'A few minutes ago. He hasn't started to type yet.'

'Put him on, will you?'

And to Lapointe:

'Well. Any photographers?'

'Yes, they were there, boss, clicking away the whole time while Mascoulin was speaking.'

'Where did he see you?'

'In the Pillar room. It was just like Saint-Lazare station! The ushers had to hold the crowd back to give us room to breathe!'

'Was his private secretary there?'

'I don't know. I wouldn't recognize him. We never met.'

'Is it long?'

'It'll make about three typed pages. Some of the reporters took shorthand notes the same time as I did.'

So Mascoulin's statement would be in the last edition of the evening papers.

'He insisted I was to bring it to him to sign.'

'What did you say?'

'That it wasn't my affair. That I would wait for your orders.'

'Do you know if there is a night session at the Chamber?'

'I don't think so. I heard them say that it would be over by 5 p.m.'

'Type it out and wait for me.'

Little Mme Gaudry was not back yet. He walked up and down the pavement for a while and saw her arrive, carrying a shopping bag of provisions, her son trotting at her side. She recognized him.

'Is it me you want to see?'

'Just for a moment.'

'Come upstairs. I've just been doing my shopping.'

'Maybe it isn't worth while coming up.'

The boy was pulling at her sleeve, asking:

'Who is it? Why does he want to talk to you?'

'Be quiet. He just wants some information from me.'

'What information?'

Maigret had pulled the photograph out of his pocket.

'Do you recognize him?'

She managed to free herself, bent over the piece of shiny paper and answered quite spontaneously.

'Yes, that's him.'

It established that Eugene Benoit, the man with the cigar, had been in two places: first in the Boulevard Pasteur where he had probably taken possession of the Calame report, then in the Rue Jacob bar, where he had gone up to Piquemal and with whom he was seen leaving in the opposite direction to the School of Engineering.

'Have you found him?' asked Mme Gaudry.

'Not yet. It won't take us long, though.'

He hailed another taxi to take him to the Boulevard Saint-Martin, regretting that he had not taken a P.J. car, for it meant having to discuss his expenses with the accountant.

The house was an old one. The lower part of the window panes, on the ground floor, was grimy, and on it, in black letters, were the words:

THE BENOIT AGENCY
INVESTIGATIONS OF ALL KINDS

On both sides of the doorway name-plates announced an

artificial flowers business, a Swedish masseuse and other pro-
fessions, some of them of the more unexpected kind. The stairs
on the left were dark and dirty. The name of Benoit appeared
again on an enamel plate attached to a door. He knocked,
knowing beforehand that there would be no reply, for there was
a heap of handbills pushed under the door. After waiting for a
moment, to ease his conscience, he went down and finally found
the lodge at the bottom of the yard. There was no concierge in
it, only a shoemaker who used it as a workshop.

'Is it long since you saw M. Benoit?'

'I haven't seen him today, if that's what you want to know.'

'And yesterday?'

'I don't know. I don't think so. I didn't notice.'

'And the day before?'

'Nor that day either.'

He had a mocking air about him and Maigret pushed his
badge under the man's nose.

'I've told you all I know. I don't mean any harm. The
tenants' business doesn't concern me.'

'D'you know his private address?'

'It would be in the ledger.'

He rose reluctantly and went to fetch a filthy register from a
dresser in the kitchen, and turned the pages with fingers, black
with wax.

'The last I have is the Hôtel Beaumarchais in the Boulevard
Beaumarchais.'

It was not far away and Maigret walked there.

'He moved three weeks ago,' they told him. 'He only stayed
here for two months.'

This time he was directed to a rather shady pension in the
Rue Saint-Denis, in front of which stood a huge girl who
opened her mouth to say something, then recognized him at the
last moment and shrugged her shoulders.

'He has room 19. He's not at home.'

'Did he spend the night here?'

'Emma! Did you do M. Benoit's room this morning?'

A head came over the banisters of the first floor.

'Who's asking for him?'

'Never mind who it is. Tell me.'

'No. He didn't spend the night here.'

'And the night before?'

'No.'

Maigret asked for the key of the room. The girl who had answered from the first floor followed him to the third, on the pretext that she was showing him the way. As the doors were numbered, he had no need of her at all. But he asked her a few questions.

'Does he live alone?'

'Are you asking me if he sleeps alone?'

'Yes.'

'Quite often.'

'Has he got a regular girl-friend?'

'He has plenty of them.'

'What kind?'

'The kind that is willing to come here.'

'Are they often the same ones?'

'I have seen the same face two or three times.'

'Does he pick them up in the street?'

'I'm not there to see.'

'He's not been here for two days?'

'Two or three days. I'm not quite sure.'

'Do men sometimes come and see him?'

'If you mean what I think you mean, he's not that type, and the hotel isn't, either. There's one of those kind of places farther down the street.'

The room revealed little to Maigret. It was a typical room for a place of that sort, with a brass bed, an old chest of drawers, a dilapidated arm chair and hot and cold running water. The drawers contained some underclothes, an unfinished box of cigars, a broken watch, fish-hooks of different sizes in a cellophane bag, but no papers of interest. In a suitcase with expanding sides he found only shoes and dirty shirts.

'Does he often stay away at night?'

'More often than not. And every Saturday he goes to the country until Monday.'

This time Maigret drove back to the Quai des Orfèvres where Lapointe had long since finished typing Mascoulin's statement.

'Get me the Chamber on the phone and find out if the deputies are still there.'

'Am I to say you want to speak to him?'

'No. Don't mention either me or the P.J.'

When he turned to Lucas, the latter shook his head.

'There was one other call after the first two. They've been
checked. Torrence is still on it. There was nothing there.'

'Nothing to do with Piquemal?'

'No. The taxi-driver was quite certain it was, but his client
was traced back to his own house and it wasn't Piquemal.'

There would be new leads, especially in tomorrow's post.

'The session in the Chamber finished half an hour ago,' Lapointe announced. 'It was just a vote on . . .'

'I don't care what the vote was on.'

He knew Mascoulin lived in the Rue d'Antin, two steps away
from the Opéra.

'Are you busy at the moment?'

'No, nothing important.'

'In that case come with me and bring the statement with
you.'

Maigret never took the wheel. He had tried several times,
after the P.J. had been provided with a number of small black
cars and he had forgotten he was driving, he was so deep in
thought. Two or three times, he had remembered his brakes
only at the last moment and now he had no wish to repeat the
experience.

'Do we take a car?'

'Yes.'

It was as if to apologize to the accountant for all his taxis that
afternoon.

'Do you know the number in the Rue d'Antin?'

'No. It's the oldest house.'

The house looked respectable, old, but well maintained.

Maigret and his companion stopped in front of the lodge
which was like the sitting room of a petty bourgeois family and
smelt of floor polish and velvet.

'M. Mascoulin.'

'You have an appointment?'

Maigret took a chance and said yes. At the same time the

woman in black looked at him, then glanced at the front page of the paper and back at him again.

'I suppose I have to let you go up, M. Maigret. It's on the first floor on the left.'

'Has he been living here long?'

'It'll be eleven years in December.'

'Does his secretary live with him?'

She gave a little laugh.

'Certainly not.'

He got the impression that she had guessed what he was driving at.

'They work late at night?'

'Often. Almost always. I think M. Mascoulin must be the busiest man in Paris, to go by all the post he gets here and at the Chamber.'

Maigret was tempted to show her Benoit's photograph and ask if she had seen him before, but she would probably talk about it to her tenant and Maigret was not prepared to show his hand just yet.

'Are you connected with him by private telephone?'

'How do you know that?'

It was not difficult to guess because beside the ordinary instrument there was another, lighter one, attached to the wall. Mascoulin took no chances. And she would warn him of Maigret's arrival as soon as he and Lapointe were on the stairs. It was not important. He could have prevented it by leaving Lapointe in the lodge.

To begin with, no one answered the bell but a little later Mascoulin himself opened the door, without even bothering to show that he was surprised.

'I thought that you would come in person and that you would choose to come here. Come in.'

The floor was littered with newspapers, periodicals, parliamentary debates, reports. There were more of them in a room that served as a sitting-room and that was about as attractive as a dentist's waiting room. Obviously Mascoulin was interested in neither luxury nor comfort.

'I expect you would like to see my study?'

There was something insulting in his irony, in his manner of pretending to guess his visitors' intentions, but the superintendent retained his composure.

'I'm not one of your fans coming to ask for your autograph,' was all he replied.

'Will you come this way?'

They went through a padded double door and found themselves in a spacious study, both windows of which looked out on to the street. Green filing-cabinets covered two of the walls. There were law-books that one finds in every lawyer's room everywhere and finally here too the floor was littered with newspapers and files, as many as in any Ministry.

'May I introduce René Falk, my secretary?'

René Falk was not more than twenty-five, blond, frail, with a strangely childish, petulant expression.

'Pleased to meet you,' he murmured, looking at Maigret in much the same manner as Mlle Blanche had looked at him the first time she met him. Like Mlle Blanche too, he was no doubt fanatically devoted to his employer and regarded every stranger as an enemy.

'You've brought the statement? With several copies, I presume?'

'I've brought three copies; two of them are for you to sign, as you wished, and the third for your files or for whatever purpose you choose.'

Mascoulin took the documents, passed one to Rene Falk, who began to read it at the same time as his boss.

Sitting at his desk, he took a pen, added a comma here and there, deleted a word and then murmured, turning to Lapointe:

'I hope this doesn't offend you at all?'

When he came to the last line, he signed, carried over the corrections to the second copy which he also signed.

Maigret stretched out his hand, but Mascoulin did not give him the pages. Neither did he carry over the corrections to the third copy.

'Correct?' he asked his secretary.

'Yes, I think so.'

'Put them through the machine.'

He looked maliciously in Maigret's direction.

'A man who has as many enemies as I have cannot afford to be careless,' he said. 'Particularly when there are so many people determined to keep a certain document from the public eye.'

Falk opened a door and left it open behind him so that a small room was visible, no doubt previously a kitchen or bathroom. A photostatic machine was standing on a white wood table. The secretary pressed some buttons. The machine gave a buzzing sound as he pushed in the pages one after the other, at the same time as other sheets of special paper. Maigret, who knew the system, but who had rarely seen a machine of this kind in a private house, followed the operation with apparent indifference.

'Marvellous invention, isn't it?' Mascoulin said, his lips curving in the same ugly smile. 'A carbon copy can be disputed. But you can't argue with a photostat.'

A faint smile flickered across Maigret's face and the deputy noticed it.

'What's in your mind?'

'I was just wondering if, out of all the people who have had the Calame report in their possession recently, one of them had had the idea of having it photostated.'

It was not inadvertently that Mascoulin had let him see the machine. Falk could easily have disappeared with the documents for a moment, without the superintendent knowing what he was going to do in the next room.

The pages came out through a slot and the secretary spread them out, still damp, on the table.

'It would be a nasty trick to play on anyone interested in hushing the affair up, wouldn't it?' Mascoulin said with a leer. Maigret looked at him in silence, his expression perfectly neutral, and at the same time at its most ominous.

'Yes, a nasty trick,' he repeated. And an imperceptible cold shudder ran down his spine.

Chapter Eight

It was half-past six when the two men reached the Boulevard Saint-Germain and the yard of the Ministry was empty. As Maigret and Lapointe crossed it in the direction of the stairs leading to the Minister, a voice sounded behind them.

'Hi! You two, over there! Where are you going?'

The guard had not seen them come in. They stood still, turning to him in the middle of the yard and he limped up to them, glanced at the badge Maigret showed him, then looked at his face.

'I beg your pardon. I saw your picture in the paper a moment ago.'

'Good for you! Now you are here, can you tell me . . .' It had become a habit, this taking the photograph out of his brief case. 'Have you seen this face before?'

The man, anxious not to blunder a second time, examined it carefully, after putting on steel-framed spectacles with thick lenses. He was not saying yes or no. Before committing himself he would have liked to ask what it was all about, but did not dare.

'He's a little older now, isn't he?'

'Yes, a few years older.'

'He has a black two-seater, an old model?'

'It's possible.'

'Then it's probably the chap I pinched for parking in the yard in the space reserved for the Ministry cars.'

'When was that?'

'Can't remember the day. At the beginning of the week.'

'Did he give his name?'

'He just shrugged his shoulders and went and parked his car at the other end.'

'Did he go up the big staircase?'

'Yes.'

'Try and remember the day, while we are upstairs.'

In the waiting-room on the first floor, the usher was still at his post reading the newspapers. Maigret showed him the photograph, too.

'When might he have been here?' the man asked.

'Around the beginning of the week.'

'I wasn't here. My wife died and I had to take four days off. We'll have to ask Joseph. He'll be here next week. Am I to announce you to His Excellency?'

A moment later Auguste Point himself opened the door of his study. He seemed tired but calm. He let Maigret and Lapointe in without asking any questions. His secretary, Mlle Blanche, and his private parliamentary secretary were both in the study. The Ministry did not as yet supply its servants with radios and the one on the table, a small portable, no doubt belonged to Point – the three people in the study had probably been listening to it when the usher interrupted them.

'. . . The session was a brief one, devoted exclusively to current affairs, but the lobbies were at fever pitch all the afternoon. All kinds of conflicting rumours have been circulating. A sensational announcement is expected on Monday, but it is still not known . . .'

'Switch it off!' said Point to his secretary.

Fleury made as if to move towards one of the doors but Maigret held him back.

'You needn't go, M. Fleury. Nor you, Mademoiselle.'

Point was watching him anxiously, for it was difficult to guess what the superintendent had come for. On the other hand he looked like a man who has an idea and is so obsessed by it that he forgets everything else.

He appeared to be mentally drawing a plan of the study. He studied the walls, the doors.

'Will you allow me, Your Excellency, to put two or three questions to your colleagues?'

He turned first to Fleury.

'I imagine you were in your study during Piquemal's visit?'

'I knew nothing of . . .'

'I don't doubt it. But *now* you know. Where were you at that time?'

He pointed to a folding door that was half open.

'Is that your study?'

'Yes.'

The superintendent went and had a look at it.

'Were you alone?'

'I couldn't really tell you that. I'm not often alone for any length of time. Visitors come and go the whole day. The Minister sees some of them, the more important ones, and I see the rest, myself.'

Maigret opened a door that led directly from the parliamentary secretary's office to the waiting-room.

'Do they come in this way?'

'Usually, yes. Except those the Minister sees first and then brings to me for one reason or another.'

The telephone rang. Point and Mlle Blanche exchanged glances. Mlle Blanche lifted the receiver.

'No. His Excellency is not here . . .'

She listened, a fixed expression in her eyes. She, too, looked exhausted.

'The same thing?' asked Point, when she put down the receiver.

She nodded, keeping her eyes down.

'He said his son was . . .'

'Please . . .'

He turned to Maigret.

'The telephone has never stopped since midday. I've taken several of the calls myself. Most of them say the same thing: 'If you try to hush up the Clairfond affair, we'll break you!" There are different versions of it, some more polite than others. Some even give their names, often the parents of the children who died in the disaster. One woman was terribly distressed, and yelled at me down the phone "You're not going to cover up for the murderers, are you! If you haven't destroyed the report, show it, so that the whole of France can know . . ." '

He had dark shadows under his eyes, from lack of sleep, his face was grey.

'The President of my electoral committee in La Roche, a man who was my father's friend and knew me when I was in short trousers, rang me a moment ago, almost directly after my statement went on the air. He didn't accuse me, but I could feel he had his doubts. He said sadly "They don't understand out here, son. They knew your parents and they believe they know you. Even if you have to sink the lot of them, you've got to tell everything you know." '

'You'll be telling it soon,' replied Maigret.

Point lifted his head abruptly, not sure if he'd heard aright, and asked, hesitantly:

'You really think so?'

'I'm quite certain now.'

Fleury was leaning against a chest at the other side of the office. Maigret gave the Minister Benoit's photograph; he looked at it, puzzled.

'Who is this?'

'You don't know him?'

'His face doesn't remind me of anyone.'

'He hasn't been to see you, recently?'

'If he'd been to see me, his name would be in the register in the waiting-room.'

'Would you show me your office, Mlle Blanche?'

Fleury was unable from a distance to see the photograph and Maigret noticed that he was biting his nails, as if it was a life-long habit.

The door of Mlle Blanche's office, adjoining that of the Parliamentary Secretary, was small and narrow.

'This is where you came when Piquemal arrived and your employer asked you to leave him alone with him?'

Very tense, she nodded her head in affirmation.

'You closed the door behind you?'

She nodded again.

'You can hear what is being said in the next room?'

'If I put my ear to the door and if the conversation was loud enough, I probably would.'

'You didn't do that?'

'No.'

'Does it ever happen that you do?'

She preferred not to answer. Perhaps she might listen, for example, if Point were visited by a woman she considered attractive or dangerous?

'Do you know this man?'

She was waiting for this, for she had glanced at the photograph when the Minister was looking at it.

'Yes.'

'Where did you see him?'

She spoke in a low voice, so that the others should not hear her.

'In the office near mine.'

She pointed with her finger to the wall that separated them from Fleury's office.

'When?'

'On the day of Piquemal's visit.'

'After it?'

'No. Before.'

'Was he sitting or standing?'

'He was sitting, with his hat on, and a cigar in his mouth. I didn't like the way he was looking at me.'

'Did you see him again?'

'Yes. Afterwards.'

'Are you saying that he was still there when Piquemal left, and that he stayed in that office all the time the visit lasted?'

'I think so. He was there, before and after. You believe that . . .?'

She probably wanted to talk to him about Fleury, but all he said was:

'Sh. . . . Come.'

When he returned to the large office, Point looked at him with reproach, as though upset that Maigret should have been badgering his secretary.

'Will you need your parliamentary secretary this evening, Your Excellency?'

'No. Why?'

'Because I would like to have a talk with him.'

'Here?'

'Preferably in my office. Will it be inconvenient for you to come with us, M. Fleury?'

'I have a dinner engagement, but if it's a matter of urgency.'

'Will you telephone and say you'll be busy.'

Fleury did so. Leaving the door of his office open he telephoned 'Fouquet's'.

'Bob? It's Fleury speaking. Has Jacqueline arrived . . . ? Not

yet ... ? You're certain ... ? When she comes ask her to start
without me.... Yes.... I'll probably not come to dinner....
Later, yes.... I'll be seeing you ...'

Lapointe was watching him out of the corner of his eye.
Point, perplexed, was looking at Maigret, obviously longing to
ask for an explanation. But the superintendent appeared not to
notice.

'Are you busy tonight, Your Excellency?'

'I was to preside at a banquet, but I cried off before the others
could do it first.'

'I may possibly telephone to give you some news, probably
rather late.'

'Even if it's in the middle of the night ...'

Fleury had reappeared, carrying his coat and hat, looking like
a man who is only standing up through sheer force of habit.

'Ready? Ready, Lapointe?'

They went down the great staircase in silence, moved towards
the car which they had left by the pavement.

'Get in.... To the Quai, Lapointe.'

They did not exchange a word on the way. Fleury opened his
mouth twice to speak, but thought better of it and bit his nails
continuously.

On the dusty stairs Maigret made him go in front and walk
first into his office, where he went to close the window.

'You can take off your coat. Make yourself comfortable.'

He made a sign to Lapointe, who joined him in the passage.

'You'll stay with him until I come back. I'll be some time. It's
possible that you'll have to be on duty for a part of the night.'

Lapointe flushed red.

'You have an appointment?'

'It doesn't matter.'

'You can telephone?'

'Yes.'

'If she wants to come and keep you company ...'

Lapointe shook his head, meaning it wouldn't do.

'Ask for sandwiches and coffee to be sent over from the
brasserie. Don't take your eyes off Fleury. Don't let him telephone anybody. If he asks questions – you know nothing. I
want him to stew in his own juice for a while.'

It was the classic treatment. Lapointe had taken part in most of the inquiry, but now he was at sea.

'Go and keep him company. Don't forget the sandwiches.'

He went into the inspectors' room and found Janvier, not yet gone for the night.

'Have you anything special on tonight?'

'No. My wife . . .'

'She's waiting for you? Can you telephone her?'

He sat down on one of the tables and lifting the receiver off another instrument dialled Catroux's number.

'It's Maigret speaking. . . . Forgive me for bothering you again. . . . Something came back to me a moment ago because of some fish hooks I found. Once when I met Benoit, on a Saturday, at the Gare de Lyon, he was going fishing. What did you say? He's a rabid fisherman? Do you know where he usually goes to fish?'

Maigret now, was quite confident of what he was doing; he knew he was on the right track and it seemed that nothing was going to stop him.

'. . . What? He has a hut somewhere? Are you in a position to find out where? . . . Yes. . . . Now. . . . I'll be waiting near the phone . . .'

Janvier was still talking to his wife, asking how all the children were and they all came in turn to wish him good-night.

'Good-night, Pierrot. . . . Sleep well. . . . Yes, I'll be there when you wake up. Is that you, Monique? Has your little brother been a good boy? . . .'

Maigret waited, with a sigh. When Janvier hung up he murmured:

'We could have quite an exciting night. Perhaps I'd better ring my wife too.'

'Shall I get you the number?'

'I have to wait for an important message first.'

Catroux had promised to telephone a colleague, another fisherman, who had gone with Benoit to the river on some occasions.

It was all a matter of luck now. It was possible that the colleague would not be at home. He could be on some mission outside Paris. Silence reigned in the office for about ten minutes and finally Maigret sighed:

'I want a drink!'

At the same moment the telephone rang.

'Catroux?'

'Yes. Do you know Seineport?'

'A little higher than Corbeil, near a floodgate.' Maigret was remembering an inquiry, long ago . . .

'That's it, it's a small village on the bank of the Seine, a favourite place with rod fishermen. Benoit owns a hut near the village. It used to be a water bailiff's hut, very dilapidated; he bought it for a song about ten years ago.'

'I'll find it.'

'Good luck!'

He did not forget to call his wife, but alas he had no children to come and wish him goodnight on the telephone.

'Ready?'

As he passed the half-open door of his office Lapointe had lit the lamp with the green shade and was sitting in Maigret's own chair, his legs crossed, his expression tense, his eyes half-closed.

'See you soon, boy.'

The Parliamentary Secretary started, got up to ask something, but the superintendent had already closed the door.

'We take the car?'

'Yes. We're going to Seineport, about ten miles away.'

'I've been there before with you.'

'That's right. Are you hungry?'

'If we have to stay long . . .'

'We'll stop at the Brasserie Dauphine.'

The waiter was surprised to see them.

'So I needn't take the sandwiches and beer to your office that M. Lapointe ordered?'

'Yes, do please. But first of all, give us something to drink. What will you have, Janvier?'

'I don't know . . .'

'A Pernod?'

Maigret needed one. Janvier could see it and he had one, too.

'Will you prepare us a couple of sandwiches each.'

'With what?'

'It doesn't matter. With some paté, if you have it.'

Maigret seemed to be the calmest man in the world.

'We are too accustomed to criminal cases,' he muttered to himself, his glass in his hand.

No reply was needed. He was mentally making one himself.

In a criminal case, there is usually one guilty man or a group of guilty men acting together. In politics it's quite different and the proof is that there are so many parties in the Chamber.

This idea appeared to amuse him.

'A great number of people have an interest in the Calame report, and from different points of view. It's not only the politicians who would be in a mess if the report were published. Nor only Arthur Nicoud. There are some for whom possession of the report would provide hard cash, those for whom it would mean power.'

There were few customers there that night. The lamps were lit, the atmosphere was heavy as before a storm.

They ate their sandwiches at Maigret's usual table and Maigret was reminded of Mascoulin's table at the 'Filet de Sole'. They both had their table in different places, and in even more different surroundings.

'Some coffee?'

'Yes, please.'

'A brandy?'

'No. I'm driving.'

Maigret took none either and a little later they left Paris by the Porte d'Italie and drove along the road to Fontainebleau.

'It's funny to think that if Benoit had smoked a pipe instead of those stinking cigars, our job would have been infinitely more difficult.'

They were crossing the suburbs. Soon they had only large trees on both sides of the road and cars with their lights on, going in both directions. Many of them overtook the small black car.

'You don't want me to put on any speed?'

'It isn't necessary. Either they are there, or . . .'

He knew men of Benoit's type well enough to be able to put himself in their place. Benoit did not have much imagination. He was just a small-time trickster and his little intrigues had not brought him much luck.

He needed women, never mind what kind of women, a loose bohemian life, in places where he could behave rather ostentatiously and pretend to be a hefty lad, with, at the end of the week, a day or two's fishing.

'As far as I remember, there's a little café in the square at Seineport. Stop there and we'll make some inquiries.'

They crossed the Seine at Corbeil, followed a road along the river with forests on the other side. Four or five times, Janvier had to brake sharply to avoid the rabbits and every time he growled:

'Get out of the way, you little idiot!'

From time to time a light showed through the darkness, then there was a knot of street lamps, and the car stopped in front of a café where some men were playing cards.

'Am I to come in, too?'

'If you'd like a drink.'

'Not now.'

Maigret went in and had a quick drink at the counter.

'D'you know Benoit?'

'The one from the police?'

At Seineport Benoit had not considered it necessary, after so many years, to disclose that he was no longer in Security.

'D'you know where he lives?'

'Did you come from Corbeil?'

'Yes.'

'You must have passed him. Did you see a quarry about a mile from here?'

'No.'

'At night you can miss it. His house is just opposite, on the other side of the road. If he's there, you'll see a light.'

'Thank you.'

One of the card-players lifted his head.

'He *is* there.'

'How d'you know?'

'Because yesterday, I sold him a side of lamb.'

'A whole side for him alone?'

'He doesn't stint himself, it seems to me.'

A few minutes later, Janvier driving very slowly, pointed to a spot of light in the wood.

'This must be the quarry.'

Maigret looked on the other side of the road and about a hundred yards away, on the river bank, saw a light in a window.

'You can leave the car here. Let's go.'

There was no moon, but they soon found a thickly overgrown path.

Chapter Nine

They walked silently, unheard by whoever was in the cottage, one after the other. That part of the river bank must once have belonged to a large estate and the cottage would doubtless have been the gamekeepers's lodge.

The grounds were neglected now. A broken-down fence surrounded what used to be a vegetable garden. Through the lighted window Maigret and Janvier could see the beams of the ceiling, white-washed walls, and a table at which the two men were playing cards.

In the dark Janvier looked at Maigret as though asking him what they were going to do.

'Stay here,' whispered the superintendent. He himself, however, moved towards the door. It was locked and he knocked on it.

'Who is it?' a voice came from inside.

'Open up, Benoit.'

There was a silence, the sound of steps. From his place at the window Janvier could see the former policeman standing by the table. He was hesitating as to what he should do, then pushed his companion into the next room.

'Who is it?' repeated Benoit from the other side of the door.

'Maigret.'

Another silence. The bolt was pushed back, the door opened.

Benoit looked at Maigret's silhouette, a bewildered expression in his eyes.

'What do you want with me?'

'Just a little chat. Come, Janvier.'

The cards were still on the table.

'All alone?'

Benoit did not answer at once, suspecting that Janvier had been watching at the window.

'You were perhaps playing patience?'

Janvier said, pointing to the door:

'The other one's in there, boss.'

'I thought so. Bring him in.'

Piquemal would have found it difficult to run away because the door led into a sink-hole without any communication with the outside world.

'What do you want with me? Have you got a warrant?' Benoit blurted out trying to regain his composure.

'No.'

'In that case . . .'

'In that case – nothing! Sit down. And you, Piquemal. I hate talking to men who are standing up.'

He fiddled with some cards on the table.

'Were you trying to teach him the belote for two players?'

It was probably true. Piquemal had probably never played a game of cards in his life before.

'Are you going to sit down, Benoit?'

'I have nothing to say.'

'Very well. In that case, I'll just have to do the talking, won't I?'

There was a bottle of wine on the table and only one glass. Piquemal, who did not play cards, did not drink either, nor did he smoke. Had he ever been to bed with a woman? Probably not. He was looking at Maigret savagely, like an animal at bay.

'Have you been working for Mascoulin for a long time?'

In fact, in this setting, Benoit made a better impression than in Paris, perhaps because he was in his natural element. He had remained the peasant who must have been the braggart of his village and he had been wrong to leave it to try his luck in Paris. His tricks, his shady practices were those of a peasant at a fair.

To give himself courage, he poured himself some wine and added mischievously:

'I needn't offer you any?'

'Thanks. Mascoulin needs people like you, if only to check on the information that comes in to him.'

'Go on talking.'

'When he received the letter from Piquemal, he realized that it was the opportunity of a lifetime and that he had every chance, if he played his cards well, of holding a large number of political figures at his mercy.'

'As you say.'

'As I say!'

Maigret was still standing. His hands clasped behind his back, his pipe between his teeth, he paced up and down from the door to the fireplace, stopping from time to time in front of one of the men, while Janvier, sitting on the corner of the table, listened attentively.

'What surprised me most was that having seen Piquemal and having actually laid hands on the report, he should have sent him to the Minister of Public Works.'

Benoit smiled knowingly.

'I only understood it just now, when I saw the photostat at Mascoulin's place. Shall we take events in their chronological order, Benoit? You can always stop me if I'm wrong.

'Mascoulin receives Piquemal's letter. Being a cautious man, he calls you and tells you to make inquiries. You realize that it is a serious, genuine document, that the chap is indeed well placed to get hold of the Calame report. At this stage you tell Mascoulin that you know someone quite important in Public Works – the parliamentary private secretary. Where did you meet him?'

'It doesn't concern you.'

'It's unimportant anyway. He's waiting in my office and we'll be able to settle details like that shortly. Fleury is a poor creature, always short of funds. But he has the advantage of being

359

accepted in circles where scum like you find the door shut in their faces. I dare say he's given you the odd tip before on some of his friends, in return for a few notes.'

'Do go on.'

'Now perhaps you'd like to go along with me. If Mascoulin himself takes the report from Piquemal he is practically forced to make it public and to explode the whole scandalous business, for Piquemal is an honest man in his way, a fanatic, whom you would have to kill to silence him. To take the report to the Chamber would of course put Mascoulin in the limelight for a time. But it would be more interesting to hold on to it, and keep all the people the report compromises in suspense. It took me quite a long time to work that one out. I'm not vicious enough to put myself in his shoes. So Piquemal goes to Mme Calame where he knows, because he's seen it before, that there is a copy of the report. He slips it into his brief case and rushes to Mascoulin, Rue d'Antin. Knowing that he is there, there is no reason for you to follow him, as you know what's going to happen and so you dash to the Ministry of Public Works, where Fleury brings you to his office. Under some pretext or other Mascoulin keeps Piquemal with him while his smooth secretary photographs the report. With all the appearance of an honest man, he then dispatches his visitor to the person it concerns, that is to say, to the Minister. I think that's correct, so far?'

Piquemal was looking intensely at Maigret, deep in his own thoughts, in the grip of a violent emotion.

'You are there, in Fleury's office, when Piquemal hands over the papers. All that you have to do now, is to find out, through Fleury, where and when you can get hold of them. In this way, thanks to the honest Mascoulin, the Calame report will be placed at the disposal of the public. But, thanks to you, Auguste Point, the Minister in question, will be unable to present it to the Chamber. So there will be a hero in the story – Mascoulin. There will be a villain, accused of having destroyed the document to save his face, as well as the face of all his colleagues who are compromised – a certain Auguste Point, who has the misfortune of being an honest man and of having refused to shake dirty hands. Quite clever, isn't it?'

Benoit poured himself another glass, which he began to drink slowly, glancing uncertainly at Maigret. He seemed to be asking himself what card it would be in his best interest to play, as he had done at the belote.

'That's almost the whole story. Fleury told you that his boss had taken the Calame report to the Boulevard Pasteur. You didn't dare to go there at night, because of the concierge, but the next morning you waited until she had gone to do her shopping. Did Mascoulin burn the report?'

'It's not my business.'

'Whether he burnt it or not, it doesn't matter, because he had the photostat. That was quite enough to keep quite a number of people at his mercy.'

It was a mistake, Maigret realized afterwards, to insist on Mascoulin's power. If he hadn't – would Benoit have acted differently? Probably not, but it was a risk to take.

'The bomb exploded, as foreseen. Other people were searching for the document for different reasons, among others a certain Tabard, who had been the first to remember Calame's part in the affair and to allude to it in his paper. You know that wretched Tabard, don't you? It wouldn't have been power he would have got from the report, but hard cash. Labat, who worked for him, probably knocked his heels around Mme Calame's place. Did he see Piquemal leave her house? I don't know and it's possible that we'll never know. But it has no importance. Anyhow Labat sent one of his men to the widow, then another to the Minister's secretary. . . . You remind me, all of you, of a lot of crabs crawling and scratching about in a basket. Others, too, more officially, asked themselves what exactly had happened and tried to find out.'

He was referring to the Rue des Saussaies. Once the President of the Council had been informed it was natural that a more or less discreet inquiry should be made by the Security Department. From then on the situation became almost comical. Three different groups had chased the report, each for quite specific reasons.

'The weak spot was Piquemal because it was difficult to tell if he might not talk under interrogation. Was it you, I wonder, who had the bright idea of bringing him here, or was it Mascoulin? You're not prepared to say. Well, it doesn't matter.

Anyway the point was to withdraw him from circulation for a while. I don't know how you went about it or what story you had to tell him. He'll talk when he sees fit to do so, when he realizes that he's been nothing but a pawn in the hands of two blackguards, a big one and a small one.'

Piquemal gave a start, but remained silent.

'Well, that's about it, this time. We're outside the Seine department, as you will no doubt point out to me, and I'm acting in excess of my duty.'

He waited for a moment, then murmured:

'Put the handcuffs on him, Janvier.'

Benoit's first reaction was to resist and he was twice as strong as Janvier. Then, after a moment's reflection, he stretched out his wrists, and chuckled to himself.

'It'll cost you something, the two of you. You realize I haven't said a word.'

'Not a word. Will you come with us, too, Piquemal, please? You're perfectly free, but I don't suppose you want to stay here?'

As they went out Maigret turned back to switch off the light.

'You've got the key?' he asked. 'It would be better to lock the door, for it'll be some time before you're fishing here again.'

They climbed into the small car and drove in silence.

At the Quai des Orfèvres they found Fleury still sitting in his chair. He jumped when he saw the former inspector of the Rue des Saussaies in the doorway.

'I needn't introduce you . . .' growled Maigret.

It was half past eleven. The P.J. building was deserted, with lights only in two of the offices.

'Get me the Ministry.'

Lapointe dialled a number.

'I'm putting you on to Superintendent Maigret.'

'Forgive me for disturbing you, Your Excellency. You weren't in bed, I hope? You're with your wife and daughter? . . . I've got news, yes. . . . It's important. . . . Tomorrow you'll be able to give the Chamber the name of the man who burgled you in the Boulevard Pasteur and took away the Calame report. . . .

Not at once, no. . . . In an hour . . . perhaps . . . or may be two.
. . . Yes, wait for me if you prefer. . . . I can't guarantee it won't
be the morning.'

It lasted three hours. For Maigret and his men it was an old,
familiar routine. They all stayed together for a long time in the
superintendent's office. Maigret doing the talking and stopping
now and then in front of one man or the other.

'Just as you please, boys. I've all the time in the world, you
know. You take one of them Janvier. . . . This one, I think . . .'

He pointed to Piquemal who so far had not opened his
mouth.

'And you can get busy with M. Fleury, Lapointe.'

Thus, in each office, there were two men, one questioning, the
other trying to keep silent. It was a test of endurance. Sometimes Lapointe or Janvier would appear in the doorway, make a
sign to the superintendent and then they would both walk out
into the passage, and talk in undertones.

'I have at least three witnesses to confirm my story,' Maigret
said to Benoit. 'Among them, and this is the most important
one, a tenant from the Boulevard Pasteur who saw you enter
Point's flat. You still refuse to talk?'

In the end Benoit made a statement that was characteristic of
him:

'What would you do in my place?'

'If I were as much of a blackguard as to be in your place, I'd
make a clean breast of it.'

'No.'

'Why?'

'You know very well why.'

He couldn't move against Mascoulin! Benoit knew well that
Mascoulin would always manage to wriggle out of the mess
somehow and God alone knows what would happen to his ac-
complice.

'Don't forget that he's the one that has the report.'

'So?'

'So nothing. I'm keeping my mouth shut. They'll charge me
with burgling the flat in the Boulevard Pasteur. How long will I
get for that?'

'About two years.'

'As for Piquemal, he came with me of his own accord. I never threatened him. So I didn't kidnap him.'

Maigret realized he would get nothing further from him.

'You admit you went to the Boulevard Pasteur?'

'I'll admit it if I can't do anything else. That's all.'

And a few minutes later it became impossible for him to do anything else. Fleury had collapsed and Lapointe came to tell his chief.

'He knew nothing about Mascoulin, had no idea until tonight, who Benoit was working for. He couldn't refuse to help Benoit because of certain transactions between them in the past.'

'Did you get him to sign a statement?'

'I'm doing it now.'

If Piquemal was an idealist, he was an idealist who had gone wrong. He continued in fact to keep silent. Was he relying on the possibility that this would bring him something from Mascoulin?

At half past three Maigret, leaving Janvier and Lapointe with the three men, drove in a taxi to the Boulevard Saint-Germain where there was a light in a second floor window. Point had given orders that Maigret should be taken immediately to his flat.

Maigret found the family in the small sitting-room where he had been received before.

'You have the document?'

'No. But the man who stole it from the Boulevard Pasteur is in my office and has confessed.'

'Who is it?'

'An old Security man who went crooked and works for anyone who will pay him.'

'Who was he working for this time?'

'For Mascoulin.'

'In that case ...' began Point, his expression darkening again.

'Mascoulin will say nothing, he'll be quite content to wait, and then when the need arises, he can put pressure on anyone who is compromised. He'll let Benoit take the blame. As for Fleury ...'

'Fleury?'

Maigret nodded.

'He's a miserable creature. He found himself in such a position that he couldn't refuse . . .'

'I told you so,' interrupted Mme Point.

'I know. I didn't believe it.'

'You're not made for political life. When all this is over I hope you . . .'

'The essential thing,' Maigret was saying, 'is to establish that you didn't destroy the Calame report and that it was stolen from you as you said.'

'Will they believe me?'

'Benoit will confess.'

'Will he say who he did it for?'

'No.'

'Neither will Fleury?'

'Fleury didn't know.'

'So that in the end . . .'

A burden had been lifted from his heart but there was nothing to celebrate in it. Maigret had undoubtedly saved his reputation, but Point had lost the game. Unless at the last moment, and it was very unlikely, Benoit decided to tell the whole truth, the real winner was Mascoulin. Mascoulin himself was so confident of his victory that even before Maigret had come to the end of his inquiry he had purposely shown him the photostatic machine. It had been a warning. It simply meant – To whom it may concern – take care!

Anyone who had something to fear from the publication of the report, whether it was Arthur Nicoud, still in Brussels, a politician or anyone else, each one knew now that Mascoulin had only to lift a finger, and they would be finished, their careers ruined.

There was a long silence in the room; Maigret was not feeling very proud of himself.

'In a few months, when all this is forgotten, I'll hand in my resignation and go back to La Roche-sur-Yon,' murmured Point, staring at the carpet.

'Is that a promise?' his wife pleaded.

'It is.'

She had no reservations about her happiness, because her husband meant more to her than anything else in the world.

'Can I call Alain?' Anne-Marie asked.

'At this hour?'

'Don't you think it's worth waking him up for?'

'If you wish . . .'

She, too, did not quite realize what the situation meant.

'Will you have something to drink?' murmured Point, looking almost timidly at Maigret. Their eyes met. Once again the superintendent had the impression that the man beside him resembled him like a brother. Both had the same heavy, sad expression in their eyes, the same hunched shoulders.

The drink was merely a pretext to sit down together for a moment. The young woman was telephoning.

'Yes. . . . It's all finished. . . . We mustn't talk about it yet. . . . We must let Papa surprise them all, when he goes up to the tribune in the Chamber.'

What were the two men to say to one another?

'Your health!'

'Yours, Your Excellency!'

Mme Point had left the room and Anne-Marie soon followed her.

'I'm going to bed,' murmured Maigret, as he stood up. 'You need it even more than I do.'

Point stretched out his hand, clumsily, as if it were not an everyday gesture, but the expression of a feeling that he was too shy to admit.

'Thanks, Maigret.'

'I did what I could.'

'Yes . . .'

They walked to the door.

'In fact, I too refused to shake his hand . . .'

And on the landing, before turning his back on his host:

'He'll get what's coming to him, one of these fine days.'

More about Penguins

Penguinews, which appears every month, contains details of all the new books issued by Penguins as they are published. From time to time it is supplemented by *Penguins in Print*, which is a complete list of all books published by Penguins which are in print. (There are well over three thousand of these.)

A specimen copy of *Penguinews* will be sent to you free on request, and you can become a subscriber for the price of the postage. For a year's issues (including the complete lists) please send 30p if you live in the United Kingdom, or 60p if you live elsewhere. Just write to Dept EP, Penguin Books Ltd, Harmondsworth, Middlesex, enclosing a cheque or postal order, and your name will be added to the mailing list.

Note: *Penguinews* and *Penguins in Print* are not available in the U.S.A. or Canada

Georges Simenon

The Fourth Simenon Omnibus

The Man With the Little Dog, *Maigret and the Headless Corpse*,
The Little Saint

A trio of stories in which Simenon uncovers three sides of man's
nature, from the macabre through the stunningly tragic to a joyous
celebration of life.

In *The Man with the Little Dog* we meet Felix Allard, once successful
but now a virtual recluse, and his dog – Bib. He decides to start
a diary in which he unfolds his past and the catastrophic events –
of fraud, embezzlement, and murder which left Felix's life in ruins.

Of all the dangerous and complex cases that he has solved
Maigret and the Headless Corpse comes close to defeating him. In
the faint grey light of an early dawn a man's arm is fished out of a
Paris canal. In the cold-blooded jigsaw of the case only one piece is
missing – the corpse's head.

The Little Saint is little Louis, illegitimate son of a street seller,
small and delicate and something of a freak in a violent world,
but destined to be a singularly gifted man. Of this story Simenon
himself has said, 'If I were allowed to keep only one of my novels,
I would choose this one'.

Also available

THE FIRST SIMENON OMNIBUS
*The Neighbours, Maigret and the Nahour Case, Monsieur Monde
Vanishes*

THE SECOND SIMENON OMNIBUS
The Accomplices, Maigret's Pickpocket, The Patience of Maigret
Many of Georges Simenon's numerous novels, including the
Maigret series, are available in Penguins

NOT FOR SALE IN THE U.S.A. OR CANADA